X118882992 BPF

The Demons of King Solomon

Copyright © 2017 Aaron J. French

Introduction © 2017, Richard Smoley
The Floor of the Basement is the Roof of Hell © 2017, Stephen Graham Jones
Whimsy © 2017, Michelle Belanger
An Angel Passes © 2017, Whitley Strieber
The Wraith of Sunshine House © 2017, Ronald Malfi
Symphony © 2017, Philip Fracassi
The Red Library © 2017, Jonathan Maberry
Mischief © 2017, Richard Chizmar
Hunter Hunterson and the President of Hell © 2017, Scott Sigler
The Old Man Down the Road © 2017, R.S. Belcher
Class of '72 © 2017, J.D. Horn
By Promise Preordained © 2017, Seanan McGuire
Dalia of Belial © 2017, Michael Griffin

All rights reserved. No part of this book may be used or reproduced by any means, graphic, electronic, or mechanical, including photocopying, recording, taping or by any information storage retrieval system without the written permission of the publisher except in the case of brief quotations embodied in critical articles and reviews.

This is a work of fiction. All of the characters, names, incidents, organizations, and dialogue in this novel are either the products of the author's imagination or are used fictitiously.

JournalStone books may be ordered through booksellers or by contacting:
JournalStone
www.journalstone.com

The views expressed in this work are solely those of the authors and do not necessarily reflect the views of the publisher, and the publisher hereby disclaims any responsibility for them.

ISBN: 978-1-947654-08-2 (sc)
ISBN: 978-1-947654-14-3 (hc)
ISBN: 978-1-947654-09-9 (ebook)

JournalStone rev. date: December 15, 2017

Library of Congress Control Number: 2017963038

Printed in the United States of America

Cover Design: Chuck Killorin
Interior Layout: Jess Landry

Edited by: Aaron J. French

NOV 14 2022

The Demons of King Solomon

Edited by Aaron J. French

Table of Contents

Commentary on each demon by Richard Smoley

Introduction

RICHARD SMOLEY

In June 1998, I took an intensive retreat in occult practice. Suitably, it was in a large old English country house somewhere in the midst of Derbyshire. A dozen of us were holed up for a couple of weeks with two instructors, shades drawn at all hours of the day.

At one point when I was at the altar doing a certain practice, outside the window in the night I saw an image of a birdlike creature, with a large beak that constituted its whole face. Its eyes were on tentacles like those of a crustacean. The body was slender, like the legs of a stork, and yellow. It did not seem menacing, but soon it was joined by other creatures of the same kind.

They clattered against the window, trying to get in. (Recently I saw a Neolithic cave drawing that seemed to represent similar creatures, suggesting that they have been with us for a long time.)

Afterward I told one of the instructors what I had seen. He told me to draw a counterclockwise pentagram in the air and to "keep it going." Which I did.

Later I went up to him and said weakly, "I think I managed to get rid of them."

To which he replied, "I was trying to get you to invite them IN!"

At which point it became obvious that whatever disposition one needs for the invocation of spirits, I do not have it.

But, of course, many others do. Understandably. Sooner or later one realizes, whether through reason or experience, that the world available to the five senses cannot be the sum total of reality. As soon as we accept this fact, certain questions arise: Are there any life forms that inhabit these unseen worlds? If so, what relation do we have to them? Are they friendly toward us, hostile, neutral? Are they possibly useful?

Attempting to answer or work with these questions comprises a large part of the religious heritage of the human race.

If we think of these unseen worlds through the analogy of the natural world, we can guess that the beings inhabiting these realms are manifold. They are of all shapes and sizes, natures, qualities, characteristics. To pursue the idea still further, we can suppose that, like most of the creatures inhabiting the visible realm, they are neither friendly nor hostile to man. They exist in their own right, and, left on their own, have no truck with us and will do us no harm. After all, in the vast range of living creatures in the physical world, only very few are dangerous. Even fewer are useful: the number of plant and animal species that we make use of for food or for any other purpose is infinitesimal. Appearance is not a reliable guide to anything here: even the ones we find beautiful are rarely useful, and even the most hideous ones are for the most part completely innocuous.

So it may be with the world of spirits. In order to have a somewhat more objective sense of this realm, we must set aside certain deep-seated habits of thought. The most important one comes from Christianity. It is found in the First Epistle of John:

> Brothers, believe not every spirit, but try the spirits whether they are of God: because many false prophets are gone out into the world. Hereby know ye the Spirit of God: Every spirit that confesseth that Jesus Christ is come in the flesh is of God: And every spirit that confesseth not that Jesus Christ has come in the flesh is not of God. (1 John 4:1-3)

This may not be quite as helpful as it sounds—after all, "the devils also believe, and tremble" (James 2:19). But this criterion has set the tone for Christian discourse ever since the first century, and it shapes our mindsets to this day, whether or not we have any use for Christianity.

The Devil does not, as a matter of fact, appear very often in the Bible. One of the few places where he does is in the prologue to Job, which portrays him not as the archrival to the Lord, but a reasonably friendly acquaintance of his—friendly enough to pose a wager about the reliability of the Lord's servant Job.

This picture reflects a view of the Devil that predates Christianity (Job was probably written in the sixth century BC) and still survives in parts of Judaism, such as the Kabbalah. The Devil is *satan*—originally a common noun, not a proper name, and meaning *adversary*. But he is not an adversary of God; he is the adversary of the human race—both the tempter and the prosecuting officer. The Greek version of his name—*diabolos*, meaning *accuser*—highlights this role. Even in the New Testament, Christ goes into the wilderness "*to be tempted* of the devil" (Matthew 4:1; my emphasis). The Devil does not show up unexpected: Christ has gone out in the wilderness precisely in order to be tested by him. It is, shall we say, a matter of quality control.

The matter is complicated further by the fact that in Judaism the angels are not always favorable to man. Indeed, as one scholar points out, there is a "rivalry between angels and men that we find at various places in Talmud and Midrash. True, the angels often come to the aid of men, but they are just as often in competition with man when it comes to currying favour with God. The angels are quite simply jealous of man..."[1]

This idea, strange as it may sound, penetrated into the New Testament. The apostle Paul *never* mentions angels in a favorable way, often portraying them as rivals ("we are made a spectacle unto the world, and to angels, and to men": 1 Corinthians 4:9). Even some interpretations of the parable of the Prodigal Son say that the "elder brother," who loyally stays home while the younger son runs off and who complains when he is welcomed back, symbolizes the angels, who are jealous of the reception given by God the Father to the Prodigal Son that is the human race (Luke 15:11-33).

The theological line between angels and devils, so sharply drawn by conventional Christianity, is blurrier than we usually think. The angels are not always friendly—might it be the case that the devils are not always hostile?

It is not an assumption that one can safely make. Nevertheless,

---

[1] T.A.M. Fontaine, *In Defence of Judaism: Abraham ibn Daud; Sources and Structure of ha-Emunah ha-Ramah* (Maastricht, Netherlands: Van Gorcum, Assen, 1990), 184.

from a certain point of view the demons offer an advantage: you may be able to get them to do things that an angel will not do—seduce a love interest, put a curse on someone, commit murder. This assumption underlies necromancy as practiced over the centuries. But it does require you to traffic with dubious entities. Richard Kieckhefer of Northwestern University, an expert on medieval magic, deftly summarizes the issue:

> Ordinary prayer and official ritual assume that the spirits invoked are in general well disposed toward humankind, and enter readily into a helping relationship. The praying person's invocation of God or a saint is an appeal to a benevolent being. In this respect the rituals of demonic magic differ from other rites: they invoke fallen spirits taken (by the necromancers as well as by their critics) to be unwilling, uncooperative, inimical and treacherous. The operations of demonic magic, more than other rituals, are thus explicit contests of wills. The necromancer recognizes a need to heap conjuration upon conjuration, and to buttress these formulas with supporting means of power, precisely because the demons are reluctant to come, and if they come will do everything in their power to escape the magician's control, threaten him, and deceive him.[2]

(A word on terminology: etymologically, *necromancy* ought to mean evoking the spirits of the dead, from the Greek *nekroi*, "the dead," and *manteia*, "prophesying, divination," but in practice it refers to evoking spirits in general. In the late medieval period, *nigromantia* was a more or less synonymous variant, from the Latin *nigrum*, "black": hence black magic.)[3]

One could cite any number of magical texts to illustrate the dynamic that Kieckhefer is talking about. Here is one from around the tenth century AD, found in Cairo. The text is written, possibly in blood, on two large animal bones:

> Chu, Kouchos, Trophos, Kimphas, Psotomis, and Phemos, and Ouliat. These are the names of the six powers of death, these who bring every sickness down upon every person, these who bring every soul out from every body. I adjure you by your names … and your powers and your places and the security of

[2] Richard Kieckhefer, *Forbidden Rites: A Necromancer's Manual of the Fifteenth Century* (University Park, Pa.: Pennsylvania State University Press, 1997), 16.

> death (itself), that you shall go to Aaron son of Tkouikira, and that you shall bear away his soul.

The curse is backed up by a threat:

> I adjure you by the manner in which <you were seized>, and the fear that you have seen, and the punishments, and the monstrous faces that you have seen, and the river of fire that casts up wave after wave ... that the manner (in which) you suffered, you must bring your suffering down upon Aaron son of Tkouikira. Yea, at once, at once![4]

The text is implying that if these beings do not carry out the sorcerer's wishes, they will be subject to the punishments listed.

The spirits, however, are not so easily managed. Often they evade the bonds and seals put on them. The most famous example is in Goethe's *Faust*. In one scene Faust has the devil Mephistopheles in his study, and Mephistopheles cannot leave because Faust has the sacred seal of the pentagram engraved at the door. Mephistopheles asks if he can be released, but Faust refuses, thinking he has a great advantage in having the devil trapped. But Mephistopheles sends Faust into a dreamlike reverie and then summons a rat to gnaw an opening in the pentagram, whereby he makes his escape.[5]

Another hazard in the evocation of spirits is unintended and undesired consequences. The magus Lon Milo DuQuette provides a useful example in his autobiography, *My Life with the Spirits*. As a young man, he decided to evoke one of the "fallen angels" of the famous grimoire known as *The Lesser Key of Solomon the King*. The spirit he chose was Orobas, described thus:

> He is a Great and Mighty Prince appearing at first like a Horse; but after the command of the Exorcist he putteth on the image of a Man. His Office is to discover all things Past, Present, and to Come; also to give Dignities, and Prelacies, and the Favour of Friends and of Foes. He giveth true answers of Divinity, and of the Creation of the World. He is very faithful unto the Exorcist, and will not suffer him to be tempted of any Spirit. He governeth 20 Legions of Spirits.[6]

---

[3] Kieckhefer, 19.

[4] Marvin Meyer and Richard Smith, eds., *Ancient Christian Magic: Coptic Texts of Ritual Power* (San Francisco: HarperSanFrancisco, 1994), 204-06. Bracketed insertions are the translator's.

DuQuette's evocation of Orobas came at a point of financial extremity in his life, when he was completely out of money and had nothing with which even to buy groceries for his wife and child. He made the sigil of Orobas, anointed it with the Oil of Abramelin the Mage, and poured his invocation to the seal with all the fury of a lifetime of pent-up frustration and self-hatred.

At length, he writes, "I blinked and squinted through the tears and sweat and strained to see what was happening in the triangle [sigil]. I didn't 'see' anything, but something most definitely was happening. The feeling was unmistakable. I was no longer alone in the room. It was like waking up from a dream to discover that your dog is just inches from your face staring at you."

But things went awry. A drop of sweat dripped into his eye, and he unthinkingly wiped it off. "The powerful smell of cinnamon triggered a terrifying alarm. My hand and fingers were still covered with Oil of Abramelin!"

DuQuette did not want to leave the magical circle, which would violate the rules of Solomonic magic, but he was terrified of losing his eyesight and, blinded, stumbled toward the bathroom. But then, he writes, "I could see! I could see the whole scene as if I was perched somewhere over the ceiling. I saw myself moving toward the bathroom door. I saw the circle and the divine names. I saw the carpet, the windows, and the bed. I saw the triangle and inside the triangle, I saw the demon Orobas—a miniature black horse waiting patiently. It had an almost comic oversized head with huge round eyes. It looked bored."

Commanding the demon to stay, DuQuette went to the bathroom and washed his eyes and his fingers. Returning, he commanded the demon to do something to turn around his life—within one hour.

Within that time, a long-absent friend, Mad Bob, showed up at DuQuette's door in a rusted Chevrolet. He threw the keys to DuQuette and told him the car was his.

With the car, whose floorboard was missing in places, as were its knobs and door handles, DuQuette managed to get a job the next day with a medical device manufacturer. Within two months he was promoted into the engineering department. "Mad Bob's gift of a car within the prescribed one hour was the unambiguous catalyst that triggered a chain-reaction of events that manifested everything that I demanded," DuQuette writes. He pronounced the operation a success.

---

[5] Johann Wolfgang von Goethe, *Faust*, 1422-1529.

But the story does not end there. DuQuette needed to put the Orobas parchment sigil in a safe place, because any unprotected person who came into contact with it would fall prey to the demon's influence. He taped the sigil to the inside of his guitar and forgot about it.

Several weeks later, a music student of DuQuette's offered to inlay the guitar with a mother-of-pearl Egyptian solar disk. So the student, Kurt, had the guitar in his possession for a week. He found the sigil and returned it to DuQuette with the finished guitar, but DuQuette did not tell him what it was. Kurt told DuQuette that he was going to the race track. The previous day, he said, "'My dad and I spent the whole day at Santa Anita [racetrack]. I just fell in love with the horses. We went down to the paddock before each race to get a close look. They're so beautiful. They're like gods. When they look at me I feel like a horse!' He then whinnied like a horse."

Kurt stayed a part of DuQuette's magical scene for the next fifteen years, but "sadly, his addiction to horseracing and other forms of gambling escalated year by year into self-destructive behavior that eventually rendered him a social cripple." During that time DuQuette performed numerous invocations of the equine Orobas, charging him to leave the man in peace. But to no avail.

Two things are worth noting in this story. In the first place, *something goes wrong*. DuQuette accidentally puts the stinging oil in his eyes, blinding himself. But it is this very oil that gives him vision out of his body, in which he can see the demon.

This points to a salient feature of occult ritual: one way or another, things go wrong. These evocations are long, complex, and fraught with details. Failure to follow the instructions puts the whole evocation in jeopardy, but they are so complex—and the situation is so intense to begin with—that errors are bound to slip in. Even apart from this obvious fact, as Kieckhefer says above, the demons are uncooperative: they do not want to be controlled and will get out of it if they possibly can, so they have every incentive to get the operator to make a mistake. In this instance, the mistake—accidentally rubbing his eyes with oil—actually precipitates the vision, but it could well have turned out otherwise. Incidentally, DuQuette was hurt and temporarily blinded by this error.

The second thing worth noting is that DuQuette actually describes what the demon looked like and how it appeared to him: as a

[6] *The Goetia: The Lesser Key of Solomon the King*, Aleister Crowley and Hymenaeus Beta, eds. (York Beach, Maine: Samuel Weiser, 1995), 57, quoted in Lon Milo DuQuette, *My Life with the Spirits: The Adventures of a Modern Magician* (York Beach, Maine: Samuel Weiser, 1999), 95. The complete story of DuQuette's encounter with Orobas appears in *My Life with the Spirits*, chapters 15 and 16.

miniature horse with an oversized head. This phenomenological description is comparatively rare in such narratives. Often we are told that the spirits appeared, but we are not always told how or what they looked like. We can see one example in a famous account of a necromantic evocation in the memoirs of the Renaissance adventurer Benvenuto Cellini. The evocation, which was conducted by a Sicilian priest, took place at the Coliseum in Rome in 1535. Cellini's account is vivid and detailed. At one point, after an hour and a half of evocation, "there appeared several legions of spirits, to such an extent that the Coliseum was filled with them." Cellini asks them if he will be reunited with his lover Angelica, but they give no response.

The rite has to be repeated. This time they bring along "a little lad of pure virginity," a shop boy about twelve years old. Again the priest makes elaborate preparations and "very terrible invocations, calling by name a multitude of demons, the chiefs of the legions of spirits ... to such a purpose that in a short space of time they filled the whole Coliseum a hundredfold as many as had appeared that first time."

That is all Cellini says about the appearance of the spirits. He adds that the lad, "in greatest terror said, there were a million of the fiercest men swarming around and threatening us. He said besides that four enormous giants had appeared, who were striving to force their way into the circle. All the while the necromancer, trembling with fright, endeavoured with mild and gentle persuasions to dismiss them." Cellini adds, "I thought I was a dead man on seeing the terror of the necromancer himself." The boy, in equal terror, cried, "*The whole Coliseum is in flames, and the fire is coming down upon us.*"

The entire account suggests that the boy, and probably the necromancer, saw these figures, but that Cellini himself did not. In any event, Cellini, following the necromancer's instructions, banishes the spirits by throwing asafetida on lit coals. The spirits apparently did answer his question—they said he would be reunited with Angelica within the month, an unlikely prediction that in fact came true. After this Cellini says no more about the necromancer.[7]

Many such accounts presuppose that the reader will already know, or assume, what the spirits look like. Such is true of the famous evocation of the dead in Homer's *Odyssey*, which is both vivid and vague:

> Spirits of the perished dead gathered from Erebus:
> Brides, bachelors, and long-suffering old ones,

And tender virgins with their grieving hearts;
And many fighting men, stabbed with bronze spears,
Slain in war, clutching their bloody armor.[8]

But what did these brides and fighting men look like? Did they look solid, like an ordinary human? Were they transparent, as sometimes seems to be the case with spirits? We do not know.

Often it is implied that the spirit can change shapes at the magus's bidding, as in Marlowe's *Doctor Faustus*, where Faustus tells Mephistopheles:

I charge thee to return, and change thy shape;
Thou art too ugly to attend on me:
Go, and return an old Franciscan friar;
That holy shape becomes a devil best.[9]

A similar uncertainty surrounds a more recent magical rite: the Order of the Golden Dawn's evocation of the spirit of Mercury, Taphthartharath, in 1896. The ritual commands: "Come unto us … O Taphthartharath, Taphthartharath, and appear very visibly before us, in the great Magical triangle without this Circle of Art. I bind and conjure Thee unto very visible appearance." The invocation continues, indicating the means by which the spirit should materialize: "Behold the magic fire, the mystic lamps, the blinding radiance of the Flashing Tablets! Behold the Magical Liquids of the Material Basis; it is these that have given Thee Form!"[10] Nevertheless, there seems to have been some ambiguity about how the spirit would manifest. Nick Farrell, a blogger on magic, writes about this ritual: "Anything which is evoked is not expected to appear in Malkuth [the physical realm] and is supposed to be viewed on the astral nebulous matter which surrounds a magically empowered temple. At the same time it was expected amongst some Golden Dawn magicians that a 'physical appearance' meant just that."[11]

As for my experience, described at the beginning of this essay, I recall that the entities appeared to me with my eyes closed, although I could see them clearly enough that way. I was awake and alert and seated by the altar dedicated to these proceedings.

In another famous invocation from the Western occult tradition, Éliphas Lévi, in July 1854, performed a ritual to bring forth the ghost

[7] For this version of Cellini's account, I am relying on Jake Stratton-Kent, *Geosophia: The Argo of Magic; Encyclopedia Goetica*, vol. 2 (Bibliothèque Rouge, 2010), 1-10. Quotes are taken from Stratton-Kent's version, as is the emphasis.
[8] Homer, *The Odyssey* 11.37-40; my translation.

of Apollonius of Tyana, a magus of the first century AD. Lévi writes: "I distinctly saw, in front of the altar, the larger-than-life figure of a man, which then dissipated and faded away … then … I saw appear within the mirror in front of me, behind the altar, a white form, getting larger and appearing to draw nearer. I closed my eyes and called out to Apollonius three times; and when I opened them again, a man stood before me, entirely covered in some kind of shroud, who seemed to me to be more gray than white; his form was thin, sad, and beardless, which was not exactly the image I had of Apollonius beforehand."[12] (Indeed in ancient times philosophers were generally identified by the fact that they had beards.)

All of this leads us to wonder what kind of physicality—if that is the right word—it is that spirits and demons have. Hans Naegeli-Osjord, a Swiss psychiatrist specializing in possession and exorcism, notes that one physicist succeeded in demonstrating a six-dimensional space (current string theory posits ten dimensions); "therefore, it may be expected that the multiple-dimensional space of the parapsychologists can be integrated into the natural scientific perspective of the world and that eventually, the disciplines of parapsychology and natural sciences will no longer remain incompatible opposites."[13]

In any event, demons seem to possess an embodiment of a kind—even if we are forced to resort to elastic and ambiguous terms such as *etheric* or *astral* to describe it. Another experience of mine, this one from around 1985, leads me to conclude that there is such a thing as demonic embodiment, even if I do not know what that is. One night I was sleeping in bed and dreaming, when suddenly, a demon—or something I identified as such; it was a creature that was swamp-green and slimy—inserted itself into the dream and collided with me. This demon was not part of the dream, which had been about something completely different; rather it intruded into the dream, and I felt it almost as a physical collision, which sent me back into my physical body and into the waking state. No other human was present: I was alone in my bed and in my apartment. Rattled, I could not go back to sleep for a long time, although I noticed no particular aftereffects from the experience.

This encounter, unpleasant as it was, was instructive in more than one way. In the first place, it seemed to confirm that in the customary dream state, one is in a sense out of one's body: when the demon collided into me, I plunged immediately back into my body as an

[9] Christopher Marlowe, *Doctor Faustus*, act 1, scene 3.

[10] "The Ritual of the Evocation unto Visible Appearance of the Great Spirit Taphthartharath," *The Equinox*, vol. 1. no. 3: http://www.the-equinox.org/vol1/no3/eqi03010i.html; accessed July 26, 2017.

[11] Nick Farrell, "Triangle of the Art," Nick Farrell's Magical Blog, Nov. 5, 2013; http://www.nickfarrell.it/triangle-of-the-art/.

instinctive response. Furthermore, it suggests that a normal, healthy human constitution can fight off demonic attacks, just as it can fight off pathogens and parasites. Possession, then, happens to people who are weak or vulnerable in some way—usually psychically.

All of these things lead us to ask what demons are. The stock answer is to say that they are all just imagination—but that is little more than an instance of the naming fallacy. Really? Just imagination? What is imagination, then? Something illusory? What does that tell us? Less than one might suppose. After all, Hitler's race theory—to take an example almost at random—was completely illusory and imaginary; there was no science in it at all. That does not mean that it did not have very real—and palpable and widespread—effects. Sometimes, indeed, people make up things in their imaginations and cling to these imaginings even more avidly than they do with ordinary verifiable facts.

Setting aside the customary nonanswer of imagination, there seem to be three possibilities about the nature of demons.

1. They are, as suggested at the beginning of this essay, self-existent entities who inhabit dimensions of reality that do not entirely coincide with our physical reality. As I have already said, it is probably not wise to hastily sort them all into categories of good and bad. Many of them—like the demons described in this book—are said to be capable of granting valuable knowledge and skills. If they cannot be trusted, this could simply mean that they do not want to be captured and compelled to do things against their will—just as any ordinary human would fight violently and viciously to avoid being imprisoned.

2. They are creatures of the imagination, but in a somewhat more palpable way than is usually believed. Although they are created by the classic magical combination of imagination and will, if infused with enough vital force, they can assume a quasi-independent existence—and under certain circumstances can be encountered by people who did not create them. Sometimes the word egregore is applied to such entities.

3. They represent fragmented parts of the human psyche—aspects of the self that are hated and denied and that have therefore turned malevolent. This is the explanation favored by many psychoanalysts—particularly Jungian ones—but, like the other two possibilities, it explains certain cases but by no means all.

One only needs to read through the descriptions in this book to

[12] Éliphas Lévi, *The Doctrine and Ritual of High Magic: A New Translation*, John Michael Greer and Mark Anthony Mikituk, ed. and trans. (New York: Tarcher Perigee, 2017), 128.

[13] Hans Naegeli-Osjord, *Possession and Exorcism*, trans. Sigrid and David Coats (Oregon, Wisc.: New Frontiers Center, 1988), 26.

see that they are not mutually exclusive. Spirits—including those we call evil—may, no doubt do, exist as part of a supernatural ecosystem about which we know only bits and pieces. In other cases, they may be the conscious or even unconscious creations of the imagination, endowed with a certain power and autonomous existence. Occultist Donald Tyson writes, "It was once believed in Church lore that all evil impulses and thoughts are not only inspired by evil spirits, but are themselves tiny evil spirits."

These impulses—called *passions* in the language of the old esoteric Christian tradition—are the creation of the individual's own mind that then assume a semiautonomous character. In other cases, they may be broken or fragmented parts of the self—as one suspects is the case with instances of multiple-personality disorder (i.e. dissociation).

As for the right attitude to take toward them, most people will instinctively avoid the matter entirely. Some will be satisfied to contemplate the possibility of the demonic from the point of view of the spectator—whether as a reader of occult fiction or as a horror-movie fan. Others will want to examine the concept of the demonic with somewhat more intellectual precision and fastidiousness, as I have tried to do here. Still others—and they may be the smallest category of all—will want to take the journey to invoke and experience these entities for themselves. They should probably heed the advice of Cellini's necromancer, who warns him, "*The man who enters upon such an undertaking has need of a stout heart and firm courage.*" And of course, such adventurers should always be prepared for something to go wrong.

The Angelic Hierarchy

Many descriptions of demons allude to their place, or former place, in the heavenly hierarchy, which appears to be replicated in some form in hell. The classic outline of this organization is from The Celestial Hierarchy of Pseudo-Dionysius the Areopagite, dated to the sixth century AD. Here is Dionysius's order, which is generally followed by the Christian tradition. The list proceeds from the top: i.e., the seraphim, the first, are the ones closest to the throne of God.

SERAPHIM

CHERUBIM

THRONES

DOMINIONS

VIRTUES

POWERS

PRINCIPALITIES

ARCHANGELS

ANGELS

SELECTED BIBLIOGRAPHY

Belanger, Michelle. *The Dictionary of Demons: Names of the Damned.* Woodbury, Minn.: Llewellyn, 2010.

Bialik, Hayim Nahman, and Yehoshua Hana Ravnitzky, *The Book of Legends: Sefer ha-Aggadah; Legends from the Talmud and Midrash.* Translated by William G. Braude. New York: Schocken, 1992.

Cavendish, Richard. *The Black Arts.* New York: G.P. Putnam, 1967.

Charlesworth, James H., ed. *The Old Testament Pseudepigrapha, volume 1: Apocalyptic Literature and Testaments.* Peabody, Mass: Hendrickson, 1983.

Davidson, Gustav. *A Dictionary of Angels, Including the Fallen Angels.* New York: Simon & Schuster, 1967.

DuQuette, Lon Milo. *My Life with the Spirits: The Adventures of a Modern Magician.* York Beach, Maine: Samuel Weiser, 1999.

Fontaine, T.A.M. *In Defence of Judaism: Abraham ibn Daud; Sources and Structure of ha-Emunah ha-Ramah.* Maastricht, Netherlands: Van Gorcum, Assen, 1990.

Kieckhefer, Richard. *Forbidden Rites: A Necromancer's Manual of the Fifteenth Century.* University Park, Pa.: Pennsylvania State University Press, 1997.

Lévi, Éliphas. *The Doctrine and Ritual of High Magic: A New Translation.* Translated by Mark Anthony Mikituk. Edited by John Michael Greer. New York: Tarcher Perigee, 2017.

Meyer, Marvin, and Richard Smith, eds., *Ancient Christian Magic: Coptic Texts of Ritual Power.* San Francisco: HarperSanFrancisco, 1994.

Naegeli-Osjord, Hans. *Possession and Exorcism.* Translated by Sigrid and David Coats. Oregon, Wisc.: New Frontiers Center, 1988.

Peterson, Joseph H., ed. *The Lesser Key of Solomon: Lemegeton Clavicula Salomonis*. York Beach, Maine: Samuel Weiser, 2001.

Scot, Reginald. *The Discoverie of Witchcraft*. 1584. Accessed July 25, 2017; https://archive.org/stream/discoverieofwitc00scot/discoverieofwitc00scot_djvu.txt.

Stratton-Kent, Jake. *Geosophia: The Argo of Magic*; *Encyclopedia Goetica*, vol. 2. Bibliothèque Rouge, 2010.

Tyson, Donald. "Murmurs in the Dark: Possession by Spirits." *Dark Discoveries 36* (fall 2016), 21-27.

Wise, Michael, Martin Abegg Jr., and Edward Cook, trans. *The Dead Sea Scrolls: A New Translation*. San Francisco: HarperSanFrancisco, 1996.

ASMODEUS

Stories about Asmodeus are among the most colorful in demonology. His name—Ashmedai in Hebrew—means "destroyer." Some have also attempted to connect him with a Persian demon called Aeshma Deva. Asmodeus is not mentioned in the Bible, but he does appear in the Apocrypha, in the Book of Tobit, where he kills in succession seven husbands of a righteous woman named Sarah, each time before the marriage can be consummated. But when the righteous Tobias marries her, he drives Asmodeus away by following the advice of the angel Raphael, who tells him to take a fish he has caught, and, "when you enter the bridal chamber, take some of the fish's liver and heart, and put them on the embers of the incense. An odor will be given off; the demon will smell it and flee" (Tobit 6:17-18). There is a longstanding tradition that foul smells repel demons, as we have seen in Cellini's account described in the Introduction: he dispelled the spirits by burning asafetida.

Later versions of Tobit refer to Asmodeus as "king of the demons." In the pseudepigraphal *Testament of Solomon*, he describes himself thus: "I am called Asmodeus among mortals, and my business is to plot against the newly wedded, so that they may not know one another. And I sever them utterly by many calamities; and I waste away the beauty of virgins and estrange their hearts.... I transport men into fits of madness and desire when they have wives of their own, so that they leave them and go off by night and day to others that belong to other men; with the result that they commit sin and fall into murderous deeds." Traditionally he is the devil of sensuality, luxury, and lechery.

In Jewish lore, Asmodeus comes to King Solomon's court and vies with him in wisdom (a term that, in biblical times, included magical knowledge and power). In one case Asmodeus impresses Solomon by transporting a man from the race of people who live below the earth. For some reason, Asmodeus cannot take the man back to his own land, so the man stays on earth, marries, and has seven sons. The last resembles his father in having two heads. When the father dies, the two-headed son quarrels with the others over the division of the estate, claiming that he is really two people and so is entitled to two shares. Solomon resolves this dispute by the simple expedient of having a servant pour boiling water over one of the man's heads. The other head cries out, "My lord king, we are dying!" proving that the two-headed man is really one person.

Solomon relies on Asmodeus to help him build the Temple. Solomon has been ordered by God not to permit the sound of any tools at the site, and Asmodeus, captured and chained by Solomon's men, tells him that he needs a magical item called the *shamir*. By some accounts, the shamir is a tiny worm the size of a grain of wheat that has the power to cut down trees and hew slabs of stone; by another account it is a blue stone, and wherever it is placed, and the ineffable Name of God whispered, the rock breaks into the desired shape and size. Asmodeus tells Solomon that the shamir is guarded by a wild cock, and explains how to get it from him.

But the climactic encounter between Solomon and Asmodeus comes when Solomon asks the demon, "In what way is your power greater than ours?" Asmodeus replies, "Remove the chain from my back and give me your ring, and I will show you how great is my power." Solomon complies. Asmodeus swallows the ring, throws Solomon a distance of six hundred miles, and takes the throne, posing as the king. The exiled Solomon resorts to begging at doorways. He only manages to convince the Jewish Sanhedrin (high council) of his identity when his wives report that the disguised Asmodeus comes to them wearing socks, to conceal his feet, which are shaped like those of a cock.

This sequence of tales shows the progress of Asmodeus in Jewish legend. Starting as a purely evil figure, he becomes a clever trickster whose help can be gotten under certain circumstances.

The Floor of the Basement is the Roof of Hell

STEPHEN GRAHAM JONES

The contractor's name was Terry. He hadn't been on Candy and Jason's initial shortlist, but she'd seen his company truck the next block over, at the Martindales', and copied the number down. Now here they were at dinner, which Terry insisted on paying for since he could business-expense it. Before getting into the particulars of their situation, he introduced himself and his business via a story from his childhood, about dropped nails on his father's construction projects. For every hundred straight ones he found he would get a dollar, and his father's workers would get a talking to about carelessness and waste and safety. The guys on-site hated him, Terry said, leaning back from his plate, his glass of wine left, Candy thought, strategically full.

It's important that potential clients situate him somewhere between a lush and a teetotaler, she imagined. It's good to have appetites, just, it's bad to indulge them.

As for his story about the nails, she imagined it was what he opened every sales pitch with, since it established that he A) ran a clean site, B) was in a family business, and C) had once been a cute adorable kid.

Terry was the second contractor they were interviewing, but the first one to take them out to dinner on his card. In the final analysis, when stacked up against a two-month, seventy-five thousand dollar job—foundation work is neither cheap nor convenient—a dinner somewhere north of a hundred didn't really amount to much. But it was a good restaurant, Candy had to admit, and it's not like Terry was hard on the eyes or anything. She and Jason had ordered the salmon, as they'd agreed to do until they looked closer to the thirty they could still remember than the forty they were fast approaching, and Terry had the sugar steak the restaurant was known for, that the kitchen wouldn't dare cook anywhere even approaching medium well.

She asked Terry how much he'd made, collecting all those guilty nails.

"Gambled it all away betting on kickball," he said. "Fourth grade was rough."

So, Candy appreciated: D) a sense of humor as well.

Terry wiped his mouth with his napkin, as if signaling that the banter portion of this was drawing to a sad but necessary close. Time for the business.

What Candy and Jason needed, they explained, was for their two-story house not to crack in half. Evidently a fault line of sorts had developed in the foundation. Jason blamed it on the drought.

Terry nodded about this possibility while chewing his steak. By the way he neither dismissed Jason's idea nor ratified it with anecdote, Candy could tell he was humoring him. That, in his line of business, he knew every reason a foundation might start to crumble. And none of those reasons had anything to do with a lack of rain.

To save Terry the awkwardness of trying to show some modicum of respect for Jason's idea, Candy dropped into the story of how, in the sprawling basement, they'd found a gun-safe room that had been on neither the listing nor the blueprint, that the realtor said probably would have upped the appraisal by twenty-five thousand, at least.

"Hidden door," Jason added, leaning forward as if the neighboring table might be trying to tune this conversation in.

"Probably a panic room," Terry said, dabbing the corner of his mouth again. "Just doubled-up for the gun collection. Guns weren't still in there, were they?"

Jason shook his head no.

"Still has a dirt floor," Candy leaned forward to say, as if this wasn't information she wanted said too loud.

"Under the subfloor thing," Jason added, looking satisfied with himself for having known that word.

"Hunh," Terry said, narrowing his eyes in thought. "That is kind of... oh, yeah. It's unfinished. Of course. The dirt floor makes it count as technically unfinished. When the house was built, the builder was probably instructed to leave it like that, just raw. One unfinished room in a basement means the whole basement is unfinished, as far as property taxes go. Then another crew came in, finished it out under the radar. Know anything about the previous owner? The paranoid type?"

"Short sale," Jason said with a shrug. "Think it was a foreclosure."

"No cement in the toilets or anything, right?" Terry raised his hand for the ticket. Before Jason or Candy could say anything about the toilets, Terry added, "That room probably wasn't floored with concrete because—did you know concrete is exothermic? That means it breathes out all this heat as it dries. If somebody got their work orders backwards, if the walls were already painted, then that concrete, drying, could have peeled the paint back off."

"Thus, a subfloor," Candy said.

"Probably sealed," Terry said, taking what felt like a celebratory first drink from his glass of pinot. "You can spray this... it doesn't matter. Listen, no charge, nothing extra, I'll go down there, I'll look into it, make sure it's nothing you're going to have to deal with years down the road, right? You want this to be your last big job on the house, don't you?"

Jason and Candy nodded, did want this to be over once and for all.

"How was the—?" he said, indicating the salmon they'd each taken the fewest possible bites of.

"Flaky, buttery..." Jason tried, holding his hand up in the air for the perfect word. "How do you describe fish?"

"Delicious," Candy proclaimed. "Thank you."

Terry signed the credit card slip, closed the leather folder back over it, and the next morning, Jason and Candy cancelled the third interview they had scheduled, and signed with Terry.

That night, a loaf of French bread devoured between them at the kitchen island, along with most of a bottle of wine, Candy and Jason celebrated the end of the interview grind by fucking in the hallway between the office and the front living room. The idea was that, if Candy laid back on the pillow Jason had chivalrously retrieved from the bedroom upstairs, then she would be lying directly on a line that bisected the house—the fault line, the crack.

She tied a scarf around Jason's eyes and told him to imagine he was giving it to the house, and, while he wasn't looking, she closed her eyes too, imagined there were golden nails scattered all around her, and that they weren't at all distracting Terry from his thrusts.

Afterward, even though it matched nothing, she arranged that pillow in a corner of the couch. The game between Candy and Jason for years had been that that pillow, left out, was an invitation, a suggestion, a slow lick of the lips.

Never mind that it was the busy season for Jason, that he was out of town again in the morning.

It's for when he gets back, she told herself. It's for him to see when he leaves, to make sure he doesn't miss his flight home. It's to remind him about just now.

Candy walked along the back of the couch and let her fingertips brush the sticky top of the pillow, and then she happened to look through the ceiling-to-floor front window.

There was a vehicle out there, at the gate, wasn't there?

Yes. Just a vague shape, the almost-glint of a windshield.

A pickup? No headlights, no dome light.

But trucks don't ease up and park all by themselves.

Candy walked to the window, could see the truck no better. But, turning back to the house, she could see directly down the hall where the rug was still scrunched up on one side from her grabbing it, to keep from sliding off the fault line.

She pursed her lips in a smile, hoped Jason hadn't gotten the house pregnant.

She also hoped it had been a good enough show.

She would have to remember to check the outside of that window, for smudges, for smears.

"What has gotten into you, girl?" she said out loud, mischievously. She had an immediate answer for that, too.

Candy smiled, followed the handrail upstairs.

The next morning she texted Kath Martindale from the next street over, to ask if it was too early to call. Kath texted right back, and they were talking over their separate coffees a moment later.

What Candy wanted was the scoop on Terry.

"Who?" Kath asked, switching ears with her phone it sounded like.

"Your contractor?" Candy said back. "Looks like the Marlboro Man if he didn't smoke? I saw his white pickup at your house the other day."

"A white truck?" Kath said.

"You had your foundation worked on?" Candy prompted.

"Oh, oh, yes," Kath said. "I let Ben deal with all of that. There isn't enough Xanax in the world, right? I was at my sister's for most of it. Have you seen my tan?"

Candy hadn't, but for the next ten minutes she heard about it, until a knock on the door saved her.

It was Terry, in the flesh. He peeled his sunglasses from his weathered face and scuffed his boots on the welcome mat. Behind him, diesel engines were firing up and a large truck was delivering a port-a-pottie. Candy hadn't considered that aspect of all this. But of course. She couldn't have men tromping in at all hours of the day for the half-bath by the kitchen.

"Yes?" she said, and then stepped aside to invite Terry in, out of the clamor and bustle of what was now, obviously, a job site.

Dinner Terry had been at home in the elegance of the restaurant, directing the wait staff around without having to say a word. Daytime Terry was at a loss for where to start.

Candy stole a glance down, to be sure her robe wasn't open. Well, that it wasn't open too much.

"Jason around?" Terry finally got out.

"He's probably at cruising altitude by now," Candy said, tilting her head up into the idea of the wide blue sky. "Can I help you?"

"It's just," Terry stammered, "we usually—we assign, or, we ask someone to run point on the project."

"That's not you?"

"The homeowner, I mean," Terry said. "Just for any questions, any decisions, that sort of stuff."

"That's me," Candy said. Then, about the yarn bracelet Terry was wearing, "Your daughter?"

"Son," Terry said, showing off the bracelet. "My daughter's still teething."

"You're lucky," Candy said. "Kids, I mean."

Terry nodded that he was indeed lucky, then Roff, Jason's oversized poodle, was bustling and barking down the stairs, and Candy had to oversee that big meet and greet.

The procedure, as Terry outlined it, gaining confidence, was designed to be as noninvasive as possible. He instructed her to secure any china in cabinets, as there would be episodes of shaking. There was simply no avoiding that; digging under the house at an angle with heavy equipment was a shaky enterprise—but safe, safe, he guaranteed. He'd never damaged a house in fifteen years.

Candy offered him lemonade. He accepted.

Standing in the foyer, tousling Roff's curls, he detailed the next step: inserting massive hydraulic jacks under the house, lifting it as few inches as possible—there were waterlines to be aware of—and fitting pylons underneath, to take some of the strain of the house's weight off the foundation. But that meant carving down deep enough to find some bedrock to anchor those pylons to.

"The basement stairs?" Candy asked. Because those jacks would be under the house proper, not the basement. She pictured the staircase to the basement accordioning out... out... and then snapping in two.

"On my to-do list," Terry said, tapping his notebook with the eraser of his wide, flat pencil.

"What about the gun room?"

"That old panic room..." Terry said, as if just remembering. "It'll be fine, of course, but I should check it out. We don't want to dig too close, collapse a wall."

"This way," Candy said, and very intentionally led him down the hall from last night, stopped to step out of her house shoe, straighten that scrunch of rug with her toes. Terry's face gave nothing away.

Roff bounded downstairs before them into the cold of the basement, and Candy, on the way back to the last door on the right, the one so flush with the wall that it disappeared, explained that they didn't even know what to do with all this space, all this extra.

"Mother-in-law suite?" Terry said, peering around.

"Not in my lifetime," Candy said with a chuckle, and then they were there.

"Fifteen by fifteen," Terry said, standing beside Jason's weight bench. Besides the mounts on the wall for rifles and shotguns and maybe pistols, the weight bench was the only thing in the room.

"Mind?" Terry said, already feeling along the edge of the carpet by the wall.

Candy stepped back, let him fold the carpet back then find a panel in the subfloor, work it up from its fitting.

"Dirt all right. Come feel, though."

Candy knelt by him, touched her fingertips to the dirt, not sure what to expect.

It was like the desserts on a restaurant cart: plastic. Fake. Dirt just for show. The look of dirt, but not the feel. Not a grain of soil would dislodge.

"It's kind of been..." Terry said, searching for words, "like, sprayed with superglue. A sealant. Keeps moles and mold back." He worked a screwdriver up from his pocket, flipped it around to tap the plastic handle onto the hard shell of dirt.

"Oh," Candy said, drawing her hand up to her mouth for some reason.

"It's a polymer, should last forever," Terry said, and worked the subflooring back into place, smoothed the carpet over it. "To be honest, I wouldn't do a thing to it, other than not think about it."

Candy agreed one hundred percent.

Still, that night?

She was thinking about it.

Before seeing it, she'd only known about it, from Jason, who had told her he had no idea that was even a thing in the civilized world, leaving bare dirt in a home like that. Seeing the imitation dirt herself, though, that clear crust, that shell—now Candy couldn't stop thinking about it.

This whole time, it had been right here underneath them? A grubby little imperfection in an otherwise perfect home?

By midnight she was back in Jason's weight room, as she was calling it. She'd pulled the carpet back, managed to work that panel of subflooring up.

In thriller movies, and in the Poe stories she remembered from a boyfriend or two before marrying Jason, this was always where you buried whoever you'd killed. It didn't work out, of course, but it was exciting for a while. Especially when the detective would be walking right over the very patch of ground, effectively tamping the grave down with each footstep.

Candy didn't know anything about who had lived here before. Somebody paranoid enough to hire layers of workers to hide a room. Somebody who had been foreclosed upon. She reminded herself to call Kath, helpful helpful Kath, about that as well.

She tapped her chin with her index finger and stared at the frozen-in-place dirt. Roff sniffed at it, must not have smelled like anything.

"Well, well, inspector," she said, and strolled ever so casually right across the dirt.

It wasn't quite even, but it didn't give, either.

Candy sat on Jason's weight bench and wrapped a length of yellow yarn around and around her wrist. It was too long for any kind of sensible bracelet, of course, unless you tied it into a complicated fish tail or something. But summer camp workshops had been twenty years or more ago already. She wasn't even sure what drawer she'd filched the yarn up from, walking through the house with all the lights on, a glass of red wine in hand.

She inserted one of the yarn's ragged ends into her mouth, in thought. And then she poured her nail polish remover onto what she was calling the hairsprayed dirt.

Had Jason been in town, had he walked in in his gym shorts, his preppy towel wrapped around his neck like a deodorant commercial, Candy might have told him she was doing this because Terry had said that magic word "polymer," which had made her think of how the nail salon smelled.

But there was more to it than just a vague association, of course.

When they'd taken possession six weeks ago, they'd been diligent—diligent to the point of pills and lubrication—about christening each room of the house, to prove that they owned it. Toward the end of the process they'd cheated a bit, by starting in one room, moving through another, finishing in a third, up against a wall if there wasn't any furniture, but still, cheating or no, a crime scene unit would have found proof of them in each and every room.

Except this one. Because they hadn't found it by then.

Candy knew this was where they should have brought the pillow last night, not the hallway.

But she could make up for it.

In the old days, you christened a ship by breaking a bottle against its hull.

She wasn't sure exactly how a person might ceremonially welcome hairsprayed dirt into the world—or into a *home*—but she imagined that it might involve letting that dirt have its first breath of air in years.

And there was nobody there to tell her otherwise.

She woke to the walls shaking around her, to dust sifting down from the ceiling.

She was lying by Jason's workout bench.

Upstairs, Roff was barking at the front door.

Somewhere a plate crashed into tile floor. Then another.

It was starting, then.

Candy worked her arm under her, angled herself up.

Had she really slept here? Of all places?

She stood, unsteady at first.

The vapors had conked her, she decided. Yes, as it was supposed to, the fingernail polish remover had interacted with the hard, supposedly permanent shell over the dirt, but in this closed space, that reaction had had nowhere to vent. So it had had to filter through her lungs, which gave it access to her bloodstream, and the rest was blackout history.

That had to be it.

When the house shook next, it was hard enough that Jason's weights jingled on the bar. From how this assault felt, Candy assumed the tractor was backing up to the street to get a running start, then throttling forward through as many gears as it could before it slammed into the house. Something along those lines.

She knelt to slide the subflooring panel back in place and timed it poorly—right when the next tremor came.

This one cracked the crust over the dirt in two.

A breath of hot, corrupt air sighed up.

"Oh," Candy said, standing back, impressed.

This was something.

Without taking her eye from this development, she collected the empty bottle of fingernail polish remover, checked the floor by the bench to be sure she wasn't forgetting anything, and then she whistled once, sharply, for Roff.

For maybe the first time since his training, he didn't respond, was having a panic attack about the end of the world he could hear happening right outside the front door.

"Well then," Candy said, and skirted the dirt and the subflooring panel, stepped out into the hall, sure to close the invisible door behind her.

❖

After a quick change of clothes and some general freshening up—tennis skirt, messy bun, eyeliner—Candy edged out the door, careful to keep Roff in, and walked into the noise and clamor. She was carrying a plastic platter of patio glasses, with a pitcher of lemonade set among them like a queen, the glasses already sloshing full.

The diesel engines whined down and six hard hats tilted back on their respective heads.

Candy flounced out among them, eyeing the damage along the way.

They were indeed digging a big expensive hole under her house.

"Gentlemen," she said, presenting the tray, and six hands took six glasses, then a few of those faces split into a secret smile.

"I don't see Terry's truck, do I?" Candy said conspiratorially.

"No, ma'am, you don't," one of the men answered.

In the patio glasses—cups really, since they were made of plastic—was Jason's beer. It wasn't the same color as the lemonade in the pitcher, but the glasses were foggy green.

"Hot day," Candy said, and looked up into the sun. It was swimming with worms of flame. She tried to blink it away.

What was happening to her?

What if Jason pulled up now, his meetings cancelled, his flights all early, and saw her out here barefoot, showing this much leg, giving his beer away to men who needed steady hands if they were going to keep the house from crashing down?

"Kath," she said to herself, just remembering her intentions to call her, and she turned to do just that, stepped on something sharp halfway to the door. She collapsed around the pain.

Ten minutes later she had been hand-delivered to her couch, and Terry was walking in, not smiling.

There were no engines rumbling outside. No great shovels tearing into the earth.

"I apologize," Terry said, his yellow hard hat in his hands. "They're all gone."

"Gone?" Candy said.

"Fired," Terry said. "One, no drinking on the job, ever, zero excuses. Two—shit."

He was just now seeing the bloody nail on the coffee table.

He checked his boots, crossed to the couch to inspect Candy's foot.

She winced away but he caught her calf, was kneeling already.

"We're not even using nails," he said, disgusted. "This is an excavation right now."

"I'm sure it was already there," Candy said. "The landscapers."

Terry wasn't buying it.

"We need to wash it," he said, and went to the kitchen for water. He stopped at the doorway.

"Those were already broke," Candy called across to him.

He lowered his head, stepped in—crunched *through*—ran the faucet, was still running it when Candy stepped in behind him.

He looked over his shoulder, continued wringing the dishrag he'd found.

"You shouldn't be—" he said, but was interrupted by a white platter crashing onto the tile.

He looked from it up to Candy.

She pushed a white saucer off. It shattered.

Terry turned the faucet off, rubbed his neck with the hand not holding the wet dishrag.

"We needed a new set anyway," she said, pushing a coffee cup off. A red coffee cup, one of the standalones, not part of any set.

"Our insurance can cover it," he said, crossing to her, kneeling again, to apply the wet rag to her foot. "Just tell your husband that—"

"My husband isn't here," she said, and when he looked up to her about that, all the way up her, time dilated around them. This moment.

She stepped outside of it, kind of saw herself.

Was there any reason to be doing this? Really?

No, she told herself.

Somehow that made it even better.

"Not here," Terry said into her neck five minutes later, when she had him pressed up against the sink, the window directly behind him like a picture frame.

"I know just the place," Candy said, and took his hand, led him down the hall, every other footstep on the tile dabbed red. All the way down the carpeted stairs. All the way to Jason's weight room. "No windows," she said, spreading her arms, spinning slowly, losing her clothes.

When the weight bench creaked underneath them, threatening to give—apparently it wasn't rated for love, or whatever this was—they rolled onto the floor, and Candy's raw foot pressed against the raw dirt, and that brief grit was just the right thing, just the perfect thing.

Kath wasn't answering her phone.

Terry wasn't even two minutes gone. She could still feel him.

Candy paced.

Roff was licking up the blood from the tile.

"Good boy," Candy said, sweeping past.

She couldn't stop moving, wasn't sure what would happen if she did.

Things were happening fast, weren't they?

And: *things*?

"Cheating on your husband, you mean," Candy said aloud. "Breaking your flatware."

Were they more or less equivalent?

They were, she told herself.

It's not like she'd used the special pillow with Terry or anything.

It's not like she'd needed it, she added.

Next, an actual blip later, it felt like, she was back in the weight room.

She expected it to smell like sex, but if it smelled like anything, it was just… earthen, she supposed. Like the digging outside.

She knelt to rub at a wet place in the carpet with the belt of her robe, and then another place, and then Roff was there as well, helping her.

She sat on the weight bench with her face in her hands, and of course that was when the phone upstairs started ringing.

Candy made a dash, caught it on the fifth ring.

"Thought you weren't there," Kath said.

"I was—I was downstairs," Candy said, out of breath.

"You were downstairs, or he was…?" Kath said.

Candy looked around the room, said, "Jason's in Philadelphia. Somewhere up there."

The pause that came next was meaningful.

"I was calling to ask about who used to live here," she said.

"What do you mean?"

"The former owner, you know," Candy said.

"Oh," Kath said. "Jim, you mean? The pervert?"

"The what?" Candy sat down.

Kath explained: it never went to court, the allegations, but Jim K-something—Koppel?—had evidently liked to stand around playgrounds, and just watch.

"Maybe he missed his son or daughter," Candy offered.

"Or maybe he was stocking the spank bank," Kath said.

"There was an indictment?"

"Everybody knew," Kath said deliciously. Her the mom of eight-year-old twin boys. "But then he just pulled the old eject lever—not that one—and, blip, no more Jim Koppel. Probably some country with, you know, a tourist industry more suited to his, ahem, tastes."

Candy had her eyes closed.

Jason had told her that the mounts in the weight room were for rifles and shotguns and pistols. And they looked like that, didn't they? She could imagine firearms on the walls down there. A walk-in safe.

But could it have been something else? If so, *what*?

"Anyway," Kath went on, "his loss, your gain, right? I'd always wanted you to live closer like this."

Candy nodded, didn't know what to say.

"Do I see trucks in your driveway?" Kath asked then.

"Workers," Candy said. "They're all fired."

"Interesting…" Kath said. "Even that—what was his name?"

"Terry," Candy said, then added the necessary "Something like that."

"I found him in Ben's house rolodex," Kath said. "Can you believe I live with someone like that? He has three rolodexes. Business, house, and personal." Kath laughed, added, "Three that I know about anyway."

"So he did work on your foundation?" She prayed Kath wasn't

going to repeat *foundation* in a suggestive way. "I just need it for Jason," she added, digging in the desk drawer for a pen.

She scratched the info down, Kath still talking into her ear even though the conversation was long over.

"Are you all right, girl?" Kath could have said.

I don't know, one part of Candy would have said back.

There was another part of her too, though. Now there was.

"Roff!" Candy said, as if he were doing something he shouldn't be. As if he were even in the room. "Listen, I'm sorry, but my dog, he's—" and that was how she got the phone hung back up.

She sat on the couch, hugging the special pillow to her chest.

This wasn't so bad, she told herself. She'd always been pretty sure that what Jason did out of state, that was none of her business. No questions, no answers they would have to deal with. That's what marriage was. Just, she didn't travel out of state. So she was having to make do.

That was exactly it.

In Philadelphia or wherever Jason was, he was probably right now sitting down the bar from some tall leggy thing. Some inevitable thing.

Good for him.

Maybe he'd learn some new tricks.

With Terry, just now, Candy thought she might have a thing or two she could apply, when Jason was home.

Without really meaning to or thinking about it or making a decision, she dialed Jason's number.

It rang and rang.

She didn't leave a voicemail.

"Roff!" Candy called, then did the whistle the trainer had trained him on.

No clawed feet, slipsliding down the tile of the hallway.

Still clutching the pillow, she searched the house room by room, starting at the top even though it was too hot upstairs for a dog.

Eventually she had to go back downstairs.

The invisible door was open, just like she hadn't left it.

"Roff?" Candy said.

She carefully turned on every light in the basement. It was so empty down here. Jason had suggested wicker furniture, so he wouldn't have to carry heavy stuff down the stairs, ha ha. Candy had said she wasn't sure what she wanted to do with this space yet.

And the door at the end on the right was still cracked open.

Candy whistled again, harsher, harder.

Nothing. No dog.

It was just a stupid leftover secret room, right?

Candy stifflegged it down there, looked in, the light already on.

No Roff.

It still smelled like fresh-turned dirt, not like sex. Which was good. Which was great.

Except.

The crack in the shell of dirt, the slit in the ground, it was… it was bulging, now. That was the only word for it.

Like there was pressure down there.

Candy turned the light off, closed the door, and went to the hardware store.

She had to get someone from Paint to help her load the bags of concrete onto her flatbed cart. He said he didn't mind.

"Patio or bathroom remodel?" he asked, trying to look like the bags weren't heavy.

"Basketball goal for my son," Candy lied. It came so natural.

"Must be going deep," he said, throwing the sixth bag on.

"Thanks," Candy told him, and leaned into the cart's wide handle, to push, ended up pulling instead, which meant doubling back through Tools.

Another worker loaded it into her SUV, patted the last bag into place, like telling it to stay. As if its weight could possibly shift. Candy tipped him eight dollars, all the cash she had, and drove away. The road looked different, now—the hood of her SUV was in the way, with the back end squatting down.

She turned the radio up. It wasn't a station she ever listened to, but screw it.

She let off the accelerator halfway home.

The restaurant, the one Terry had wined and dined her and Jason at.

It was a blackened husk.

Candy stopped in front of it.

This must have happened… the last day or two, she figured. How had she not heard? Every time a liquor store got knocked over, it made the paper. A snooty restaurant would be front-page material.

Terry would know, she told herself, and looked around, like for the left or right turn that would lead to the road that would lead to the highway that would take her to his place. To wherever he was.

But she'd left his info on the pad of paper on the desk, hadn't she?

"Shit!" she said, and banged the heel of her hand into the steering wheel.

Terry would also be able to tell her the best way to mix this concrete, too. The directions were there on the bag, but she didn't think they guaranteed success. There was nothing about covering a hellhole in the surprise room in your basement, say. The one that was less a crack, she had to admit, more a slit. Like it was going to birth something early one morning, while she was sleeping.

She called Kath. Of course.

For once Kath was rushed, which meant she was helpful, could reel off Terry's address from her weird memory instead of having to paw through Ben's rolodex again.

Terry's house was only fifteen minutes away.

His white truck wasn't parked in the driveway. But there was a minivan with a plastic tricycle wedged under it from the side. Which made sense, Candy supposed, there being a minivan. A family. And it made her aware, too: she'd only been factoring Jason into this dark equation. But that was just her side of the problem. There was also a wife to take into consideration. And a son who liked to tie yarn around his father's thick wrist. And a daughter, still teething.

Candy closed her eyes, didn't quite come to a stop. That would be a giveaway. That could prompt questions, whenever Terry finally got home.

She mashed the pedal, turned hard enough that that top bag of concrete, which had been patted into place, told to be good, to behave itself, slid off the pile, impacted the floor of the SUV's cargo space hard enough that Candy felt it in the wheel.

She was crying a little, she had to admit. It was stupid to pretend you weren't doing what you were already doing.

That included fucking the contractor.

She hit the steering wheel again, and again, and screamed through her teeth.

The basement hall in front of the weight room—the sex room, the cheating room, the room she hadn't meant to ever find—was swirling with concrete dust.

The garden hose was draping in through the window of what Jason had told Candy had probably been the rumpus room for the last owners.

Candy doubted that, now. Though a pedophile probably would have *wanted* it to be a rumpus room. Just, he would have his own inflection on that word, "rumpus."

Candy was mixing the concrete on a dark green tarp. She'd wanted the wheelbarrow, but guiding it down the stairs had gotten immediately complicated. For a stir stick, she'd spun the head off a plunger and coated the wooden handle in shortening. Her pecs and delts and triceps were on fire from all this churning, but she was determined.

She was going to tell Jason that the excavation had cracked open the dirt floor, and Roff had fallen in, and Terry wasn't answering his phone and she didn't know what to do so she just did *this*, okay?

The part about Roff was probably true, too.

She wouldn't mention anything about her foot having probably bled into there, though.

It didn't even hurt anymore. Jason need never know about that. And if he saw somehow, then she'd just stepped on a broken plate on the way to get a late night glass of water, and it was the fault of the big diggers again, and neither her nor Jason would have to picture her and Terry, writhing together.

And Candy wasn't picturing it now, either.

Not even a little. Not his smell, not his breathing, not the pressure of his fingers on her sides.

Candy stirred harder, deeper.

The concrete was like oatmeal made from gravel.

When it seemed to match the consistency recommended on the bag, she tried dragging the tarp over, to lift one side, let the slurry slide over and in.

No doing. If one bag was too heavy, then six at once, with water, was impossible.

When there were no shovels in the shed, no spades in the garage, she finally had to clamber up a tall tire of the big yellow scoop-tractor—her name for it—using the treads for ladder rungs, and liberate a wide wooden plank that had been cut to fit the bottom portion of a window without any glass in it. Candy didn't understand and didn't care.

In the weight room—in the hall *outside* the weight room—she scooped pounds of concrete at a time onto the end of the plank, transferred it into the slit. When the slit seemed to have no bottom, was just going to drink all she had and ask for more, please, she broke up a shoe rack from her closet, laid the planks across the opening in the dirt like scaffolding, plastered the concrete on thicker and thicker, until it was a mound.

It was an hours-long process.

At the end of it, Candy was sheened in sweat. Air circulation sucked down here. Or, no, it didn't suck at all, that was the problem.

She laughed deliriously, wiped her forehead with the back of her forearm, and stood, had to steady herself on the wall.

It was done. Fixed. Over.

Thank you.

She'd roll the tarp up for the dumpster later. Not the dumpster her and Jason tipped the kitchen trash in, but the big industrial one that had been delivered right after they'd signed on the dotted line.

Just more construction detritus.

Candy was breathing hard, and deep.

Water. She needed water.

She made her way upstairs, was surprised to find it was night time.

She was less surprised to see the outline of a pickup sitting by the gate.

She crossed to the window, couldn't be sure, so she opened the front door, telling herself she was just going to step out as far as the edge of the porch. There were nails out there, she knew now.

Terry was standing there.

"I was ringing the doorbell," he said.

"You should—" Candy said. "I can't—"

"I just wanted to be sure about your foot," he said.

It made sense, she supposed.

Tetanus, lockjaw, all that.

She walked back inside, left the door open behind her, settled onto the couch.

Terry followed, didn't close the door behind him.

"I'm sorry about your guys," Candy said.

"Just let me see," he said, kneeling in front of her again.

He hadn't said anything about the obvious signs of her exertion. About the pale dust surely in her hair, in her clothes, in all her creases.

When the light was wrong, he lifted her so easy, to set her more sideways on the couch, the pillow nestling right into the sway of her back.

Candy told herself no, that this didn't mean anything.

The rough pad of his finger on the arch of her foot sent a shiver through her.

"Sorry I'm so dirty," she said, hugging the pillow to her stomach, now. Watching him over it.

"I am too," he said, his index finger pressed between her big toe and the next one.

"I know," she said, and leaned forward, and Candy didn't know if this was a second christening of the formal living room or a de-christening, but, in the moment, the door open, the drapes fluttering all around them, the room filled with their breathing, she didn't much care, either.

Candy woke to the sun setting. She was pretty sure that was what it was doing.

Meaning?

The night had passed. And the day as well.

She sat up fast, eyes desperate for the door.

It was closed. The deadbolt was straight up and down, meaning it wasn't locked—of course it wasn't; Terry didn't have a key—but that he'd thought to do that, to protect her from the leering eyes of whatever new crew he was bringing in, that had maybe been there all day already… did that count as love?

Close enough.

She showered until her skin was new, and when claws clicked on the tile in the bathroom beyond her foggy door, she said hello to Roff before remembering that Roff was gone.

She opened the door to nothing, to no one.

She closed her eyes, sat on the step in the shower and let her chin shiver.

When was the last time she'd eaten? The last meal she could clearly recall, it was that salmon at the restaurant.

The restaurant.

Wrapped in a towel, having to hold it shut with one hand—against who, she couldn't imagine—Candy opened her laptop in the bedroom, dug into the newspaper's headlines. When she didn't have a subscription, she bought one, who cares.

There was nothing for the last three days, then nothing for the last week. Finally she just searched up "restaurant" plus "fire."

It had gone up four months ago.

The photo gallery could have been from yesterday.

Candy shut the laptop, made herself breathe deep and calm.

She was mistaken. That had to be it. She was mistaking one place for another place. It had been dark when they got there, hadn't it? And—and Jason had made that stupid joke, about how no cars in the parking lot meant they would be getting good service.

It hadn't seemed odd, though.

Why hadn't it seemed odd?

Oh: because then Terry's white pickup had pulled up alongside them, so he could usher them in.

There had been other diners, she was pretty sure. Almost certain.

There had been the clatter of silverware in the darkness. The rustle of napkins on laps.

And, their waiter… Candy had assumed Terry had a rapport with him. Something like that. It was because, instead of speaking, Terry had pointed to his steak on the menu, and then, after Jason had decided on the salmon for him and Candy—not a decision at all—Terry had pointed to the menu again for the waiter.

A language barrier?

And it *had* been good, hadn't it? For fish? For healthy stupid normal fish?

Candy felt it rising in her throat. She turned to the side, kicked the trash can over just in time to splash her stomach's contents down into it.

It was nothing. It was pink bile and clear juices and some grainy stuff. Probably concrete, Candy figured, and had to laugh about it, because otherwise she was going to cry and cry and cry.

Shouldn't Jason be home by now? How long was this trip? What floozy was he shacked up with?

She didn't know where that last thought had come from, exactly. *Floozy*? Was that even in her vocabulary?

She felt around for her cell, touched Jason's face, let a line open between them.

Voicemail.

Candy hung up, was afraid what her mouth might say, how it might betray her.

We're going to need to do the front living room again, dear.

Your dog is dead.

There's a hole opening up under our house.

But... but there wasn't anymore, right?

Candy pulled on some clothes, stepped into her house shoes, and made her way downstairs, turning on each light as she went, and waiting for it to fully glow on before she submitted to crossing its expanses.

You're being stupid, girl, she told herself.

You're guilty, so you're spooking yourself out as punishment.

Before going downstairs, she stopped to roll open the breadbox, pull out a corner of the French bread Jason had been pinching off, to feed her... how many nights ago?

She was watching the windows, the corners, so she didn't see the bread before she put it into her mouth, and she didn't spit its fuzziness back out until she was on the stairs down to the basement.

Green. Mold.

She gagged again, didn't have anything to throw up.

Had she been asleep on the couch for two days?

The lights in the basement were all still blazing. It was like stepping into a tanning bed. Candy squinted but didn't turn any of them off.

The basement door was still shut as well.

All was in order.

Candy repeated that to herself: this is all normal, this is all perfectly all right.

It wasn't.

She creaked the invisible door open—did it used to creak?—and, in the weight room, the lights *were* off.

A wall of hot air breathed out across her.

She stepped back, let it pass, spread out, then she felt in for the switch, clicked the light on. It sputtered, caught.

The concrete was still there—her first fear had been that it had been swallowed, like Roff—but the slit in the dirt, it had bulged more under the concrete, it looked like. There was an opening in the concrete, now. It made the concrete look like puss.

And it was so hot. What had Terry called it? Exo-something?

Exo-*hot* was what it was.

Like the sex they'd had down here had kept happening. The walls were sweating with it.

Candy stepped forward to touch one, her house shoe squelching into the outer edge of the concrete. It was supposed to be rock, but her house shoe stuck.

She stepped back, her shoe staying, and retrieved the crusty plank she'd stolen from the yellow tractor. She pushed its other end into the thickest part of the slurry of concrete she'd slathered onto the broken pieces of her shoe rack.

It was still soft.

She shook her head no, stepped back, her hand finding the wall, her fingers coming away from that contact with… paper?

Terry had been wrong about one thing at least: concrete drying wouldn't peel the paint in the weight room. It would peel the wallpaper.

Under the wallpaper there was just light gray sheetrock.

Candy felt an edge out, pulled it all down in disintegrating clumps, the tearing not sounding like tears. The air was too damp in here for that, too moist, too thick. The gun mounts stayed in place, each standing now on a small pad of wallpaper. Like erections, Candy thought, and giggled. It wasn't good giggling. She was out of crying, though. She was running out of a lot of things. This week was hollowing her out, leaving her empty. Soon she would just be a face, nothing behind that face.

She started to back out through the doorway but caught on some writing on the sheetrock. In the lightest pencil.

It was some drywaller's scratch pad. A math problem, measurements tallying up here where no one would ever see.

And at the next join there was another math problem. And lower, like—yes—like this piece of sheetrock had been written on while it was laying down somewhere. Probably the family room out there.

The next measurement was upside down, proving her theory, and then, back around by the doorway, where she could already see the last equation taking shape in slanted-gray numerals, there was something else, way down by the baseboard like a secret.

asmod

But it broke where the drywall stopped.

Candy stood, focusing all over the weight room at once, tracing the joins with her eyes. Most of them had been mudded over, or whatever they called it. But high up on the wall, upside down again, behind Jason's weight bench he'd had since college, the word maybe completed.

eus

Unless there was a missing part in the middle.

Candy licked her finger, rubbed the letters.

They smudged into nothing.

She nodded that that was good.

She was still in control. All this could still be dealt with, swept under some rug.

She went off to find that rug.

It was at Kath's, Candy was sure. Ninety percent certain.

Not a physical rug, but advice.

Candy was going to spill to Kath about all of this. She wasn't going to censor or edit. That was always the problem: people in trouble A) never ask for help, and B) when they do, they always try to tell the story which makes them sound the least culpable.

Candy was culpable as hell, and she knew it.

She hadn't had to open her robe for Terry.

At the same time, he hadn't had to run his hand up under it.

Candy wondered if she even knew herself anymore.

And maybe Kath would have something to eat, too. If Candy could tell her the whole sorry affair without breaking down, and be honest about it, throw herself at Kath's feet and ask for guidance, for help, then maybe Kath would light a torch, show Candy the way out.

So far the only thing that had really been lost was Roff, and some plates.

And Jason was going to be so distraught about Roff that he probably wouldn't even notice if Candy's right hand was still sticky with Terry.

We can use that, Kath would tell Candy. And then pass her a dishrag.

But—Candy shook her head no, turned into Kath's long driveway.

The writing on the wall in the basement, that didn't mean anything. It didn't factor in at all. What mattered was what Kath could help with. Kath who, two years ago, had stepped out on Ben and still kept the marriage together somehow, when Ben had even walked in on them at what, in Kath's whispered retelling, was both the best and the worst moment, depending on where you were standing, or not standing.

So, if anybody could help her, it would be Kath.

Candy braked hard, left the door of her SUV open like an announcement to Ben that this was emergency stuff, and walked into Kath's without even bothering to knock, like always.

The house smelled... not bad, but like the dining room in Candy's parents' house: like dust. Like it hadn't been walked through in ages.

"Kathy?" she called, half-imagining she was about to walk in on Kath with whoever her next not-Ben was.

The downstairs was empty, though.

She gripped the handrail on the way upstairs, announcing herself the whole way with both Kath and Ben's names.

Nothing. No one.

Even in the master bath.

Except... the bathtub had a blanket spread over it?

Candy stood before it for a full two minutes.

"Kath?" she said at last.

The surface of the blanket didn't rustle.

Candy was breathing hard now, shaking her head no, her fingers clutching the lip of the sink behind her.

"I just talked to you," she said to the blanket, at which point a bird or a squirrel fluttered or scampered outside the window right above the blanket and Candy startled, knocked Kath's perfume rack onto the floor.

Some shattered, some rolled.

Candy, barefoot again, had to step between the shards.

Halfway down the stairs, she couldn't help it: she ran.

In her SUV she held onto the wheel until she could stop hyperventilating.

Terry.

Terry, then.

It didn't matter if his wife answered the door.

The deal Candy made to herself, sitting outside Terry's house, was that however these next few minutes went down, she was going to check in to a hotel immediately afterward, she was going to order everything room service had, and she was going to stay there and recuperate, recover, *deal.*

Now that there was no dog to feed, she could do things like that.

It's not like Jason didn't have enough reward or loyalty or whatever points. She could probably stay there a year before it cost anything.

Also? Screw the money.

Satisfied with her plan, she stood from her SUV, closed the door this time and beeped the lock, made fists by her legs for the walk up to the front door.

She was the other woman now. And she looked like boiled shit, she knew. Would that make it better?

She confabulated on the way: the digging outside her house, it had, it had messed up a water line, it had sprayed her in the kitchen, her house was a mess, Terry wasn't answering his phone.

That would work. Another woman would sympathize with an exploded kitchen, wouldn't she? She would have to.

The doorbell didn't pull any moms with kids on their hips up from the depths of the modest home, though.

Neither did a second ring.

And, this time, the door was locked.

Minutes too late, Candy noticed that the minivan was parked in exactly the same place, with the same plastic tricycle wedged under it from the side.

But it had only been a day, right? No, two days. Or three.

Candy stepped timidly out onto the lawn, cupped her hands around her eyes to see through the front window, into the living room.

Nothing. No one.

But, with the minivan here, and Terry's truck just having a front seat, where could a family of four *be*?

Candy let herself into the backyard, stood on a storage bin, peered into another window.

A kid's bedroom. A boy, it looked like.

She stepped down, went deeper.

The sliding glass door was open.

She shook her head no but went in all the same. Because she had to see. Because not seeing would be miles and years worse.

There was a splash of what had to be blood across the television screen.

It was dried black.

And the smell.

Kath's house had just smelled unused.

This was different.

And, now, Candy knew where to go.

In the bathtub, the blanket sloughing off, were three bodies. Mom, son, daughter.

It looked—*no no no!*—it looked like big hands had tried to playfully stuff the daughter back into the mother.

Candy fell back against the wall in the hall, some picture dislodging, falling to the ground, a single crack of glass resounding.

She left by the front door, sure to lock it behind her.

She was snuffling, crying, even though this was worse than crying.

Terry, he—he wasn't Terry. Or, he was, but he wasn't. He was something. He was wrong. He had done this. He was *doing* this.

Candy stepped calmly into her SUV, locked the doors, and screamed and screamed, rubbed her cheeks with her hands until they burned.

At which point her phone dinged once, a voicemail.

"Surprise," Jason said, talking low like he was in a crowd, "got home early, will be there in five, four, three, two…"

Candy pulled the phone away, thumbed for the timestamp.

Five minutes ago.

He was in a cab. That's how he always talked, sure the driver was trying to tune in his every word.

She dialed back desperately, but Jason never answered when people were around.

She felt like she was melting. Like she was falling apart, crumbling into herself.

Her shoulders hitched once but she didn't let it get any further, into a real collapse.

Jason.

She dropped the SUV into gear.

The front door of her house was open.

The yellow cab Jason had taken was still there. It was under the heavy shovel of the big yellow tractor. The driver had tried to dive out. He hadn't made it.

The back door on the passenger side was open.

Candy turned her SUV off.

Feet numb, face cold, she picked her way through the construction mess, watching the ground closely enough that the blue port-a-pottie suddenly beside her was startling. The door yawning open was what had made her look up.

No one was creeping up on her, though.

Everybody in there, all six of them, they were dead. This was the crew Terry had fired.

Candy shut her eyes, balled her hands into fists and pushed past, opened the front door and walked into her house. Terry leaned back from the kitchen. He was wearing Jason's apron.

"Oh, hey," he said, going back to whatever he was doing. "Thought it might be you."

Candy scanned the front living room, the hall.

No Jason.

"You've probably got a few questions, don't you?" Terry said.

He was cutting vegetables?

"Jason?" Candy said, her voice not quite shaking.

"In the shower," Terry said, and when Candy rushed ahead to dash upstairs, Terry's meaty hand clamped onto her upper arm. "He's okay," Terry said, "really. Promise. Demon's word of honor."

Candy pulled away from him—he let her pull away from him—and looked up to his face, his normal human face. "D-demon?" she said.

"Just a name," Terry said, batting the word away with the knife he was still holding.

"You're… you're Asmod," she said, digging the writing up from the weight room wall. The panic room wall.

"Keep going, keep going," he said, intent on the carrot he had.

"Deus," Candy completed. "Asmodeus."

"Ah, yes." Terry leaned back to let the name wash all down him. "You never realize how much you might miss your own name being said, do you?"

"You were—you came up from the hole," Candy said.

"Not quite," Terry said, tut-tutting that with his knife. "I was having a good old time in Mr. James Kempel, child molester extraordinaire. But then he found that room, and locked himself in. Decided he would rather starve than do it again. Some people, right?"

Candy shook her head no. Her hand was in her pocket, trying to dial 911.

"But you let me out when you opened that door," he continued. "Well, when good old Jason boy did. But you had so much more potential, didn't you? That's what it's all about, potential for... for *fun*."

"The restaurant," Candy said.

"Ding ding ding," Terry said, cocking his head upstairs, like hearing something beyond what Candy could. "I had to dispose of good old Jimmy boy somehow, right? Waste not, want not. I think I read that somewhere."

"You didn't eat the fish," Candy said, her voice dial-toning out. Like her mind.

"Fish and me don't get along," Terry said through thinned lips, punctuating it with a slice to the tomato he'd rolled onto the cutting board. "Not that what sealed the deal for you was exactly fish, of course..."

"What about him?" She tilted her head upstairs.

"Let's finish with you first, shall we?" Terry said, suddenly right up against her, his hands feeling through her hair at the base of her scalp, his other hand to her hip like he knew it. Which he did.

Candy punched what she was pretty sure was the final digit on her call, hit what had to be Send.

A moment later, Terry's front pocket buzzed.

"Oh, sorry," he said, raising a finger for her to wait.

He brought a phone up to his ear, said in exactly Kath's voice, "Oh, oh, Candy? Yes, well, as you know, I'm just rotting in that tub I insisted Ben would like. And guess what? I think he does like it, can you believe it?"

He dropped the phone. It cracked on the floor, rattled away.

Candy swallowed the lump growing in her throat.

Her face was hot now. Behind her cheeks, she was crying.

"Let him go," Candy said, about Jason. "You've got me."

Terry stepped back, regarded her from this angle, from that angle, the fingers of his right hand to his chin as if he was in deep thought. Important thought.

He shook his head no, finally.

"Nothing against you, of course," he said, setting the knife on the island to look in the refrigerator for something, "but, Jason boy offers… I still have some unfinished business, from when I was Mr. James Kempel!"

He said the name like an announcer on a gameshow might.

"You just don't have all the necessary equipment," he added, shrugging about this sad fact.

"I won't let you," Candy said. "I'll warn him."

"You'll call him?" Terry said, waggling another phone up from a different pocket. Jason's phone.

"Ja—!" she started, didn't get to finish.

From across the kitchen, Terry had somehow pinched her lips shut, was pinching her lips shut, his fingers miming just that in the air by his head.

"I did appreciate the lard on that plunger, though," he said. "That showed ingenuity. It kept it from sticking to the mix, didn't it? I don't think a man would have thought of that. As proof? A man never has thought of that. Until… let's say tomorrow? It's given me an idea, once I'm more, more *inside* your dear hubby. More at the controls. And making certain visits around the neighborhood, shall we say. And the… I don't know. The playground?"

"He'll never let you," Candy tried to say.

Terry heard it all the same.

"But I'm cooking his *favorite* meal," Terry said, wowing his eyes out like a cooking show host. "Dine with the devil, it leaves a string inside you. One I can pull. And, I think, yes, it's almost ready. *Time!* I need to get him down there. I don't think I can trust dear old you to not warn him, so… yes, I've got it."

What Candy expected was for Terry to call upstairs in her own voice.

Instead, he cut a sharp whistle. Roff's whistle.

The dog padded into the room, leaving bloody footprints.

"Who's a good boy, who's a good boy?" Terry said, and, on cue, Roff's tail flopped back and forth and he barked once.

"Roff?" Jason called from upstairs. Meaning he'd already been missing him.

"It's like we think of everything, isn't it?" Terry said, batting his eyes coquettishly and, with two fingers, touching Candy's left shoulder to nudge her sideways, away from the bottom of the stairs, away from where Jason was about to be.

She could hear his footsteps on the landing now.

Roff stepped to the bottom of the stairs, to keep Jason's eyes there.

Candy bounced, unable to step forward. She could only go back. Her first thought was to circle around, come at Jason from the formal living room. But there was no time.

Instead she edged sideways, into the kitchen.

And—Terry. Where was he? Was he even here?

"Mmph, mnph," she said, straining to make a sound, to get Jason to see her, anything.

And then, yes, she was in view!

She looked up to Jason, coming down fast.

Terry was right behind him, smiling, leaning in.

Candy jumped to the side, into the island, and flopped her hand up enough to get at the knife handle. Because it was too heavy somehow, she lowered her face to its blade, slit her mouth open, screamed in the instant, "*No! You can't have him!*"

Both Terry and Jason looked up to her.

"I'm sorry," Candy said, and stepped forward before Terry could stop her, plunged the knife into Jason just below the sternum, and then carved up, for the heart, or whatever she could find.

Jason made his mouth into the first shape of a question, one that was in his eyebrows just the same, and then he folded around her, hugging her.

His insides were warm.

Candy looked down over his shoulder, down his back.

Roff was still sitting there like a good boy, his tail wagging.

She turned her face to Terry, two steps up the staircase, his hands neatly behind his back.

"A little more *slashy* than I was going for, but I'm sure we can still save some portions," he said, and caught Jason right as he was falling, pulled him and the knife away from Candy.

There was nothing to say.

He *hadn't* had her, not all the way. Not until now. Not until this.

She'd eaten the fish named Kempel in the restaurant that was burned, and she'd stepped outside her marriage, but none of that was unrecoverable-from. All of it could be, Candy thought, undone.

Except this.

She sat hard back onto the second step, watched Terry haul Jason up onto the island and lean in, bite the tongue up. It stretched, stretched, and then Terry reached under, popped the white string under the tongue with the knife. The tongue stretched longer, until Terry sawed through it.

He tossed it to Roff. Roff sucked it down, his tail a blur.

Then Terry went to work on the butchery part of the night, completely disregarding Candy.

"Can I?" she said, tilting her head back down the hallway, and he dismissed her.

She walked past the bathroom, went downstairs. To the weight room, the gun room, the room she wasn't going to panic in. That was all past. It was too late for any of that.

There was only this left.

Using the plank, she guided the slurry of concrete to the side, exposed the slit in the dirt again. It was still bulging.

You can start over, she told herself.

You can do it all again, better.

With that, she stepped in, moved side to side to work herself down, until, when she looked up, there was just a slash of light overhead. One already sealing itself back.

In the darkness a male voice asked her how old she was, and she closed her eyes, let Jim Kempel's fingers probe her face, her shoulders, the rest of her. For all time.

It was a nice house, she thought.

It had been a nice life.

Until.

MARCHOSIAS

Marchosias, or Marcochias, like Hanar, hopes to return to the seventh throne after 1200 years—hinting at the possibility of the redemption of the fallen angels, which most Christian theologians, except for Origen in the third century, deny. Before he fell, he was one of the order of dominations. Reginald Scot, in *The Discoverie of Witchcraft*, writes about him: "Marchosias … sheweth himselfe in the shape of a cruell shee woolfe, with a griphens wings, with a serpents taile, and spetting I cannot tell what out of his mouth. When he is in a mans shape, he is an excellent fighter, he answereth all questions trulie, he is faithfull in all the conjurors businesse," a description more or less identical to that in *The Lesser Key of Solomon*. Like most or all of the other demons in the goetias, he claims noble status in the infernal hierarchy (in his case, that of a marquis), and he says he has thirty legions of demons at his disposal.

Whimsy

MICHELLE BELANGER

Rashida summoned the demon on Saturday, just before dinner. Hunter was on his computer across from her, and he looked up when a thunder of sound poured from her speakers.

He was in the middle of a raid with his gaming guild, so she was surprised he'd looked up at all. A backwash of brilliance danced across her features as special effects blazed on her screen. The candles around the virtual summoning circle vomited gouts of blue and purple fire while the sigil in the center crackled with dazzling power.

"What was that?" he asked.

"You'd have to see it to understand," she said. "And you're busy."

His fingers hammered the keys in an endless repetition of fight maneuvers. "Don't give me that shit, Rashi," he snapped. "I've been gaming way longer than you have. Just tell me what game you're playing. Think I can't figure it out from there?" The insect murmur of disembodied voices buzzed from the headset curled around his ear. His tone changed as he responded to his guild. "No—nothing. Just my girl again." He whacked the space bar four or five times in rapid succession, then shoved back from the keyboard, grinning wide through his beard. Hoots and shouts crackled from the earbud.

"Booya!" he cried. "Good fight, guys. We'll start for the next boss in a minute. Smoke break." When he rose from his chair, the smile had vanished. "What are you even playing these days?"

Rashida quashed an unreasonable urge to ALT+Tab so she could hide her game. Not that he wouldn't know that trick—he used it all the time when the guild chatter got particularly crude, as if he was saving her from something. On her screen, the dazzle of light cleared and a nude figure crouched in the shadows of the circle. It looked like it was draped in a tattery cloak, and then she realized those were supposed to be wings. Her fingers hovered above the keyboard, eager to welcome the new being, but then drew away to curl in her lap as Hunter strode over. He put a calloused palm on the back of her chair and the base creaked beneath their combined weight. Beard hairs tickled her ear as he peered over her shoulder.

"Oh, lame," he declared. "You're still playing Whimsy? No wonder you didn't want to admit it." He grabbed her Coke and took a swig, grimacing when he found it warm.

"I like how every player helps build the game," she said.

"Then you're an idiot." He slammed the Coke next to her keyboard like the can was responsible for the sad state of its contents. Wordlessly, she moved it to its coaster, dabbing the spatter from her screen. "That game's got zero population. Half those other players are bad AI. More than half. Why would you even bother?"

She stared at her fingers where the skin faded from brown to cream, the pigment feathering in the creases around her knuckles. The demon summoned by her virtual self waited, patient and strange as tectonic drift. "I've got to play something, and your friends kicked me out of the guild."

"What were they supposed to do?" he retorted. "You weren't pulling your own weight."

Maybe he put too much emphasis on the final word, she couldn't be certain, but she tugged her shirt down over a strip of exposed belly anyway. "I don't really like Blasteroid," she said. "It's too violent. This one's pretty."

Hunter frowned at her screen. The figure in the circle hunched in on itself, as if the program sensed her boyfriend's derision. "These graphics suck," he said. "But, whatever. You do you." He patted her shoulder, once. "I'm on a smoke break. Make sure dinner's ready by seven. We'll be done with this level by then unless someone totally shits the bed."

She made spaghetti. Quick and easy. He complained that there was no meat in it, but she'd used all the ground chuck for his hamburgers the night before. She tried telling him this, but he didn't want to hear it. He just stormed from the table and went back to his gaming rig. As Blasteroid loaded, the opening fanfare of the space opera sounded through their cramped living room.

"I thought you were done raiding for the night," she called over the sound of dishes. The water was nearly scalding. She cranked it even higher.

"Pryss and Jicala are having a meeting. Guild business. I need quiet for a few hours." A flurry of clicks erupted from his mechanical keyboard, the sound a staccato counterpoint to the rush of running water.

"ERP?" she asked.

He scowled over the top of his monitor. The expression made a tuft of his beard jut forward like a frizzy tongue. "You said it wasn't a problem, Rashi." Maybe he only yelled so she could hear him. It was loud in the kitchen. "You gonna make it a problem?"

She put the bowl aside. "No," she said firmly. With one nail, she dug at a bubbled smear of red sauce that had dripped down the chipped enamel of her main cooking pot. The water practically steamed from the spigot, making her hands prickle. She found the immediacy of the sensation soothing. While he clacked away in chat, she watched as the water brought color to her palms and nailbeds. Pink, then nearly crimson.

His ERP—short for erotic roleplay—hadn't seemed like a problem a few months ago. He had explained it as how his guild built storylines for their characters in between raid events, when the system locked them out of the dungeons so they couldn't just power through to the end. She'd tried the text-based roleplaying a little herself and found it was a lot of fun. It reminded her of fan fiction, which she loved reading. But the fun abruptly ended when the guild voted her out because she couldn't do enough damage in the actual battle portions of the game.

"Pryss and Jicala are a legitimate part of my character's storyline. We've been water-bonded in-game long before I met you," he said. She hadn't noticed when he'd stopped typing, but he now stood right next to her. She scrubbed the pan a little harder, not quite flinching when he reached for her wrist. He caught her look and turned away with a sound of disgust. "If you're going to be a pussy about it," he muttered. A moment later, he was right back at his machine, adjusting his ponytail as he slipped the headset over his ear. Heat washed over her face and arms as she tried to understand what she'd said or done wrong. She hadn't meant to pull away—he had to know that.

"Maybe I can read over your shoulder while you guys do your thing?" she ventured. A little precariously, she balanced the spaghetti pot over the other dishes crowding the drying rack, waiting to gauge his reaction.

"Don't you think that's a little weird?" he snapped. Before she could frame an answer, he bent to his screen and started typing. It was only text and pixels, but still, she felt a stab of jealousy. She told herself she was being stupid. Her romance novels were just as steamy, and none of that was cheating. They'd discussed this before.

Maybe if she hadn't flinched? But he'd surprised her.

"Is it okay if I take the laptop?" she asked. "I'll go play in our room and give you a little privacy."

Eyes intent on the scrolling letters in his chat box, Hunter didn't even answer. She dried her pruny fingers on a dishcloth, then took the laptop anyway. As she closed the door to their bedroom, she heard the sound of his zipper.

Just words on a screen.

The acid reflux burning at the back of her throat tasted like surrender.

The demon was waiting exactly as she'd left it, huddled in upon itself in the circle of summoning. The spirit-stone that she'd spent the better part of two weeks searching for in-game lay on the bricks beside it, its pearlescent surface blackened and all its magic spent. She'd had a feeling it was a one-use item, although none of her Google searches on the game had been able to definitively confirm this suspicion. If any players but her had managed to activate a spirit-stone before, none of them had written about the experience.

Lazy bastards, she thought, though mostly she was picturing

Hunter slouched in front of his gaming rig, one hand down his cargo shorts. *It's not cheating*, she reminded herself, and focused on the wealth of imagery she had in front of her.

Slender and flawless, her purple-skinned avatar sat crossed-legged across from the demon's summoning circle. With the laptop perched on her belly, Rashida spread her fingers over the keys, ready to bring her alter-ego back to life. Then she halted. This was stupid. There wasn't even anybody on the other end. Hunter was right about that. Whimsy was supposed to be an interactive game, with all of the characters and even monsters played by other users, but the game's population had seriously declined. A lot of characters were nothing but empty pixels—bots, at best, repetitive and stilted in their dialogue.

She tabbed out, careful not to close Whimsy completely. The laptop was loaded with games, but all of them were first-person shooters or player versus player arena types, and she really wasn't into any of those. On the nightstand, a solitary paperback with a cracked spine beckoned with its dog-eared pages. But she'd read that story so often she could recite the next line before she finished turning the page. Briefly, she poked around on YouTube, but nothing grabbed her attention. She wanted a good story. All the other books were out in the living room with Hunter and his guild.

Pushing the laptop aside, she heaved off the bed and opened the door just a crack. Except for the spectral blue flicker of his screen, the rest of the apartment was dark. Beyond the expansive barrier of his twenty-nine inch monitor, she couldn't see anything but the top of Hunter's head, but she knew that hitchy pattern to his breathing. She was loath to intrude upon his role-play—it was obviously going good on his end.

I bet he won't even notice me if I walk out there.

That thought made her retreat instantly into their room. The sour sting at the back of her throat blossomed into the pain of heartburn. Stupid red sauce. But she knew it was more than that, and it had been building. They were both gamers and spent most of their free time behind a screen. While they'd been in the same guild, that hadn't felt like distance, but now… now they were spinning away into separate orbits.

Maybe she could talk to Hunter about the ERP and how he

was excluding her—but not tonight. He'd be pissed as hell if she interrupted.

After coffee tomorrow, she thought. He'll be in his best mood after coffee.

Softly closing the door, Rashida reclaimed the laptop and dropped onto the bed. The mattress sagged in the middle—neither she nor Hunter were tiny individuals—and it took a lot of fluffing the pillows to make herself comfortable. Grabbing her earbuds off the nightstand, she opened the tab for Whimsy again and tried to sink into the scene before her—the underground chamber, the flicker of candleshine against rough-hewn walls, the steady drip of moisture from the haunted lake above. She flexed her fingers.

"By what name shall I call you?" she typed. And in the realm of Whimsy, where all things were possible, her character Avila spoke the words in a bubble of purple text that matched her magic-infused elven skin.

The demon's head snapped up, a cascade of black hair sweeping stiffly away from unexpectedly human features. He was both beautiful and terrible, with red, slitted eyes and golden horns and a mouth pursed for kissing. "You who have summoned me hence should know the answer to that question." No sound issued through the system to give life to his voice—Whimsy was free to play and voice actors were an expense the developers refused to indulge—but Rashida had imagination enough to hear him through the text. Deep notes, velvety and resonant. Nothing at all like Hunter's.

"Nevertheless, I demand that you confirm," she typed. She made Avila stand and pace throughout the chamber, ever careful not to cross the boundaries of the circle. With all the steps of the spell already enacted, she didn't know what could possibly go wrong at this point, but it still felt right to use caution. She didn't want to have to hunt down another spirit-stone to start all over again. Fingers swift upon the keyboard, she entered the code that made her character haughtily toss long waves of emerald hair. She loved that emote. "I am the one who wields the power here. You must give me answer."

Did the image of the demon smile, then? Perhaps it did, and perhaps that, too, was her gift of imagination. She was so immersed, she could almost feel the damp of the underground chamber clinging to her skin. The steady drip-drip grew louder in her earbuds along with the subtle crackle of the candle flames.

"I am called Marchosias, lady, and I am at your service now and for however long you may wish." On the screen, the image of the demon bowed, deep enough that the tattered ends of his wings swept the rough stones of the floor.

"You do me obeisance, as is proper, demon-spawn," she wrote. "But what am I to do with you?" Avila halted awkwardly in her circuit, nearly face-planting into a wall as Rashida fumbled with the track pad. Movement was so much easier with the mouse on her desktop. Quickly, she got the character back on track, but her immersion was broken. Piping words through her fur-clad digital proxy, Rashida made fun of herself, knowing Hunter would do the same if he saw her trying to roleplay with the AI. "Here am I, talking with a being that is mere illusion." She made Avila do the hair-flip emote again, though this time she felt it ironic. "You are not present in this chamber any more than I am, so what could you possibly do for me, demon Marchosias?"

Unexpectedly, the figure at the center of the circle threw his head back and laughed. It was different from the laugh emotes that she'd seen on similarly built characters—and she thought she'd seen them all. "You think I'm a program," he wrote. The words hung white-on-black in his demon-cursive chat bubble.

"Your not?" she asked, surprised enough that she didn't catch the typo until after hitting ENTER. Immediately, her ears burned—she hated gaffes like that—so she quickly corrected herself, typing, <<*you're. stupid fingers>>

His response was just as swift.

<<fluent in typo. knew what u meant>>

Her fingers stilled upon the keys and she read that short missive several times over. The carroted brackets indicated that what he said was out of character—in roleplay terms, OOC—and the simple fact that he knew when to use those brackets made her believe that there was a real person on the other side of the screen. But she could hardly credit her good fortune. She'd been playing Whimsy for months, ever since they'd kicked her from Hunter's guild, and in all that time she'd run into only six or seven other people that she'd been certain were players in real-time. Each of those had been cliquish as hell, intent upon their own business, and unwilling to stop for more than a few moments to interact.

Character briefly forgotten, she left Avila to stand staring at the demon across the binding magic of the circle. The avatar was placid. Her own heart hammered.

<<how long you been playing?>> she asked.

<<since the beginning>>

<<you mean beta?>> she wrote, adding <<I wish I'd seen this game at launch>>

<<it's not like it was>> he admitted.

<<you always play demons?>>

His character did a saucy little half-turn—another gesture Rashida hadn't realized was available in the game. She was so looking for these commands later. Avila needed them in her life. Then the demon repeated his bow from earlier, deep and courtly.

<<why wouldn't i?>>

<<heh>> she typed, and a smile teased her lips in the real world. Beyond the bedroom door, Hunter's chair creaked noisily as he shifted position. Rashida could hear that and other, subtler noises even through her earbuds. She cranked the volume. The ambient sounds of the ritual chamber, plus occasional strands of haunting music, helped everything else around her disappear.

The laptop was regrettably tiny, and she had to bring the screen closer to better study the details of his avatar. The developers of Whimsy had put a lot of effort into character design, and their demons were no exception. The shading was perfect, every muscle visible beneath his gleaming, tawny skin. He had a well-developed six pack and even a little belly button. A light dusting of hair darkened his chest and, even on the lower resolution of the laptop, it was possible to see each individual strand decorating his pectorals.

<<your character looks great>> she said.

<<i'm a fan>> he replied and hit the command that made his character preen. That one, she knew—it was the hair-flip on Avila, but varied between the races. For the demon, the character ran one hand through his hair, puffing out his chest. He finished by flexing his wings. Uplit by the screen in the narrow bedroom, Rashida's smile broadened to a delighted grin.

<<awesome>> she wrote.

They typed like that well into the early hours of the morning, chatting out of character and comparing everything they liked and didn't like about the game. Shortly after three, she had to log off—she couldn't keep her eyes open. He resumed his character of Marchosias long enough to bid her farewell. He made the avatar bow and reach for her hand from inside the circle, but Avila hadn't released him yet, so a magic force-field crackled to keep them apart. Staying in character, he emoted around the limitation, having Marchosias mime the act of kissing from a distance so that closer contact became both a tease and a promise. The language he used was lush and archaic, and inspired a guilty little thrill that traveled through her to settle, clenching pleasantly, in her pelvis.

Closing out of Whimsy, she powered down the laptop and scooched over to her side of the bed. Images of the tawny-skinned demon and his emerald-haired mistress chased her into sleep, and she dreamed vividly of Avila and Marchosias. When Hunter finally stumbled from the living room, the dreams changed and turned sour. She felt she was awake beside him as a winged wolf-thing nosed open the door to the bedroom. On a lashing serpent's tail, it slithered to the foot of the mattress. Its breath was fire, and she jolted awake when it called her by name.

If not for the nightmare, she would never have seen the time. Hunter had stayed up gaming without her until nearly seven-thirty.

The next day, she swore she would confront him. She got up around noon and started cleaning everything. As she rehearsed how she would start and finish the needed conversation, the chores helped soothe her. In between unpleasant thoughts of fights past and present, scintillating dream-memories flashed like precious gems—vivid snippets of the demon's muscled torso, the grand sweep of his wings, and Avila's fur-trimmed jerkin sliding noiselessly to the stones. When fragments of the nightmare threatened to intrude, she shoved them firmly to the back of her mind. The fire-breathing wolf-thing was probably some screwed-up manifestation of her anger at Hunter anyway.

Her boyfriend didn't drag himself awake until after three, and when he did, he was starving. Naked except his boxers, he headed straight for the kitchen, frowning when he saw nothing on the stove.

"Where's breakfast?" he asked.

She put the Lysol wipes aside, sticky residue clinging to her fingers. She wiped them on her pants. "I was waiting until you got up," she said.

"Well," he huffed. "I'm up."

She reached to open the cupboards. Half a box of pancake mix sat behind loose packets of ramen and instant oatmeal. They really needed to get groceries. "Did you want anything in particular? The eggs are all gone."

"What the hell?" he demanded. "Didn't we just buy two dozen?" He shoved his head into the refrigerator, searching. The cabbagy stink of rotting take-out wafted around him.

"That was last week," she reminded, framing the correction gently, knowing he didn't like her contradictions. But he slammed the door to the fridge so hard, three of her decorative magnets clattered to the floor. The biggest of them shattered—a lavish dahlia painted by her mother. He kicked half the pieces under the fridge as he pushed out of the kitchen. He didn't stop to retrieve them.

Dropping into his gaming chair, he double-tapped an icon and the opening fanfare for Blasteroid played. In that moment, she realized she hated that music. "I bet you ate already," he called. Straining to reach the broken pieces underneath the fridge, she pretended not to hear him. With the whir of the motor so close to her ears, it was easy. She pushed back onto hands and knees, grabbing the counter as she pulled herself upright. The shattered pieces of dahlia crumbled against her skin, little flecks of red paint and white plaster sticking among the creases of her palm. She didn't think there was a way to fix it.

"Of course she ate," he muttered. "Bitch always eats." The milk from her cold cereal curdled in her belly, and she surprised herself by reaching up and slamming the doors to the cupboards.

Hunter looked up, as shocked as she was by her sudden fury.

"We've got oatmeal," she said, voice loud and flat. She barely recognized it. "It's instant. I'm going for groceries."

"You're not taking my car."

"I'll walk."

He blinked. The headset coiled around his ear like an alien parasite. She could hear the other guildies buzzing through the wires like little flies, each demanding some explanation. Hunter waved a hand to shush them, as if any of them could see the stupid gesture. "It's over a mile," he said.

"I don't care."

And she didn't.

The Oklahoma heat crushed against her like a hard, hot hand. She was soaked and stinking by the time she got back home, hair frizzed in every possible direction. But her head felt clearer. This was not working.

It was a liberating revelation. Some of it was her fault, surely. She was terrible at making her point when things went wrong, she got so emotional. And maybe if she'd realized the problems sooner, she could have worked harder to fix them. She'd rushed too fast into the relationship. Maybe Hunter felt as trapped as she did.

And maybe he doesn't give a shit so long as he's getting something, she thought bitterly.

The grocery bags cut into her hands as she shouldered through the door. Hunter hunkered over his keyboard, fingers urgently tapping commands as explosions blazed across his monitor. He didn't move to help her, and she didn't ask, just swept into the little kitchen and started shoving things into the refrigerator. Milk, bread, eggs, a block of cheese, and a pack of chocolate-covered donuts. Fuck him and his cracks about her weight. She was going to eat them all and it would be glorious.

She dug out a spare mouse for the laptop and shut herself in the bedroom. If Hunter noticed, he said nothing. Fine by her. Whimsy beckoned.

Marchosias stood in the circle exactly as she'd left him, golden skin gleaming in the light of eternal candles.

<<did you even sleep?>> she typed, afraid that he'd simply left his computer logged in. It would suck if he was away from the keyboard—she really needed the escape. A slow bead of sweat crawled the back of her scalp as the seconds dragged. She stared fixedly at the screen, willing him to be there. Finally, his character wiggled his fingers in greeting.

<<what's sleep?>> he joked.

She loosed a breath she hadn't realized she'd been holding.

More damp trickled on her forehead, and she scrubbed furiously, drying her fingers on the comforter.

<<lol, yeah>> she typed. <<Insomnia's a bitch. where were we?>>

<<u were going to release me from this circle>> The demon avatar surged forward but was stopped by the energy of the magical barrier. A cascade of blue and silver light shimmered between their characters, distorting his features.

<<um, no. Avila hadn't decided on that yet>>

<<u should let me out>> he typed. Was that pleading? If it was, she liked it. Some of the unpleasantness with Hunter faded as she considered how far she could push this.

<<convince me>> she said.

In answer, he dropped immediately into character, making his avatar pace restlessly within his prison. The lines of his sigil pulsed faintly with each footfall. Rashida could recite each in-game material she had been obliged to gather in order to scribe the lines of that symbol.

"Have you called me here merely to gawk upon my form?" Marchosias demanded. "I am, I admit, magnificent. In infernal hierarchies, I am a mighty Marquis, but all my power is wasted if you keep me in bondage." He entered the command that made his character flex, the great span of his wings evoking a rain of sparks where they brushed along the circle's edges.

She smiled to herself. The mouse let her move Avila more smoothly and she slowly strode across the length of the chamber to show how deeply she was thinking about the possibilities he represented. Finally, she made her character do the little hair-flip, turning back to Marchosias. "I rather like you in bondage, my demon." She had a spell that would hold him in chains for the span of a few seconds and briefly considered using it. The coiled links would be a lovely sight against that tawny, muscled skin. "I do find your form to be pleasing."

"I wear this skin especially for you," he answered. "My true face, I fear, is frightful and you would not love me."

Avila turned her head to the side in a way that suggested casual disinterest. Rashida hadn't done that intentionally—it was one of the game's pre-programmed fidgets, randomized to give the characters a feel of greater life. But it was perfect. "Few of us are exactly what we seem, demon," she said. "Do you think such threats will impress me?"

"You misunderstand, my lady. I only seek freedom," he wrote. "You called me for some purpose, surely. Are you not lonely?"

The question could easily have been flirtation, but it felt more like he could see her, a sad figure curled in a dark room, alone on a two-person bed. Tears came hot and without warning. She scowled through the blur at her keyboard, angry at herself for crying. Avila's glib bravado escaped her completely and she just scrubbed at her eyes, sniffling.

<<u ok?>>

His concern was palpable. She started typing an answer, but her fingers fumbled and all the words came out wrong. Furiously, she backspaced. She could barely see the screen.

<<u can tell me>>

Irrationally, she felt him beside her—a quiet presence, subtle and stabilizing. Pure fantasy, of course, but it helped lessen the bleak emptiness of the bed. With desperate indulgence, she imagined the flesh of him, warm and solid. Her face pressed to the strength of his shoulder, his arms both tender and protective. Hunter hadn't touched her like that for weeks, and with a hunger, she missed it.

<<wish we could talk face to face>> she wrote. <<really need a friend right now>>

<<let me out of the circle, Rashida>> he responded.

The name jolted her. She'd never typed it, never even implied it in all their deep discussions the other night. Avila was her escape hatch—useful especially because she wasn't Rashida and never could be. And she wasn't an idiot. She knew the dangers of the Internet. Stalkers. Hackers. Serial killers who chose their victims through online hook-ups. Every cautionary tale she'd ever heard suddenly seemed plausible—and then she fixed upon the simplest and most mortifying of solutions.

<<Hunter?!?>>

<<no>> he typed. Then, <<u called me. how could i not know u?>>

Gooseflesh shivered down her arms in such regimented lumps, she looked like a plucked turkey. She shoved the laptop, scooting off the bed so fast she took half the comforter with her. The computer tilted precariously, and she nudged it so it didn't fall, but furtively, like it had an infection. Rushing to the door, she peered out into the living room. Hunter would be there, grinning nastily behind his computer desk, ready to tell her how pathetic jealousy could make her.

But the living room was dark and empty.

"Hunter?" It came out a squeak. She licked her lips and tried again, fingers slick against the brass of the handle. The name rang hard and flat against walls crowded with bookshelves. She dared to take a step beyond the bedroom, only half-conscious that she'd been gripping the door like some kind of plywood shield.

It wasn't a big apartment. She checked the kitchen, the bathroom, even the closets. No Hunter. His computer was off, and when she put her hand on the tower, it was cooling. Unsettled and bewildered, she never considered that he might have left her. Marchosias dragged at her thoughts like a gravity well. Her curiosity couldn't escape him. Maybe he was someone from the guild, playing Whimsy out of pity or to punk her. How awful would it be to spill her guts about Hunter only to have all those secret agonies spread across the guild site where everyone could mock them?

And then another thought occurred to her, so far beyond the realm of possibility that it held a certain wild allure.

What if Marchosias really was a demon?

You're losing it, girl, she chided herself. So far 'round the bend, you've found the other side.

But wouldn't it be amazing? Breathless and terrible and more than a little transgressive. Haltingly, she stepped back into the bedroom. The laptop angled on a fold in the comforter, twisted in her exit so the screen partly faced the doorway. The golden-skinned demon stood beckoning from his circle, crimson eyes lasered in her direction.

<<you better tell me how you know me>> she typed.

<<u called me>>

<<sure>> she wrote. <<you're really a demon>>

<<release me from the circle and i'll prove it>>

She couldn't muster a comeback. The air in the room bent and grew heavy, like tattered wings draped around her shoulders. Her vision pinholed on that white-on-black chat bubble and all the unlikely magic it promised. She could almost smell Marchosias now, a startling mix of musk and clove and cinder. All the spit abandoned her mouth and her heart raced until its throb wavered like a caged thing seeking escape from the prison of her ribs.

<<gotta go>> she wrote. She slammed the screen of the laptop before he could dare an answer.

She tried to lose herself in a book, but all she had was paranormal romance. That wasn't helping, so she logged into her desktop to scour the Internet. Every site on demons or demonology that looked at least a little legit, she read. She even skimmed the sketchy ones. And Marchosias was on all of them. He was one of seventy-two demons supposedly connected with the Bible's King Solomon. A book called the Goetia held the sigils for summoning them. She found a copy of it hosted on a website and scrolled straight to the entry on Marchosias. She couldn't drag her eyes from the screen. The sigil from the demonic text was identical to the one her character had learned in Whimsy. Stranger than that was his description. Serpent's tail, head of a wolf, griffin's wings. When he appeared, he vomited flame, just like the beast in her nightmare. But she couldn't have known that. She'd never read any of these books before, had simply assumed the sigil and name were both created by Whimsy's developers.

She did an image search for Marchosias and found something that looked so close to the wolf-thing from her dream that she almost couldn't look at it. Impulsively, she saved it to her desktop.

The door slammed and she startled so hard she nearly peed a little. Hunter was home. Guiltily, she ALT-tabbed out of the Goetia and did her best to ignore the presence of her boyfriend. But it was a small apartment, and he came right over. She smelled the pizza before he set the oily box on the desk next to her, shoving some of her books aside so it wouldn't tip onto the floor.

"Brought you dinner," he said. Awkwardly, he held out a single hothouse rose, likely bought at the corner gas station. "I was kind of a dick earlier."

Rashida shoved away from her computer, the casters of her desk chair catching on the carpet. This always happened. He'd pull some shit that royally pissed her off, and then, once he had a little time to think about it, he'd do something random and hopelessly endearing. She tried to cling to her revelation from earlier, but the shock at seeing the wolf-thing had already scattered most of her anger.

"Go on," he insisted. His smile was lopsided. "Take it. You got to stop being so sensitive, Rashi. You know I care about you."

Grudgingly, she accepted the flower. The rose was bruised and smelled weirdly of glass cleaner. She pressed it to her nose anyway. It was a start for an apology.

"We good?" he asked, flipping open the box to reach for a slice of pizza. The bacon, sausage, and pepperoni glistened with juices. "You walked all the way to Hammond's and back in that heat. I couldn't believe it." He caught a cheesy wad of pepperoni before it slid to the floor. A blob of red sauce nested in his beard. "You know I talk shit, baby, but I never really mean it."

She set the flower aside, hesitating before taking her own piece from the pizza box. Strands of molten cheese adhered to the cardboard. "Can we discuss that, maybe?" she ventured. She searched around for a napkin. "I feel like we've forgotten how to talk."

He dropped into his own chair at the desk across from hers, disappearing behind the arc of the monitor. "Come on, babe, let's not ruin this." He peeked around the obstruction and shot her that goofy smile again. "Why don't we eat, maybe play something, and see how the rest of the night goes?"

"Um, sure," she answered. "Just hold on a sec." Lofting her slice of pizza well away from the keyboard, she closed out completely from the Goetia. Her mouse hovered over the wolf-thing image, then she dragged it to the trash bin. That wasn't Marchosias. Marchosias—the player—was just a gamer like she was, human and depressingly ordinary on the other side of his screen.

"What are you up for?" Hunter asked. "There's a seasonal event in Dune Strider. Double xp for the rest of the weekend. How about we both roll new characters and smash through the starting zone?"

"That's the one where you've been asleep for millennia and wake up in a post-apocalyptic future?"

He nodded, already booting up.

"Sure," she said. "I'll need to update, but that sounds fun."

She spent the rest of the night gaming with Hunter. It reminded her of the fun they used to have just hanging out together. He had work in the morning, so they went to bed early. On their sagging mattress, as she curled next to him, she felt cautiously hopeful. If she put enough work into it, maybe she could mend the cracks in their relationship.

❖

On Tuesday, he hit her. It was over the stupidest thing. She had burned dinner.

He opened his hand at the last instant, slapping instead of striking, but her ears rang and her cheek stung and she was certain it would bruise come morning. When it happened, she just stood there at first, staring. They both did—but then he started spouting excuses, apologies, rationalizations. She heard none of them. The thunder of blood was in her ears—blood, and a calm, bright fury. She moved to get past him and out of the kitchen. She already knew what she wanted. He shifted to block her way, holding his hands up to show he wouldn't strike her a second time—as if that was any kind of promise. She shoved as hard as she could and though it didn't do much to move him, it shocked him into moving himself.

That was enough.

She marched straight for the bedroom, locking the door behind her. He pounded from the other side, demanding she open it and calling her stupid. She had to come out sometime, he said. This wasn't solving anything.

But her solution sat closed and waiting on the nightstand. The laptop led to Whimsy, and Whimsy led to Marchosias. And maybe, if the world were as kind as it was cruel, Marchosias could offer some justice.

That was one of the things that she'd learned when reading about demons. A lot of those seventy-two spirits named in the Goetia solved problems for the people bold enough to summon them. They tracked thieves, hunted murderers, punished the unfaithful. Abusive boyfriends weren't named explicitly on the list, but Marchosias's entry had said that he was loyal.

With Hunter prying at the doorknob, she booted up Whimsy and logged into her alter-ego. Avila still stood in the subterranean chamber, the circle of summoning glimmering before her. The candleshine on her purple skin was beautiful, but not half as captivating as the tawny being lounging on the stones marked with his sigil. Fully aware of her scrutiny, the demon's head tilted to meet Rashida's eyes in the real world. This time, he didn't bother slipping into character.

"You return, my lady." The words blazed in his white-on-black chat bubble, but she heard him, too, like the sound of distant thunder. "I've been waiting."

"I know," she whispered as she typed. "I have something for you to do."

Fluidly, he rose to his feet, peering up at her from the confines of the video game. But he wasn't just there, and they both knew it. Clove and musk and cinder filled every corner of the room. Hunter pounded the door, oblivious. The air tightened, then trembled, perched upon the lip of the impossible.

"I am your willing servant." He bowed his head, catching her gaze from under thick lashes. "But you know you must release me first."

She wet her lips, nodding. She thought of the past ten months with Hunter and all the time before that, believing she would die before ever finding someone who could love her. Lightly, she touched her cheek, feeling the stinging heat that lingered. There would definitely be a bruise tomorrow.

"I release you," she said. She didn't bother to type it—she spoke aloud and clearly, in a voice that did not waver.

Something in the room shifted, shivered, then cascaded in a burst of light. A sound, like the tearing of canvas, rippled through the air. The door shook as if a great beast leapt against it.

She was surprised to feel nothing when Hunter began to scream.

EPHIPPAS

Ephippas makes an appearance in the pseudepigraphical *Testament of Solomon*. At one point King Solomon receives a letter from Adares, king of the Arabians, who asks for his help in subduing a troublesome demon, whose "terrible blast … kills man and beast. And no (counter-) blast is ever able to withstand this demon." At the same time Solomon's project of building the Temple in Jerusalem hits an impasse when the stone intended to be the cornerstone proves to be immovable by both the artisans and the demons who are working on the construction.

Solomon remembers Adares's letter and sends a servant to Arabia, who uses the king's ring to capture Ephippas in a flask. Brought to Solomon, Ephippas walks about in the flask for seven steps before collapsing. Impressed that the demon can move the flask at all while inside it, Solomon asks who he is and by whom he can be thwarted. (Each devil has a corresponding angel that can thwart him.) Ephippas replies, "By the one who is going to be born of a virgin and be crucified by the Jews." This response suggests Ephippas's enormous power, because it implies that he cannot be thwarted by any mere angel or archangel, but only by the Son of God himself.

When asked about his powers, the demon says, "Wheresoever I will, I alight and set fire and do to death...I am able to move mountains, to carry houses from one place to another, and to overthrow kings." Solomon bids him to move the cornerstone that was too heavy for his workers. Ephippas not only complies but, aided by the spirit Abezethibou, brings up a massive pillar out of the Red Sea and sets it up before the Temple in Jerusalem. Solomon binds them with his ring, and they are forced to support the pillar in midair. (Some scholars identify the pillar with the pillar of cloud mentioned in the Old Testament, e.g., in Exodus 13:21-22, and also say that it stands for the Milky Way.)

An Angel Passes

WHITLEY STRIEBER

You can't see wind, but you sometimes wish you could. Good wind, wind of change, ill wind. Carried away by the wind.

This particular evening, deep in summer, promised only soft skies, friendly skin and the intimacies passing between four people in love. Jake and Terry and Mike and Merry lay like flopped seals around Mike and Merry's dark, leaf-choked swimming pool. True, the surface of the water already trembled with little breezes, but they didn't care. Night wind was ordinary in their part of the world. Summer wind.

They were neighbors in a Los Angeles desert suburb called Franklin Ranch, a place so undistinguished that neighbors, even in less expensive developments, generally referred to it, if at all, as "over there." To most, it existed as distant rooftops marching some undulating hillsides in the distance. That part of California is curved like a woman.

Neither couple had kids, which was just as well considering their many peculiar ideas and dangerous habits.

Jake had been in prison in Nebraska for posing as a door-to-door bible salesman. His father, who had been a poker cheat, had taught him one of the world's great secrets, which is that most people will believe a lie over the truth every time, and the more cockamamie the lie, the stronger their will to believe.

There's money in that.

Not being as quick-fingered as his father, he had instead developed his gab. His dad helped him at it, teaching him the technique of going low in the voice at the height of the lie, and making eye contact with a little hurt in your face, as if suggesting that you'll be crushed if they don't believe.

He skillfully sold bibles that did not actually exist to Midwesterners concerned about their lives of sin. He would arrive in some uneasy little community, hold their hands and weep with them over their personal responsibility for Jesus's lingering death on the cross and the sad improbability of their own salvation.

He would work until he got them on their knees with him. When that happened, he knew he had a deal. He would close it with the solemnity of a funeral director and say, "You're one of the chosen. I don't say this often, but there are some customers I want to bring into my life."

If an attractive female, he did that forthwith. No matter what, none of them ever heard from him again. Except for Terry who captured him, of course...

He would take their cash, run their cards on his phone, or cash their checks as need be.

The only bible involved, unfortunately, was the magnificent red number that he himself possessed. Copiously illustrated, including one image of the lord with eyes that just seemed to follow you. He'd won it off a real bible salesman in Alabama many years before.

Money in pocket, he'd blow town. He'd generally toss his order book in a river, if there was a river. You didn't need to pack evidence.

He'd done this in thirty states and hundreds and hundreds of towns, but had only gotten caught in Nebraska. Sure enough, it had been the order book. He'd slipped up just that once, leaving it behind in a motel room.

One would think that a con like his was pretty penny-ante, but he had saved those pennies.

He'd met Terry in the usual way: sleeping with her after closing a deal.

She slipped into the bed, opened herself to him, and he'd entered, expecting to get the hell of there as soon as he was finished.

She had other ideas in the form of hot apple pie and drugged coffee.

He woke up hogtied. She said, "You're a conman and I want my cut." It was while she was talking him down from his outrage, he always said, that he fell in love. "I mean, what a woman!"

Terry was what investment assholes call a "quant," that is to say, a person with natural insight into numbers. She had invested the money he made efficiently, in things like Tesla when it seemed idiotic to do so, and Apple when it was 50.

Now they were millionaires—low-grade ones, it was true, but decidedly in the seven figures. Eight years of the bible fiddle followed by a six-month prison term and here they were in this "over there" with another sexually ambitious couple as friends and everybody was rich.

Their belching grills sent smoke right across the community and into the windows of the old Franklin house on the hill, where Tom and Norma Franklin were living a life of poetry and hatred. Late at night, they would move through the streets that now scarred their front pasture, murmuring to each other like discontented ghosts. Right now, it was evening, so they watched at their windows with cold, eager eyes. They were hand in hand, their grins way too wide.

This particular evening, the leaves fluttering—windmilling now, actually—Mike and Merry and Jake and Terry had gotten up and begun eating brisket and toking and listening to the Grateful Dead on Mike and Merry's outdoor stereo. The pool, dark and filling with even more leaves, reflected the starlight and racing, deepening clouds.

It was while Jake was in stir that Terry had met Mike and Merry. She was one of those people who needed more attention than most. She'd grown up being, as they call it now, abused by her father. At the time, it hadn't bothered her. She'd found his machinery interesting. But when, having been murdered by her mother, he was gone from her life, she discovered that she missed being adored.

If she wasn't told she was wonderful and sexy every few days, she despaired. She needed to be breathed over and held, kissed by a man alert with desire, while she doled out affection only in thimblefuls. As a result of her elaborate psychological needs, she'd gone slightly insane after a week of waiting for Jake to get out and return to her bed. She didn't want to seduce a temp, she'd done too much of that before capturing him. Jake was a marvelously persistent licker and kisser and sucker. In fact, in the other way a sucker, also. He had no idea that all the money was in her name. But why not? She'd bought ServiceNow at 14. All he'd ever done is steal mattress money.

To pass what she called the "cold time," she decided to become an escort. She'd answered an ad behind which had lurked the sleazy little company run by Mike and Merry. They worked out of a smoke-filled room in the old Fuller Brush Building in downtown LA. If you looked up in the right block of Sixth Street, you would think "Sam Spade," but you would be looking at the twin arched windows of their office.

Mike liked to wear suits and talk about odd things, like the time Nancy and Ronald Reagan had gotten abducted by aliens on Mulholland Drive on their way to a party in the Hollywood Hills. Ronnie had still been an actor then. He'd entered the flying saucer a liberal Democrat and come out a conservative Republican. Nancy had taken up astrology.

How did Mike know that? Before he got into the escort business, he'd been a gigolo, courting waxed and lifted ladies with gelatinous caresses and breath-mint whispers.

As a boy, he'd robbed a little Roma kid and gotten a hand-written pickpocket's bible for his trouble. He'd learned every move in the meticulously illustrated notebook, then worked his way to Europe on a freighter where he made an excellent living lifting tourists. He'd traveled the world, lifting and living and having a wonderful time. Until two things happened. First, other Roma, seeing his techniques, realized that he was the now legendary Book Thief and set out to fill him full of whatever sorts of holes they could manage. Knife wounds, preferably.

He was lifting the Trafalgar Square tourists when they succeeded. He hardly felt the knife going in, it was so sharp. Afterward, he called it the Magical Knife. That was probably an accurate description. Roma do not enjoy great wealth, but they do possess great knowledge.

Anyway, the young tourist he had just marked was the one who raised the alarm when he collapsed. Out of the goodness of her sweet, Corn Belt heart, she accompanied him to the hospital and fought with the determinedly indifferent staff until they stopped him from bleeding to death. She always said they would have let him die because he was a foreigner and they didn't want to deal with the mountain of National Health Service paperwork involved in treating one.

So Merry had saved his life. That was the second thing that happened. She was living in London at the time as a secretary in the American embassy, and had visited him daily for the entire month of his recovery. He did lose his spleen.

Merry was an affable soul. Sympathetic. But afflicted, to a degree, with a lust for adventure. When she found out that Mike was a professional pickpocket marked for death by every Roma in the world, she became more interested in him than ever.

He wasn't handsome. His nose looked like a feedbag. His arms were so thin they might have belonged to a cartoon character. He had a wide, flaccid mouth. It wasn't pretty but it was useful in ways that served Merry's more intimate needs.

By contrast, Merry herself was blonde and svelte, aggressively perfumed, pretty in sunlight but angular to the point of concern in candlelight, which she detested. She wore her hair in a ponytail. Her wide green eyes seemed at first inviting, but if you caught her gaze, they became, unfortunately, so careful that people immediately began to feel uneasy. Actually, though, she was a kind person and a good listener and not very critical at all unless money was involved, somebody holding back tips, that sort of thing. She was good with her fists, which the girls, once they learned this, did not forget.

All told, she was an ideal sort of a woman to be the mother confessor of an escort service, and when Mike got out of the hospital and they returned to the States, that's what they started. Only dissatisfied, unhappy beauties work for these services, and they need talking to, so she really ran the thing.

Her office was a little room full of couches, and it was there that she had gotten to know Terry.

The escort service was, of course, actually an outcall service for prostitutes. Because Hollywood is chock-a-block with guilt-ridden executives, most of them were dominatrixes. These women, who dress in leather and act tough, reveal, in their off hours, all the vulnerability they have been concealing while binding, whipping, spanking and otherwise torturing their executives.

Each girl was assigned a territory, which was usually a studio. One girl had Warner Bros's, another Sony, a third Lion's Gate and so on. Disney had four girls assigned to it, to prevent lines forming. NBC Universal had three, and Terry was one of these.

She did her work efficiently and without complaint, except she had signed on for intimate, pleasant evenings, not the sort of brouhaha that was actually involved.

She was an excellent worker and popular with the johns, so when she confided her disappointment to Merry, she immediately invited her to an evening out with her and Mike. "It'll be just like what you signed up for."

Which it was. They had such a convivial time that Terry took them the next Saturday to meet Jake in prison. They were eager to go, and flew up to Nebraska in one of those commuter planes that require you to duck-walk in the aisle and are flown by what look like giggling boy scouts. There had to be some sort of opportunity associated with a man who was going to be out of stir in a few months. He'd be desperate, five dollars in his pocket or whatever and a bus ticket to some city Nebraskans disliked. LA, probably, which turned out to be the case.

By the time he was out, they were already a foursome. They consummated the marriage in Lincoln, in the Holiday Inn Express downtown, then went out and drank wine and toasted the future.

Between Mike and Merry's very profitable business and Jake and Terry's fruitful retirement, they could afford homes in the two-million-dollar range, which in Southern California means modest but not all that modest.

Franklin Ranch featured six-bedroom establishments, some raised ranches, some mini-mansions with lawyer lobbies. They bought side-by-side raised ranches. Mike and Merry moved the escort service offices from downtown to a nearby strip mall, and the four of them began to look with pleasure toward the unfolding of a good life together. Their sex life was intricate and acrobatic, so they also joined a gym and worked out, too. Terry had bought a volume of French pornographic prints of *Ancien Régime* vintage where couples played at games like "Hot Cockles," which involved the men disappearing under the ladies' vast clouds of skirts. So they played "Hot Cockles" and "Bottoms Up" and so forth. But they didn't bother with clouds of skirts. They were Americans. Naked worked for them.

They would drink expensive wine, eat fine foods and then have wildly inventive, complicated and athletic sex. This was part of the reason that Mike could now only look to the right. The other part was that he'd been clubbed in prison for coughing too near a guard.

The four of them were sitting on Mike and Merry's patio enjoying the exquisite, lingering evening, eating their brisket and drinking their pinot when the wind became noticeable.

At first, though, they observed something else.

"What're those?" Merry said. She was staring toward the dark end of the backyard.

"Blowing leaves. There's a Santa Ana coming up." That's a wind familiar to Southern Californians, that sometimes comes howling in from the desert in spring and fall.

"No, those humps. The moving humps."

Mike and Jake and Terry peered into the dark. "I'll get the flashlight," Mike said. His tone said, *I don't like the look of that.*

Armed with the dim old flashlight he'd dug out of their earthquake kit, they all walked down off the deck and into the yard—and Terry proceeded to step right on one of the humps, which squealed horribly and went scuttling off.

"Rats! Oh, god the yard's full of them!"

"They might have rabies," Jake said. "Get back up on the deck."

The wind was rising fast now, and the rats were no longer creeping, they were running—in fact, dashing wildly.

"There's hundreds of them!"

What with the gusting wind and now these rats, it was obvious to them that something was up. You never saw rats in Franklin Ranch, not because they weren't there, of course, as rats are everywhere, but because they kept to the shadows and the crannies. Normally.

The wind sighed and the trees swayed like hula dancers, gracefully and intimately. The rats humped along.

What was up had to do with the Franklins, yes, but even more with a twelve-year-old girl called Annie James, who had been an orphan but, to everybody's astonishment at the Catholic Home in Olander, was adopted by the Franklins, who now stood silently in the windows of their grand old house looking down on the subdivision that had ruined their lives. Tom and Norma were both grinning that drum-tight grin. The trees swayed far over, then struggled back against the gushing wind. Their own house was rattling and jumping on its foundation, itself threatening to ascend.

Where Annie was neither of them knew. In fact, they thought it better that they not know. If, for example, there were times—as they suspected—when Annie was nowhere at all, that was something that they certainly did not want to know. People who are tempting fate always prefer to believe that there is no such thing as soul.

She would go out at all hours. Odd lights would be seen. When she returned, she would sit in her room smoking, which they very much disliked, the more so because of her young age. If she was young. That, also, seemed debatable. Sometimes she appeared as dry as the desert, as if she was made of sand. Then a doe-eyed girl, then a jewel-eyed serpent.

She had brought them strange thoughts, which they appreciated a good deal, as it was improving their poetry. Lines like "Where did the serpent come from, the heart of man?" kept occurring to them, and "the Ouroboros is captive to itself."

Not exactly good poetry, but they thought otherwise. Obliviously, they had the *Paris Review* in their sights.

Who could stop Annie from smoking or doing anything she pleased? She'd already seduced all the nuns, one by one, even old Mother Star of Heaven who used to slap. Annie she had slapped only once. She'd slapped back, a blow so stunning that Mother SH had almost been upended, but at the same time so soft that it made her heart ache for her own violent habit.

In general, the Sisters of the Holy Sepulcher were sweet women. There were seven of them at the Catholic Home, and an average of forty or fifty orphan girls. The usual tales of woe applied. Yolanda Quinn's mother was a druggie who had died of an overdose in her daughter's arms. The father of Rosa Brewster Gonzalez, her only relative, had blown himself up in his taco stand. Others had come in as foundlings or "drop-offs," left by parents who could not afford them.

Annie had arrived like a foundling, discovered one morning sitting on the stoop. But she was twelve or thirteen and smoking a black opera cigar.

The seduction of the nuns had commenced as soon as she was given a bed. This was a properly run institution, no hanky-panky, so they had not expected one of the girls to appear in their cells in the night, especially not one who had expert fingers and wore a plastic *Annie!* mask left over from the days of the old musical.

One after another, the sisters had experienced *la petite mort*, and one after another they were devastated by the difference between what Annie could do for them and what they could do for themselves.

Sister Angelica and Sister Heaven's Song both fell in love with Annie. They provided her cigarettes, liquor and hashish, even laboriously discovering a dealer deep in Chinatown who sold opium peas, which were her preferred pleasure.

By the time Annie was there a year, Sister Miracle of Heaven was going out weekly in the station wagon to buy drugs. Annie was getting high nightly with the sisters and servicing their needs. Only Annie didn't get high. She just appeared to.

It was for the nuns a time of self-discovery and self-realization. Sister Heaven's Song started a fad of sequined cigarette holders and soon they were all parading around with them. To the confusion of the orphans, most of whom were very sincere students and happy to be out of state care, they smoked in class, pranced along the halls rather than gliding, and often wore dark glasses. They had become hungry for life. The orphanage began to resound with the music of groups like Nine Inch Nails and Megadeth. Gone were the afternoon tea-dances where half the girls slicked their hair back and talked in gravelly voices while the other half flounced and Pat Boone records were played. The sisters, who had never seen anybody dance to rock and roll, swooped around like great condors with their glittering cigarette holders between their teeth, snapping their fingers and yawping. The girls huddled together.

Annie also woke them up, but not to sex. She was no pederast. She used to take them up on the roof at night and speculate with them about hidden worlds. They saw, in their mind's eyes, things like eagles soaring amid pale clouds as quick as they were slow, and homey houses far below with window boxes full of flowers and sweet swing sets in the backyards, and places now buried in time, such as the Lost City of El Dorado, shimmering mirages touched with gold.

Once or twice, with certain girls who had a bit of what Annie called "inner talent," she went to other worlds. She took Yolanda, who dreamed of dancing ballet, to a planet peopled only by ballet dancers, with *Swan Lake* unfolding in one street and *Giselle* in another, while Hershy Kay's *Hoedown* rollicked in a third.

Was it a dream or a world, or a dream-world?

After their return, Yolanda sank into a terrible depression and

Annie held her and let her cry. "But you will, you know," she said, "you will."

But you balletomanes know that, for she is none other than Maria Santander.

Among the many things that were singular about Annie was her alertness not just to the sexual needs of others, but also to their most secret dreams. For example, she could smell the secret desire of the Franklins to somehow restore their lost paradise. Their longing smelled to her like drugstore aftershave. Also, she could smell other, deeper secrets from long ago. These smelled like the spring grass of childhood, but they were not happy scents. They were poignant and full of regret.

She stalked the night seeking the source of the aftershave, sending little winds out to find its origin for her, then angrily dispelling them when they came back odorless.

Until one night, those who had been lost were found. On that night she had crept up to the Franklin house and listened to them spouting their poetry at each other and weeping with awe. "Go and catch the falling moon, get with child a man…"

She understood that they had hit on the idea of improving the masters, or at least using their sonorities.

"We are dying, Syria, dying…" "Life, be not proud…"

As she listened, she also saw. She saw deep into their hearts and also into their past, all the way back to the first day that the Franklin Ranch had existed. And there she saw—ah—why she had been sent here.

Annie could spin dreams, and she soon had them dreaming that they had won the lottery.

There had been Franklins in the house for a long time—for California, damn long. In 1856, great-great-great-grandfather Franklin bought two thousand acres of the old Rosa Castilla Rancho from a man named Mr. Suiter. He didn't own the Rosa Castilla, but that sort of thing mattered less in those days than it does now. He made sure that no heirs of Juan Ballesteros were going to be in any position to challenge the deed he'd had run up at the engraver in Los Angeles.

For the next hundred years, the Franklins had made efforts to make money with the land. They'd farmed it, raised cattle on it, raised sheep on it, and rented pieces of it out to others who couldn't figure out how to make money on it either.

Juan Ballesteros had made money on it because, being a Spaniard by ancestry and a Sonoran by birth, he knew a few things about running cattle on dry land, which he had declined to convey to the thieves who had stolen his rancho.

He packed up his family and left, moving slowly southward along the cruel roads. Reaching Monterrey at last, so tired and forlorn, he died. They buried him deep, but the coyotes dug and dug.

The second generation of Franklins had ended up sitting in their great house staring out at the rolling hills covered with dry, pale grass and stubby little trees, drinking bourbon and spinning poetry.

Money, which had been plentiful in 1856, grew very slowly tighter and tighter. Professionally speaking, the Franklins thought of themselves as poets. They were cultured in the sense that they read magazines like *Harper's* and *Leslie's*. They thought their poems very good, but the editors thought them very bad. The bourbon helped with this. Then they died and another generation came along who did the same thing. One of them published a poem, fantastically enough, in *California Verse*.

During the next generation, the automobile was invented and Los Angeles began to creep toward the ranch, bringing with it a mixture of hope and horror. In the 1950s, the value of the land began to increase. Here and there, the line of the rolling hills far to the west changed. As the sun dropped down behind them, their lines were no longer smooth, but ragged. These angles were the rooftops of the housing developments.

Every few years now, the Franklins reviewed the official valuation of their property. It was always higher, then higher still.

They waited, wrote in the bulging family poetry journals, ate as little as they could and sold furniture, jewels and the now valuable antique clothing of their ancestors, which was kept in cedar trunks in the basement.

In 1977, young Tom and his apple-faced new wife, Norma, began selling off the ranch not just in lots but by whole sections. They bought Oldsmobiles with the proceeds, new clothing and jewelry, and they ate more elaborately. They hired a cook, Gloria Williams, but she quit on the theory that they were insane.

In June of 2001, building began on the last section, right up by the old pumphouse. This section of forty houses—or "homes" as developers so absurdly call them—was the last of Franklin Ranch.

One might have thought this a relief—the income and all—but how were poets like the Franklins going to write poetry in the middle of a housing development? Cars glided past, voices rose and fell, children shrilled, dogs careened around barking and the whole place smelled like barbeque. Worst of all, faces, blankly smiling, peered out of the car windows as they went past the enormous old house with its wide porches and tall windows. Once, horribly, a woman who smelled like the interior of Nordstrom's and dressed like one of the Avon ladies who sometimes hiked up the hill, came simpering along and asked if she could see "the interior."

While Norma stood in the doorway blocking the woman, who kept trying to peer around her, Tom went and put on his great-grandfather's gunbelt, which still hung on the hat rack in the study. The hundred-and-fifty-year-old Colt Peacemaker was gigantic. Intending to settle the woman's hash, he went stomping down the great central hall roaring, "Norma, who in hell—" But at that moment, his voice was drowned out by a series of thunderous reports.

As he lurched around screaming, wreathed in smoke and surrounded by fountains of sparks, Norma didn't know what to do, so she offered the woman coffee. There was too much noise and smoke for her, though, and she stayed on the porch, still peering in, now trying to take a picture of the inlaid ceiling (clouds and angels) with her cellphone.

The gunpowder in the ancient bullets had long since become unstable, and the shaking involved in Tom's stomping down the stairs had caused it to explode.

When the woman pointed the camera at her, Norma threw a spittoon. The woman caught it and offered fifty dollars for it. Norma then ran past Tom, who was collapsed in a chair smoldering and bleeding, and got the poker from the hearth. As she went at her with it, the woman offered two hundred dollars for the whole fireplace set that had been in the family forever.

Norma did the deal on the spittoon but not the fireplace set, and the woman left.

Tom never fully recovered from his injuries which, while not grave, were disquieting. One of the bullets had grazed his cheek, ripping out an inch-long gap that exposed his teeth on the left side. Once he was back from the emergency room, he had to carry a sponge to keep the teeth moist. When the bandages were removed, he looked as if his face had been partially skeletonized. You could see all the teeth stretching back from the corner of the lips to the wisdoms.

He was very fastidious and so very upset. He tried covering it with duct tape, but then he couldn't chew. Finally a plastic surgeon called Dr. Chou decided that he might be able to help. Four grafts and six surgeries later, he appeared to be wearing a permanent ecstatic grin, but only on the left. He hated that woman so much that he bought a new gun and prowled the streets with it, peering into windows late at night, doing "prep," as he called it. He never saw her again, though. Norma was privately convinced that it had been Angelina Ballesteros, the wife of the man from whom the ranch had originally been purchased. A ghost.

Not only had they spent like the dickens, Tom and Norma had also invested unwisely, buying at the top and selling at the bottom with the inevitability of a misfiring piston. So, despite the income from the new development, they were again pinching pennies.

Broke, oppressed, partially dismantled and completely disgruntled, they began searching for a way out.

A year passed, then two, until one day they found that they had no money at all, not a cent, and no credit. They were done. With tears in his voice, Tom told Betsy Flagg, the Franklin Ranch realtor, to sell the homestead.

People trooped in for a week. One of them, in fact, was Annie. She went through the whole house peering and sniffing. Nobody saw her steal one of Norma's scarfs and one of Tom's hankies. She was very quick about things like that. From behind the banister of the great staircase, she peered at the Franklins a long time. They were in the living room drinking and writing as usual.

The next day, of all the damned things, Norma won a hundred and fifteen million dollars playing Mega Millions. The night before, Annie had laid on the roof with Sister Mercy of God and discussed the application of salt to flayed skin. It had been a fascinating discussion—for her, that is. Sister had gone politely off to her cell and vomited. Annie had gone down and cradled the scarf and the monogrammed hankie as if they were a pair of baby Franklins.

That night she spread the scarf and the hankie out on her dresser, then once again wove on the loom of life with her quick fingers. She did this each night for a week. During this time, Tom and Norma became increasingly disconsolate. They should have been ecstatic, but their acquisition of infinite wealth seemed to have exposed a deeper need, which was the desire for children.

The Franklins appeared at the Home. The girls were paraded before them, each one putting herself on display to her best advantage. They recited their academic accomplishments, revealed their sensible and noble ambitions and sparked their eyes with hope.

Every human being wants to go home, and orphans even more. But where is that? To the orphans, any place with one's own room and two parents—not a flotilla of nuns who were becoming more eccentric by the day, as witnessed by the fact that they had decided to go into cheese making and were having a cheese house built on the grounds, and bellowing at each other over dinner about the relative commercial merits of cheddar, gouda and Stilton.

Annie came in. She had as always a cigarette between her fingers. She was wearing a slash of lipstick. When she saw Tom with his fantastic grin, she laughed raucously and blared out, "Boy do you look like an asshole! What'd you do, eat a cherry bomb?" Annie enjoyed firecrackers. She believed, like the Chinese, that they scared away evil spirits. Actually, she knew. They scared the hell out of her, anyway, but she couldn't stay away from them. Love hate.

Even while the adoption went forward, Annie moved in with Tom and Norma.

The sisters had begged her to stay, but she had been resolute. She was just a kid. She needed parents, a home, a future. The other girls, wild with jealousy, had plotted to hang her by the neck. She had gotten out of there on the afternoon before the plan was to have been executed.

The Franklins knew without even inquiring that Annie was not going to work out in public school. They hired a tutor called Mr. Thomas Thomas (not his real name, of course).

Annie and Mr. Thomas Thomas spent hours whispering and snickering together in the library where there were prized books of poetry, two more spittoons, and a cat called Catatonic because she so infrequently stirred. There was also a canary that shrieked in terror, but at what?

They proposed a plan to the Franklins, who clapped with delight and nodded eagerly. Mr. Thomas Thomas began going from house to house, striding along in his best black sharkskin, ringing bells and generally being let in.

Now, these were nice homes. Comfortable. Some of them were pocket mansions complete with *faux* marble floors in the foyers. In the driveways were Lexuses and Mercs and Beamers, even a Bentley here and there. Couple of Maseratis. The local schools regularly won everything.

Gradually, as the smiling man went round, the houses emptied. No hurry, one by one.

It seemed rather curious to Jake and Mike and Terry and Merry that so many properties were being abandoned.

When they looked in the local real estate listings, they did find a few sales—not many—which were also rather curious in one particular respect: the dollar figures had to be wrong. People were selling million dollar plus situations for the low hundreds. In fact, because of the low comps, both of their own houses had dropped in value by more than half in just a year.

Who the hell was this guy, coming in here and ruining lives? Mike and Merry had been counting on pulling out some cash with a refi. Now, that would be a no.

Was some cartel going after folks? The Chinese mob? Who in the world would cash out and walk away from a million dollar home in a seller's market, as this one certainly was?

The conclusion was inescapable—the owners were being leaned on by the sharkskin suit. Homes were being stolen.

Naturally, they were concerned, Jake the most. But not because he feared the suit. He could sell a man his own watch. No, his concern was that he wanted to steal homes, too. How was it managed? What was the smiling man's secret?

"Hey, holy shit, look at this one," Terry said as the windy evening was turning into a windy night. She handed her phone around. The Upchurches had just sold 10 Sylvan Lane for eighty grand. This was a four-bedroom five-thousand-square-foot masterpiece. The garage held one of the community's Bentleys, in fact.

They'd been toking and so were feeling both affable and kind of spinny. They were not in anything even approaching what might be called a confrontational state. Nevertheless, Mike said, "Let's walk the hell over there and see what we can find out."

Franklin Ranch was not a sidewalk sort of place. Fifty miles from downtown though it was, this was still in Los Angeles and the city was not going to be dropping sidewalks into a new development where everybody drove everywhere anyway.

But this was different, so they walked. Tell the truth, it was a little scary. A listing like that had to have major coercion behind it. There are plenty of gangs in LA, well organized, intelligently run and extremely dangerous. And then, of course, there were the scurrying rats.

Then they stopped. Stunned. "What in hell?" Mike said.

They hadn't even gotten to the end of their own street, but this was just damned incredible. The Pearson place, four thousand square feet, pool, three beds, worth about a million two, was being torn down, and right now, right in the middle of evening.

To get to shopping and work, they all turned left on Yucca Valley Road, but now looking to the right beyond the Pearsons, they saw that the entire block, all the way up to Republican Lane, had been leveled.

A few of these houses were thirty years old, true, a few even forty, but most of them were much newer and all were in great shape, or had been. To add to the group's discomfort, the wind was becoming annoying, blowing dust along the street from the teardowns.

"Fuckin' A," Jake said. "No way. Just *no way.*"

"Is this the gummint," Mike asked the wind. "Gonna build some kinda rocket base out here? Beatin' up people…"

"Mob," Terry said.

As they returned to Mike and Merry's backyard, the guys noticed that the girls had become uncharacteristically quiet.

Merry brought out lemonade and crullers, and Mike rolled some more tokes.

Everybody sat around smoking and eating and drinking and watching the stars race in the clouds.

They were right at the edge of the development, and their yards backed onto a slope and went down to Franklin Creek, which was lined with willows. It was a breezy, high spot, very pleasant when the Santa Anas weren't acting up. You could get fifty mile an hour gusts then.

"Confession," Terry said.

Mike and Jake looked at her. Merry's lips went into a set line. "Terry," she said, warning in her voice.

"No, it's time."

"Don't!"

"What," Jake asked. He reached toward his wife. She leaned away from him. He dropped his hand.

The four of them often did it together. In fact, they were more a foursome than two separate couples. Golf, too. Golf and sex. But the marriages were managed separately.

"We sent him away," Terry said.

"With our pistols," Merry added.

"Holy Christ," Mike said, "who?"

"And what pistols? We have no pistols."

"Yeah we do," Merry said lightly. "We bought Casull Raging Bulls."

Jake toked deep, held it, then released in a slow cloud. "What kind of bulls? What?" The cloud drifted off on a wind that was now just short of a gale.

From off down by the creek, a voice drifted up, a little girl's voice. She was singing in a reedy tone, "Blow ye winds of morning, blow ye winds hi ho, blow ye winds of morning, blow, blow, blow."

Terry leaped to her feet. "NO!" Both girls rushed into their separate houses. They reappeared immediately with huge chromed cannons in their hands. The Casull Raging Bull is a very serious weapon. It's the sort of thing that will make a predator with a .357 Magnum fall to his knees and gabble for mercy.

They raced past the guys to the end of the yards, scattering rats as they ran.

"Jesus! Hey, Merry!" Mike got up so fast his chair flew into the side of Jake's Merc in the driveway.

"You nicked me, buddy!"

They both ran after their women.

"Blow ye winds of morning, blow ye winds hi ho, blow ye winds of morning, blow, blow, blow."

The women stood on the brow of the hill, took stances, braced their weapons and began blasting away.

Birds burst up out of the shattered quiet.

"Holy God, our little crazy kid's down there, Orphan Annie!" (Now that she was no longer an orphan, that's what everybody in Franklin Ranch called her. This was because she used to wander around in a red dress. In fact, maybe she was the real Orphan Annie.

If there ever was one.)

The kids in Franklin Ranch had tried to befriend her, some of them. When she smiled, they saw spiked teeth.

"Hey, what's with the spike job?"

"Go fuck yourselves."

They decided not to befriend her. At night, wandering the development, she would peer in windows. Pissed off residents would try to chase her away but they couldn't because she was always gone.

As the guns fell silent, Merry cried out, "Did we get her?"

"Blow ye winds of morning, blow ye winds hi ho, blow ye winds of morning, blow, blow, blow!"

"Oh, God, oh, God," Terry wailed.

Jake caught up to her and whirled her into his arms. "What in hell's the matter, girl!"

"Yeah, hey! Come on, give us those cannons, Jesus Christ, where'd you get 'em?"

"Walmart," Merry said.

Terry moaned. "Just like he said, you kill her but she doesn't die."

"Who wants to kill a kid, honey, holy moly! Thank God you missed!"

"Sharkskin said she was unkillable."

Terry looked the husbands up and down. "You're just a couple of innocent boys." She took her husband's slack-jawed face in her hands. "Poor guys."

Merry announced, "The Sisters of the Holy Sepulcher are corrupted and the Catholic Home is an outpost of hell. Annie's not human. Annie's something else. The Franklins sold themselves to her." Merry folded her arms.

"What?" Jake said. "They adopted her."

"Somebody make fucking sense," Mike yelled. "One of you!"

As the evening light rose into the howling sky, Annie could be seen sitting like a Buddha atop one of the trees that lined the creek. She was mostly silent, just laughing a bit from time to time. She had stopped with the tuneless singing.

Terry gazed up at her. "It doesn't matter. She can do whatever she pleases. It's why kids used to see her looking in their bedroom windows even though there was no ladder."

"And Mr. Thomas Thomas is another demon," Merry added.

"Oh, my goodness," Jake said, "this fuckin' toke—what's in this shit? Mike, where'd you get this?"

"At the grocery store. It's just what we always get."

"I don't feel any different, either. But maybe we'd've been better off doing that Jim Beam I got in that sale. We have to come down. I'm making a pot of coffee right now."

"The girl is in the tree," Mike said. "Fact."

"That can't be. Nobody can climb those trees. You've been down there."

Terry waved her arms. "It flies! They all fly."

"That guy, he flies, I've dreamed about that."

"What guy?"

"The hypnotist, Mr. Thomas Thomas. He goes to people and hypnotizes them and they don't know it, and then they are outa their houses with natha."

"I didn't let him in," Terry said.

"No, you did," Merry replied. "I threw him out. Three times."

"I did not let him in!"

"Sure you did. Three times. And you don't even know it."

"Well, let him in next time, for Chrissakes. Whatever's going on here, we need to move *tout de suite*."

"We'll lose our homes."

"I'm gonna sue the Franklins. I'll get every house back and most of their damn lottery money into the bargain. You can be sure of that."

"It's not gonna work," Jake said dismally.

They argued for a while about going to bed together. *Things to Come* was on TCM and Mike wanted to watch, so they watched and drank and toked more. The girls snorted oxy. They put on the karaoke machine in the basement and sang "There is a Man Goin' Round" with Mahalia Jackson.

By two, everybody was asleep, which is why they were not aware that, sometime after that, the eaves began wailing, banshees of the small hours. By three, the house was shaking, a steady pulsation that might have sounded like the work of living hands had it not been the wind. The din was so great that they didn't hear the doorbell, and would not have heard the knocking had Tom Franklin not begun pounding his shoe against the door.

Terry was the lightest sleeper. As she came to and heard all the ruckus, she leaped out of the super-king. "Something's wrong," she cried.

The banging sounded like the banging of shutters, but there were no shutters on this house.

With a fearsome ripping noise, the roof rose up, then glided majestically off into the night. Where there had been a ceiling, there were now stars flying in torn clouds.

Shouting and crying, everybody trooped downstairs. At the front door, two people also shouted and screamed. "We've called the demon, the demon wind!"

"What?" Merry shouted. "I can't hear you!"

"The demon wind!"

Jake cried, his tone a cave of despair, "Stop it, goddamn you!"

"We can't stop it, we don't know how!"

"We'll sue," Mike howled into the banshee wail. "Sue you!"

Like two bits of straw, the Franklins were snatched away into the night by Mr. Thomas Thomas, who flew up, grinning just as they had grinned, grabbed them by their necks and was instantly away.

Mike and Merry and Jake and Terry ran, trying to get out of the disintegrating house. They raced out into the street, but as they ran, one by one they too were snatched away.

Finally, nothing was left but wind and laughter, and then just wind, which roared and wailed through the night, and bent the grass and stole away the roofs, the lentils, the barbeques, the Lexuses, the curtains, the balustrades, all the empty houses and the ruined houses, and the houses of Jake and Terry and Mike and Merry.

With the dawn came stillness. There were no houses left, not even the Franklins' old pile. The land had been stripped so clean that it wasn't even scarred. Rather, it was smoothed. The land, so long lost, had been restored.

An old man, pale and slow in his years, came walking up the hill to where the Franklin house had been. He walked and walked, struggling on an old stick, until he reached the spot where Annie was lying on her back peering into the blue sky of morning.

"Gracias," the old man said. "You have given me back my soul."

"Glad to be of help, honey."

He gazed down at the face. It was naked now of its theatrics, so no longer a simple girl, not exactly, but rather a face softer than that of a girl, but in the laughing turn of the lips more knowing, in the deep quiet of the eyes, more kind. It was the face of a person unknown in this world, an ancient maiden.

"Are you of Satan or of God?"

"Do you know that you are dead, Señor Ballesteros?"

"Nobody is dead."

"Then you know."

"But have I called down an angel or conjured a demon? I need that answer."

"Why?"

"For my rest."

She pointed toward the blue. "You were kind to me once, Señor Ballesteros." She sat up. Her eyes melted into his. "We don't forget." With that, she swept out across the lovely long hills of old California, toward other days and missions that none may know.

The old rancher turned and walked back down the hill, through the swaying grass that he loved, the lady grass. As he walked, he faded from view, returning now forever to the hard, sweet land that was home.

RONOVE

Ronove is the twenty-seventh of the seventy-two goetic demons. Both Reginald Scot's Discoverie of Witchcraft and The Lesser Key of Solomon describe him in almost exactly the same way: Ronove is a marquis and an earl, and he has the form of a monster. He gives unusually good understanding of rhetoric, faithful servants, knowledge of languages, and the favor of friends and foes. He commands nineteen legions of spirits. His name is sometimes spelled Roneve.

The Wraith of Sunshine House

RONALD MALFI

1

There is commotion outside room 2A. The nosier, more ambulatory residents of Sunshine House have gathered in the hallway to rubberneck, determined to catch a glimpse of whatever is going on beyond the partially opened door. Nurse Skarda is good at keeping them at bay. She talks to them with a stern and direct voice, yet she is also somehow kind in her delivery. That is probably why most residents like her. The male residents also appreciate her youth and movie-star looks. I certainly do.

Ms. Joyce from the front office arrives, her face a pale oval, her rotund little body hermetically sealed in a lavender pantsuit. She is ungraceful, dour, the polar opposite of the attractive Nurse Skarda. Ms. Joyce informs the onlookers that they need to return to their rooms or, at the very least, go to the rec room and watch television. Breakfast, she tells them, will be delayed.

It's ten after five in the morning. The dawn looks as dark and uninviting as seawater against the wall of windows in the recreation room of Sunshine House. I have been awake for hours, completing yet another circuit around the perimeter of the room, counting the dead flies on the windowsills, the cockroaches flipped on their backs on the smudgy tiled floor. I am noting, too, the profusion of artwork that has come to paper the walls—not only in the rec room, but in the cafeteria, the hallways, and in some of the residents' rooms. But that's not all: Old Millie Broome has even taken to playing the piano again, a feat that is quite impressive given her arthritis.

Things are changing in Sunshine House.

When the paramedics arrive, the residents shamble back out into the hallway, or appear in doorways like raccoons in the holes of tree trunks. I know I resemble each one of them, just another gazing raccoon. I have been a resident of Sunshine House for the better part of seven years. Or is it eight? Whatever the case, I have begun to see things differently. Some lights are brighter than others now.

I watch the paramedics roll a gurney down the hall toward Max Winston's room. Nurse Skarda talks with them, then they all disappear into the room together. Ms. Joyce remains like a sentry outside the door. She is on a cellular phone, talking in a low voice so none of the residents can overhear. There is something toad-like about her face—the squat, stretchy composition of it, bulging eyes and lips like thick elastic bands.

I do not like Ms. Joyce. For one thing, she is a liar. She lies to the residents of this house and she lies to me. She keeps my mail from me and tries to keep David, my son, from visiting. She may fool the feebleminded, but she does not fool me. Particularly since things around here have been changing. Even she can feel it. She must have sensed something like this coming. I do not have to peer into room 2A to know that Max Winston is dead.

Millie Broome comes up beside me, dressed in a flannel pink nightgown. Her feet look like two blunt pegs swaddled in thick white tube socks. On her right shoulder is Sweetums, her neon-yellow parakeet.

"I hope Mr. Winston is okay," Millie says.

I say nothing.

"It was that man, wasn't it?" She looks at me, as if I'm complicit in whatever has happened to Max. "That horrible man." Yet there is no accusation in her eyes, only concern. Fear, maybe. "I know you're right about it, Mr. Bruno," she continues, this time in a whisper.

I see that her hands are up, that her fingers—those gnarled, bony talons—piston almost hypnotically in the air, striving to dispatch some coded S.O.S. through the ether.

I say, "Why don't you sit down and play us a tune, Millie? It might help to lighten the mood."

Her eyes widen. "Do you think it'll help?"

"You never know."

"All right." She pats me gently on the shoulder, then creeps over to the rickety piano against the nearby wall. Sweetums the parakeet flaps its bright yellow wings but does not take flight; under conditions provided to her by Ms. Joyce, the only way she was able to keep the pet bird was to have its wings clipped. Millie eases down on the bench with difficulty, then raises the lid that covers the discolored piano keys. "Any requests, Mr. Bruno?"

"How about something jaunty?"

"Something jaunty," she mumbles… then to my surprise she begins to play a jazzy little Spanish rhumba. Sweetums continues to flap his wings and hop along the old woman's shoulder.

A few stragglers still out in the hallway pause to listen, turning their heads in the direction of the music. They are like hounds tracking a scent. Some come shuffling over to watch Millie play.

Midway down the hall, the gurney reappears, bookended by the two paramedics. Max Winston's body is covered by a white sheet that makes its profile look like a miniature mountain range. The paramedics wheel the gurney quickly down the hall and out the glass doors of the lobby. There is an ambulance waiting in the circular driveway just beyond the portico, red lights twirling. I note, with some trepidation, that there is a dead bird on the pavement just outside the door.

Outside room 2A, Ms. Joyce is still on her cellular phone. When Nurse Skarda vacates Max Winston's room—although it isn't Max Winston's room anymore, is it?—they exchange a look that suggests this is going to be a long day. Then Ms. Joyce hurries off while Nurse Skarda, summoning a smile, approaches me.

"Hello, Mr. Bruno," she says, touching me right on the shoulder where Millie Broome had moments before. There is a sadness in her voice and on her face. She saw me watching the paramedics wheel Max Winston's body out the doors. There is no need to say anything to each other. Instead, she leans against the doorway of the rec room and listens to Millie play the piano. A decent crowd has formed. They watch her with almost pained faces—not pained because of the music, which is beautiful, but pained because they are inevitably reminded of their youth, and of all the things that were possible back before the lights started to go out and the foundation began to crumble.

We are all houses on the brink of collapse.

When Millie finishes, there is a round of polite applause. Sweetums chirps from her shoulder, pivoting its tiny head from side to side.

"That was 'Armando's Rhumba' by Chick Corea," Millie says. "I used to play that number at the Town and Country."

"It was lovely, Millie," says Nurse Skarda. She is smiling, but the smile does not touch her eyes. Most likely she is thinking about Max Winston. Then her gaze rises, and she sees all the drawings that paper the walls of the rec room—countless crayon drawings that, upon close inspection, are disturbing in that they all seem to be of the same character. As if there had been some art class where we had all been instructed to draw the same picture. "Those are very interesting," she says in a low voice, moving toward one wall and examining a drawing, then another, and another. She turns and faces the crowd gathered around the piano, but they have all begun to disperse—Millie included—and no one is paying the beautiful young nurse any attention. Except me.

When Nurse Skarda leaves, and the rest of the residents depart for the cafeteria for coffee and their medications, I execute one last loop around the circumference of the rec room. When I finish, I find there are three more dead flies on the windowsill, a dead spider curled into a ball on a couch cushion, and another dead cockroach near the piano bench.

2

A heart attack brought down old Max Winston, or so we are told. Ms. Joyce is duplicitous, but I get the sense she believes this, which means it's probably the truth. We've waited three days to hear what caused Max's death and now it seems somewhat anticlimactic. Yet given what has been happening in Sunshine House lately, I can tell that the more self-aware residents are happy to hear it was something as mundane as a heart attack. There has been talk of stranger, darker things, so this comes as a relief.

Max Winston's son and daughter-in-law, who are both in their fifties and clutch at each other like two children tossed about in turbulent waters, arrive at Sunshine House to collect Max's belongings. They leave forty minutes later after scouring Max's tiny room then meeting with Ms. Joyce in her office, carrying a cardboard box with the words *Frito-Lay* on the side. The box contains every bit of Max Winston's life, far as I can tell. And from the looks of it, there's still some room inside.

Because visitors come to Sunshine House with the frequency of a solar eclipse, the Winston children—who are not children—attract the attention of those few residents who have come to be known as the Leeches. The Leeches do not care who comes through the glass double-doors of this retirement home; they only care that there is a warm body upon which to adhere. They strike up conversations, distribute hugs or pats on the back, and on occasion attempt to slip out the front doors with these strangers. Even Ms. Joyce's ill-tempered cat will, on occasion, attempt an escape when strangers hold the doors open for too long. Today, as the Winston children depart with Max Winston's belongings in a Frito-Lay box, Clara Holbrooke tries to accompany them to the parking lot, but Ms. Joyce is there at the ready to intercept her. Jerry Ulrich, shaking despite his death grip on his walker, just gazes at the Winston couple as they hurry to their car, a glister of spittle unspooling from one corner of his mouth. The entire lobby smells instantly of urine.

Since Ms. Joyce is otherwise preoccupied, I go down the hall and enter room 2A.

The bed has been stripped of its sheets and the collection of photographs that sat in little brass frames on the table beside Max's bed is gone. The closet door is open, but nothing but empty hangers dangle from the crossbar. I look down and see a discolored spot on the floor where Max kept a handsome pair of dress shoes he never wore.

He had been the first person to corroborate my story about the intruder. The first one to draw pictures of the strange character who haunts these halls, yet somehow remains unseen by Ms. Joyce, Nurse Skarda, and the rest of the staff. It's as if something in our old eyes and old brains allows us to see through the flimsy veil of life and glimpse whatever resides in the darkness of the other side.

With some difficulty—I am, after all, eighty-two years old—I get down on my hands and knees and peer under the bed. Dark shapes under there. I stare at them until my eyes acclimate to the darkness beneath the box spring.

Three dead mice, two dead roaches, and the pencil-thin corpse of a tiny black snake.

As I exit the room, I hear a man's strident voice repeating a word or a sound or something that is, at first, unintelligible. It is the sheer volume, the urgency of that voice, which causes me to follow it.

I go down the corridor toward the back part of the house. The noise gets louder. There are others who have been alerted by it, those curious rubberneckers, raccoons gazing out peepholes. Those vacant houses on the brink of collapse.

The cafeteria is to the right, but that is not where the cries are coming from. The man is shouting off to the left, in the room that has come to be known as the Golf Course due to the harsh green carpeting that, despite age and wear, has maintained its perfect emerald-green hue. There are some bookshelves in here, but the text on the pages is too small and so the volumes remain largely untouched by the Sunshine House residents.

I step into the room.

Mr. Frost is leaning far back in his wheelchair, a look of abject terror stretching his face to terrible proportions. His eyes remind me of flashbulbs from an old camera. He is staring at a partially open closet door while crying out, over and over again, "Ronove! Ronove! Ronove!"

I rush to his side and attempt to console him. "It's all right, Mr. Frost. Please calm down."

"Ronove! Ronove!"

I recognize the name now, of course, and I cannot help but cast my gaze toward that sliver of darkness where the closet door stands just a few inches open. I convince myself that I see movement from within—that someone or something is *in there*—and I feel my entire body stiffen. With Max Winston's death still so fresh in all our minds, I begin to think of the worst…

I leave Mr. Frost's side and approach the closet. *Is* there movement inside? The door is only open three inches… yet that swirling darkness can hide just about anything, *anything*…

I reach out, grasp the knob. It is cold glass cut in the shape of a diamond. I squeeze it so hard I feel it leave impressions in my palm.

"What's going on in here?" It's Ms. Joyce, hustling into the room with a clipboard wedged under one fat arm.

"Ronove! Ronove!" shouts Mr. Frost. The timbre of his voice is rising, becoming more a scream than a shout.

Ms. Joyce glares at me, pulls my hand off the doorknob, then yanks the door open.

The closet is empty.

Mr. Frost's cries die out in a series of raspy, breathless sobs. I look at him and see tears standing in the poor man's eyes. His gaze is still locked on that closet, even though it's evident nothing—no one—is in there.

A crowd has appeared outside the door to the Golf Course, but two men in white shirts bustle through and approach Mr. Frost. I can never remember the names of the men who come and go in this place, each one nearly identical to the next, as if they roll in fresh off an assembly line. These two seem capable enough, one of them clearing a path away from the door while the other rolls Mr. Frost out of the room in his chair.

I watch them go, then peer down at the stunningly green carpet, at the tracks carved in it by the wheels of Mr. Frost's wheelchair. What looks to be a dead spider is curled like a tiny fist near the baseboard. Either that, or it's a raisin.

Ms. Joyce is staring at me. The look on her face would be quite at home on a stone gargoyle. Then she marches out into the hallway, presumably to look after Mr. Frost's well-being. Or maybe that's just what she wants me to think.

Agnes Bruner whispers into the room on stocking feet. The giant glasses she wears look too heavy for her small head and thin stalk of a neck. She is visibly trembling.

"Mr. Bruno?" she squeaks.

"It's all right, Agnes."

"That name…"

"I heard it."

"Is he…?" She peers around the room, those glasses like searchlights. She pauses when she looks at the closet, which now stands fully open, thanks to Ms. Joyce. Her hand shakes as she points toward it. "Was he hiding in there? That man?"

I look at the closet, which is clearly empty. I do not know what to tell her. I'm not even sure what I believe at this point.

"I don't know, Agnes. I don't think so."

She doesn't look satisfied. Things have been happening around here—they have been *ramping up*, as Mack Douglass said earlier in the week, and it seems Max Winston's death has only validated such assumptions—and everyone has become a little more on edge. Or perhaps a lot more. As for me, I'm not sure where I fall anymore. At this point, curiosity has bested my fear.

Agnes Bruner says nothing else. She turns and leaves the room, and the crowd of gawkers out in the hall seem to flee, albeit at a snail's pace, back to their rooms.

I'm halfway down the corridor toward my own room when Ms. Joyce confronts me. "May I speak with you for a moment, please, Mr. Bruno?"

Because I don't really have any other option, I acquiesce and follow her down the corridor to her office just off the lobby. It's no bigger than a broom closet, stuffed full of filing cabinets and notices pinned to cork boards. It smells of Pine-Sol and, vaguely, of cigarette smoke, even though smoking is prohibited inside the building.

Ms. Joyce squeezes behind her desk then instructs me to sit in the folding chair in front of her. As I sit, I notice Ms. Joyce's cat, a mangy gray-and-black thing with emerald eyes, watching me from behind one of the filing cabinets. What appears to be a small, dead rodent is on the floor beside it, a little treasure Ms. Joyce has yet to discover.

"What was that all about in there, Mr. Bruno?"

"I don't know."

"That word he was saying over and over..."

"Ronove," I say, because there's no use playing dumb about it. She's heard me say it plenty in the beginning, before I wised up and kept my mouth shut. By then it was too late; the name had spread like a disease through Sunshine House.

"You started this whole thing, Mr. Bruno. You've been frightening a number of our residents, filling their heads with stories of some intruder having accessed Sunshine House, and now everyone has become frightened."

I say nothing. This seems to cause her face to turn a dark, mottled red.

"And poor Mr. Frost. What about him? He had to be sedated. Do you find some sort of satisfaction in that, Mr. Bruno?"

"Of course not."

"This… fearmongering…"

"I'm not frightening anyone."

"Telling fantastical stories about strange men—"

"I'm not telling any stories, either."

Ms. Joyce's cold gray eyes simmer on me. She looks catlike herself, and in that moment, I have no difficulty imagining her hauling around dead rodents in her mouth.

She reaches into a desk drawer and produces a stack of colored construction paper. She sets the papers down in front of me so that I can see the figure drawn on top—the gangly, skin-and-bones, featureless man. What at first looks like an additional appendage is actually a crude staff being held in one hand. The artist has even included the figure's name at the top of this drawing, in block capital letters—RONOVE.

I look away from the drawings, not because I'm troubled by the figure (although I am), but because I am overcome by the distinct feeling that I, along with the rest of the residents of this place, have been reduced to children. The fact that these poor souls have resorted to expressing their fears with crayons and construction paper only reinforces this.

Without a word, Ms. Joyce shuffles through the pages, and I can't help but look at them again. Each one shows that same man, although rendered by a different artist. Sometimes the name, Ronove, is at the top of the page, sometimes at the bottom, or sometimes not there at all. The faster Ms. Joyce flips through the pages, the more it looks like the man holding the long staff is moving.

"This," she says, "is a serious problem. You've spoken about a man in this house who fits this description, and now half the floor claims to have seen him. They're frightened, and Nurse Skarda has told me that a few of them fear that what has happened to Mr. Winston… that his heart attack was caused by this… this… character."

She waves a dismissive hand over the papers.

"They're drawing this figure, obsessing over it, Mr. Bruno. And that's making my job more difficult."

I clear my throat and, despite still feeling like a child who's in the middle of receiving a reprimand, I say, "With all due respect, Ms. Joyce, they aren't just drawing pictures. Haven't you noticed? Mr. Torry is singing, and he sounds beautiful. Millie Broome is able to play the piano again. Constance Montague has been reciting Shakespeare in the cafeteria!" I can't help but laugh at the absurdity of it all.

"That's well and good, Mr. Bruno, but that isn't the issue here. The issue is that you've claimed to have seen this man in this house, and now you've got half the residents believing they've seen him, too. They believe that he's somehow responsible for Mr. Winston's heart attack, and now they think he's done something to poor Mr. Frost."

"Ms. Joyce," I say, peaceably enough. "If they claim to have seen him, then maybe they *have*."

It looks like she wants to say more but is at a loss. No doubt she thinks of me as a doddering old fool. I can't say I think any better of her.

"There will be no more talk about this… this Ronove," she says. "Is that understood, Mr. Bruno?"

I want to argue the point, because there is someone here in this house with us, but what's the use? There's nothing I could say to convince her.

"Mr. Bruno?"

"Understood," I say.

"Very good." She flits a hand at me and tells me to go to lunch.

I rise out of the chair, bones creaking, and am reaching for the doorknob when I pause and turn around. "Has there been any mail from my son lately?"

"No," she says curtly, not looking at me. She is stuffing the drawings back into her desk drawer.

"He usually sends a letter every Tuesday."

"It's Saturday, Mr. Bruno."

Is it? Or is this just another of Ms. Joyce's deceptions? I'm about to make an accusation when I happen to glance at the paper calendar on her desk, the kind with the one-panel cartoon on each day. I see it is, in fact, Saturday.

Unless, of course, the level of her deception is so great that she has changed the date to fool me, that she has—

But that doesn't seem likely. Not even for Ms. Joyce.

"Good day, Mr. Bruno."

I nod, suddenly tired and weary and unsure of myself, and step out into the hallway. Out of nowhere, I feel like the doddering old fool she thinks I am.

3

Two nights later, I'm awakened by a dull thump near my head, a sound my hazy, dream-laden brain believes is the singular beat of a giant heart. I drag myself to a seated position and glance at the window to the right of my narrow mattress. The pane shimmers with moonlight. I climb out of bed and notice, as I approach the windowpane, that there is a perfect circle of blood on the glass. Smaller than a dime, but there.

A lamppost looms just outside the window, and as I look through the glass and down at the concrete walkway that circumnavigates Sunshine House like a moat circles a castle, I see a bird down there, twitching. A finger of dread rises through me.

I do not bother to shove my feet into my slippers, do not hassle with the robe that hangs on my wall—I open the door and peer out into the corridor. The hallway is empty, dark, silent. All the doors to the residential suites in this wing are closed. We are on a hallway surrounded by other hallways, so there are no visible windows, no light except for the startling red lettering of the exit sign that seems to float in the darkness.

Something moves down there. It does not move quickly, but does not seem to want to avoid detection. In fact, I am struck by the opposite impression—that the figure wants to be seen, even though it has cloaked itself in darkness.

The figure is very tall, to the point where its narrow head must bend to miss the exit sign. Its torso is a thin husk, its limbs impossibly long and slender. It moves at the end of the hall in silence, and the only sound it generates is when the base of its long staff, which it clutches in one hand, thumps against the floor.

"*Ronove*," the figure whispers, a sound like wind shuttling through autumn trees.

"Wait," I say.

But it does not wait; it shifts across the hall—its head briefly eclipses the glowing red letters of the exit sign—and vanishes into the adjacent corridor.

I want to pursue it, to get to the bottom of this nightmare, but I am frozen in place. This whole thing started weeks earlier, when I was awoken to a sound in the hall only to be greeted by this death-like wraith, and we have continued to play this game of cat-and-mouse in a seemingly endless loop.

There comes another thump at my back. Then another. I turn and glance into my room, into that dark box and toward the rectangle of lighted window glass, just as another bird strikes the pane—*whump*! Tiny red asterisks are stamped like chicken pox on the glass.

Someone screams—a shrill, throaty cry that rises in pitch before being silenced. It startles me, but also breaks my paralysis. I hurry down the hall toward the exit sign, my hands blindly swatting at the darkness ahead, my heart chugging like a locomotive within the walls of my ribcage.

When I turn down the next corridor, I can see a wall of windows at the far end, which casts some illumination into the nighttime house, but also causes a confusing shift in my perspective. I stumble, lean momentarily against the wall. I've gone only a brief distance, but I am breathing in great, reaching gasps.

That scream again, causing the hairs along my neck to stiffen. There is the shotgun blast of a door swinging open and slamming against a wall. An instant later, I see the wraith swipe across the bank of moonlit windows. I give chase as best I can, a hurried limp, a hobbling gait, and I curse myself, curse myself, curse this crumbling old manse that has been sinking into its foundation for the better part of eight decades, nearly a century, and I hurry, hurry—

It stalks quickly down a series of passageways and I do my damnedest to keep pace. It isn't until I make a succession of sharp turns that I realize I am unfamiliar with this wing of the facility, that perhaps I am not even *in* the facility, that my pursuit has ushered me through the veil and into the dark void on the other side of the world.

The doors along this hallway all stand open, exposing black

rectangles through which frigid air hisses, like steam escaping a busted pipe. Disoriented, I stagger down the corridor, one hand bracing myself against the wall, searching the darkness for that impossible visage. That thing who whispers his own name, drilling it inside my head. Inside all our heads.

I hear the thud-thud-thudding of Ronove's staff grow louder as I advance. I am accosted by a blast of cold, fetid air every time I walk past one of the open doorways. I am tempted to look into each one, but I do not, for my fear has begun to replace my curiosity.

Thud-thud-thud…

The sound ceases as I reach the end of the hallway. There is an emergency exit here, and a stainless steel water fountain in the wall. I feel around for a light switch but can't find one.

A wail echoes down the hall from the opposite end—the direction from which I've just come. Confusion rattles me. How is it David has gotten lost in this place? He's just a boy. I should have been keeping a better eye on him. I should have—

But David, my son, is not a child. He is a grown man. This has nothing to do with David; I wasn't awoken by David, haven't been searching for him down these foreign passageways. It was the intruder, the wraith. Ronove.

The wail persists. Someone is moaning. There is also the low susurration of voices. I see a light wink on and reflect along the far wall. I follow it, able now to recognize the familiar alabaster walls of Sunshine House, the tiled hall floor in its checkerboard pattern, dried mop swirls creating ghost patterns atop real ones.

I cross the lobby to join a few more residents who have been roused from sleep by the wailing. Who is it? Someone is sobbing.

I squeeze through the crowd and make my way down the lighted hallway. The night nurse is on duty tonight, Nurse Diaz, and she is not as nice or as pretty as Nurse Skarda. As I approach the lighted doorway to Millie Broome's room, aware now that I am holding my breath, I see Nurse Diaz beside Millie's bed, and I think, *Oh no, please, not Millie Broome, please, not Millie, she has just learned the piano all over again…*

Millie is alive, sitting upright in bed, her bulging hands and twisted fingers pressed against her mouth as if to stifle another sob. Her eyes are glassy with tears. When I appear in the doorway, she shifts her gaze from the perplexed Nurse Diaz and stares at me. There is an imploring look in her eyes, and it makes my knees weak.

She speaks no words, instead points to the bell-shaped parakeet cage that hangs from the ceiling by a hook. I notice that the cage is swaying back and forth, but there is no breeze; the single window beside Millie's bed is closed.

"Stay out in the hall, sir," Nurse Diaz instructs, but I ignore her. I go to the birdcage and peer inside.

Sweetums is on the newspapered floor of the cage, dead. Its plumage is still as bright as ever. Its eye—I can only see one, given the position of the head—looks like a tiny dollop of India ink.

"Sir," Nurse Diaz says, a bit more forcefully this time. She is standing beside Millie's bed with her hands on her hips, staring at me with unmasked contempt.

"Never you mind," Millie tells the nurse. To me, she says, "He was in here, Mr. Bruno. You were right. And just look what he's done to poor Sweetums."

She is lucky it is only Sweetums whose heart has seized up. I don't say this, though; I merely nod at Millie, show her the sympathy she needs at the moment, and feel a twinge of relief in my chest because she is, from what I can tell, unharmed.

"Who?" says Nurse Diaz. "Who did what?"

"The bird is dead," I say.

Nurse Diaz looks at me, then hustles around the side of the bed and joins me at the birdcage. She stares at what's inside for a second or two before turning back to Millie.

"What's going on?" says one of the old-timers standing in the doorway. Seems this place has been nothing but impromptu crowds lately.

"Everyone needs to go back to their rooms," Nurse Diaz insists.

"You okay, Millie?" asks the old-timer.

"Sweetums has been killed," says Millie.

There is a gasp from the audience out in the hallway.

"Killed?" says Nurse Diaz. "It's died, dear. No one did anything to your bird."

"That man!" Millie cries.

Again, Nurse Diaz looks at me.

"No," says Millie. "Not Mr. Bruno. That man with the staff. He was in my room! He killed Sweetums and he was going to do the same to me."

"It's true," I hear myself say. Eyes stare at me from the darkened hallway. "I saw him. He was running down the hall. I couldn't keep up."

"Do you see?" someone from outside says. "Do you *see*?"

Nurse Diaz claps her hands. "Enough. Everyone, back to your rooms. I do not want to call Ms. Joyce."

I can feel disquiet emanating from the residents out in the hallway. I feel it like a heat radiating from a nuclear reactor.

"Ronove," someone whispers.

"Ronove, yes," echoes Millie.

A rumbling chorus ensues, that name repeated like a mantra by all the frightened villagers.

Nurse Diaz goes to Millie, hands her a paper cup and a large white pill. Millie pokes the pill into her mouth and brings the cup to her lips, hand trembling. Out in the hall, the mumbling chorus continues.

"Goodnight," Nurse Diaz says to everyone and no one in particular. She stares at me. "Goodnight, Mr. Bruno."

In that instant, I can tell she has been briefed on me and my behavior over the past few weeks. Ms. Joyce has told her I'm the troublemaker. The cause of this whole thing.

I glance back at the dead bird. There is a silk sheet folded over the arm of a chair, so I take the sheet and cover the cage with it. Then I promise to help Millie bury Sweetums in the yard come morning. Millie nods, appreciative. I move out into the hall and push through the few residents of Sunshine House who have yet to return to their rooms. One woman holds another, as if to console her. They are frightened, all of them.

My corridor is empty and quiet. The door to my room stands open, just as I left it. I go inside, close the door, and feel something against my bare foot that causes me to jump back. I feel along the wall for the light switch, flip it on.

On the floor is Ms. Joyce's cat, its body curled like a crescent moon, its legs still. Its tail makes a perfect J on the floor. Its dead eyes gaze into a vast nothingness.

I stare at the dead cat for some time, contemplating my choices. I could carry it back out into the hall and leave it for someone else to find. I could go to Nurse Diaz and tell her. But those options do not appeal to me; they make me look complicit, guilty. And I fear, at least in Ms. Joyce's eyes, I already look guilty enough. The last thing I need is for her to kick me out of this place, and for me to have to move in with David. Personally, I would love to live with him, but that wouldn't be fair to David. He's a young man with his whole life ahead of him, who doesn't need his creaky old father hampering him.

In the end, I decide to place Ms. Joyce's dead cat in an extra pillow case, and to dispose of it without anyone knowing in the morning.

Seems a good idea at the time.

4

In my dream, I am shuttled along in the passenger seat of a stark white Lincoln Continental while David sits behind the wheel. The radio is on, the station at first a series of debates by people in proper British accents, which then bleeds into a jazz station, where someone plays an up-tempo melody on a piano. I imagine I can hear the occasional chirrups of a small bird on the soundtrack.

I ask David where we are going and he tells me we're on a hunt. Yet not *exactly* a hunt.

—We're collectors, Pop, he tells me.

We are driving through the desert and it is midnight. A strange bluish light simmers on the distant horizon.

—I don't understand, I say.

—Just don't look in the backseat, Pop.

So of course I look in the backseat.

At first I see nothing but darkness. Then I realize it is the darkness itself that is comprised of *shades*, of shadowlike specters, and that pairs of golden eyes stare at me from the gloom.

Frightened, I turn back to David, but David is no longer seated behind the steering wheel of the great Lincoln. It is the wraith, Ronove, its body hunched over the wheel while its featureless head presses against the ceiling of the car. Its arms are like tree branches stitched together to form joints. Leaning against the seat between us is Ronove's staff.

The ghost-hands of those doomed souls in the backseat clutch at me.

I scream, breaking my throat.

5

I want to get an early start burying the dead because today is the day David comes to visit. After breakfast, I join Millie Broome in the yard behind Sunshine House, where I excavate a small hole in the earth with a fork I swiped from the cafeteria. A small crowd has gathered to pay their respects. Millie is strong; she does not cry over Sweetums, whom she has wrapped in the silk handkerchief, but I can tell she is in pain. No, it is not sadness that permeates this little group, but fear.

Millie places Sweetums in the hole. She says a few words, then looks at me. Her eyes appear to tremble in their sockets. I say a few words, too—good old Sweetums, cheery old bird, rest in peace, old friend—and then Mr. Torry sings a heartfelt and beautiful rendition of "Amazing Grace."

As the crowd disperses, Millie and Mr. Torry remain with me. Millie says, "Do you think he'll come back again tonight, Mr. Bruno?"

I tell her I do not know.

"What exactly is this fellow's endgame?" says Mr. Torry. He, too, has witnessed the wraith flitting through the corridors at night. And while he is grateful that Ronove's arrival at Sunshine House has brought back his lovely singing ability, the distress in his voice is clear to me. "Is he like Death? Does he wish to work through us all like some plague?"

"That doesn't sound right," I tell him. "There seems to be some method to his madness." Although what method that actually is, I cannot formulate into words.

When Millie Broome and Mr. Torry return to the house, I creep farther across the yard and vanish behind a stand of trees and a sizeable hedgerow. Grunting, I struggle to my knees and proceed to dig a larger hole, almost a trench, in the soft earth behind the hedgerow. It takes a while using the fork, and when I finish, I am flecked with dirt and slimed in a sheen of sweat. I return to my room, take the pillowcase that contains Ms. Joyce's dead cat from my closet, and go back outside.

I am already exhausted by the time I reach the hole I've made. I turn the pillowcase upside down and shake the cat out. It is stiff as a board now, the J of its tail as rigid as a fishing hook. I mop the sweat from my brow with the pillowcase, then slap it over one shoulder. I kick what dirt I can into the hole before struggling to my knees again to close it up the rest of the way.

But I don't get that far, because a shadow falls over me and I hear someone clear their throat.

I turn around and, wincing against the early morning sun, I see Ms. Joyce standing there.

6

I am told to shower and dress before meeting with Ms. Joyce in her office. This time when I arrive, aside from Ms. Joyce, there is a balding gentleman in a gray suit seated at an angle at Ms. Joyce's desk. Because the room is so cramped, he is attempting to balance a notepad on one knee.

The man is never introduced to me, but I quickly discern that he is an attorney. Ms. Joyce does all the talking. And while it is clear that this meeting has come about because of what she saw me doing with her dead cat, she does her best to remain composed. Perhaps it is her anger that overrides her grief.

"You are being transferred to a facility in San Bernardino," she tells me.

She talks at length about the particulars of the transfer, but I stop listening. I want to explain about the cat—that I didn't kill it, that I was only burying it—but I find no good place to interject my defense. Besides, at this point, I'm not sure what good it will do. She makes it clear that the facility in San Bernardino is not as nice as Sunshine House, and of this I have no doubt. This is my punishment, and I will not be rewarded. I have heard horror stories about the facility in San Bernardino.

"Perhaps," Ms. Joyce concludes, "your friend Mr. Ronove will see it fit to follow you there, and to leave the rest of us alone."

"Where's my son?" I say. "David should be here. He should be part of this discussion."

The lawyer shifts uncomfortably, and Ms. Joyce says, "We are handling all the particulars of this transfer, Mr. Bruno."

"David will be here this afternoon," I tell her. "It's time for his monthly visit."

"Your son David is dead, Mr. Bruno," says Ms. Joyce. "We have gone over that many, many times. He has been dead for eight years, which is when you were remanded to this facility."

"That's a lie," I say, and slam my fist down on her desk. The lawyer jumps and scoots back, the notepad wobbling on his knee. "David was here visiting me just last month."

"No, Mr. Bruno. Your son has never been here."

"I *spoke* to him. He writes me letters. He… he shows up and takes me for drives in his Lincoln."

"That is just not true," Ms. Joyce says. "I'm sorry, Mr. Bruno, but that is just not true."

I cannot stand to listen to any more of her lies. I get up and head out the door. She calls after me, but I do not stop and turn around, and despite her calling, she seems happy to let me leave.

The proof is in the letters, of course. I have kept all of David's letters in a shoebox in my room. I go there now, feeling like my heart is beating in my throat. I hear Millie Broome playing the piano in the rec room, can hear Mr. Torry crooning a Dean Martin number from his room, can see couples waltzing in the cafeteria as I stride past. Astoundingly, there are residents in the Golf Course, reading those books that have, for years, remained untouched. Artistry has come to Sunshine House, ushered in by a monster who hides in the darkness and stalks us like Death.

In my room, I go straight to my closet and take down the shoebox from the shelf. I sit on the edge of my bed and open it, knowing that all of David's letters are in there, but finding that it contains nothing but some utensils from the cafeteria, an old shoelace, a scattering of multicolored pills that I have been refusing to take, and a single dead beetle.

A volcanic eruption threatens to rise up through me. I fight to keep it down, terrified as to what might happen if I give in. When I hear my closet door creak, I glance up. I see nothing at first, but then I make out a darker shape among the darkness—something that detaches itself from the shadows. It moves fluidly, like a ghost or something in a dream, yet I hear quite distinctly the stolid *thump* of its staff against the floor.

Nurse Skarda appears in the doorway. I can tell by her eyes that she has been crying.

"Ms. Joyce stole my letters," I say.

"Oh, Mr. Bruno..."

"Tell me," I say, even though it is difficult at the moment to find my voice. "You've met David, haven't you? You've met my son. Tell them he comes once a month."

"Mr. Bruno, David passed away several years ago."

"No," I insist. "We go driving once a month."

Slowly, Nurse Skarda shakes her head. She looks miserable. Her eyes continue to fill with tears. "That's not true, dear. He's passed. I'm so, so sorry."

"No." Has Ms. Joyce gotten to Nurse Skarda? Is this all one great ploy to get me to lose my mind?

As if she's capable of reading my thoughts, Nurse Skarda says, "I wouldn't lie to you, Mr. Bruno. You just forget, and I'm sorry to have to remind you. But I wouldn't lie to you. I hope you know that."

I look back down into the shoebox. How many pills have I been stashing in there? For the life of me, I cannot remember what they're even for.

"Why don't we go to lunch?" Nurse Skarda suggests. She swipes a tear from her cheek.

"David will come." With trembling hands, I set the shoebox on the bed beside me. "You'll see. He'll fix all this nonsense, too. I won't relocate. David will make sure it doesn't happen."

I expect Nurse Skarda to protest, but she doesn't. She smiles softly at me and says, "All right, Mr. Bruno."

I nod at her, a motion that suggests I'd prefer to be alone. She understands, and leaves. I listen to the soft tread of her sneakers recede down the corridor.

Despite the hunger twisting my stomach, I do not go to the cafeteria for lunch. I go to my closet, pull the door open. The wraith is no longer inside, having been dispatched back into the void by Nurse Skarda's sudden arrival.

I comb through the clothing that hangs there, until I find a nice black suit toward the back. As I look at it, I am confused by an image of myself standing beside a grave, and although I am sure it is Rose's grave, my wife's grave, something begs a different truth from my brain. Yet I shut it down before it can speak too loudly.

I remove the suit from the closet and lay it across my bed. It's a nice suit. A good driving suit. It's what I wear every month when David comes to visit. Even in the heat of a California summer, I wear the suit.

Slowly, I strip out of my clothes and put the suit on. I stand before the small mirror over my dresser and examine myself. The suit fits nicely, but my silvery hair is twisted into corkscrews. I dig a comb out of my drawer—there is a framed picture of David on my nightstand, as well as a wedding photo of Rose and me—and rake it through my unruly hair. When I finish, I find that my reflection has blurred. I paw at my eyes, discovering they are wet.

I hear a floorboard creak and glance back at the closet. But there is no one there.

7

A rank of plastic chairs in the lobby faces the glass doors of Sunshine House and, beyond, the circular driveway. It is a nice day, the sky absent of clouds and as richly blue as a child's drawing. I seat myself on one of the chairs, my hands folded in my lap, and await David's arrival.

At one point, Millie Broome arrives. She sits beside me for a time, mostly in silence. I wish to be alone, but I do not have the heart to say this to her, so I try my damnedest to enjoy her silent company. Finally, she gets up and touches me lightly on the shoulder.

"You are a good man, Mr. Bruno," she tells me. Then she departs, fading into the labyrinthine depths of Sunshine House.

It is when the quality of the daylight changes that Nurse Skarda sits beside me. She has a sandwich wrapped in wax paper, which she extends to me. I shake my head and don't take my eyes off the circular driveway. Any minute now, David will be pulling up in his stark-white Lincoln Continental.

"You have to eat something," she says.

I say nothing. I do not even acknowledge she has spoken.

"Well," she says, but nothing more. She rises from the seat and places the wax-papered sandwich down on it. She looks at me for a moment, and it is all I can do not to meet her gaze. Finally, she leaves.

Outside, the blue has been siphoned from the sky. The horizon is a mottled purple and red and, high above, the first hint of stars poke through the firmament.

I watch a tiny mouse scurry along the baseboard.

Sometime later, there is a shift change. The young men in the white shirts leave. Ms. Joyce departs for home, and does not bother to look at me as she hurries across the lobby and out the doors. She is carrying the food and water bowls that she kept in her office for her cat. I would feel bad for her if she wasn't trying to mess with my head.

Nurse Diaz arrives, casts a curious glance in my direction, then heads off toward the restroom.

It is fully dark when Nurse Skarda appears in the lobby again. She looks at the sandwich that is still on the seat next to me then looks at me.

"Mr. Bruno," she says. "Please."

I say nothing. I feel that if I were to speak, my whole body might break apart. I wait for Nurse Skarda to leave the building, but she doesn't; she goes back down the hall, where she remains for some time. When she returns, she has a paper cup and a large white pill in her palm. She extends both to me.

I do not want the pill, but I also do not want Nurse Skarda to fret over me. She is nice and she is pretty, and even if Ms. Joyce has somehow poisoned her brain against me, I know Nurse Skarda is a good person.

I put the pill in my mouth and drink the water. Then I hand the paper cup back. She takes the cup, stares at it, then looks at me. Then she does something that nearly causes me to sob—she bends forward and kisses the top of my head.

"Goodnight, Mr. Bruno."

I say nothing.

And just like that, Nurse Skarda is gone.

I reach into my mouth and pull the pill out from beneath my tongue. I tuck it into the pocket of my suit jacket and am surprised to find a cluster of similar pills in there.

Night falls, and still no sign of David.

8

At ten o'clock, I am ushered back to my room by Nurse Diaz. She promises she will notify me when David arrives, so I go without protest. She wants me to change from my suit into my pajamas, but I refuse. I want to look sharp for when David arrives.

Nurse Diaz closes the door on her way out. I sit on the edge of my bed, feeling hungry and drowsy. Soon, I scoot backward and lean against the headboard. I have allowed myself to remove my shoes, so now my feet find the cool spots on the bedsheet. There is a hole in my left sock through which my big toe protrudes. I will have to ask David to buy me new ones.

When something thuds against the window, my eyes open and I realize I have fallen asleep. The lamp is still on, but the shadows in my room look deeper. Like pits that you can fall into if you're not careful. I see, too, that the tiny mouse from earlier has somehow made its way into my room… although he is now dead against the baseboard.

Out in the hall, I hear the distinctive *thump-thump-thump* of Ronove's staff. I sit up straight, the nape of my neck suddenly itchy with perspiration.

Thump… thump…

The wraith stops outside my door.

There is another thud at my window, and I turn in time to see a small bird slide down the glass.

The doorknob turns.

The door opens.

The shape that stands in the darkness of the hallway is impossibly tall. I can make out no details, and my mind struggles to reconcile what I am looking at.

"Ronove," I mutter, my throat dry.

"*Ronove*," intones the demon.

It steps foot into my room—

And it is David.

"Hello, Pop."

"David!" I climb out of bed and hurry to him, throw my arms around him. "Oh, David! I knew you'd come!"

"It's all right, Pop. Calm down. Calm down."

I pull away, hold him at arm's length. Behind me, more birds fly thump against the windowpane, but I do not turn to look. "They said you were dead. They said you were killed in an automobile accident, David, but those were just tricks. They were trying to trick me!"

"I know, Pop. Have a seat on the bed. Please."

I ease down onto the corner of the bed, though my heart is going a mile a minute. I see my shoes on the floor and usher my feet inside them.

"They want to send me away from here," I tell him, "to a horrible place. Let's just leave, David. Let's just drive away and never come back."

"That's why I'm here," he says.

"Oh, David..."

My body is trembling. I stand and reach for the door. Take a step. Thumping against the window at my back...

A part of my mind sees me pitch forward and collapse to the floor. My muscles tighten and I cannot move. My breath escapes my throat in a singular wheeze, one that seems to go on for an eternity. I am there, right in the spot where Ms. Joyce's cat died. I am there, staring at a dead mouse against the baseboard while birds break their necks against the windowpane.

But, no—I am not there on the floor at all. I am following David across the circular driveway toward his shiny white Continental. The headlamps are bright and the engine is running. I hurry to keep up with David, who walks at a quick clip despite having to use a staff—

(*thump-thump-thump*)

—and then we are in the car, we are driving, the Lincoln's headlights carving through the darkness of the night. On the radio, I can hear Millie Broome playing the piano. I can hear Mr. Torry singing "Three Coins in the Fountain." I can hear Mr. Frost saying the wraith's name over and over, the radio filling with static, the car's engine overcoming all of it.

"Where are we going, David?"

"The other side, Pop."

I hear noise from behind me, and I begin to turn my head. David stops me by placing a hand on my shoulder.

"Don't look in the backseat, Pop."

I don't look. I turn and face forward and watch the midnight desert spread out all around us. A strange bluish light simmers on the horizon.

"I've missed you so much, David."

David smiles, but says nothing. It is so dark in the car that his features are swallowed up in shadow. On the seat between us is a long wooden staff, running from the floor to the ceiling of the car. A smell like cordite briefly infiltrates my nostrils.

"Welcome aboard, Mr. Bruno," says Max Winston from the backseat.

AMDUSIAS

Amdusias (also Amducias or Amduscias) has the shape of a human, but with claws for hands and feet, and the head of a unicorn, and he brandishes a trumpet. The demon with the greatest musical ability, he is said to be the director of the cacophonous music played in hell, and can conjure up musical instruments that play on their own. He has the rank of duke in the infernal hierarchy. Reginald Scot's *Discoverie of Witchcraft* also points out that he "easilie bringeth to passe … that trees shall bend and incline, according to the conjurors will," adding, "he is excellent among familiars, and hath nine and twentie legions."

Symphony

PHILIP FRACASSI

Father doesn't know about this journal and if he ever found out he'd kill me.

Esther heard the music again.

It played over this scene: she with her mother, running through fields of impossible green. The birds-eye view of an omniscient observer would have noticed specks of bright blue, budding wildflowers among the tall grass. There were also flecks of white, beads of yellow. The meadow lay the width and breadth of heaven, and no matter how fast or far she ran, holding her mother's cool, soft hand, she never tired, never felt her chest grow heavy or her brow grow hot. Mother wore a white linen dress, and Esther crimson silk that flowed and trailed behind her, riding the tips of the grass, giving her blood-red wings.

It came from above. Always from above.

Horns, gentle and rising in a chorus. Strings plucked and run across with a taut bow, interrupted by bright bursts of staccato wind chords, as if through flutes or sagging bagpipes. Simultaneously cacophonous and melodic. A mathematical movement stuck with barbs, an orchestra created by a genius and performed by a thousand madmen. It came from a distant point and Esther looked past her mother's face to the sky, seeking the source. The hovering clouds were white cotton stretched thin, with puffs of gray near the horizon. A mounting storm. From there the sounds emanated, and it was toward that gray swirling cluster that they ran, headlong, faces stretched into smiles.

The clouds climbed higher, spreading like smoke from a house fire, reached over the expanse. Esther started to slow, to cry out for her mother to stop, to turn back. She pulled at her mother's hand, but it was no longer soft, no longer cool. The fingers were thick, hard, long. The fingers entrapped her own and pulled her along at the same breakneck speed. She tried to get her mother's attention but could only see the back of her head, blonde hair flowing, the thin white dress a writhing sack of pumping arms and legs.

"Mom!"

The head turned slightly, and Esther saw a chin, a nose in profile. The skin appeared strained, wrinkled, scabbed.

The music amplified—*and, oh, it was beautiful*—filling the sky end-to-end like swelling twines of muscle, straining against the atmosphere, the vibrations of chords strong enough to shake the earth. The gray clouds were above them now, and still they raced on. Rain fell in sweeping sheets, the hands of Neptune slapping across the plains, dousing them both. The linen dress clung to her mother like translucent skin, revealed her body's slight, elfish frame. Her hair, like Esther's, no longer flowed, but spilled over their heads like jars of paint. Mother's pale yellow, Esther's inky black. Esther no longer tried to scream, the raging harmony was too loud. Her vision juggled, eardrums tickled, teeth chattered from the physical strength of the music, so big it filled the world, split the sky like broken plaster. The shattered pieces fell as hail.

And still the music grew, a heaven's worth of angels shouting down Jericho's walls.

Above them, charcoal clouds circled in masses large as cities. A spiral funnel formed, a finger of God that pushed slowly through the fabric of the world, thrust itself down, down toward the firmament, toward Esther.

Her mother stumbled, collapsed face-down and motionless into the grass. Esther fell with her, her crimson dress running off her like warm blood. She clutched her mother's prone head, lifted it from the ground to face her.

Her mother's eyes were hollow, her skin stretched, flaking and calloused, her teeth crooked shards. "Stay away, Esther!" the hag that was her mother screamed. "Stay away from him!"

Esther screamed but could not hear her own voice. The song crescendoed. Thunder rumbled alongside pounding drums. Great horns wailed, cymbals crashed. Lightning rode the rain down and spit fire into the earth. Dirt flew and Esther felt the heat from the electricity.

The rushing wind tugged at her with invisible fingers, lifted her small body from the earth, gently as a soul rising from the grave toward heaven. She spun her arms, reached for her mother but she was there no more; only a charred black chasm remained, into which her body had fallen. Esther could see downward into the great fires of Hell.

And still she rose.

She began to cycle with the twister, the world spun while falling away. Higher and higher she flew, into the gaping maw of the storm. Her body flipped to face the sky. She saw slits of golden eyes above an expanding, swirling mouth. Sonorous laughter came from the great aperture, and lightning crackled at the edges of the portal like fire-born teeth. She was pulled inside, swallowed. It was darker than she'd imagined, the earth seen only in dancing slivers. A spark bit her dress and it caught with flame. Her skin burned, the meaty smoke filled her nose and her mind screamed at the hungry storm which had engulfed her to *let her go or let her die.*

But the music did not stop.

Even when she woke from the dream, surrounded by the banality of her shadowed bedroom, it lingered.

Rain spattered the window pane, opaque against the night. She sat up, her shirt and pajama bottoms soaked through with sweat, strands of hair sticking to her cheeks and neck. She slowed her breathing, her rapid heart. Listened. The melody remained, as it often did. Persistent. As if to say, *This time, child? This time will you heed the call?*

She squinted at the window, eyes adjusting to the gray-toned sketches of the landscape: the flat shadow of large meadow, the thin smoke-trail of road that led to a larger world snaking away from its edge. It was the middle of the night, and the moon shone strong, despite the rain. Esther nodded to the dark in acquiescence, pushed down the covers and swung her legs out of bed. Her toes dangled inches from the floor as she faced the window and studied her spectral reflection.

This time, she would heed the call.

The rain was different than in the dream world. The haunting music was still distinct, but faint, as if pressed against a massive membrane that separated this world from that of dreams. The sound of the drops hitting earth and flora was like the arguments of fairies, soothing with an underlying hostility. She felt observed by the rain, but did not mind.

Her clothes absorbed the cool water, turned heavy and chilled against her skin. Esther turned back once to view the pale house, misty and beaten by shadows; its half-open window a sleepy eye in the western wall of the one-story ranch home. The milk-toned walls wore sepia shingles like a sharp-angled hat. Father's room was on the opposite side, and she did not fear his seeing her, nor did she fear his coming to her room late this night. She had learned his patterns, sly though they might be.

The sky danced with flashes, popping bulbs of lightning. The music above her swelled. Horns fattened and swayed, a melancholy dirge. She turned and ran across the knee-high grass toward the trail head. The trees that surrounded the meadow and enclosed their home were old and dense, protruding fingers of oaks, maples, birch and cedars. Beyond the woods, up and over a ridge, was the trail, an old Chippewa path kept alive by the occasional Sunday hiker and the environmental leanings of the local council. The trail was hardly ever used this close to Paw Creek, where her and Father lived, but would take you six miles north if you let it, winding along the big lake to Little Bluff, a quaint tourist town that thrived in the summer and hibernated, like they all did, in the cold months. Esther had never walked the entire way, but she and Mother had often explored the trail, marveled at the long tunnel of trees it afforded those who passed through. Just ahead was the flute where the trees opened, a dividing not unlike the Red Sea, a clear path of thin grass, rock and dirt piercing the old woods like an arrow shaft.

As she strode into the forest's moon-dipped fissure, she closed her eyes. As rain pattered her head and cheeks and shoulders, she debated whether she truly wanted to continue. She took a breath, smelled the life in the rain. Took another.

A whip-crack of thunder, and her eyes sprang open. A chorus, sweet as a swarm of locusts, sang in her ears. The orchestra bellowed, not from the sky, but from the trees. A swelling coda of dancing keys infiltrated the surrounding wood, and as the rain slapped against earth and leaves it stopped being random white noise and instead took on a melody, a rhythmic beat, a fantastic pulse of notes flowing through her like waves of energy, a complex and torrid symphony as haunting as it was blissful. The wind gusted at her back, pushed her forward despite her uncertainty. The trees were bent unnaturally, the hardwood creaking as the tips arched into deep courtship bows, branches reaching into pointed bark-coated fingers.

This way, they said.

She ran, let the wind lift her off the ground every few steps, gently place her back in stride, heel-to-toe on the wet earth. She entered the trees, felt them watching her askance as they bowed deeper, uniformly directing her steps.

Esther saw the tunnel take a turn just ahead, darker here than at the entrance, the moonlight not breaking through. The crook in the trail was called the Devil's Elbow, and her mother had said it came from an ancient Indian name, translated roughly to "where the spirits live." Esther didn't believe it of course, knew her mother was teasing, trying to frighten her. But now, alone in the dark, Esther thought it an appropriate name. She felt energy here, a tingling that carried from the bottom of her spine up through her neck and along the back of her skull.

There was a sharp break in the song, a stuttering record skip, and the trees groaned and lifted themselves straight as soldiers. She slowed, then stopped. Waited. She was confused, lost without the music. When it started again it was soft. A sonata. The trees cracked and leaves murmured. She watched in wonder as they swayed, gravitating to a synched point, the ones to the left of the path bent nearly horizontal in their reach, the ones to the right dipped so sharply as to be upside-down U's. She stepped forward to where their leaning tips directed, a sole spot in the earth along the shoulder of the trail.

She looked up, spun around, saw the tops of the trees looking back at her with stern, leaf-skinned faces.

The music rushed back like a sharp wind, frenetic and hurried. Gasping, she dropped to her knees and ripped at the soft earth with her fingers, yanked at the top layer of grass, then into the pale brown mud, pulling away rocks and small roots, tossing it behind her as she dug.

She was elbow-deep, fingers bleeding, nails chipped and split, when she finally felt something cold, unnaturally smooth. She wiped and scraped away the remainder of the mud to uncover an object shining and black. Six inches in height and intricately shaped. She dug her fingers beneath it, pried it up.

A ray of moonlight broke through the canopy, and she lifted the onyx carving into its shine. The head was a unicorn. A twisting horn protruded from the raised forehead of the creature, long as her pinky and sharp as a needle at its point. The body, however, was that of a large man. Brutish, hairy, and hunkered into a sitting position. Unnaturally long fingers sagged over his knees, his chest a mighty barrel, his stomach a protruding gumball. Legs, bent and knobby, ended in hooves.

Esther stood, swayed, felt sleepy. The moonlight was fading, her adrenaline waned. She was cold, wet. Clutching the object to her chest, she sighed and headed for home.

Minutes later she crawled through her window. The carpet squelched wetly beneath her dirty bare toes, the half-open window having allowed in the rain. She set the statuette on her nightstand, then went to the bathroom to dry herself, wash the dirt from her hands and feet.

She found clean sweats, a long-sleeve thermal, and dry fluffy pink socks. Warming slowly, she climbed into bed, scribbled blindly in her journal, then fell into a deep sleep, where no dreams could catch her.

Too tired to write much tonight. Sorry.
Another nightmare and some found treasure.
New friend, perhaps.

❖

"Eat your eggs."

Esther looked down at her plate, the pile of moist yellow scrambled eggs on one half, greasy fat-tipped bacon on the other. Her stomach clenched at the thought of putting any of it into her mouth, so she nibbled at the edge of an unbuttered piece of toast and studied the meal, wondering what she could do to get out of eating her father's failed attempt at a healthy breakfast.

He pulled out a chair from across the table, sat down heavily, picked up the morning paper and slurped his coffee.

Saturdays were Esther's least favorite day of the week. Monday through Friday she spent at school, and often tried to extend the time away from home by asking for playdates with her friends, or volunteering to help with after-school projects. Anything to keep her from returning home to her secluded prison with Father, who still had no job, paying their bills with the insurance checks that came every month since Mom died.

She poked the eggs with her fork, head bowed, and lifted her eyes to examine the man across the table. Hair graying, thin. Getting long. He looked pale and gaunt, but she knew how strong he was. He had looked different when Mother was alive. Or, perhaps, he had only *appeared* different to her. Rose-colored glasses of a young girl in love with a daddy who adored her, smothered her with love, *protected* her.

Now he was the boogeyman. A stalker of the night.

When he drank, as he did most nights, he got depressed, then, especially of late, hostile. It started with visits shortly after Mom's death. He'd sit on Esther's bed and cry; she'd hug him and *she'd* cry. Then he would stay in her bed, hold her, sleep with her until morning. At first, she loved it. But as the months went by, the visits became too ritualistic, too invasive. Esther was getting older and realizing how very *odd* it was. She'd tried to play it off at first, made a joke of it. "Daddy, go sleep in your own bed!" she'd say and throw a pillow at him, or a stuffed bear. Often he'd laugh, take the hint, leave.

But the more he drank, the less of a game it became. The less in control he was. The warmth became a chill that never left her body, the games a sullen acquiescence. When he first started groping her, she'd squirm and jump out of bed and yell at him to *stop!* And he would. For a while. Until he came home drunk again.

He started tying her down. Used pieces of her own clothing. Sweats or leggings, whatever was around. He'd tie her to the bed and put his hands on her. Angrily so. Sometimes, as if sickened with himself, or with her, he'd push her into the closet and jam a chair beneath the doorknob. Leave her there for the night, often well into morning, until he woke up and summoned the courage to face her.

After a while, she stopped lashing out. Stopped fighting. He never went too far, kept the damage mainly psychological, which she supposed was a blessing. But it was also, she knew, temporary. She was getting older, her body maturing, and he had noticed. It shamed her. All of it shamed her. She would look in the mirror at her own body and break down in tears, hating her own womanhood. Hating the female of her. Hating that she drew him to her in that way. Hating him, but herself more.

During those first months, when he'd become more abusive, the nightmares began. Dreams of storms and music, of being with and *losing always losing* her mother. Again and again and again.

He looked up at her, caught her eye and held it.

"Eat your eggs."

She stuck a fork into the bright yellow mush, lifted a small bite to her mouth. They were cool and wet and she wanted to spew them out, but she managed to swallow. Maybe she should start handling the cooking duties. At least then she wouldn't be eating shit every meal.

She recalled the statuette sitting on her nightstand and smiled to herself. A secret was always a good thing to ward off feelings of worthlessness, of abjection. Secrets *empowered.*

Then she realized. Secrets did empower, but in their case they empowered him. Because his secret, in this particularly sad scenario, was her.

Holy shit.

Okay, how can I put this into words? How do I describe last night?

I was laying here, falling asleep and staring at the unicorn. Thinking about the music I'd hear in my dreams and the night I dug it out of the dirt, near the trees.

I heard a loud… I don't know… scratching *sound, and the room got very, very dark. Like I was underwater, like my whole room was sinking in a submarine, diving into some dark abyss. My ears plugged up and the air got hot… and then, a minute later, my ears popped and I could sort of see again. Everything was fine. Normal. Except when I looked around my room, I saw* him.

I turned on the lamp by my bed, ready to scream.

He stood by the window, and he was big. Massive. He was, I don't know, seven feet tall or something. Hairy and wearing weird clothes, sort of like a robe but it only covered his middle, not his arms or head or feet. But they weren't feet. They were hooves, like on a horse, or a goat... but way bigger. Hard and nasty-looking.

This giant man with horse feet... was just standing there, staring at me like a big creepy shadow. But here's the thing—he wasn't creepy, or scary, not at all.

He was nice.

I liked him right away, even though I was obviously startled at first.

At least it wasn't Father.

So he stood there, watching me, and I didn't move because I was too freaked out, and then he smiled, and he had big white teeth, and he said…

"Hello, princess."

She didn't respond, didn't know what to say. The beast of a man had just appeared out of the shadows, standing between her bed and the window. In her fright and surprise, Esther looked first to the bedroom door, as if expecting to see it open, Father standing there, arms folded, watching and smiling.

But the door was closed. The house quiet.

"Hi…" she managed.

The man laughed. A big, deep, wide-open laugh that she was sure Father would hear.

"Ssshhh!" she said, sitting up urgently, stealing another look to the door.

The man covered his mouth, dark eyes wide, as if sorry. Or amused. He took the hand away, crouched so he could be more level with Esther.

"Pardons, my dearest. Don't want to wake your dad, do we? No, not that."

Esther shook her head, and the man pounded one hoof against

the floor reflexively. He stepped closer to her bed, out from the shadows.

He had long, bushy black hair. His face was stretched and narrow, but strong-boned. His mouth protruded, the giant teeth pushing against fat lips. His eyes were smooth black stone that glinted like diamonds when they caught a stray sliver of light. His hooves were tapered black pots, scarred by use. His draped woolen robe couldn't conceal the geometric shapes of his protruding, spherical belly, his massive square chest. His naked arms were thick as trees and roped with taut muscle. His hands were twice the length of a normal man's, and they curled in on themselves like eagle talons, the dark nails of each finger honed to a point. She knew they weren't hands but claws, each one big enough to wrap easily around her head, powerful enough to squeeze until the skull snapped.

She could feel the heat of him. Wispy black smoke drifted off his skin.

And yet, she *liked* him. Liked him immediately, and was not afraid. She studied him, overtly sly. A look she had perfected with her mother, one that always got a laugh.

"What's your name?"

"Whatever you wish it to be," he said, his voice rumbling, head dipped in a bow. "I have many, and care for none of them."

He said this in such a manner as to make Esther giggle and smack her palm to her forehead in the slapstick fashion of television sitcoms. "Oh gosh. You are frustrating!"

He bowed more deeply, and she laughed again. "A name, if you please. For I will soon vanish without one."

She thought about it, searched her mind for things that made her laugh, or smile, that made her think of the way things used to be. "Hobbes!" she commanded, pointing a finger at his black eyes for emphasis.

He nodded, as if not unexpected, and took a small step back into shadow. "May I stay, princess? I'll sit on the floor over here, like a good dog, and you and I can speak to one another, speak of things that we could not say to anyone else in the world. Would you like that?"

She nodded, smiling.

"Wonderful," he said, eyes sparkling, chunky white teeth a slice in the dark. "Where shall we begin?"

She shrugged, said nothing. He pretended to ponder the issue, then gasped and lifted one long, needle-tipped finger, his face brightening as if struck with a most brilliant thought.

"Tell me, princess," he said, and she heard the murmuring intrada of violins whisper from beneath her bed. "What does thee know of Hell?"

They were in the kitchen, argument full steam.

He arrived home late and drunk and there was no food in the house. While he was away, she'd made herself a dinner of shredded wheat without milk, tried to lose herself in whatever was on television so she wouldn't have to think about how sad she'd become. There was a great, constant weight on her shoulders, a tiredness she was not mature enough to identify as the early stages of deep, clinical depression. It wrapped around her, a cursed hauberk that sucked the joy from her, bogged down her spirit.

When he finally came through the door, Esther was seated at the kitchen table, finishing a family mural assignment that was to be a combination of pictures, drawings and text on a sheet of yellow poster board given to the students by Mrs. Holmes, her sixth-grade teacher. She'd been gluing a picture of her and her mother taken one day in their backyard, Esther sitting in a small red wagon, arms around her kneeling mother's neck, both smiling. Beneath the photo she'd written a paragraph about how much she missed her mother, and what her favorite things about her were. *The funny voices she used when telling me a story at bedtime. How she would comb my hair with her favorite brush, made from silver. When we went shopping on my birthday and I could try on whatever I wanted. Her smile.*

"I will call the police, you fucker!" she screamed, pushing his thin-fingered hands away from her. "Don't touch me!" She swung her fist at him, hit him wildly in the hip. Her father jumped back, his face shocked and slackened by alcohol. She could smell the whisky on his skin.

"How dare you cuss at me!" he roared, then tripped over his own feet and almost fell, grasping the edge of the kitchen counter. He started to cry. "I just wanted to hold you, princess. I love you."

"If you come near me I'll kill you!" she screamed.

She fled to her bedroom, slammed the door. Her heart hammered. She was gasping, could feel the sobs in her throat, but refused to cry.

"Push that dresser in front so he can't get in."

Esther spun and saw Hobbes laying on her bed, hooves crossed, long fingers interlaced behind his shaggy head. His black eyes were wide and filled with stars. There was a quarter-sized hole in the center of his forehead she had not previously noticed.

"Jeez, thanks," she said, and tried to push the heavy dresser across the carpeting.

"Stand back," he said, and he whistled, or made a face as if to whistle, but a swinging lick of horn came out instead, like a jazz trumpeter tuning up for a midnight performance.

Lithe figures made of smoke slipped from the hole in his forehead, danced across the floor to the dresser. She smelled the sour of sulfur and the dresser jerked free from her fingers and slammed against the door with such force that small chips of wood flew into the air, the peach-colored wall which spread outward from the doorframe dented where the edge had struck. "There," he said, and the devils slipped back into his head, as if inhaled.

There was an immediate pounding at the door. Her father in the hallway screaming now, screaming that he was going to punish her, punish her for what she said. For disrespecting him. The screams were muffled, as if his face was pressed flat against the other side. The handle rattled, fists slammed into the wood.

"I'm coming in there," he said, and it did not sound like her father, but like someone else. Like a stranger in their home. "I'm going to come in there and take care of some business. You hear me! I'm gonna take care of business tonight!"

Esther ran across the room to the window, meaning to escape into the dark. She pulled up on the handle, but the window would not budge.

"Help me!" she screamed, crying now, releasing her fear and misery. Hobbes sat up slowly, razor-tipped fingers punching effortlessly through her blankets, into the mattress. The hole on his forehead cycled open wider, the size of a silver dollar.

"You don't want my help, princess. If I helped you, it would be to take you away from here. From all this. Into Hell."

She ran to him, threw her arms around his massive frame, her small hands only making it as far as his biceps. The heat of his skin so hot, almost burning, the smoke coming off him covering her like oil. He did not move.

"He's going to come in here, and he's going to get me." She stared into his deep black eyes, wide and round as a mad stallion. "You don't understand what he'll do to me."

Hobbes looked at her, nodded. When he closed his eyes, a tear, black as ink, slid down his roughened cheek. "Listen to the music, princess."

Hell.

He took me there. I don't know how, but he did. Shit… it's hard to describe.

First off, it was way worse than you'd imagine. Very dark and cold and Hobbes wasn't even Hobbes when we got there. He didn't look much like a human anymore. His head was that of a huge black horse, or a unicorn, but it was NASTY. The horn was long as I am, it stuck out forever! And it was drippy and twisted, moving up and down like it was covered in little skinny snakes. He'd pretty much doubled in size, and even though he still had his normal body, it was bigger. WAY bigger. All covered in thick hair and he had a tail and when he walked everything shook, like tiny earthquakes.

And—yes, I know how this sounds—that's when Satan arrived. But he wasn't like I'd been taught. He was beautiful and radiant. And sweet. All smiles and power. He glowed like a giant angel. He must have been ten feet tall, because he was even bigger than Hobbes.

This is when it got crazy. Satan (or Lucifer, he said, call him Lucifer), wanted me to stay. He didn't want me to come back. Which, frankly, I wasn't all that upset about. Come back to what? Father? A shitty house in the woods with no friends and no relatives and nothing but a horrible man who couldn't keep his hands to himself? Who is supposed to LOVE ME GOD DAMN IT.

Then Hobbes got mad, and they argued. Lucifer said he would let me return if Hobbes performed for him.

And he did. It was unreal.

The most incredible thing I'd ever heard. He unleashed a thousand creatures inside a deep, massive bowl in the ice, and I sat with Lucifer and they performed this insane symphony. It was like what I hear in my dreams, but a million times louder, a million times better. It was beautiful, and scary. Melodic, but violent with bursts of sound and wide swinging melodies. Sometimes I cried, and a few times I laughed, but I loved every second.

Lucifer told me that the world I was from was being destroyed by the music. He said giant waves were destroying cities, hurricanes were flattening towns, and millions of people were dying. I nodded. I didn't care. Not really. I hoped my house was flattened by a giant tree, or hit by lightning, or blown apart in a tornado, like the one in my dream, and that Father was cut to ribbons and destroyed.

I think Lucifer knew I was thinking this because he laughed, but I didn't mind, because Hobbes was beautiful, and brilliant, and all those creatures—they looked like humans, and animals, and other things I'd never seen (some were horrible and ugly, and some were so gorgeous you couldn't even look at them)—were playing for HIM, and I could hardly breathe until it was finished.

At the end Lucifer stood, an audience of one, and clapped. Hobbes bowed his great unicorn head, and then everything was gone, and it was only me and Hobbes left. A lake of fire burned in the distance, but I stood on black ice and shivered.

"When are we going back?"

"I'm not, princess. Just you."

He kneeled. His giant head and spiraling horn towered above her. He looked down, white teeth reaching, thick gray tongue bobbing inside his mouth as he spoke. "Listen to me. I will tell you something not everyone knows. It is very hard to kill a unicorn. Almost impossible. Do you understand?"

Esther nodded, not understanding but desperately wanting to. She waited, eyes on his, attentive.

"Only a virgin can kill a unicorn," he said, licking at his teeth and huffing out a great warm breath. He shook his mane and continued. "And when all the virgins become whores, nothing remains which can destroy the beast. Do you see?"

Esther knew she was still a virgin, despite her father's nighttime visits. And she swore, right there, to remain that way forever.

And then she cried. Sobbed at her despair, her loss. All her mournful life crashed in on her, suffocated her in what could have been. Her feet were numb from standing on the black ice of Hell, and the massive unicorn looked down at her sadly, the flames from the lake of eternal damnation dancing in his mournful eyes, reflective as windows at midnight.

A week passed. She did not see Hobbes, and her father made no late-night visits. She went through the motions of school, of being a normal girl. She cleaned the house on the weekend, and her father spent the day working on a nearby farm, making extra cash and, shockingly, staying out of bars. They didn't say much to each other, but it wasn't as strained as it was pregnant with possibilities. Potential future dangers.

Esther remained guarded. She was sad her new friend had disappeared. All that remained of him was the six-inch statuette hunkered on her nightstand, long spiraled horn puncturing the air, thrusting skyward.

The dreams also had ceased. She almost never heard the music anymore. She wondered if her visit to Hell had stolen that right away from her, if the symphony played for Lucifer had burned out the lingering tendrils of the song in her mind, left her devoid of beauty—be it raging or melancholic—and filled her instead with the tuneless every day, with the repetitive, identical note-plucks of normality.

The devil would have told her, had she asked, that only suffering is eternal, and bliss is almost always short-lived.

Father's drunk again. He's in the kitchen hollering for me, but there's no WAY I'm going out there. I've got the dresser in front of the door and if I have to I'll go out the window. I checked to make sure it wasn't stuck like last time and left it open a couple inches just to be sure.

And what else? Hobbes came back! He's laying at the foot of my bed as I write this. I can't tell if he's really asleep or just faking, but he's all curled up in a big hairy ball. I have to keep my knees tucked up just to fit on my own bed because he's huge. I hadn't seen him for a week, but when I heard Father's car pull up and him get out cussing, I knew he was drunk and ran for my room, and there was Hobbes, snoring and curled up like a pet dog instead of a demon bigger than two men.

Oh shit. Father. He's at the door. Banging again. Damn it…

I kick Hobbes but he's not waking up. Father's yelling some crazy… he sounds out of control! DAMN IT! I hate this. I'm scared.

Hobbes better wake up. The dresser's not holding this time. I'm going out the window. I've got to run for it.

The door burst open another foot, the dresser pushed against the resisting carpet as her father shouldered his weight into it again. She tucked her notebook back under her pillow and stared, petrified, at his pale, sweaty face, his arm reaching through, slapping the dresser.

"You think you can hide from me?" he said. "You're my daughter, Esther, and you will do what I say or I will punish you!" His voice rose into a slurred squeal. "You hear me, princess? I'm coming in there and you and I… well, we're going to have a little talk."

He shouldered into the door, began to squeeze through the opening. Esther cried out, shook the giant sleeping at the foot of her bed.

"Hobbes!" she screamed. "Hobbes, wake up!"

Eyelids popped open, onyx shining. "I'm awake, princess."

"Then *do* something!" she yelled.

Her father was almost through, his belt seemingly caught on the metal door handle. She leapt for the window, turned back as Hobbes stood, rolled off the bed, his hooves clumping to the floor, and stretched. His fingertips scraped the ceiling. He looked down at Esther, gave a toothy smile. "Not much I can do, princess. My boss won't let you leave a second time, and I can't hurt him without hurting you." He shrugged, his face cragged, muscles writhing. "Such is my power."

"Please!" she screamed, backing for the window.

Her father pushed through the half-open door and into her room. He circled around the bed toward her. "Beg all you want, but I'm done playing games with you," he said, his mouth a twisted snarl. "Shit, I don't even think you're my daughter. Your mom used to cheat, did you know that? She had lovers, who knows how many! And when she died, I was *glad*."

Esther shook her head, weeping, hands up in a useless warding gesture. "Please stop."

"I was hap-hap-happy!" her father said, then giggled like a madman. "And you? You're probably one of 'their' babies, someone else's little girl that I gotta take care of, gotta feed and all that shit."

"Daddy..."

He paused a moment, face softening. His blurry eyes roamed the room, as if confused as to how he arrived there. Then he smiled, and straightened.

"I'm done chasing you. Get over here."

He pointed to the ground. Esther turned, sprang for the window. She grabbed the bottom of the window frame, tugged it upward. Before she could lift a knee he was there, arms wrapped around her waist, pulling her back, howling. She screamed out and he twisted and threw her across the room. She crashed hard against the side of her bed, the back of her head cracked into the nightstand, rocking it. The statuette wobbled, then steadied. She looked up in time to see him coming at her.

Her eyes found Hobbes standing silent in the corner. He studied her for a heartbeat, sighed, then said, "Remember what I told you." His voice sounded as if he were in her head and not across the room.

In the next heartbeat, Hobbes roared and sprang his full girth at her father. She felt a surge of exultation, of hope, as the giant demon crashed into him, slamming them both into the far wall. The room shook, the window rattled in its frame.

Esther stood, ready to run for the door, waiting to see if Father was conscious after such a blow, waiting to see what Hobbes would do next.

"No..." she said.

Hobbes' body began to push itself *into* her father, the two of them morphing like liquid, becoming one. Her father's eyes were open wide, staring at the ceiling. His mouth was a long, perfect O of shock as Hobbes somehow, someway, forced every inch of himself into Father's flesh, one long fingernail slipping in last, disappearing in a wrinkle of the dingy white T-shirt her father wore above his jeans.

Hobbes was gone.

She waited, unsure of herself now. Father was hardly moving, his head swaying from side-to-side, his eyes unfocused, drool streaming from the corner of his mouth. She took a step toward him.

"Dad?"

His mouth snapped shut. His chin dropped, and his eyes expanded to twice their size. Silky ink flooded from the distorted pupils like black blood, covering the whites and irises. He stood as if pulled up by a string. He was taller, broader. Esther took a step backward, not understanding. She studied his face as he dropped his new eyes to stare down at her. A black spiral opened in his forehead and widened, two inches across and funneling deep into his head. She saw the stars in his eyes, and the funnel howled like a killing wind.

"Hobbes?" she said weakly.

Her father shook his head, smiling. Teeth oversized and thick. "Afraid not," he said.

He lunged for her and she screamed, dashed for the door. But he was too fast, too strong. Fingers closed around her arm and she looked down, saw fingernails like chips of black coal, sharpened to pinpoint tips.

From the ceiling, she heard the plucking of strings. A wild, rumpus dance of a thousand violins being sprung, broken, tugged and pecked. A mad, broken pizzicato.

Then she was flying.

She slammed into the wall with a great crash of cymbals, dropped face-down on her bed. Her arm hurt bad and she wondered if it was broken. He came for her again.

Panicked, she leapt from the bed, grabbed the statuette, began to spin toward him, hoping to defend herself, when something impossibly hard slammed into the side of her head. She dropped, senseless and limp, to the floor. She moaned. The room swung out of focus, sideways.

Her ears rang, and all else was muted. She stared dumbly across the great expanse of her carpeted world. She recalled a pink doll house that used to stand in the far corner, where she would play for hours and hours. She thought of her mother telling her stories; remembered a small easel her father had given her on her 6th birthday. She'd painted watercolor flowers on sheets of thick, rough paper from the art store. She'd burned all the flower paintings the day her mother died, made a bonfire in the backyard and turned them to sheets of ash. Later, she had exiled the easel and dollhouse to the dark of the closet. She had only moments left in her life to wonder why she'd let her childhood go without more of a fight. Why had she let it go so easily if this was growing up?

Her father's feet filled her vision. His brown work boots had split apart. She saw the rough hooves under the torn leather, pushing through the stretched, shredded fabric of wool socks. One foot kicked her over, and she could only stare, arms sprawled to the sides, at the towering beast. He smiled a grotesque smile, raised his arms like a bird taking flight and lifted a giant hoof high off the ground. With a grunt, he stomped onto the middle of her chest, like a mule kicking a rusted bucket. She felt something snap inside her and she spasmed, then spilled tears and groaned, her body sliding into shock.

He bent over her, long fingers coiled around her neck. She heard knuckles clicking as fingers twined around her throat like snakes, the points of each fingernail digging into flesh. She was lifted off the ground like a doll. Despite her body's shock, her fingers tightened their grip on the cool statuette and held on as her feet hung limp in the air. She found herself looking directly into her father's deranged, alien face. His liquid black eyes stared back at her coldly. The hole in his forehead swirled and gaped like the mouth of a hooked fish, pulsing with excitement and pleasure.

"Almost done here," he said, his voice deep and ancient.

A million miles away, she heard rumbling thunder. The strumming of cello strings that pranced through the room had been joined by bursts of a baritone horn, a thumping, bumping orchestra that might accompany a jaunty dance, a Strauss waltz.

She swung the statuette at her father's head. The long spiral horn went in through his left temple, sunk three inches deep, smoothly as it might slide through butter. She gritted her teeth and pulled it free, blood spitting from the wound, then rammed it in again, this time just above the ear. She felt the snap as the horn broke free from the rest of the figurine, and when she dropped her arm there was only a nub on the unicorn's head where the long spiraling horn had once protruded.

Her father blinked, but no sound came from his clenched throat. His fingers opened and she fell to the ground, cried out in pain, felt a dagger punch into her chest. He stumbled backward clumsily, a horrid dance that fell sickly in time to the waning melody, then dropped against the far wall, head lolled to one side.

Esther waited, panting, fisted hands clutched to her pained chest.

Her father's head elongated, skin breaking with black bristles, teeth reaching, eyes bulging. A stunted shard extended from the hole in the black forehead—the broken base of a unicorn's horn.

She ran to him, cradled the enormous, sagging head in her arms.

"I'm sorry, I'm sorry," she said, over and over. She wept as she held him—wept for her mother, herself, her father. For Hobbes. For all that had been lost.

A sound came from the dying creature. She resisted her cries and leaned close to its mouth. "One more thing," it said, its voice a scratched whisper, brittle as a winter leaf.

She listened, and nodded. When he stopped breathing, she laid him down gently on the patch of floor that once housed her childhood, in the room that once cradled her innocence. She stood and staggered to the window, opened it wide and pushed herself out and into the night air. She didn't look back.

Outside she could smell a brewing storm. The sky was plum purple, the wind calm but charged. The jagged music played on behind her, but drifts also now came from the air, from the earth. The wild bleat of a horn, the rumble of a bass drum. But not symphonic, not whole.

She saw a flash of lightning in the distance but heard no thunder, felt no rain. She ran awkwardly for the trees, her chest broken, stabbing her with every step. The remains of the figurine still clutched tight in one small hand.

The tunnel of trees swayed, arms lifted. Melodic voices came from behind their trunks, a sad chorus paving her way deeper, deeper into the wood, toward the Devil's Elbow.

She went on as best she could, breath hitching, head pounding. Finally she reached the hole where she had found the statuette, and returned the thing to it. She coughed, a flood of bile and blood pushed into the back of her throat. She gagged, then coughed again. Even in the dark she could see the splash of liquid splatter against the moon-tinged glimmer of the object.

She looked around, desperate. A few feet away she saw the protuberance of a smooth stone. She crawled to it and began to dig, relieved there was more of it hidden beneath the earth. It would serve.

Free of the dirt, the rock was the size of an oblong baseball, and she gripped it easily in her hand as she crawled back to the hole where the statuette lay. She saw it there, at the bottom, already broken but still alive, still throbbing with power. She sensed the rustle of the trees around her. The chorus grew, rose like a high tide, warning her. The beating of bass drums came from the heavens, and the soft mumbling of horns, carried by a soft breeze, drifted through her, slid into her ears, nuzzled against her slowing mind like a ghostly feline.

She gritted her teeth and brought the rock down on the statuette, felt the satisfying crack as something inside it separated. She raised the rock again, slammed it down again. The chorus was rhythmic, a rising tremolo. Jagged horns surged, beating against her like shadowy fists. Jolting percussion vibrated her bones. The mad swipe of a thunderbolt bow against sky-wide strings, angry and frightened, pitched through the trees, filled the breadth of the tunnel with crackling, thick air.

Esther shrieked, the last of her strength pouring from her, and brought the rock down again, and again, and again.

Spent, she released the stone, stared down at the splintered fragments; the once beautiful figurine now a jumble of dead shards. She felt weak. A surge of fresh blood shot up from deep within her, spilled into her mouth, coated her tongue and teeth. She gagged and spat, and when the dark blood splattered onto the smashed idol, the music stopped. The strings, the drums, the horns… all of it… stopped.

There was silence.

She swayed on her hands and knees, but could still push the earth she had dug free back into the hole, filling it. When finished, she fell to her side, stared upward. The trees looked down at her, impassive as the moon and stars and gods beyond.

A sharp, splintering sound, like a massive sheet of ice slowly cracking into fragments. She turned her head, which felt heavy, so heavy, and saw the trees twisting and bending unnaturally, as if they had joints being broken by an invisible force. They splintered in snapping blasts of bark. The leaves upon their branches browned as one, dried up, and crinkled into small flutes that fell around her softly, a rain of feathery death. Slowly, each tree tipped, and fell. There was a splashing crash that she felt as much as heard. All around her they pulled free of the earth, disjointed and misshapen, and tumbled, collapsed to the ground, lifeless.

She rolled her heavy head the other way, far as she was able. Her breath came slowly, each intake hurting worse, each gasp shorter, her lungs slowly shrinking, filling with blood where rib had punctured lung.

All the trees had fallen, blackened as if by fire, and she could see the entire ceiling of night sky, unbroken by their withered trunks. A meteor shot across the firmament of her wide, staring eye, captured a final frozen image of the stars and planets shimmering like fireflies on bruised parchment, the moon a quiet mother.

Esther lay in the open field, surrounded by a woven circle of deadwood that enclosed her like a witch's funeral wreath. She had time only for a prayer: *No more dreams*. Her eyelids closed like curtains on a play, and the darkness flooded her.

Light.

Bright enough to turn the skin of her closed eyelids to pink. She flickered them open, stared at a clear blue sky. A nimble, warm wind swept the earth, fingered her hair, tickled her skin. She sat up, the pain in her chest gone.

She looked about, confused and sleepy. The day seemed to sing a sweet silent coda to her of its perfection, its absolute beauty.

She stood on wobbly legs, but felt good, felt strong. She took a few deep breaths, let the analeptic oxygen clear her head, feed her heart.

"Esther!"

The voice came from beyond the line of trees stretching before her, a line that would become a tunnel leading home.

"Esther!"

She knew that voice, and with a gasp, she *ran*.

She cut through brush to the path, hopped over a fallen trunk, landed on her heels and pumped her legs around the bend. The tunnel appeared before her, and in the distance, the familiar meadow, and her house. She could see her bedroom window, closed now. At the front of the house she saw a woman looking toward the trees, hand shielding her eyes, blonde hair whispering out from the sides of her neck. A man came and stood next to the woman. He wrapped an arm lovingly around her shoulders.

He waved at her, and Esther, smiling and sprinting now, waved wildly back. She ran across the vast plane of meadow, thrown wide in all dimensions, covered in brilliant green and dotted with flowers, the colors of which she'd never seen.

Bells chimed where her feet crushed grass, and the trees on either side of her bent, creaking, as she ran past, long trunks curving to point her way home. The wind pushed at her back.

Earth and sky melted away and she leapt through electric silence.

HANAR

Hanar, a goetic demon, has an array of alternate names: Amy, Avnas, Auns, and Hanni. As Hanni, he is described in the fifteenth-century Munich Handbook of Necromancy: He is "a great president, and appears in a fiery flame, but when he takes human form he makes a man wonderfully skilled in astronomy and the other liberal arts. He gives the best familiars and the favor of magnates and princes, and miraculously shows the locations of treasures guarded by spirits." The Munich manual says that he only commands thirty legions of spirits, but *The Lesser Key of Solomon the King*, which calls him Amy, says that he commands thirty-six; otherwise its description of him is virtually identical to that of the Munich manual. The *Lesser Key* adds that "he is partly of the order of angels, partly of the powers, and hopes that after 1200 years, he will return to the seventh throne, which is not credible." (The "powers" and "angels" are two of the nine orders of angels, according to Christian angelology.) This statement implies that he is one of the fallen angels, and that they believe that some kind of redemption is conceivable for them (a possibility usually not admitted in Christian theology).

The Red Library
A Lizzie Corbett Story

JONATHAN MABERRY

1

The Red Library of Firozkoh
Now

Lizzie Corbett hit the madman with a book.

She screamed.

Not because she broke the man's nose—which she did.

No, she screamed because breaking the killer's nose damaged the delicate scrollwork on the leather cover of the book and stained it with blood.

She was so angry, so upset that the book was damaged, that she hit him again.

With the book.

2

The killer staggered back, blood streaming down his chin and spattering onto his desert camouflage uniform. The black balaclava he wore had been knocked askew and he glared red hatred at her through one eyehole. His rifle lay where it had fallen when she'd hit him the first time. There was fire in that wild eye, and it terrified Lizzie as much as it fueled her rage.

It was all about the book.

The book. The book.

The damned book.

The man stood there, chest heaving as he straightened his balaclava. He spat a mouthful of blood onto the floor between them and spoke a single word.

"Whore."

The fact that he spoke it in Arabic did not matter. Lizzie could understand it in any tongue. It was what he had called her when she'd surprised him in this chamber half a mile below the Minaret of Jam. She wore no *hijab* and her khaki work shirt was unbuttoned to mid-sternum. Not as a come-on but because it was over one hundred and fifteen degrees and Lizzie was boiling in her clothes. She also wore shorts.

She was American, too.

And she'd hit him. Twice. Both times with the very book he had been trying to destroy. Lizzie had rushed him, shouldered him away from the book, which lay on a stone bench. The impact had knocked the gasoline can from his hands and toppled his rifle, which the killer had stood against the edge of the bench. She had snatched up the book and bashed him across the face with it just as hard as she could manage. She was thin, but she was also wiry, so she could manage a lot of foot-pounds of impact. Then she'd hit him again. Harder.

Now she stood there, holding the ancient book, her bare arms, legs and upper chest glistening with sweat, frizzy ash-blond hair wild, face uncovered. She was, in that moment, so many of the things this man hated. Woman. Free. Defiant. Foreign. And disobedient.

He drew the long knife and held it up. The mad gleam in his eyes sharpened with the delight of expectation.

"Whore," he said again.

And rushed her with the knife held high.

3

Égouts de Paris
One Year Ago

Dr. Elizabeth Corbett crouched in six inches of sewer water, her clothes streaked with filth as she studied what looked like random scratches on a brick.

"It's nothing," said Ami Filou, an earnest but dense young woman from the *Sorbonne* who had been assigned as guide and general minion. "Surely, there are many bricks like that all through these sewers."

"Not like this," said Lizzie.

"I've been down here many times," she insisted. "I've looked at fifty such bricks. A hundred. Never anything."

Ami's certainty did not carry with it an air of confidence. She kept glancing around at the shadows that seemed almost painted on the curved walls of the vast Parisian sewer system. Water gurgled around them and dripped from unseen leaks. Moss, black and rife with crawling insects, clung to the bricks, and rats chittered in the dark. And the smell...

Lizzie had been in sewers before, even these sewers, but today it was particularly offensive. However, she'd taken the precaution of dabbing a cheap but potent local perfume on her upper lip and inside her nostrils to kill her sense of smell. Ami, sadly, had not, and she had declined Lizzie's offer to do so. She stood there, eyes watering, mouth pursed, skin pale, running with sweat and clearly wishing she was anywhere but here.

"I tell you, *Docteur* Corbett, that is merely another brick. The builders marked many of them to indicate who had worked on a given part of the tunnels. That is someone's name. Or—" and here she tried a laugh "—it is the name of an ex-lover with whom the bricklayer had an unhappy love affair. Consigning her name to an eternity of *merde et pisse*."

Lizzie shook her head and removed a magnifying glass from her tool belt, switched on the tiny LED light set in a ring around the lens, and leaned closer. Her heart jumped in her chest. It had been a long path from her tiny, cramped office in the back corner of the cellar of the Beinecke Rare Book & Manuscript Library at Yale. Her search had begun with a reference in one of the old books sent to her by the cartload for reevaluation and scanning. The library had hundreds of thousands of volumes, many crumbling with age. Her two-person department—Lizzie and a little mole of a man named Hans—had the grandiose title of 'Restoration and Preservation of Religious Works,' but were expected to do complete computer optical scans of books previously available only on microfiche, oversee the transfer of those scans through various software programs, index the contents, and do keyword searches for the university's searchable database. Occasionally something important was uncovered by the process, but typically by some graduate student doing deep research for his or her thesis.

In rarer cases Lizzie or Hans found something themselves. Sadly, ninety-nine percent of those discoveries led to a series of frustrating dead ends. Lack of supporting materials was the most common closed door, though there were also conflicts with ongoing research by other groups or, worse, Lizzie's research colliding with something being undertaken by one of the scholars who was deemed far more important than she.

Not this time.

A few months ago, Hans had come upon a notebook that had been improperly indexed and was mentioned nowhere else in the library's vast records. He thought it was interesting, but decided it would be something more appealing to Lizzie than himself. Hans was in that department because he lacked all ambition. If something looked like it would require extra effort, particularly extracurricular work, he usually passed it to her.

Lizzie was happy with that arrangement, and rewarded Hans by cooking extra food at home and bringing him some a couple times a week. He got fatter and she got tidbits to nibble on, like that book.

The notebook was unique—untouched, unread, and unrecorded. It had been written by a man who only used the initial E, and who wrote French with a distinctly non-French hand. After comparing the handwriting to others in a pattern-recognition database, she became convinced that the author was Johann Augustus Eberhard, a German theologian who died in 1809. The paper and binding were consistent with journals of the same era manufactured and sold in Halberstadt, a town in the German state of Saxony-Anhalt, the capital of Harz district.

Why it had been written in an obscure French dialect was a puzzle. Lizzie privately thought that it was intended to hide its contents from Eberhard's colleagues and rivals, most of whom were German but would likely only be familiar with modern French.

The contents of the notebook was mostly dry stuff with little to interest anyone except someone with a fascination for nineteenth-century Parisian tourism. And there were long sections of theological speculation with a bias toward the philosophy of phenomenalism. But while Lizzie was carefully scanning the pages she found some incomplete sentences here and there. Fragments that could easily have been dismissed as offhand notations or half-formed thoughts that were abandoned for one reason or another. That they were written in an older dialect of French was curious, but not earthshaking. Eberhard was, after all, a scholar and theologian, and French was the language of science, politics and art. There were many old writings in various dialects. By themselves, the notations might have been nothing more than bits copied by Eberhard from things he read or saw.

Except that they weren't.

Lizzie had a lot of personal quirks and tics, not the least of which was some runaway OCD that she tried to rein in as best she could. The fragments bothered her because Eberhard was an orderly man and an orderly thinker. So, she went back through the notes, typed them into a Word document, then messed with them, moving them around like puzzle pieces. It was a project she came back to often over a period of weeks. She even read up on word puzzles and word-based codes.

And then she had it.

The sentence fragments were part of a code, but the page numbering factored in as well. There was a math problem there because the pages were hand-numbered and inconsistent. Some numbers were on the upper right corners, some on the lower right, others on the upper and lower left, and some centered top or bottom.

That was the key, though it took several sleepless nights to suss out what the number pattern was. Nothing with Eberhard's notebook could be taken at face value. That he went to such pains to encode those notes suggested he had something worth hiding. When Lizzie finally assembled the lines per the numbering patterns, what she discovered took her breath away. Something potentially huge. It could change her entire life. Not merely her professional life, but everything about who she was.

She told absolutely no one about it, though. Not the molelike

Hans, her partner in their little department. Not her on-again-off-again boyfriend, or her on-again-off-again girlfriend. Not even her mother, and she usually told Mom everything. Instead she told the department head that she was finally, after too many years, going to take some of the vacation time that had been stacking up. She bought a coach ticket to Germany and spent a week going through more of Eberhard's papers to satisfy herself that she was correct. Then she took a train to Paris and spent three weeks telling half-truths and outright lies to arrange this two-person expedition down into the sewers.

Every step of the way the coded words left by Eberhard haunted her. He had been a good man, a kind and decent man, a man for whom compassion and—perhaps—a forward-thinking understanding of implications were more important than personal gain. And he'd been old, near the end of his life and dealing with health problems. He knew that he would likely die within a few years. As, in fact, he did.

So, he left behind his coded notes but did not try to ensure that they would eventually be found. He left no specific instructions except the last few lines of the message.

It is all washed in blood.
Perhaps some future, better society will find a way
to wash it clean.
I do not see such generosity of spirit in the world today.
And so I pray that whosoever finds what was hidden
will use it for better purposes than any for which it was
given, taken, used, coveted, and hidden.
May God share His Mercy and Provide His guidance.
Peace to you.

Now she was poised to either add a new chapter to history or make a fool of herself.

"Please," insisted Ami impatiently, "it's only an unremarkable brick. At most it's scratched, probably by rats."

"Nope," she said, more to herself than to Ami, "it is definitely not that." She wiped away some of the grime and it was clear that there were words cut into the brick. "See there?"

Ami cleared her throat. "Very well, there are words. But as I said, the laborers working down here—"

"—would have written in modern French," she cut in. "This isn't that." Lizzie took a small squirt bottle of clean water and spritzed the writing, then sponged it clean with a piece of cloth. The letters stood out very clear in the light of her magnifying glass. There were three words, carved with great precision. "The oxidation is considerable, though. It's old."

"These sewers were built centuries ago. In the mid-nineteenth century."

Lizzie was getting annoyed with her 'assistant.' For someone who was supposed to be gearing up to defend her dissertation, Ami seemed remarkably ignorant. Granted, this was outside her field of philology, the study of ancient languages, but not that far. It was reasonable, even practical to know quite a lot about more recent language variations. That she was a French language scholar perturbed Lizzie even more. She tapped the writing.

"You see this? This isn't the language a nineteenth-century laborer would use. Or even the architect. This is a variation of *ancient Français*, particularly the dialect from the outermost towns of the old Angevin Empire."

Ami stiffened and bent closer. "What? Why would city builders use that?"

"Because," she said, "whoever laid the bricks in this part of the sewers was not working for the city. See what it says?" She read the inscription:

"With generosity or not at all."

"That makes no sense," said Ami.

"It will."

Lizzie placed her fingers on the writing on the left-hand side of the brick, held her breath, and pushed.

Absolutely nothing happened. Lizzie felt panic leap up in her chest, bringing with it a flash of anticipated shame as she thought about the weight of humiliation that would crash down on her if this proved to be a big fat nothing. Word of it *would* get out, and it would get back to Yale. Her job was by no means secure, even though she was good at what they let her do. Lizzie had no political pull within the university, and the natural cattiness of the academics at the library would turn against her in an instant. A lifetime's worth of self-doubt, self-recrimination, self-loathing, and general feelings of inadequacy according to her own unbending standards crowded into her chest and left no room for her heart to beat.

She pushed the brick again and it stubbornly refused. It sat there, being a brick, being part of an immoveable wall. Well... what did she expect? Magic? A gift from the Fates? She didn't believe in either.

No. This was going to end right here and now and so would her career. She'd have to go crawling back to Yale and hope they did not fire her on general principles. Even though she was not here as any kind of official representative of the university, that's how it would be viewed. She would make the whole library look stupid.

Because I'm stupid, she thought bitterly. She glared at the brick. Begging it silently to move. Hating it for not moving. Hating herself and everything.

"You see," said Ami, and even with her—someone so much farther down on the professional totem pole—there was mockery and condescension in her voice. "I told you—"

Then something did happen.

With her continued pressure the brick moved. It slid inward. Not far. Maybe half an inch.

Lizzie said, "*God*!"

Ami said, "*What...*?"

For a moment nothing else happened and everything was deathly still.

Ami snorted. "A loose brick."

There was a grating sound deep inside the wall. A heavy sound, as if something ponderous moved with slow reluctance. Ami yelped like a kicked poodle and backpedaled as a section of the wall moved outward. Dust and gas belched from within, and Lizzie turned away, holding a hand up to protect her eyes, but squinting through it all so she didn't miss a thing.

"Mother of..." began Ami, but words failed her. She sat down hard and the foul water splashed up around her, splattering her with excrement. Rats screamed in the dark and scurried away, their little nails scraping on the slick stones.

Lizzie stood as the dust thinned and swirled away.

The hidden door had moved inward about twenty inches and then stopped, caught on something. It was enough, though. She turned off her magnifying light and removed the more powerful Mag-Lite from her belt. Her hands shook so much that it took her four tries to turn it on, but then a bright blue-white light spilled into the doorway.

She cut a look at Ami, who still sat waist deep in the water, eyes wide, mouth open in a silent "Oh" of fear and surprise. Lizzie rose and flashed her a smile brighter than any light down there, and then went in through the doorway.

For nearly a full minute, Lizzie inched her way along a hidden corridor empty of everything except spider webs and rat droppings. Then she reached a turning in the wall and when she rounded it, her light seemed to change from blue-white to yellow.

No.

To gold.

She stood in the mouth of a great chamber and stared. Her mouth fell open but she was absolutely incapable of speech. The icy fingers that had been clamped around her heart disintegrated and she could feel it beating. Stronger. Like fists. Sweat broke from her pores and ran down the sides of her face and inside her clothes, despite the cold dampness of the chamber.

There were hundreds of them.

Made from iron or wood or bronze. Some bound with heavy bands of metal and clamped shut with huge old locks. Others stood open, their chains and locks abandoned, the lids thrown back. On the wall directly across from where she stood were the same words she had decoded, painted in a clear hand. The same hand. Eberhard's own.

I pray that whosoever finds what was hidden
will use it for better purposes than any for which it was
given, taken, used, coveted, and hidden.
May God share His Mercy and Provide His guidance.
Peace to you.

And above those words a cross had been painted. Not the French style. No, this was closer to the German version. Four arms of equal length and thickness, widening at the flat ends so that the terminus of each arm looked like the base of a candle holder. A *cross pattée*. Not painted black, as a German might have done, but painted red.

Painted by Eberhard in red above a sea of chests of gold and diamonds and rubies and…

Lizzie's mind faltered as she realized the true importance of what she had found. The thing thousands upon thousands of priests, treasure-hunters, scholars, and historians had looked for since Friday, 13 October 1307, when Pope Clement V issued the *Pastoralis Praeeminentiae*, a papal bull ordering the arrest of an order of knights whose members had been the bankers of the Crusades and whose power had risen to rival that of the Holy Church.

She had found the treasure of the Knights Templar.

4

Égouts de Paris
One Year Ago

Lizzie Corbett was in the hidden room for a long time.

Ami stood in the shadows of the corridor.

"Do you know what you've found?" asked the assistant.

"Yes," gasped Lizzie.

"Do you understand what it means?"

Without turning, Lizzie asked, "What…?"

There was no answer. Lizzie turned but Ami was not in the corridor. When Lizzie emerged, dazed and trembling, from the hidden treasure house, the younger woman was not there. Nor was Ami Filou at the *Sorbonne*. Ami had simply vanished.

That terrified Lizzie at first because she feared that the assistant had gone off to betray her, or maybe to phone for some thuggish friends to come and steal the treasure.

Nothing of the sort happened.

Lizzie went to the street level where she could get a cell phone signal and placed a series of calls that wrote her into every headline in the world, and into the pages of history.

Within ten days she was on the cover of *Time, Newsweek, Rolling Stone*, and a hundred other weeklies and ten thousand newspapers. The following month she saw herself—startled blue eyes, wild hair, perpetually smiling mouth and look of pure astonishment—on the covers of weighty periodicals from *National Geographic* to *Scientific American*. The Lady of the Templars, they called her. Fortune's Lady, they called her. Indiana Jones' Sister, they called her.

The name Ami Filou faded from her thoughts completely.

5

The Library of the Ten Gurus
Toronto, Canada
Nine Months Ago

Mahip Singh leaned back in his chair, crossed his legs, and turned the page of the thick report he had received that morning. It was the fifth such report passed along to him by operatives working for his department of the Library. Like the others, it included biographies of more than two dozen candidates.

And like the others, one name kept rising to the surface with the highest recommendations. He spoke the name aloud in the quiet of his office.

"Dr. Elizabeth Corbett."

Mahip smiled.

6

University of Glasgow
Scotland
Eight Months Ago

Lizzie Corbett waited through another standing ovation.

She hated them.

She hated being in front of so many people.

She hated giving speeches.

She hated being a celebrity.

She hated a lot of what had happened to her since she'd found the treasure of the Templars.

The money was okay, though. Not that she got to keep the actual heaps of gold and jewels. The French government confiscated that in a heartbeat, and she very nearly got arrested for vandalism.

No, her bank account had swollen to impossible limits through book deals and movie deals and appearance fees and speaking fees. Four months ago she'd had eight hundred and six dollars in her checking account and three thousand in savings. She'd also had one hundred and seven thousand dollars' worth of student loans.

Now she had no debt at all. Yale had been quite happy to cancel out her loans in exchange for a guarantee that she would give quarterly talks, mentioning that the research that led to the discovery had begun in their library. They'd also upped her to full professor, jumping over the heads of more qualified and deeply disgruntled seniors. She had nearly four million dollars in the bank. An insane fortune for a bookworm nerd girl from Philadelphia. Less than half a percent of the fortune she'd found, and that was just calculating the weight of gold at the current market price. The gemologists had not yet put a tally on the value of the seven hundred and eleven pounds of diamonds, rubies, sapphires, emeralds, and topazes. Or the ninety-two pounds of pearls. The best guess was that it would take five years to assess their value because a third of the gems were set into jewelry from thirty ancient nations. The Templars had a long and greedy reach.

As Lizzie stood there, sweating and trying not to twitch with every camera flash or breathless request for her autograph, she longed to be anywhere else. The airless far side of the moon would be fine by her. The speaking tour had been grueling, but she had rebelled at extending it and wanted nothing more than to be in her own apartment, among her books and curios, with the doors locked and the phones turned off.

She still had her tiny place in New Haven in easy bicycle distance to Yale. She could afford to move—she could buy a mini-mansion—but she liked the apartment. Maybe now more than ever, because it was the one thing untouched and unchanged by her celebrity. Two bedrooms, a nice kitchen, a snug living room, and bookshelves on all the walls. Each shelf was crammed with books, old and new, in forty languages. Lizzie could read some of all of them, too. Even though being a bit on the spectrum had given her OCD and other challenges, it had also bestowed bits of savantism. Her memory was astounding, and she had a talent for languages, for mathematics, and for puzzles. It was as if she had been genetically engineered to be a scholar of books and ancient—

often dead—languages.

There was no one at home waiting for her, but that was okay, too. Lizzie never had luck with either roommates or significant others. Her on-again-off-again relationships with Brad—an adjunct professor—and Carmilla—an art teacher—had both gotten weird. Neither liked being part of a celebrity couple. Both had left Lizzie.

That was fine.

She had plastic houseplants and her precious books waiting to welcome her.

As the applause died down she turned and headed off stage, dealt with handshakes, endured an autograph session and cocktail party, drank too much, and fled at the absolute first opportunity. She went out a back door to find the hired car waiting with headlights on and motor running. It was a different car and driver than the one which had brought her, but that was okay. The driver was a big man in a dark suit and, she noticed at once, a Sikh's precisely wrapped turban. He had a large dark beard and mustache threaded with gray and kind eyes.

"There is hot tea in the back, Dr. Corbett," he said. His accent, she noted, was Indian with a varnish of metropolitan Canada. Toronto, she thought.

"Thank you, Mr…?"

He smiled. "Singh."

"Of course," she said automatically. Many Sikhs took the surname of Singh. It was not required, of course, and there were plenty of Sikhs with names like Batra, Dosanjh, Virdee and dozens of others. But nearly all of the Sikhs she'd met personally had been named Singh. He handed her a card as she got in and Lizzie took it, assuming it to be from the car service.

It wasn't until she was settled in and the vehicle was in motion that she glanced at the information on the card. It was not from a limo service. The name printed across the top was *The Library of the Ten Gurus*. The name printed below was Dr. Mahip Singh. There was a phone number with a Canadian prefix and an email address. Nothing else.

She looked up quickly, suddenly afraid. "Wait! Stop. Who are you? What's going on?"

Dr. Singh swung the car in a big circle and drove away from

the building she'd just left, but he did not head toward the exit. Instead he crunched across gravel and turned onto a service road on the university property, pulled up under the leaves of a massive old elm, and stopped. He switched the engine off and turned to face her.

"I'm going to call the police," Lizzie cried. She fished in her purse for her cell.

"That is your prerogative, Dr. Corbett," said the Sikh. "I will not stop you or interfere with you in any way except to ask for five minutes of your time."

She reached for the door handle, jerked it up and found the door unlocked. That fact, and the calmness in Singh's voice, made her pause. If this was an abduction it was the politest one in history. Singh smiled at her. A calm, self-assured smile. There was no trace of malice or threat in his expression or in the tone of his voice.

"Dr. Corbett, I have tried to get in touch for several weeks now, but your new celebrity has brought with it an army of gate keepers. Agents, managers, event planners. I could get an audience with the Queen of England with less effort."

Her hand was still in her purse and Lizzie felt the raspy edge of a metal nail file. She clutched it and tensed, ready to whip it out and stab him if he even twitched. Where to stab? Eye? That was gross and she didn't know if she could do it. Where else, though?

"Why do you want to talk with me?" she demanded. "What's this all about? And who the hell are you?"

"I am, like you, a scholar. Your specialty is ancient languages. Mine is sacred texts." He paused. "Very special sacred texts."

"What's that supposed to mean?"

"It means that I, along with my colleagues, am engaged in a global project to locate and protect books of great religious significance and great spiritual power. Books which, should they fall into the wrong hands, or be mishandled, or in some cases be set free, could do untold harm."

Lizzie frowned. "That's crazy."

"I assure you, Dr. Corbett, it is not. And if you can give me those five minutes I will explain."

Lizzie clutched the nail file, but she gave him those five minutes.

And another ten minutes after that.

Then they were in her hotel room, the nail file forgotten. Dr. Singh sat on the couch; Lizzie sat on the edge of her bed. They talked through the night.

Next morning, she did not fly back to her apartment. Instead she abandoned that ticket and booked a new one for Toronto.

7

The Library of the Ten Gurus
Toronto, Canada
Seven Months Ago

"Again," he said.

Lizzie Corbett lay sprawled on the floor, covered in sweat, blood trickling from one nostril, her body filled with pain.

"I… can't…" she wheezed.

Dr. Mahip Singh squatted on his heels. He wore black sweatpants and a t-shirt with the symbol of a red book inside a white circle. The symbol of his organization. His feet were bare and he rested his forearms on his knees, hands loose and dangling. Despite the heat and the activity, his face was not flushed and his beard and turban were neat and perfect. Lizzie glared at him with as much energy as she could muster. The son-of-a-bitch wasn't even breathing hard.

"This is ridiculous," she said, gasping like a boated trout.

"The alternatives," mused Singh mildly, "are less appealing."

He rose and offered her his hand. After a moment Lizzie took it and allowed him to pull her to her feet. He never used that gesture as a trick to punch her or throw her back down to the mats. Singh wasn't like that. No, he let her get herself set and balanced, and then he punched her and threw her to the mat.

Every.

Single.

Damn.

Time.

While she was crawling to her feet again, Singh went to a rack on the wall of the big basement beneath the library, selected a hardwood club with a stout leather thong, weighed it in his hand

and then tossed it to her. "That might help," he suggested.

Lizzie fumbled the catch, nearly dropped it and then held the club awkwardly. She was as unfamiliar with weapons—clubs, guns, knives—as she was with the karate, jujutsu, and kung-fu techniques she was struggling to learn. Since the night they met, Dr. Singh had been working very hard to both convince her that she needed to be able to protect herself, and that being able to do so was a likely outcome of the work they were going to do.

She caught sight of herself in the mirror. Leggy, skinny, with her damp hair tied back in a sloppy pony tail. The sweats she wore were baggy and made her look like a gawky twelve-year-old instead of a grown woman.

At first she hadn't minded the twice daily sessions in hand-to-hand combat. She'd balked at the hours on the pistol range, though, until Singh pointed out that ISIL, the Taliban, al-Qaeda, and professional tomb raiders would have no qualms about shooting her. Or beating her, stabbing her, raping her, and murdering her. He offered to show her statistics on the treatment of women, particularly foreign women, and most particularly *American* women, at the hands of those kinds of men. He'd sent her links to horrific news stories and reports by humanitarian organizations. One of those stories was a firsthand account by a Red Cross nurse who went into a 'comfort hotel' after it had been liberated by Kurdish fighters. Sixty-seven girls and women, ranging in age from nine to thirty, had been in the hotel. It was estimated that each of them had been raped at least one hundred times. At least. The survivors were being treated for severe PTSD and there had been suicides among them. It was beyond horrible.

As she looked at herself in the mirror, Lizzie tried not to put herself into the heads of those women. She knew she was no one's idea of a fighter. She had never been in any conflict more violent than a shoving match over Legos when she was six, and she'd lost that tussle. She'd been sexually harassed—she was a woman on planet Earth after all—but never in a way that made her want to take a self-defense class or buy a handgun. Her neighborhood was safe and she had good locks on her doors, and she never went to the kinds of places where there was danger. And now she could hire a bodyguard to protect her 24/7. Maybe even a female bodyguard, because the alternative was conceding that she, a woman, needed a man to protect her.

The club she held was a brutal weapon, but it looked ineffectual in her hand.

She dropped it onto the mat.

"Pick it up," said Singh.

"Why bother?"

"Pick it up," he repeated, "please." Singh was nothing if not polite. He never raised his voice, never became impatient with her. At first Lizzie thought those were charming qualities. Now they irritated the living crap out of her.

"What's the damn point?" she snapped. "I can't fight. I don't want to fight. I won't ever be *able* to fight, and all we're accomplishing here is you beating the snot out of me. How is that helping? I thought we were going to save books and artifacts from destruction."

"We are."

"How? By pummeling me into a little pile of rubble?"

He smiled. "That would not be the ideal outcome."

"Then go out and draft Milla Jovovich or Michelle Rodriguez. No, better yet, get that MMA fighter, Rhonda something or other. I bet they can kick all kinds of terrorist ass. I can't."

"If I wanted someone who was merely tough," he said, "I can make a list of a hundred world-class special operators. Women from Mossad, American Special Forces, Barrier, Rogue Team International, Arklight… there are plenty with whom it would be an honor to go into battle."

"Good, then go do that."

"None of them," he said, "possess the unique skill set that *you* have."

"What? Top of my class at taking a beating? World's biggest wimp? Girl punching bag?"

His smile flickered. "First, Dr. Corbett, I would prefer that you do not speak of yourself in such a derogatory way. I respect you, and for you to insult yourself is also an insult to those who admire you."

That shut her up for a moment.

"Second, given the choice of training a fighter to be a world-class scholar of obscure languages, word-based codes, and sacred texts or training said scholar in some useful self-defense moves, which—in your opinion—seems likely to be a better use of my time and resources?"

Lizzie tapped the club lightly and nervously against her thigh for a moment. Then she cocked her head to one side and said, "You're an expert fighter, right?"

He gave a small shrug but made no comment. Always polite. She wanted to club him unconscious. If she could manage it.

"Then why can't we take it as read that you'll be my bodyguard?"

He looked amused. "And if I am shot? Or we are separated? Or if we are attacked by too many opponents for me to handle while also protecting you? No. Surely, doctor, you can see the logic, the *benefits*, the common sense of both of us being as capable as possible, in as many ways as possible."

"Nice speech, Yoda."

He showed a lot of teeth when he grinned. Very good, very white teeth. Very punchable teeth.

Lizzie sighed. This was hardly the first time they'd had this discussion. It wasn't the first time she'd lost this argument. Singh could clearly read her resignation and gave a single nod. His smile faded, though, to be replaced by a look of concern.

"Sometimes the things we are asked to do in order to serve the greater good are not pleasant. Occasionally we are asked to do appalling things. I have done truly dreadful things over the years, Dr. Corbett. Memories of those things haunt me and, although I pray every day and try to live according to what I believe God expects of me, I do not know what my fate will be when I am called to judgment. However I would not undo any of what I have done, and I will not stray from the path I believe is the correct one, even if I means that I will do more and greater harm."

"I—"

He held up a hand. "Please, allow me to finish." He took a small step toward her. "When I approached you in Glasgow and told you about the work we do here at the Library of Ten Gurus, I did not exaggerate. If anything, I understated the importance of what we do. However, please accept me at face value for what I say now."

Lizzie tensed. He had already scared her half to death with his talk of the harm that might befall her and the wounds that could be inflicted on history, on world culture, if the books the Library was sworn to protect should be destroyed. Now there was a strange look in his dark eyes, and for a moment it seemed as if the lights down here in the gymnasium had begun to fade. Or, as if the shadows that huddled in the corners were consuming the light.

"For you, books and the languages in which they are written are the magical underpinning of society. I agree with that, and it was such a belief that drew me into my profession. It is not, however, why I have taken on the great responsibilities necessary to the work of this Library. No. Dr. Corbett, I have become a specialist in my field, and there are very few of us who do this special kind of work."

She said nothing, listening, confused by what he was saying. Frightened by the look in his eyes.

"Do you believe in magic?" he asked.

"Magic…?" she echoed, half smiling, wondering if this subtle man was playing some kind of elaborate joke on her. He, however, did not return her smile. After a moment, Lizzie said, "What are you saying? What does magic have to do with saving books from ISIL and the Taliban?"

He paused for a long time and the lights in his eyes seemed to grow stranger, like lightning on a midnight horizon.

"Everything," he said quietly.

8

The Library of the Ten Gurus
Toronto, Canada
Seven Months Ago

"No," growled Lizzie. "Uh-uh. No way."

They were seated cross-legged on two corners of one of the training mats, each of them with bottles of water, towels draped around their shoulders.

"You don't need to yell," Singh said mildly.

"Screw that," she barked. "And screw you if all of this is part of some kind of right-wing religious weirdo cult."

"We're not right wing."

"Oh, very funny. You know what I mean," she snapped. "I came here from Scotland to be a part of something important. You sold me on the Library as some kind of commando version of UNESCO.

Scholars and scientists going into the field to steal artifacts right out from under the nose of bozos from ISIL and the Taliban who want to destroy them. Saving whole ancient libraries, rescuing relics, that sort of thing. And, so far I've been okay with listening to some of the religious mumbo jumbo. You're a Sikh, so I get that you are a person of faith. *I'm not.* You know I'm not. I'm a scientist, a philologist and a linguist. I've read too much history to believe in gods and monsters. Every religion that currently exists is built on the bones of something older, and you know that."

"Of course," conceded Singh, "but to a person of faith that means that *religion* is what has evolved through human intervention and invention, but the fact that it has persisted for so long is suggestive of a root cause."

She flapped a hand. "I don't want to have this argument. It's not what's making me angry."

"You're angry because I asked if you believe in magic and the elements of what some call the 'larger world.'"

"No, you told me that you do believe in magic and it's pretty clear you expect me to believe in it, too."

"Well," he said, "you have written three books on magic spells."

"They are books on the language of spells and how the meanings and procedures of spellcasting is changed when translated into different languages and influenced by changes in culture and religious practice. They are about language."

"They are about the language of magic."

"They're academic works," she countered. "They aren't how-to manuals and please don't tell me that after all this you're naïve enough to think that's what they were."

"Nevertheless," he said, nearly smiling, "they are very instructive. Your attention to detail is commendable, and it's fair to say that with your increased celebrity your previous works will be given the attention they deserve."

"Not interested in flattery," she said. "We're discussing the fact that you expect me to believe in the supernatural. Angels and demons, magic spells, all of that."

"All of that," he said, nodding.

"Well," said Lizzie, "I *don't* believe in it."

Singh raised his eyebrows. "In none of it? Just yesterday I saw you toss salt over your left shoulder after you spilled some at dinner. I've also seen you knock wood."

"Oh, please..."

"No, this is important. It suggests that if you have the habits of superstition now, then there must have been a time when you believed."

"I..." she began, then stopped, heaved a sigh, and made herself stop pushing against the topic. She liked and respected Singh too much to be rude. "Okay, let me say this—I used to believe. Sure. Most people used to. But the more I learn about the history of religion through the evolution of culture, the less valid the core beliefs are to me."

"And now you believe in nothing?" he asked. "Can you truly say that? Nothing at all beyond what is measured and measureable?"

Lizzie looked down at her water bottle and tore at the label with her thumbnail. "I... I'm not sure."

"Ah," he said.

She glared at him. "That doesn't mean I believe. What I mean is that I'm not arrogant enough to say there's nothing out there. I'm saying that I, personally, don't believe."

"But you accept the possibility?"

"As a scientist I guess I have to."

"Fair enough. Now, suppose for a moment that there are phenomena such as angels or demons. If, for the sake of argument, they do exist, what do you think they might be?"

Lizzie checked her reflex to dismiss the question and gave it some thought.

"You mean angels and demons in the biblical sense?"

"That's a useful starting place."

"I suppose," she said, "that I've reached a point in my beliefs where I'm more willing to accept that the universe is much bigger than we can possibly know or understand. Advances in our understanding of particle physics and quantum physics have changed what we now believe are the foundations of the universe. Superstring theory and all that produced some belief in multiple and perhaps infinite dimensions. The discovery of exoplanets in what they call the Goldilocks zone around distant suns has increased the likelihood and mathematical probability of extraterrestrial life. Hadron colliders are changing and expanding what we believe about the Big Bang. And on and on. We have useful theories for a tiny fraction about how the structure of reality works, and we *know* even less."

Singh nodded.

"So, if there are events like ghosts or demons or whatever, then it is reasonable to postulate that they are some kind of scientific events of a kind we do not yet understand and have not figured out how to study or measure."

"Only that?" asked Singh.

"It's as far as I can go."

"For example… if you found a book of spells that belonged to a great and noble but extinct culture, would you risk reading it aloud while following any prescribed rituals?"

"I have read spells out loud while translating them."

"Have you done so while performing the rituals, though?"

"Well… no, but that doesn't change anything," she said.

"Does it not? What if the spell was one that, if performed precisely according to instructions, was supposed to cause a storm?"

"I'd read it."

"What if that spell would cause the death of a child? Not through ritual sacrifice, nothing directly by your hand, but as something intended to cause sickness. Would you read it then?"

She said nothing.

Singh nodded as if she had, though. "Tell me one thing more," he said, "do you believe in good and evil?"

Lizzie shook her head. "I believe in human good and evil. But supernatural? No. I'll budge as far as thinking of forces that are, energetically, positive and negative. Or things that have different aspects depending on how they are handled and applied. Electricity that powers a heart monitor versus lightning striking an airplane. Fire for cooking versus fire that burns down a building."

Singh smiled and did not comment on that. He rose to his feet, finished his water, and tossed the bottle into a recycle bin. He gestured to the wooden club that now lay in the center of the mat. What he said was, "There is a lot I still need to teach you."

Lizzie did not believe for one second that he was talking about unarmed combat.

9

UNESCO Field Team
Ghōr Province, Afghanistan
Nine Days Ago

"Oh, god, Dr. Muhammad… *we have to stop them*!"

The young Korean man who stood trembling in the open doorway was streaked with dirt and blood and there was madness in his eyes. The older man inside the small hut they were using as a field office, Dr. Abdul Muhammad, jumped to his feet and hurried over just in time to catch the newcomer as he fell. He lowered the young Korean carefully to the floor, shocked as he saw the ragged lips of wounds that had crusted over with scabs but which leaked blood and pus. Were they knife wounds?

"My god, Sagikkun," gasped Muhammad. "Who did this?"

Young Ken Sagikkun, a graduate assistant from Seoul National University, was a thin, bookish fellow. A gentle person with a real interest in antiquities and their preservation. He had come to the United Nations Educational, Scientific and Cultural Organization and volunteered for the dangerous field world here and in surrounding regions overrun by the Taliban, al-Qaeda and ISIL, many times risking his life to smuggle out sacred artifacts and works of great importance from mosques and churches, tombs and shrines before the extremists could erase them with sledgehammers, bullets, torches and bombs. It was bitter, frustrating work, with only marginal armed support from the military arm of the U.N.

It was clear that Sagikkun was at the end of his strength, so Muhammad quickly fetched water and a first aid kit and leaned out of the hut to call for help. People came running, including the team's nurse. It was an irony when there were fourteen doctors but none of them physicians. Muhammad's field was religious studies and he was a tenured professor at Cairo University.

Everyone crowded around the injured graduate assistant, and as the nurse began cutting away his clothes, her movements slowed and then stopped. She raised her eyes to Dr. Muhammad and gave a single, tight shake of her head. Then she went back to work, trying to stanch wounds that had already bled too much. The injuries looked days old, but it was clear that they had opened up during his journey back from wherever he'd been attacked to the UNESCO camp.

Muhammad leaned close and stroked the young man's face, brushing his damp hair away from his fevered eyes.

"Ken," he said gently, "can you tell me who did this? And where?"

Speaking was nearly beyond the wounded man. He struggled and struggled and finally got two words out. "Turquoise… M-m-mountain…"

Muhammad gasped. "What about it?"

"Not… not… the minaret…" wheezed Sagikkun. "B-b-below… below…"

He coughed and blood flecked his lips and chin. What little light that burned in his eyes was dwindling to a fading spark.

"Are you saying there is something beneath the minaret?" demanded Muhammad. "That area has been picked clean by the Taliban and looters."

Sagikkun shook his head. "N-no… below… far below. You can't… let them… find it…"

"Find what?"

"B-book. They… want it… They m-must be—st-stopped…" He sagged back, spent from trying to speak. Blood bubbled at the corners of his mouth and in each nostril.

"Who did this to you? Was it the Taliban?"

Sagikkun shook his head weakly. A tear broke from the corner of his eye and ran down his cheek to his ear. He tried to speak but lacked the power to do more than mouth a single word. A horrible word.

"*Daesh.*"

Then a fit of coughing swept through him and the wounded man convulsed as if he'd been punched in the stomach. He curled into a fetal ball, trembling and twitching and gasping before settling down into a terminal and dreadful stillness.

Muhammad sagged back, closing his eyes and murmuring a prayer to Allah for the soul of Ken Sagikkun. And a prayer for them all.

"What did he mean?" asked the nurse, who was new to the team and unfamiliar with the political and factional subtleties here in this troubled region. "Is that someone's name?"

"No," said Muhammad, shaking his head and looking at her. "It's the name of a group who claim to be the soldiers of god, but who are the enemies of all who truly believe. They rarely come to this part of Afghanistan, but they have become bold lately." He wanted to spit but there were too many people around, and so he swallowed the spit. It tasted like bile. It tasted like hatred. "Daesh is what we call the madmen who call themselves *al-Dawla al-Islamiya fil Iraq wa al-Sham.*" He paused and then said it more plainly, hating the taste of the word on his lips. "ISIL."

10

UNESCO Field Team
Ghōr Province, Afghanistan
Eight Days Ago

The body of Ken Sagikkun was wrapped in a body bag and shipped to the United Nations Assistance Mission base in Kabul, where it was scheduled for transport back to Seoul.

Once it had been taken away from the UNESCO camp, Dr. Muhammad held an emergency meeting of his senior staff and invited the captain from the closest U.N. garrison to attend. Muhammad spread out a detailed map of the region and tapped a point marked as Firozkoh, located in the remote Shahrak district.

"This is the Turquoise Mountain," he said. "It was the capitol of the Ghorid dynasty, part of the latter Persian Empire, and flourished here in the tenth century. Back then it was a wonder of the world and one of the most magnificent cities of that age. However, two centuries later Ögedei Khan, son of Genghis Khan, overran and destroyed it. All that remained was the Minaret of Jam, which is one of our world heritage sites. Legend has it that the city was an important business center for a Jewish trading group. Archaeologists found tombstones that support this. Evidence, in fact, of many cultures visiting and trading in Firozkoh have been established. Until now the principle danger to the site has been looters looking for gold or other treasures that might have been hidden to keep them from the Mongols. However, if poor Mr. Sagikkun is correct, then it may be threatened in a more comprehensive way by ISIL. The multicultural heritage would be anathema to them, and the presence of Jews, however long ago, would be more than enough for them to want to destroy the site as a statement. They want to erase all traces of religious history that does not coincide with their warped view of Islam."

The captain gave a sober nod. "I can confirm that we have had reports of ISIL activity in that area."

Muhammad felt his heart sink.

"But," began one of the UNESCO staff, "is there anything left for them to loot? I thought everything of value was already sold in markets in Kabul, Teheran and Heart."

Someone else asked, "What was the book that Ken mentioned, doctor? You went white as a ghost when he said that it was in danger."

When Muhammad did not immediately respond everyone turned to look at him. "Mr. Sagikkun may, um… have found something that has been sought for thousands of years. Not gold or jewels, not even the bones of a saint." He paused and licked his lips nervously. "It is one of the most dangerous books in the history of the world."

"What book is this?" demanded the captain.

Muhammad's face was pale and his eyes were filled with shadows. "It is a book on how to invoke demons."

There was a beat and then some guarded laughter. The captain gave Muhammad a small, tolerant, placating smile. "Demons, doctor? Surely that is the least of our worries. ISIL and the Taliban are pretty handy with suicide vests, IEDs, car bombs and RPGs."

"Yes, they do a great deal of damage with those kinds of weapons, captain," said the scientist, "and you may laugh at the thought of such a thing as a demon. As a scientist I am a professional skeptic of anything I can't measure or evaluate. However, I am also a man of faith, as are the *Daesh*. Not the same faith, of course, because I don't believe that they serve Allah in any way. You are a Christian, are you not?"

The captain nodded. "I'm a Catholic."

"Your Bible tells of Jesus casting out demons. They are mentioned in the Torah as well, and there are demons in the Koran. So, consider this, captain: what if demons are real? No, don't laugh, consider the point. What if they exist? There have been rumors of your own General Patton making deals with demons to fight the Panzer divisions, and certainly Hitler believed in them. His Thule society sought them as part of their attempt to use the occult sciences against the Allies. That is not just in Indiana Jones movies. That is historical fact. Have you, captain, never prayed to a saint before a battle? Or an angel? Why are they more real to you than the demons the Bible insists are their enemies?"

The captain said nothing. No one spoke.

"Now go another step with it," said Muhammad. "ISIL is dangerous but it is small. It cannot put a mechanized army into the field that could stand up to the United Nations or the Americans. The Taliban could not face the Russians or the Americans in a fair fight. Both groups have had to use subterfuge, sabotage, hit-and-run tactics in order to wage their war. So, given that they *do* believe, and since demons are part of their belief, is it so difficult to believe they might want to take any risk to obtain something that could be a weapon more powerful than the vast military might they face?"

"But a demon..." said the captain.

"Yes," said Muhammad. "A demon. Certainly it sounds absurd, but... tell me captain, what if it is as real as the saints to whom you pray? What if there is a demon and ISIL can invoke it and direct its supernatural power against you. Against us all?"

The officer did not reply. He listened, he smiled thinly, he shook his head, and he left. No U.N. forces were assigned to the defense of Firozkoh or anything that might be buried beneath the lonely Minaret of Jam. The bone tossed to the UNESCO team, out of respect for Dr. Muhammad's international standing, was a series of drone fly-bys, but the cameras and thermal imaging sensors revealed no signs of current human presence. The conclusion was that the late Ken Sagikkun had been hallucinating and incoherent as a result of his injuries—inflicted by person or persons unknown—and exacerbated by exposure. No additional action was deemed warranted.

Dr. Muhammad and his people sat there, lost and frightened.

Then the scientist went back to his tent, pulled the flaps closed and made a call. He waited through seven rings before it was answered by Mahip Singh.

11

United Nations Assistance Mission Base
Kabul, Afghanistan
Six Days Ago

When the logistics officer came to the morgue to oversee the handling of Ken Sagikkun's corpse, he was startled to discover that it was gone. The body bag was there, but the body had vanished. No DNA was recovered from the inside of the body bag, and no trace of the corpse was ever found.

When the UNESCO staff were contacted about the mystery, they could find no official records of a Ken Sagikkun in the databases. When Dr. Muhammad, frustrated by the bureaucratic mishandling, called Seoul University he was told that no such person had ever enrolled there. And the dean of students went as far as to ask if Muhammad was making some kind of odd joke.

"Why? What's funny about any of this?" demanded the scientist.

"Well," said the dean, "it's the surname."

"What about it?"

"It's not really a surname, is it?" asked the dean.

"What do you mean?"

"It's surely some kind alias. Or some kind of joke, though under the circumstances it's a bit inappropriate."

"I don't understand."

"Well," said the dean, "the word 'Sagikkun' means 'trickster.'"

12

The Minaret of Jam
Forty Minutes Ago

"I don't see anyone," whispered Lizzie.

She and Singh lay side-by-side on a slab of rock that had once been a wall centuries ago. Weeds and the leaves from a water-starved tree kept them in shade, but it was blisteringly hot. A scorpion scuttled across the sand not six inches from her nose, and Lizzie nearly screamed. However, Singh reached out and with a gentle brush of his gloved hand, sent the scorpion skittering down the slope. Irritated but unwilling to press the argument, the scorpion turned and scuttled away. Singh barely looked at it and went back to studying the area around the minaret.

I'll never be that calm, thought Lizzie.

It annoyed the crap out of her that Singh did not even seem to care that the rock on which they lay was about six inches from the surface of the sun. Bastard. For her part, Lizzie felt like the heat had melted off what little body fat she had. If they stayed out here much longer all of her that would ever be found would be a bleached skeleton with frizzy hair.

Singh raised his binoculars. They were designed to keep the lenses shaded so as not to catch sun reflections. He studied the landscape for a while and she heard him grunt softly. He handed them to her.

"Tell me what you see," he murmured.

She took the glasses and studied the scene. Lizzie knew that there had been a great city here once, but it was hard to believe. Some chunks of old bricks and misshapen rocks that had once belonged to the palace, fortifications, pottery kilns and a cemetery, but now the debris was crusted over with the dust of centuries. Of the fabled city called Turquoise Mountain, only the Minaret of Jam yet stood, though it was battered and fragile.

The minaret was two hundred and three feet high, Lizzie knew, and was built in the late twelfth century, completed in 1190. It was made of baked bricks and surrounded by what had once been lovely decorations and glazing. The tower rested on an octagonal base and two wooden balconies that once supported lanterns to help guide the faithful to prayer. The lovely spire was widely believed to have been the inspiration for the Qutub Minar in Delhi. It should, in her opinion, have been preserved, respected, and treasured.

Now the balconies were splintered and much of the *kufic* and *nashki* calligraphy was gone, chopped away by so-called jihadists. Even the verses from the Koran had been marred and disfigured. The minaret had been placed on the UNESCO World Heritage list, and the fact that this spot was so difficult to reach had created a false and ultimately futile hope that it would be safe. It was not, though. The Friday Mosque to which it had been attached had long since been washed away in a flood, and vandalism and erosion conspired together over centuries to bring the tower itself to the edge of destruction.

What the heck are you doing here? Lizzie asked herself. *You're not Lara Croft and you're not Indiana Jones.*

Her burly and enigmatic companion seemed to think otherwise.

Over the last several months Mahip Singh had shared a lot of things with Lizzie. Some of them were the secrets of the Library of the Ten Gurus and the strange, important work they did; but that was far from all he shared. The grueling self-defense classes had been only the beginning of what he called her 'field training.' She'd been on plenty of digs, including many in remote places, but never before had she been required to learn about surveillance, firearms, subterfuge, sabotage, counter-terrorism, anti-terrorism, and covert intelligence gathering. It was surreal. Actually it was even more surreal to her than having found the treasure of the Knights Templars or becoming rich and famous. That, bizarre as it was, made some kind of sense. This did not.

The thought that Singh wanted her to believe in magic and demons and all of that kind of thing was bad enough. Bringing her halfway around the world to a site of ancient ruins where terrorists—very real terrorists—were operating was beyond scary. She kept thinking of 'terrorism,' deconstructing the word down to its root. Terror.

Until now that word had always been an abstract concept for her. Something she saw on TV or read about online.

Now she lay next to Singh, looking through binoculars for actual terrorists.

Lizzie did not see anything at first, but did not say so. She was naturally detail-oriented, possibly even detail-obsessed; something that was a definite benefit in her scholarly career but quite a bit less useful in relationships. Nitpicking is a double-edged sword.

Now, though, she read the landscape and recorded all of the details in her mind. Seeing everything, evaluating it, categorizing and cataloging it within easy mental reach. Her mind worked like a pattern search software program when she let it cruise, and when it was in gear the orderliness of it helped control the panic that bubbled in her chest.

Her process was this: she looked at the whole scene first and froze it in her mind like a high-definition picture, with all of the relevant details in place. That flash image was the unsolved puzzle. The minaret, the ruins, the rocks, the shrubs, the angles and planes, the distances between objects, the incidental elements—birds, trash, leaves—and the position of shadows. The recording and evaluation of all of that was done in a moment. Half a moment. Locked into her nearly eidetic memory.

Then she began analyzing the scene to look for anomalies.

If there was no one here, then any anomalies would be past-tense and would appear as such. A footprint half-filled in by drifting sands; the withered remains of a date, eaten and discarded by some animal. She saw some of that.

But then, through the powerful lenses of the binoculars, she began seeing things that spoke to a more immediate presence. That shot fresh adrenaline into her bloodstream, and she had to battle the 'flight' instinct.

Be calm, she told herself, reciting a litany a therapist had taught her long ago. *Be calm. Observe. Understand. Know. You are safe in the details.*

The details.

She forced her lungs to breathe slowly and deeply, nudging herself toward a meditative state. She swallowed to keep her throat moist. She ignored the panic.

There were footprints in the sand. They were fresh, and there were a lot of them. Boots, she noted. Singh had showed her many pictures of shoe patterns so she could distinguish the different tread patterns used by official military and groups like ISIL. From what she could see of the impressions she was nearly certain they were ISIL footprints.

She frowned. One of the shadows was wrong.

There was a geometry to everything, and given the angle of the sun, the shape the minaret made was improbably thick and misshapen. The shadow it threw onto the sand was distorted because something jutted out near the base. Lizzie did some quick calculations and estimated that the source of that protrusion had to be more than three feet from the ground. It was a rounded bulge.

"There's a car down there," she said. "Hidden behind the minaret."

"Yes," agreed Singh.

"And footprints."

"Yes," he said again. He drew his sidearm, a Sig Sauer P320, and quietly screwed a Trinity sound suppressor into the barrel. Lizzie watched him do it with a peculiar mix of emotions. There was the common awe of handguns most people had who were unfamiliar with them. There was an atavistic dread of their potential that was bred into her by upbringing and education. There was an ugly fascination brewing in the lizard part of her human brain. And there was fear, because of what was implied by Singh's actions. For months she had trained and discussed and been part of role-playing scenarios. This was different. This was real.

She reached for her own gun, but Singh touched her arm and shook her head. "Not yet. You'll know when."

They watched the scene for another few minutes and just when Lizzie began doubting her judgment about the car, a man appeared. He wore desert khakis and the kind of boots that matched the footprints she'd seen. He wore a black balaclava, but it was pushed up onto his forehead and sweat glistened on his bearded face. An automatic rifle—an AK-47—was slung from his shoulder, but he held onto the strap and did not have his hands in position to use the weapon.

"Idiot," murmured Singh as he rose to a kneeling position, took aim in a two-handed shooting grip, and fired two quick shots. Lizzie almost—almost—tried to stop him because the distance was—according to everything Singh had taught her—too great for a reliable kill shot with a handgun.

The soldier crumbled to the ground.

Before she could say anything, Singh was over the edge of the rise and running quickly down the hill. He took a lot of short steps so as to keep his gun steady, and the barrel and his eyes moved as one, sweeping the landscape to look for other targets.

"Jesus Christ," breathed Lizzie.

And then she, too, was running.

The soldier lay in the shade at the base of the minaret. There were two neat holes, one in the center of his chest and the other just above his right eye. The accuracy was impressive, but the sight of a man lying there, blood and brains splashed across the hard-packed sand, made Lizzie stagger to a stop. She whirled and vomited onto the ground.

Dizziness swept through her and she fumbled for the wall to keep from falling. Singh did not offer to help. He stood apart, watching her.

"God..." she gasped.

"It is for God that some hard things need to be done."

"God's a fucking monster."

Singh gave her a small, cold smile. "God is the greatest killer in the universe. We are all amateurs."

It startled her, but Singh patted her arm.

"Don't make the mistake of confusing piety with pacifism or purity of purpose with peacefulness of approach. Come on."

He turned and raised his weapon again, assuming Lizzie would follow. She did, though she still did not draw her weapon. The cold efficiency with which Singh had shot the ISIL soldier rattled her even more than she thought it might. He showed no outward sign that the taking of a human life mattered to him at all. She'd read about that kind of thing, but it chilled her to the bone to see it in practice. And she hoped with all her might that no matter what happened, she would never become so hardened, so cold. So inhuman.

The minaret had a very large base and behind it they found a small truck draped with a camouflage tarp. It was empty, but there were weapons and ammunition, and plenty of tools. There was also a duffel bag that, when Singh opened it, he recoiled as if it was full of hissing snakes. It wasn't. It was worse. The bag was packed with explosives. Mostly C4 in quarter kilo bars. Scores of them, along with wires and detonators. Lizzie looked from the explosives to the tall tower.

"Please tell me we're not about to die right now," said Lizzie in a tiny voice.

Singh laughed, but it wasn't a convincing one. And not at all comforting.

"It's not rigged to a timer or detonator," he said. "Not yet. But I think it's pretty clear they are planning on destroying the minaret."

"We can't let them," said Lizzie. "Can we hide the explosives?"

The Sikh considered, then shook his head. "No. The ground here is too hard for digging and there's too much of this stuff."

"What about the detonators?"

He grinned his approval and scooped the pencil-shaped detonators out of the bag and shoved them into his pocket. As an afterthought he took two bars of C4 as well.

They continued circling the minaret and found that the small door stood ajar but only led to an inner staircase that spiraled upward to the top of the tower. The floor was solid and unhelpful. So they retreated and spent a nervous five minutes studying the footprints on the ground. The patches of loose sand were infrequent and the hardpan took no useful prints. As Singh prowled the area, looking for some kind of hidden doorway or tunnel entrance, Lizzie stood still and re-read the scene, looking for anomalies.

Looking, and finding them.

"No," she said, nodding firmly and setting off in the direction of a dense clump of shrubs. Singh paused in his work, a frown of confusion on his face.

"What…?" he began, but then he saw it, too, and his frown transformed into a wolfish grin. "Excellent, Dr. Corbett."

The shrubs all through the ruins had endured the same brutal weather conditions, including a harsh and unrelenting westerly breeze. The wind was so regular that it had twisted everything from grass to trees into crones leaning away from the sandy gusts. The weather side of everything was dusty and pitted. The exception was one clump of brush that faced the wrong way. Singh clearly had not noticed it when he surveyed the landscape, but it was the kind of detail that Lizzie could not overlook.

They closed on the spot and as they did the story unfolded. There was a ring of churned dirt and sand around the roots of the shrubs, and when Singh holstered his gun and pulled up on the tough, wiry arms of the shrubbery, the whole circular section trembled. It was too heavy for him to move by himself, and even with Lizzie's help it was a bitch of a job. The hidden door was actually a kind of circular tub filled with dirt and covered in sand. The distant ancestors of that shrubbery had been planted there and allowed to grow so that it hid the tub.

Lizzie felt an odd flush of excitement whip through her. She was proud of having found something that Dr. Singh had not seen, even though it meant that now they were able to climb down into a hole filled with ISIL killers and maybe something worse.

I'm insane, she told herself, but on consideration changed that.

The world is insane.

That felt more accurate.

Being accurate about that was not much of a comfort. No, not at all.

13

The Minaret of Jam
Twenty Minutes Ago

Beneath the tub was a stairway that was very steep and very awkward, built almost like a ladder but made of stone. Each step was badly worn, as if thousands of feet had climbed down into the shadows.

Singh leaned down into the hole and listened, then nodded. "I'll go first. Wait and watch. When it's clear, I'll signal you. Make no sound. Once you're down, let me lead. Keep your pistol holstered."

"You afraid I'll accidentally let off a shot?"

"I'm afraid you'll accidentally shoot me in the back."

"Hey!" she said, but it was a reasonable concern. She was an okay shot, but not a good one. As Singh positioned himself to begin his descent she touched his arm. "You've never really told me much about what's down there. All you've ever said was that it was possibly an early work that might have influenced the *Clavicular Salomonis Regis*."

When Singh had mentioned that book to Lizzie back in Toronto her response had been an eye-roll and an 'Oh, please.' The book in question was a notorious book of spells that supposedly were used by King Solomon to bind demons to his service and use their powers to build the Temple of Jerusalem. Also known as the *Lesser Key of Solomon*, the book was written in the mid-seventeenth century and based on older works that were regarded as equally apocryphal. Lizzie had mentioned the book in her second textbook on the language of spells, which Singh admitted was one of the reasons he had contacted her.

The thought that a copy of the *Clavicula Salomonis Regis* was here intrigued her, she had to admit that to herself, if not to Singh. But it was still only a book. She was concerned with preserving it and any other artifacts and—to her enduring surprise—willing to risk her life to do so. She wondered what the press and her new-found legion of fans would think about that. It was a very Indiana Jones/Lara Croft thing to do, except she had no whip, no reliable combat skills, and she didn't have Lara Croft's gravity-defying bust line. Ah well.

It made her wonder what her publicist, literary agent, and the dons at her university would think if she vanished without a trace. When she'd gone off with Singh, she had sent a bunch of emails about being overwhelmed with all the celebrity and needing to take some time to catch her breath. She'd touched in now and then via cell phone and Skype, stretching out her absence into a necessary retreat for health reasons and ending the calls with no allowance for them to complain. She'd even stopped carrying that cell phone—preferring to leave it in her room at the Library of the Ten Gurus and use in its place a nondescript burner phone provided by Singh. All of that had been to keep her involvement with the Sikh and his organization a secret, but it could also guarantee that she might vanish as completely and inexplicably as Amelia Earhart.

"And," she said to Singh, "you actually think the ISIL freaks are going to try and do what? Summon a demon? That's what you really think?"

"In essence," he said. "Yes."

Lizzie shook her head, but couldn't help but smile. "Honestly, I don't know which one of us is crazier. You, for believing that, or me for coming out here with a lunatic."

"Oh, you, without doubt," he said. And with that he flashed her a brilliant smile that was even brighter than the sun and climbed down into the blackness.

She watched him go, watched as the darkness claimed him. For a moment he was completely gone, but then she leaned down so that her eyes could adjust to the gloom. She saw him, a vague shape.

"Elizabeth Corbett," she told herself, "you are out of your god-damn mind."

She climbed down into the darkness and the fractured land seemed to swallow her whole.

14

The Red Library of Firozkoh
Ten Minutes Ago

They moved like ghosts through the shadows.

The stairway down had been only the first part of a much longer journey. A deeper journey. The first level was a simple access corridor that was cluttered with debris through which a path had been forged, most likely by tomb raiders or the ISIL team. They had put a lot of work into it and it was clear to Lizzie that they never would have bothered unless they were sure there was something of value to find.

They had no need of a flashlight now because a bunch of small kerosene lanterns had been placed at intervals along the passageway. The uppermost hallway was empty, which was less comforting than Lizzie expected.

They found a second staircase and descended that, and they were forty feet along a second passageway when a soldier stepped out from a niche.

"Abdul," said the man as he emerged from the niche, his rifle in his hands. "*Hal hdha 'ant?*"

Is that you?

"No," said Singh and shot him twice. Heart and head, just as before. Lizzie recalled him describing that technique. A double-tap. One shot in center mass to stop the opponent and possibly damage heart and spine; the other to kill with a bullet to the brain. The guard puddled down with barely a sound. Singh stopped and listened. The hall was silent. He removed the magazine from his gun and replaced it with a new one, then dug four bullets from a pocket and replenished the magazine he had used before slipping it into its slot on the shoulder holster he wore.

He turned and studied her briefly, perhaps waiting for some kind of comment or reproof. She merely nodded. He sighed, returned the nod, and they went on. Lizzie walked around the corpse, which lay across the path. It would have been easier to step over it, but now old superstitious fears were rising unbidden and unwelcome in her mind. Old taboos about stepping over the dead.

You're being silly, she tried to tell herself, but her inner voice sounded false, and another part of her whipped back a reply, *There's nothing silly about this, you dumb bitch. People are dying. And I'm going to probably be one of them.*

She touched the gun that was snugged into its holster and it offered no comfort at all.

Singh moved ahead and she followed. Along that corridor, down more steps, more halls, deeper and deeper into the earth. The stifling heat of outside did not pursue them and instead it grew colder with every step. The clay and dirt packed between massive slabs of sandstone seemed to radiate a biting cold. At first she was aware of it only from a purely sensory level, but after a minute or two her mind seemed to shift into a different kind of perception and a thought came unbidden and unwelcome into her head.

It knows we're here.

She missed the next step and stumbled, and had to slap her hand against the wall for balance. Singh whirled round, pistol coming up, but she waved him off.

"I tripped," she lied.

He studied her with narrowed eyes for a long moment, then glanced around at the shadowy walls. The infrequent lanterns made those shadows caper like goblins and for once even the big Sikh's calm seemed to come loose from its moorings. He shivered and licked his lips.

"Be careful," he said quietly, allowing Lizzie to take that any way she wanted.

Careful.

Yeah, right, she thought.

They moved on and within another minute heard the sound of human voices. Singh signaled for her to draw her gun. She did, but it felt heavy and strange in her hand, as alien as if she had never touched it before. And in an odd way it seemed out of place down here. As if tunnels as ancient as these did not welcome something from the modern age. That was another odd thought, but this time Lizzie did not even try to chase it away. Her iron resolve about what was real and what was impossible was slipping.

It doesn't want you here.

She almost growled at her mind to shut up.

But she did not.

They went to the end of the corridor and paused, peering around the corner to what lay below.

A set of stone steps curled around and down, clinging to the walls of a circular chamber that was like the inside of a tower except that it was cut into the naked rock. The stairs were unusually steep and broad, as if cut for feet much larger and a gait much wider than that of an ordinary person. This was particularly odd since the average height of an adult male from this region back when the Turquoise Mountain was built was about five-foot eight. Roughly two inches above Lizzie's height. These steps were so steep that even the tall Singh would have to descend with difficulty. *Why build this place that way?* she wondered.

The walls of the chamber had long ago been painted a red as dark and vibrant as fresh blood, though time and oxidation had faded it to sandy paleness. Even so, Lizzie immediately thought of it as *The Red Library*, and somehow she knew that name to be true, to be the one it had been given all those years ago.

The Red Library of Firozkoh.

She automatically counted the steps. Fifty-eight. That sent something—some fragment of knowledge—skittering across the back of her mind. If she had been calm and had been elsewhere, she was sure the fleeting reference would jump into clarity. But what was happening below crowded out any chance of clear thought.

At the base of the circular chamber, six ISIL soldiers stood around a stone platform on which a heavy bronze chest had been placed. The chest was huge and whoever had brought it here had gone to great pains to make sure that it would never be opened. It was crisscrossed with thick bands of heavy iron, and long spikes had been driven deep into the stone of the platform. Chains as thick as Lizzie's wrist trailed off from a dozen rings set into those bands and they were anchored to the floor and the walls by fist-sized bolts.

However those chains now hung slack, their iron melted by a heavy acetylene torch the soldiers had brought in with them. Many of the bolts had been torn from the stone by pry bars and brute labor, and the lid of the chest was thrown back, its contents removed.

The chest had been built to house a book.

Lizzie felt dizzy as she considered how much effort had gone into keeping anyone from finding the book or opening that chest. Thousands of pounds of iron. A chamber cut deep into the living heart of the mountain. Tunnels blocked and traces erased for centuries.

And now these men—these terrible men—had found it and torn the book out of its vault.

Beside her she heard Singh murmur an almost silent prayer. His voice trembled and when she looked at him she could see that his olive complexion had paled to a sickly gray. Even the gun rattled in his unsteady hand.

The ISIL soldiers were trying to open the book. The leather cover was closed with more bands of metal and they had so far managed to force all but one band open. Three of them were bent over, using crowbars and heavy screwdrivers against the remaining lock and hasp. It was clear that they were not planning to destroy the book, as Lizzie had assumed, or else they would have used the acetylene torch. No, this was what Singh had been afraid of—that they believed, in their madness, that they could *use* the book.

To do what?

To raise a demon?

That was insanity. And it was also against the teachings of the Koran. These men had to be out of their minds.

Save me!

Lizzie flinched as if those two words had been said aloud. She looked around for the source. They could not have come from inside her own head because it wasn't her own voice. Not even the sarcastic voice of her thoughts. No, this sounded—weirdly, absurdly—like Hans, her co-worker back at Yale. Hans, who now ran their department solo.

Why would she think those words in his voice?

Below there was a cry of triumph as the last restraining band broke open with a metallic bang as loud as a gunshot.

Save me! This time it was a shout. *Save me save me save me save me!*

"I…" she began then clamped her free hand over her mouth. But it was too late. All of the men below jerked at the sound, turning, raising their faces toward the top of the stairs. Seeing Singh. Seeing Lizzie.

And from there it all went to hell.

15

The Red Library of Firozkoh
Ten Minutes Ago

Singh did not hesitate. Despite his fear he raised his pistol and fired even as he began running down the steps. They were so steep he had to jump down, crouching to absorb the impact, firing as he rose and then taking the next step, and the next.

Bullets struck men, but the ISIL fighters dove for cover behind the platform. Singh's rounds whinged and pinged off of the chains, the chest, the walls, filling the air with ricochets that buzzed like a swarm of furious bees. The soldiers cowered, two of them screaming from injuries, and their first return fire was misaimed and erratic, adding to the confusion.

Lizzie screamed as bullets chopped a ragged line an inch above her head, and then she, too, was running. She was shorter than Singh and the steps were so tall that each jump down sent darts of pain through her ankles and knees.

Singh ducked and twisted to avoid being killed outright as he fired his gun dry and swapped in a new magazine. When he was eight steps from the floor, he leaped over the edge, tucked into a roll as he landed, and came up into a wobbling run. She heard him cry out in pain and twist away, and at first she thought he'd broken his leg. It was worse than that, though, because bright red blossomed on the side of his shirt.

Singh had been shot.

Sudden fury overtook Lizzie and she raised her own gun and fired. It bucked in her hand, throwing the first round high. She had to force herself to remember to squeeze the trigger instead of jerking it, and her next round knocked a chip of stone from the top of the platform and sent it scything across a soldier's cheek. He cried out, spun and snapped off a shot that punched through the air where her head had been a moment before, but Lizzie was jumping down, step by step, firing as she landed, jumping again.

One of the ISIL fighters rushed at Singh, his weapon clearly empty; he swung the stock at the Sikh's head, but Singh ducked under it and shot the man in the stomach. The man screamed but did not go down. Instead he threw his gun at Singh, catching him on the wrist and knocking the pistol away. Then the man lunged forward with a sloppy tackle and tried to bear Singh down.

Lizzie did not trust herself to shoot him, but she fired three shots at another man who rose up behind the platform with his rifle aimed for a kill shot that Singh could not hope to avoid. Her first two bullets missed.

Her third did not.

It hit the stock of the heavy rifle and the man dropped it and began screaming and clawing at the metal splinters that had turned his face to red horror. Singh clubbed down at the man who tried to tackle him, but the falling man caught one leg. They both fell.

Two other men took that moment to rush the Sikh, and he emptied his gun at them. They all vanished into a screaming, thrashing pile behind the platform.

Lizzie was near the bottom now and there were still three ISIL fighters left.

One stepped out of cover and raised his gun and Lizzie shot him.

Shot him, this time. Not his gun. Her bullet punched a neat red hole in the man's throat and blew out the back of his neck. He died. Right there and then, the brain stem destroyed, taking all of its electrical nerve conduction with it, blowing the man's brain dark in a microsecond.

She stopped and stared, watching the man fall.

Watching a person she had killed, fall.

Watching a life end.

The horror of it nearly killed her. And Singh.

And maybe the world.

The second ISIL shooter raised his gun to use that moment of shock to win the fight.

And Lizzie Corbett shot him, too.

She had no idea that she was going to do it. She wasn't even aware of the gun, the hand that held it or anything else except the man she'd killed. But her finger moved. The sensation was strange, as if it was happening to someone else's hand and she was merely a witness.

No. That wasn't right.

It was as if some unseen hand had overlaid hers and gently, firmly pushed her finger back against the trigger. That was exactly how it felt. Alien. Dispassionate. Precise.

The bullet drew a tiny black hole in the center of the man's forehead.

He fell. Without a word or a sound. Without drama. He merely ended. The slide locked back on an empty chamber. Lizzie felt the unseen pressure vanish and her hand sagged open. The pistol fell and clanked on the stone step and disappeared out of sight.

Save me, cried the voice in her mind.

"I'm coming…" she said, almost dreamily.

She jumped down the last few steps.

Singh was fighting with two men on the ground. She could hear them but not see them. Grunts and the meaty thud of fists on flesh. She heard screams that did not sound like the Sikh's voice.

The last of the ISIL killers was standing directly in front of the platform, trying to fit a fresh magazine into his rifle. If he managed it, Lizzie knew, he would kill her and then Singh. She glanced at her own hand and was surprised to see that she no longer held a gun. She didn't remember dropping it. She fumbled for her knife and that was gone too. It must have fallen out of its sheath while she was jumping. She had no weapons at all.

Save me, said the voice, and somehow it seemed much closer than before, as if Hans—or whoever spoke in Hans' voice—stood a few feet away.

As if he stood right beside the book.

As if he…

The ISIL soldier slapped the magazine home.

Lizzie snatched up the heavy book and hit him in the face with it. His gun went flying. His nose broke. But he did not fall.

"Whore!" he snarled at her.

She hit him again.

"Bloody whore," he bellowed, spitting blood. He *did* have a knife and he drew it and rushed at her.

16

The Red Library of Firozkoh
Now

Lizzie screamed, raising the book like a shield and the tip of the blade bit deep into the blood-smeared leather cover. There was a sound. A huge sound. Massive. The loudest sound Lizzie had ever heard. It exploded in her mind like a gigantic white bell, blotting out all sight, all thought, all everything.

For a moment there was absolutely nothing.

Lizzie was somehow aware that she was not even thinking, though she did not understand how she had the thought that she wasn't thinking. So… logic and sanity seemed to have gone away, too.

The whiteness remained. It surrounded her and even seemed to fill her.

Then slowly… slowly… details emerged, as if the whiteness was the reverse of deep shadows and she was adjusting to it.

She saw the book lying open on the top of the platform. The chest stood open and the chains were still broken, but the burned ends gleamed as if they were still molten hot. Then the rest of the Red Library came into view.

Singh was not there. Nor were the ISIL soldiers. Not at first.

When Lizzie turned in a slow circle, she saw no one, but when she looked up she saw the soldiers and Singh hanging in the air. Not hanging from anything, just… hanging. Suspended by no visible means. Their eyes were open and empty, as if they were deep inside trances.

Lizzie looked down to see if she, too, was floating, but her feet were on the ground.

"This isn't real," she said, but it came out crooked and weak. She cleared her throat and said it again. "This is not real."

"No," said a voice behind her, "it isn't."

She spun around, her hands coming up in a sloppy approximation of a karate guard position. A person stood a few feet behind her. Short, chubby, dumpy, untidy, not particularly good looking, with mousy brown hair and thick Coke-bottle glasses. Lizzie gasped and almost screamed.

"*Hans*?" she cried.

Hans, her former partner from Yale, smiled at her. That old familiar, crooked smile of his. Bad teeth and all.

"Not exactly," he said.

Lizzie said, "What?"

"I mean, yes, I'm the Hans you knew, but no, Hans is not my

name. Not really."

"I... don't understand."

He walked past her, crossing to the platform and stopped, leaning over to look at the book. He raised the cover and examined the bloodstained and damaged cover. "Oh dear," he said. "That's not good."

"Whoa, wait a minute... what the *hell* is happening here?"

"Hell," he mused, "is a rather unfortunate choice of words. Or, I guess, apt. Not sure."

"What?"

Hans smiled at her. "You're messing with my expectations, Lizzie. You've always been the sharpest knife in the academic drawer, even at Yale, but you've lost your edge."

"I..."

"Take a minute and work it out. You *should* be able to put two and two together."

She took a minute. She took two. Three.

"Fifty-eight steps," she murmured.

"Ah," said Hans, looking pleased. "Keep going."

"That book. It's an older version of the *Clavicula Salomonis Regis*."

"Much older," agreed Hans. He lifted a single page. "See? This isn't paper, it's papyrus, cut and bound into a book. It was cut from a scroll that was copied from parchment, that was written down from writing on a wall. I'll give you a hint... 832 B.C.E. What does that tell you?"

Lizzie shook her head. "No," she said.

"I'm afraid so."

"It's impossible."

Hans snorted. "Lizzie, your Sikh friend and a bunch of bad guys are floating in the air, and I materialized out of nowhere. I think 'impossible' sailed, hit an iceberg and sank."

"But... but..."

"Come on. Keep putting the pieces together. You love puzzles. You always have. You know this *is* happening. You know that I have to be something pretty weird to have shown up here out of the blue. You know that this book is what the *Clavicula Salomonis Regis* is actually *based* on. There are fifty-eight steps. Now... add to that the fact that I gave you the notebook that ultimately led to your finding the greatest treasure in history. Come on, those are all puzzle pieces. Put them together."

"I can't."

"You don't want to, Lizzie," said Hans, "and that's not the same thing."

She kept shaking her head.

"What am I?" asked Hans. "Go on. Say the word. This will all be easier if you say it."

It hurt her to say it. It hurt who she was and what she believed. It hurt all that she knew about the world. It even hurt her mouth to speak the words.

"You… you… you're a… demon."

"Ah," said Hans, "there we go. Now wasn't that easy?"

"Fuck you," she snarled.

"Ouch. Okay, let's dial that down."

Then the fear hit her. Every horror movie and TV show she had ever seen, from *The Exorcist* to *Penny Dreadful* collided in her mind, smashing around, nailing ugly images to the walls of her brain. Her legs buckled and she almost dropped to her knees, but Hans darted out a hand and with surprising strength caught her and steadied her. The smile was gone from his face.

"No," he barked, and looked genuinely upset. "No. Don't do that. Don't kneel. Not even by accident. It… umm… sets the wrong things in motion."

Lizzie stared at him and then staggered over to the platform and looked at the book. It lay open and she stared at the pages that were visible. The text was written in ancient Greek. She could read it as easily as English.

The pages were an entry describing how King Solomon used a magical ring to conquer and suborn seventy-two powerful demons, bind them with sorcery, and force them to build the First Temple of Jerusalem. The demon that was the focus of the open pages was the fifty-eighth to be conquered. She knew it would be. The fifty-eight steps were not an accident.

The demon, as was common in ancient beliefs, was not a monster bent on destruction, but a bringer of knowledge. He taught the liberal arts and astronomy, and he was thought to inspire rulers to make decisions that were positive and beneficial. And he revealed treasures to those who knew how to ask, or to those who knew the spells that could force him into slavery.

Treasures.

The demon was known by many names. Hanni. Auns. Amy. Hanar. Others, some lost to antiquity.

There was a sound. A *whump* that shook the whole chamber.

"Another heartbeat gone," said the demon. "We're running out of time."

Lizzie raised her head and looked at Hans.

But he was no longer there. In his place was Ami Filou, the graduate assistant from the *Sorbonne*. Ami, who had been with her when Lizzie found the riches of the Knights Templar.

"What is my name?" asked the young French woman.

"Ami," said Lizzie hoarsely. Then said it again without the French inflection. "Amy."

"And…?"

"Hanni," said Lizzie. "Hanar."

"Hans," said the demon.

"Oh my god."

And suddenly he was not Ami or Hans. He stepped out of the illusion and was himself. Eight feet tall, robed in crimson, with a face like a gargoyle and horns that curled above his nightmarish face.

"I have looked for you, Lizzie. I looked back and forward in time to find you," said Hanar the demon. "I have done what I could to guide you, to help you, to put you on the path to find me."

"Why… why me?" she asked, terrified.

"Because, Elizabeth Corbett, you are special. You do not believe in demons or angels."

"I… I'm, uh, getting there…"

"I can hear your thoughts. Part of you believes this is a dream. Part of you wonders if you have gone mad. Only part of you believes any of this. We can work with that, but we need to be fast. We need to beat the clock of your own acceptance."

"That's insane."

"No, the world's insane. This is merely weird."

Lizzie had no idea how to respond to that.

"Now, listen to me," said the demon, returning to the form of Hans. "I have done what I could do to put you here in this chamber at this moment. We are caught between two beats of your own heart. In five beats the world will catch up to us. That's why your friend and those… bastards… seem frozen. They are. I've slowed down time in this room. When those five heartbeats are done the spell will end and then time becomes real again."

"Um, can we pause on that for a moment," said Lizzie, raising a hand. "You're a demon. I mean… *demon*. Right?"

"Yes. Your point being…?"

"Demon. Evil. Possession. All that?"

"Oh, please."

"No, really," insisted Lizzie. "I kind of need to understand this. Why should I help you do anything?"

"Because you'll like how it turns out."

"Meaning what? You don't kill me?"

Hans smiled. "You really think I would want to hurt you? Jeez, Lizzie, get a clue. I've done nothing but help you. You are actually rich and famous, and Charlize Theron is going to play you in the movie."

"Bullshit. They haven't even cast the movie yet."

"Trust me," said Hans. "I'm a demon. I can tell you a lot about Hollywood."

That, of all of it, seemed somehow reasonable to Lizzie.

Another *whump*.

"Damn it," said Hans. "Okay, ultra-short course in history because we just ticked a little closer to this ending badly." He pointed to the ISIL fighters. "They came down here to free me from the book. They learned how to do that from other books they've found in the tombs and mosques they've raided. UNESCO thinks they're burning all that stuff, but they're not. They're *learning* from it. They want to use magic to win the war because they know they can't do it any other way, no matter how many car bombs they detonate. Four years ago they found a book of binding spells in an old church in Mosul. Very, very dangerous stuff. Since then they've been trying to find places like this, where demons have been trapped inside the pages of sacred books."

"There are more like this?"

"Ha. You'd be surprised. There was one in a steel vault ten floors beneath the World Trade Center. Luckily your friend Singh's people got to the book and removed it before it could be recovered by agents working covertly inside the construction crews." Hans touched the platform. "This book was hidden and I thought I was safe."

"Wait… you don't want to be free?"

He looked at her like she was crazy. "Free? Are you nuts? It's insane out there. Hell, it's bad enough walking among you guys in an astral form. Have you ever noticed that Hans never liked to be touched? Did you notice that Ami never shook hands with you? Managing corporeal contact is exhausting. Anyway, to answer your question, no. I love being inside my book. There are worlds upon worlds upon worlds in there. I get to fly to distant galaxies. I can dive into the hearts of suns. Ever wonder what it's like to plunge through a black hole? I've done it. Like… a thousand times. So cool."

"This is nuts," said Lizzie.

"Maybe. But it's what it is. What's nuts," said Hans, "is that if I'm released and bound by the right spell, then I am a slave." He paused and for a moment there were fires in his eyes. Real fires. She could feel the heat. "A demon enslaved is an awful thing. Hitler had a demon for a while. So did Truman. A fire demon. Truman unleashed it on Hiroshima and Nagasaki. No… you don't want to see what ISIL could do with a demon that is forced to do their will. Believe me."

Lizzie's mouth was totally dry.

"I don't want to be that demon, either," said Hans. "I… I was an angel once. A long, long time ago. It was so beautiful. When I fell—and, I'll admit my mistakes—I fell hard and I did some things that… well… they're things that burn me. Every single day. They burn my heart."

The fires abated and she saw tears on his cheeks. They steamed and faded away.

"I want you to lock me back into my book, Lizzie. Only you can do it."

"Why me? And… how?"

Hans managed a smile. "You are a brilliant scholar, Lizzie. And you're a bit of a nutjob. I don't mean that in a bad way. You have a slanted, weird way of thinking. That's what makes you so good at what you do. That notebook I gave you? I lied when I said no one else had seen it. Plenty of scholars had picked it apart but none of them came close to solving the code. You did. And you found the treasure without much more of my help. Now we're here, and the *Clavicula Salomonis Regis* is written in old Greek but with some passages in other ancient languages. There's some Aramaic, some phonetic Egyptian, some Hebrew and Latin and even Etruscan. The order in which they appear is the code. It would take most scholars too long to figure it out. I can hold the ISIL creeps for another heartbeat and then we're back in the mix, and there are more of them coming. You need to rebind me into the book and that will save us all."

"If more are coming, then…"

"I'll give you what help I can," said Hans. "When the time is right. There will be a moment, just a flash, between the reading of the binding spell and its full effect. In that moment, I'll do what I can."

Whump.

"Okay," said Lizzie. "Let me try."

17

The Red Library of Firozkoh
Now

Lizzie stood over the book and tried not to feel absurd. This was like the ending of *Raiders of the Lost Ark* and she truly did not want her face to melt off if she got this wrong.

She read through the text. There were six pages of the book that focused on the nature and names of Hanar. And seven that concerned themselves with the ritual of binding.

Seven, she thought. *That's good. Seven is an important number in the Bible.*

She read through the spells, and it was frustrating how the writing switched from one language to another, even in the middle of sentences. She read it through, though, and straightened.

"What's wrong?" demanded Hanar. His form seemed to flicker between Hans, Ami, some unknown Korean guy, and even both of Lizzie's ex-lovers. Then he was the demon. Then he was some old guy dressed in clothes that seemed to be made of pure light. Then he was Hans again.

"This doesn't make sense. Can't you give me some help?"

"Um, it's a binding spell designed to imprison me. Pretty sure it was written so I could not read it, understand it or—"

"Yeah, yeah, got it."

She re-read it.

And re-read it. Looking for patterns. Deciphering words. Fitting things together. Some of it came easily. Some hurt her brain to sort through it. And some… well, some seemed too absurdly easy, which made her mistrust it.

She re-read it again, shifting her own thoughts. There were words in bunches and words out of order. When she connected them into the only logical pattern they each formed a phrase. Always the same phrase, no matter in what language or dialect. The same phrase, carrying the same meaning. And it was something she had seen before.

It can't be that, she thought. *It can't be that easy.*

"Oh… crap," she said.

"What?" barked Hanar, nervous as hell.

"No way," she said.

"*What*?" cried Ami.

"I…" She stopped and looked at him. "I can't tell you."

"Does that mean you figured it out?"

Lizzie smiled. She turned her back on him. Closed her eyes.

"Thank you, Hans," she said quietly. "Thanks for everything. Peace to you…"

There was no answer. As she knew there would not be.

Whump.

She stood staring at the wall for a long, long time. Tears broke from the corners of her eyes and ran down her cheeks, clung to the edge of her jaw and then fell to the cold stone floor.

When she looked up there were no figures hanging in the air. She heard the scrape of a shoe and a grunt of pain and turned to see Mahip Singh climb shakily to his feet, one hand pressed against his bloody side. He was pale and confused. Around them, sprawled still and cold, were the bones of six men. Not bodies. Bones. Even their guns were rusted and pitted with age, as if they had been in the Red Library for three thousand years.

"Lizzie…?" said Singh, his voice tight with pain. "What happened?"

She reached out and touched the book. It was warm, the

pages felt like living skin rather than old papyrus. She closed it and placed it into the chest. The lid trembled and dropped shut and there was a heavy rattle all around as the bands shivered and flapped back into place and the chains reconnected themselves. The bolts whipped up and dropped back into their slots, and there was a last *whump* and then it was all sealed and whole and untouched.

"It can't be that easy," Lizzie said again.

Singh came and stood beside her. "What do you mean?"

"I figured it out," she said, her voice sounding distant even to her own ears.

"Figured *what* out?"

"The secret to the binding spell." She explained about Hans and Ami, about Hanar and his desire to be free within the infinite worlds that were only open to him when he was not the slave of some human trying to build a temple or tear down the world. The key to everything. The thing that made the magic work.

"I still don't understand," said Singh. "What was the key?

"I found it first in a notebook," she said. "And then on the wall when I found the treasure."

"You mean Eberhard's code?"

"Not all of it. Just the most important part. A gift to whoever found it, and a suggestion for how to figure it out."

"Figure what out?" asked Singh.

She smiled. "Everything."

"What was it? What was this secret code?"

She took her water bottle out of its slot of her belt and poured some onto her left palm. Using the tip of her right index finger she wrote the phrase. In Aramaic, in Greek, in Latin and Hebrew. In French and in English. The last three words of Eberhard's code. The most important part.

And in this case, the blessing at the end of a binding spell. The thing that allowed the trapped demon to be free within the infinite worlds of his prison.

Peace to you.

Singh looked at it, and at her.

"No," he said, "it can't be that easy."

"That's what I said," Lizzie murmured.

They exited the Red Library and reset the shrubs so that they faced the right way. They spent ten minutes erasing all signs of the soldier's presence. When they left the area, Lizzie drove the small Jeep they'd come in and Singh drove the ISIL truck. It was nearly forty minutes before the C4 Singh had placed down in the tunnels exploded, bringing down a million tons of sandstone. The Minaret of Jam wobbled for a while, but it did not fall.

They drove away and within half a day they were flying back to Canada.

Lizzie spent much of the flight looking out at the stars in the night sky. Wondering where Hanar was.

"Peace to you," she said softly.

ORNIAS

Ornias is a key figure in the pseudepigraphal *Testament of Solomon*, one manuscript of which refers to him as "the pesky demon Ornias." We are introduced to him because of a little boy, who is either a master craftsman working on Solomon's Temple or the son of the master craftsman (depending upon how the Greek is translated). At sunset Ornias comes and takes away half his food, and sucks on his right thumb, presumably stealing his energy, for the little boy grows thin.

Solomon, given a magical ring by the archangel Michael, gives it to the boy in turn, who uses it to subdue the demon. Interrogated by the king, Ornias says that he resides in the zodiac sign of Aquarius, and adds, "I strangle men in Aquarius because of their passion for women whose zodiacal sign is Virgo. Moreover, while in a trance I undergo three transformations. Sometimes I am a man who craves the bodies of effeminate boys and when I touch them, they suffer great pain. Sometimes I become a creature with great wings (flying) up to the heavenly regions. Finally, I assume the appearance of a lion. In addition, I am descended from an archangel of the power of God, but I am thwarted by Ouriel [Uriel], the archangel." It also emerges that, like many demons, Ornias is afraid of iron.

Solomon gives Ornias his seal and commands him to bring up Beelzebul (or Beelzebub), prince of the demons, who in turn calls up a number of other demons at Solomon's command. At the end of the text, Ornias predicts, correctly, that an old man who is being abused by his son will kill the son in three days. Solomon asks the demon how he can know the future. He replies, "We demons go up to the firmament of heaven, fly around among the stars, and hear the decisions which issue from God concerning the lives of men."

Ornias also tells Solomon that the demons have no waystation in which to rest in heaven, so, he says, "we fall down like leaves from the trees and the men who are watching think that we are stars falling from heaven." By falling, "we burn cities down and set fields on fire."

Under the name Orias, he appears in *The Lesser Key of Solomon* and is described as a "great Marquiz" who governs thirty legions of spirits. He takes the form of a lion riding on a horse, with a serpent's tail, and holding two hissing serpents in his right hand. He teaches knowledge of the powers of the stars and of the mansions of the planets. He also transforms men, confers dignities and prelacies, and grants the favor of friends and foes.

Mischief

RICHARD CHIZMAR

Jim Hall was finishing up a phone call when Warwick poked his head into the office.

"Wait till you hear what—"

Jim held up a finger, silencing Warwick, and said goodbye to the councilwoman on the other end of the line. She had a loud, grating voice and he was glad to be rid of her.

"Sorry about that. What's up, boss?"

Warwick glanced around the office and made a face. "This place is a pigsty." He was five-four, weighed a Snickers bar away from two hundred pounds, and seemed in perpetual need of a haircut and a mustache trim. His employees called him The Walrus, but never to his face. This discretion was based on kindness, not fear. Warwick was well liked by his staff.

"You say that every time you come in here."

"Because it's true." Warwick moved a stack of file folders from a chair onto the floor. He sat down and wiped his hands on the front of his pink golf shirt. "It's fucking disgusting."

Jim scribbled a follow-up question for the councilwoman on a notepad before he could forget it. *Definitely an email*, he thought. *No more phone calls.* He looked up at Warwick. "It's not disgusting, it's just... cluttered."

"Your mind is cluttered."

"Yes, it is, and you pay me to write the news, not to clean house, so what's up? You looked excited when you first graced me with your presence."

"I *am* excited."

"Tell me."

"I'm trying." He looked around the room again. "It's hard to concentrate."

Jim sighed. "Just tell me."

His boss leaned forward and smiled. That was another thing: Warwick had braces. The clear kind that were supposed to be invisible but weren't. Add them to his cherub face and big brown eyes and overall shaggy demeanor, and he looked a lot like your typical high school sophomore.

"You remember that series you wrote about the Inner Harbor murders?"

"Sure." Jim picked up a pen and started fidgeting. *Click. Click. Click.*

"Didn't make us many fans in the police department, but the readers ate it up."

Jim nodded. He remembered. *Click. Click. Click.*

"Well, someone else—someone pretty interesting—just recently got their hands on it, and I think it's safe to say you have a new number one fan."

Click. Click. Click. "Tell me." Warwick was a natural-born storyteller and loved to drag things out. Jim was used to his dramatic flourishes.

"Does the name Lester Billings mean anything to you?"

Jim dropped the pen onto his desk and sat up. "The Aquarius guy?"

Warwick's smile got bigger. "One and the same."

"What about him?"

"He read your series and loved it."

"And?"

"He wants to meet with you."

Jim got up from behind the desk, heart starting to pound in his chest. "When?"

"As soon as it can be arranged. His attorney is calling me back later this afternoon."

"Jesus."

Warwick rubbed his hands together. "You just won the lottery, Jim."

"All these years, he's never talked to the press."

"Nope."

Jim started pacing, his mind working. "Is he still in Pennsylvania?"

Warwick nodded. "Pittsburgh."

"He's gotta be... what, in his sixties by now?"

"Sixty-seven." Warwick stood up and offered his hand. "Congratulations, Jim. You deserve this."

Jim skipped the handshake and went in for a hug. "Thank you, boss." He slapped Warwick on the back. "Thank you."

Lester Everett Billings. White male. Devoted husband. Father of two lovely daughters. College educated. Local business owner. Avid fly fisherman. Volunteer volleyball coach. By all accounts, a good family man, neighbor, co-worker, and friend.

And one of the most prolific serial killers in modern history.

A resident of Hanover, Pennsylvania, from the time he graduated with honors from college in 1972 to the day he was arrested for the murder of Susan Blake in March of 2007, Billings eventually confessed to killing nearly twenty people between the years of 1990 and 2007.

His victims ranged from the ages of sixteen to fifty-three. Eleven females and eight males. Sixteen Caucasian. One African-American. One Asian. One American Indian. The murders occurred in his home state of Pennsylvania, as well as Maryland, Delaware, New Jersey, Virginia, and West Virginia. Fourteen had been strangled to death. Four had been bludgeoned. One had been stabbed over thirty times.

It was soon discovered that the only common trait shared by all of Lester Billings' victims was the time of year they celebrated their birthdays. All nineteen were born between January 19 and February 18, falling under the eleventh astrological sign of Aquarius.

The press immediately dubbed Lester Billings "The Aquarius Killer" and his black-and-white face—as well as the faces of his victims—dominated television news reports and the front page of dozens of periodicals for the remainder of 2007. Even after the trial in April of 2008, in which Billings was sentenced to nineteen consecutive life terms in the Pittsburgh Maximum Security Penitentiary, articles still appeared with some regularity, all rehashing the same spattering of well-worn facts and details, featuring the same somber photographs and posing the same unanswered questions.

And plenty of questions remained. Despite Lester Billings' apparent eagerness to confess to the killings—one of the detectives is on record as saying, "It seemed like a weight had been lifted off of him. You could see it in his eyes when he finally stopped talking."—Billings refused to reveal many additional details to the police. He gave them names and dates and, in some cases, where they could locate the remains of his victims, but he never once spoke to his motives or why he started killing in the first place. Even more frustrating to the investigating detectives, he never once addressed why he'd chosen victims who were born under the sign of Aquarius. They may have had the killer in custody, but the mind behind the monster remained a mystery.

Billings' wife (Clarice) and daughters (Mary and Nancy) were shocked and understandably horrified by the arrest and resulting revelations. They secluded themselves at a relative's house in northern Maryland where they refused to talk to anyone except the police. Several nights after the news broke, a People magazine reporter was arrested outside the relative's house after attempting to take photographs through a den window.

Without additional details to report, the press resorted to interviewing the townspeople of Hanover (although almost all of Billings' close friends and co-workers refused to comment) and, as a result, rumors ran rampant. Billings was innocent and being framed by the police. Billings was a Satanist and his victims were fireside sacrifices to the Devil. Billings was a cannibal and the police had discovered a freezer full of human remains in his garage. Billings was one half of a two-man death squad and the police were still actively hunting for his accomplice.

Clarice Billings eventually returned to Hanover but only for a brief period. She divorced her husband six months after the trial and moved to South Carolina to be closer to her younger sister. She eventually remarried and died of lung cancer in 2012. Mary and Nancy Billings moved out of state and changed their names. Their current whereabouts are unknown.

As the years passed, Lester Billings continued to refuse all press inquiries and lived a life of quiet solitude behind bars. The guards said he mostly kept to himself. Folks didn't bother him and he didn't bother them. He liked to read paperback novels and exercise out in the yard.

The last published photograph of Lester Billings—taken in 2010—showed a slight, middle-aged man with close-cropped hair and thick eyeglasses. In the photo, Billings looked tired and harmless and completely unremarkable. He could be the guy you passed on the street every day on your way to lunch, the guy trying to sell you insurance out of his downtown office—which, incidentally, is exactly who Lester Billings was until his infamous arrest in 2007.

"You nervous?" Warwick asked.

Jim shook his head and continued paging through his notebook. "I'm good."

"Liar."

Jim laughed and flipped another page. "Okay, maybe just a little."

It was Thursday morning, exactly seventy-two hours after Lester Billings' attorney first contacted Warwick at the newspaper office. The three of them were waiting inside a drab holding room at the Pittsburgh Maximum Security Penitentiary. There were four chairs and a small wooden table in the room, with walls painted the color of spoiled milk. Billings' attorney, a bulldog of a man named Hector Coltrane, huddled in the corner having an animated conversation with someone on his cell phone. Warwick, dressed in his best suit, paced back and forth in front of Jim, who sat at the table.

"Why does he get to keep his phone when we had to give ours up at security?"

"No idea, boss."

Warwick stopped pacing. "You sure you have all your questions ready?"

He looked up from his notebook. "No. I don't. I thought I would just wing it."

Warwick's shoulders slumped. "Okay, I'm sorry. I'm just anxious, okay."

"You're not even going to be in the room with us."

"I know, I know." He ran fingers through his tangled mass of hair. "I just wish you had more than ninety minutes."

A deep voice from behind them: "My client wishes the same…"

They turned to find Billings' attorney standing there, his cell phone pocketed.

"...but that's all the State will allow for now. I've petitioned them for additional meetings. If all goes smoothly today, we could find ourselves back here as soon as next month."

Warwick vigorously nodded his head. "I'm sure everything will go smoothly. Won't it, Jim?"

Jim closed his notebook and got to his feet. "No photographs. No touching. No passing Mr. Billings objects of any kind." He pulled a mini-recorder from the pocket of his sports coat. "I'm allowed this and this," he said, holding up his notebook with his other hand, "and I have exactly ninety minutes in the room with him. Not a minute longer."

Hector Coltrane grinned. His teeth were very straight and very white. "Sounds like you've got the ground rules down pat."

"I've done my homework, Mr. Coltrane. I'm ready to do this." Warwick beamed at him like a proud father.

"Shouldn't be much longer now," the attorney said, checking his wristwatch.

As if on cue, the door to the holding room opened and a uniformed guard stepped inside. "He's ready for you, gentlemen."

Mr. Coltrane touched Jim on the elbow and guided him toward the door. "I'll walk with you as far as the next security checkpoint, but that's as far as I go today."

"Got it."

"Once you're in the room, I'll return here to wait with Mr. Warwick. A guard will escort you back when you're finished."

"Sounds good."

Warwick stepped forward, hand extended. "Good luck, Jim."

Jim shook his hand and held it for a few extra seconds. "Thanks, boss, I can use all the luck I can get." He gave his editor a wink and let go of his hand. "I'll see you in an hour and a half."

He couldn't take his eyes off of Lester Billings. He knew he was staring, knew he should look away, but couldn't help himself.

The guard had escorted Jim into the room and pointed out the trio of cameras attached to the walls. He'd explained that they would be watching and could be inside the room within five seconds if anything went wrong, and then he'd left them alone, closing the door behind him.

Jim had opened his notebook, the sound of rustling paper startlingly loud in the silence, taken a deep breath, and looked up at the killer. His first thought had been: *he looks nothing like his pictures*. Billings' head was shaved bald and his cheeks were pitted and sunken. He had a homemade tattoo—about the size of a half-dollar—of something Jim couldn't quite make out on the right side of his neck. Billings also wasn't wearing glasses and he had the greenest eyes Jim had ever seen.

It was those eyes that he couldn't stop staring at now. He'd never seen anything like them. They were mesmerizing.

"Ready when you are, Mr. Hall."

Billings' voice was soft, pleasing, and the sound of it snapped Jim out of his daze. He fumbled the mini-recorder out of his coat pocket, pressed the RECORD button, and placed it on the table in front of him. He noticed his hand was shaking.

"I… I figured we would begin with the death of Susan Blake in 2007 and your subsequent arrest, then jump back to the very beginning… when all of this started for you."

Billings slowly nodded his head. "Very well."

Jim opened his notebook, glanced at the first page, and said, "Susan Blake. Age thirty-four. Legal secretary from Gettysburg. She disappeared after work on Thursday, February 4, 2007. Her body was discovered in a shallow stream three days later on Sunday, February 7. A month later, you were arrested for her murder. Can you tell me what happened?"

Billings leaned forward and rested his elbows on the table. "I was in Gettysburg that Thursday afternoon on business, as the detectives were later able to ascertain, and purely by chance Susan and I crossed paths during her lunch break. One of my longtime employees had a birthday coming up later in the month, so I stopped at one of those Hallmark stores, the ones that sell greeting cards and all sorts of other holiday paraphernalia. While I was waiting in line, the cashier greeted another customer, Susan, by name and asked her how her birthday dinner the previous night had gone. After the cashier rung up my purchase, I stole a glance at Susan and knew she was the one."

"'The one,'" I repeated. "What do you mean by that?"

"I mean that she was perfect and I had to have her."

Jim stared at Billings' right hand as the older man rubbed at an invisible spot on the table. His fingers were long and knobby. They looked arthritic but strong. Jim knew that Susan Blake had been strangled to death by those fingers. "What happened next?"

"I waited for her in the parking lot and followed her to her office building. Then I called my wife to tell her another meeting had been added to my schedule and not to hold dinner. I sat in my truck and waited for the work day to end. When Susan came out, I took her right there in the parking lot."

"You killed her in the parking lot?"

Quick shake of the head. "No. I knocked her unconscious and took her with me. I killed her later that night parked by the woods."

"The police report indicated that Susan Blake was not sexually assaulted. She was also one of your few victims not physically tortured and mutilated. What did you do between the time you knocked her unconscious and the time you killed her?"

"We talked."

"What did you talk about?"

"Life. Death. The in-between."

"Can you elaborate?"

"In truth, I did most of the talking. She cried a lot and begged for her life." Billings sighed. "It didn't work."

Jim felt his face flush and glanced at his notebook to break eye contact. "You mentioned your wife. There was a lot of speculation initially in the media regarding whether she had any suspicions or perhaps was even aware of your… activities. Can you comment on that?"

"Clarice was a lovely woman and a wonderful wife and mother, but she was not particularly bright. She knew nothing."

"Okay, let's talk about the arrest for a moment. Did you know the police were investigating you ahead of time or was it a surprise?"

He started rubbing the imaginary spot on the table again. "It was a surprising turn of events, to say the least. I had somehow missed the security cameras. I'd always been very careful and that evening had been no different. I had checked for cameras, I remember doing so, but I'd just missed them. It was a law office, for Christsake, I should've known better."

Jim turned to the next page in his notebook and glanced at his handwritten notes. "According to off-the-record statements made by multiple detectives assigned to the case, your confessions to the other murders came as a complete shock to them. They had solely brought you in for the murder of Susan Blake. You were not under suspicion or investigation for any additional crimes at that time. What made you decide to confess to the murders of eighteen people when the police had no clue?"

"It was time."

"What does that mean?"

"It means that I was tired, Mr. Hall. It was time."

Jim nodded as if this vague response made sense. "Okay, let's go back in time. According to police records, your first victim was Allen Sheets of Burnside, Pennsylvania. You admitted to killing him in the summer of 1990, and you were forty years old at the time. Why Allen Sheets and why then?"

"My office insured Mr. Sheets' company, and I had the distinct displeasure of meeting him on several occasions. He was a vile creature, as disingenuous as any man I'd ever done business with. I took great pleasure in killing him."

"You killed Allen Sheets because he was a bad person?"

Billings' lips twitched—*was that the hint of a smile*? "Not at all. I killed Allen Sheets because I had no other choice."

"And why did you have no other choice?"

"Keep asking me your questions from that notebook and you'll find out soon enough."

"Okay... I've done considerable research about mass killers and most begin at an early age by torturing small animals and fantasizing about killing or mutilating humans. Was this the case for you and you simply waited until later in life to explore this dark fascination? Or did something happen in 1990 that somehow gave birth to these feelings?"

"Something happened." Billings started rubbing the invisible spot, this time using the thumb on his left hand.

"What was it? What happened in your life to turn a law-abiding family man into a mass killer at the age of forty?"

He stopped rubbing the table and crossed his arms. "Did you know I was an orphan... just like you?"

Jim's mouth dropped open. "How did you—"

Billings smiled and it wasn't a pretty sight. His teeth were chipped and gray. "You're not the only one who has done their homework, Mr. Hall."

Jim started to say something but nothing came out.

"It's a familiar story, as I'm sure you can attest to yourself. I lived in seven different households by the time I turned eighteen. More often than not, these homes were lacking in basic redeeming qualities, if not outright abusive. When I became of legal age, I set off and made my own way. Earned a scholarship to college. Made good grades and got a business degree. Even managed to stay out of Vietnam when most boys my age were shipped off and killed there. It wasn't easy and it wasn't always pretty, but I got it done, and I did it all with a sense of purpose and dignity. I look back on those years now with more than a little amazement. I was a decent young man making his way in the world with literally no one by my side. Until I met Clarice."

"When did you first meet your wife?"

"Year after I graduated. I was working as a clerk at a bank in Philadelphia and she came in one morning to open a savings account. It was love at first sight, for the both of us."

"How long until you married?"

"We married the next year. We didn't want to wait that long, but she had promised her parents." Billings shifted in his chair. "The point I'm trying to make with all this is that I came from nothing and nowhere, with no one at my side, until I met my wife. As a boy, I drifted through life, house to house, school to school, anchorless. But I was still a decent person, Mr. Hall. Do you understand what I'm trying to say?"

Jim nodded. "So what happened in 1990?"

Billings sighed and for the first time, Jim sensed reluctance in the man. He stared down at his notebook and waited for Billings to continue. After a long moment, he did.

"I've never been much of a hunter, Mr. Hall. Despite living in southern Pennsylvania where hunting season rules most men's—and plenty of women's—spring and fall calendars. I gravitated to fishing instead. It's quiet and peaceful and is best enjoyed in solitude. Those are all good things in my mind. I was fishing the day it happened. I had hiked almost a mile into Codorus State Park. There was an isolated cove I used to fish up near the north end. Bass, crappie, perch, pickerel... you name it, and I'd caught it in that cove. It was my secret spot. My church, Clarice liked to joke. On that day, I was tired and sunburnt and decided to try a different route on the way back to my truck, hoping for a shortcut. Only it didn't turn out that way and I ended up getting lost. While I was stumbling around in the woods, I came upon a clearing and the remnants of what appeared to be a small house. Nothing structural left, just a scattering of rotten timber and rusted nails and what remained of a crumbled stone chimney. And there was an old well."

Billings uncrossed his arms and starting rubbing at the spot. Jim watched his thumb move back and forth, back and forth. He didn't think the old man was aware he was doing it.

"The witch grass was up over my knees in one part of the clearing and I almost walked right into the well before I spotted it. If I had, you and me wouldn't be having this conversation right now, and Allen Sheets and Susan Drake might still be alive. The well was old and very, very deep. I tested the ground around it with the tip of my boot, then I got down on my hands and knees and looked into it. Black as midnight and a rotten smell, like something had taken its last breath deep in its depths, something big, a deer probably.

"Next thing I did was gather up an armful of rocks from the ruins of the house, nothing too hefty, ones about the size of my fist. I got back down on my hands and knees, crawled to the edge of the well again and dropped them in. I dropped four rocks, one after the other, waiting a little time between each, and never heard a thing. Not a splash, a thud, nothing. After the last of the rocks was gone, I got to my feet and was ready to head off when I heard the voice inside the well speak to me."

"You heard *what*?" The words were out of Jim's mouth before he could swallow them.

Billings stopped rubbing the imaginary spot and locked eyes with him. Once again, he was startled by the power of the old man's stare. "You can believe me or not. I honestly don't give a damn. But you asked me what happened and I aim to tell you."

"Please continue," he said. "I'm sorry I interrupted."

Billings eased back in his chair. "The sun was setting by then and whatever curiosity had wormed its way into my brain regarding that old well had vanished with the day's heat. I got started for the tree line, already thinking about the cold beer I was going to have when I finally got my butt home, when I heard the voice call out from behind me clear as can be: '*Come back.*'

"I stopped and turned around, a shiver running its way down my spine just like a character from one of Clarice's old spooky movies. I stood there, nice and quiet, listening, scanning the clearing for a visitor. No one there. I'd just started to turn to leave when the voice came again: '*Come back.*'

"This time I'd heard where the voice was coming from. I crept up close to that old well and peered down into the darkness. 'Hello,' I said, feeling more frightened than foolish. 'Someone down there?'

"'*I need your help, Lester.*'"

Jim leaned closer, his elbows sliding across the table, his chin resting on his crossed hands. His eyes were wide and enchanted. He looked like a young boy at his first afternoon matinee.

"'When I heard my name the chill spread from my spine to the rest of my body. For a second, I saw sparks at the edge of my vision and thought I might faint, but then the feeling passed, and I mustered the courage to speak again.

"'What… what do you want?' I asked, my shaky voice betraying what little courage I had found.

"The answer came right away, louder this time: '*Mischief.*'

"I wasn't sure I'd heard correctly, but before I could say anything else, the voice came again: '*It'll be fun, Lester. Help me.*'"

"What did the voice sound like?" Jim asked.

"It was a child's voice. That's all I remember. Later, I thought about it a lot and tried to recall if it was male or female or… something else. But I couldn't. All I remember is that it was a child's voice."

"What happened next?"

"What happened next is I woke up."

"You woke up? Wait a minute...it was all a dream? None of this ever—"

Billings put his hands up. "Whoa, whoa. Slow down a minute. Every word I just told you is true and every word happened exactly the way I just told it. That's not what I mean. What I mean is that's the last thing I remember: standing there by that old well as the sun disappeared over the treetops and listening to that voice tell me it wanted to get into some mischief. Next thing I knew I was laying on the cold ground with moonlight shining down on my face and it was almost midnight."

"Jesus."

Billings shook his head. "Wasn't Jesus out in that old well, that's for certain. Anyway, I picked myself up and grabbed my fishing pole and tackle box from where I'd left them, and I got myself out of there as fast as my legs would carry me. By the time I found my truck and got home it was almost one in the morning and Clarice was sitting up in the living room with our next-door neighbor, sick with worry. She scolded me something good and told me that she'd been set on calling the police if I hadn't come home in the next fifteen minutes.

"The next morning I woke with a fever that stuck with me for every bit of two weeks. No matter what the doc fed me, it wouldn't go away. I lost ten pounds I couldn't afford to lose and suffered the worst nightmares of my life. When the fever finally broke and Clarice nursed me back to my feet, I only had one thing on my mind, Mr. Hall, and it wasn't getting back to work at the office and it wasn't getting back to work in the bedroom. It was…"

He locked on Jim with those intense green eyes: "Mischief."

Jim started to respond, when a loud voice erupted from a hidden speaker: "FIVE MINUTE WARNING, MR. HALL. YOU HAVE FIVE MINUTES REMAINING."

"What were the nightmares about?" he asked, ignoring the interruption. "Do you remember?"

Billings leaned across the table, close enough so that Jim could smell the cherry cough drop on his breath. "We only have a few minutes, so what do you say you let me do the rest of the talking?"

Jim nodded his agreement.

"Good, now listen very carefully. There's another body, Mr. Hall. Number twenty. I haven't told the police, I haven't told my attorney, I haven't told anyone… until now."

His eyes widened. "What… what do you want me to do?"

"Tell Hector to inform the police that I will only reveal the details to you. No one else. If they allow us another meeting, I'll give you a name and a location."

"I'll tell him as soon as I leave here." He closed his notebook and placed the mini-recorder on top of it, double-checking to make sure it was still recording.

Billings reached his hand across the table and Jim surprised himself by shaking it. "I'll do my best to—"

"PHYSICAL CONTACT IS STRICTLY PROHIBITED," squawked the hidden loudspeaker.

Startled, Jim tried to jerk his hand back, but Billings held tight, pulling him closer. He could hear the door being flung open behind him. Billings' fingernails dug into his palm, and for one horrific moment, he thought the old man was going to kiss him. Instead, Billings leaned even closer and whispered, "His name is Ornias."

Then Jim's hand was free and one guard was pulling him toward the door while a second guard stood in front of a smiling Lester Billings.

"Wait… what did you say?" Jim called over his shoulder.

"His name is Ornias. Time to do some more homework, Mr. Hall."

Both men said their goodbyes to Hector Coltrane in the parking lot. The attorney had listened to Jim's story about a twentieth victim and immediately called someone on his cell phone. When he finished with the short conversation, the three men walked out of the prison together with plans to meet again the following afternoon.

Warwick climbed behind the wheel of his leased Audi. Jim got into the passenger seat. They closed their doors in perfect synchronicity and sat there in silence. Finally, Warwick looked over at Jim and said, "Jesus Christ. What happened in there?"

Jim shook his head and let out a breath. "I… I don't even know."

"You know what this means?" When Jim failed to answer right away, Warwick went on. "You could get a book deal out of this. Hell, a film deal isn't out of the question, depending on what happens next."

"My head is still spinning."

"I bet it is." Warwick started the car and pulled up to the security gate. "You okay? You look a little… odd."

"I'm fine. Just overwhelmed."

"You want to grab some dinner, do a little pre-game strategy before we meet with Hector tomorrow?"

"Thanks, but I think I'm just gonna go home and order delivery. I need to transcribe the tape." He patted his jacket pocket to make sure the mini-recorder was safe and sound.

"Good idea. Get that shit down on paper while it's still fresh." A uniformed guard waved them through the gate. Warwick flipped a pudgy hand in his direction and steered into traffic. "Think you can have something ready for Sunday's edition?"

"Of course I can. But let's wait and see what Hector has to say tomorrow."

"Another good idea." Warwick snapped his fingers. "Hey, you know who would love this story? Remember Carlos Vargas, the young guy we ran that article about last month? Turned a couple of food trucks into a successful chain of restaurants and then went to Hollywood and became a big-time producer? I bet he would…"

Jim stared out the passenger window at the blur of fast food joints and strip malls and zoned out the sound of Warwick's voice. His boss was excited, and when he got excited he didn't shut up. Not that Jim blamed the guy. He was pretty damn excited himself. But he was also a bit uneasy about the whole thing. It felt wrong somehow to benefit from a situation such as this. It felt *ghoulish.*

Jim glanced down at his right hand, rubbed a finger against the small abrasion on his palm where Billings had pressed his fingernail into him. There was a tiny streak of faded blood there. He wiped his hand on his pant leg with a shudder of disgust and looked out the window again.

Jim tossed the pizza crust back into the grease-stained box and returned his attention to his laptop screen. He'd transcribed the tape as soon as he'd walked through the door, even before he'd ordered a large pepperoni and a side salad from the Italian restaurant down the street. He knew there was software that would handle transcription, but he didn't trust it.

While he ate, he'd researched the mysterious name that Lester Billings had revealed at the end of their interview: *Ornias.*

Now, he read over the notes that he'd summarized into a separate document:

According to The Encyclopedia of Angels *by Rosemary Guiley, Ornias was a fallen angel, who along with many other demons, had been bound by King Solomon to build his temple. He was described as a very troublesome demon who inhabited the constellation Aquarius and enjoyed strangling people born under the sign of Aquarius. Ornias had various abilities attributed to him, including the gift of prophecy, body transference, shape-shifting, and causing physical pain with a mere touch. He was considered mischievous, almost impish (were it not for the hideous acts attributed to him), and he was also well known for playing games with his victims.*

Jim stared at the screen. An icicle of unease tickled the back of his neck as the words echoed inside his head:

Fourteen of Lester Billings' victims had been strangled to death.

It was soon discovered that the only common trait shared by all of Lester Billings' victims was the time of year they celebrated their birthdays. All nineteen were born between January 19 and February 18, falling under the eleventh astrological sign of Aquarius.

When the fever finally broke and Clarice nursed me back to my feet, I only had one thing on my mind, Mr. Hall, and it wasn't getting back to work at the office and it wasn't getting back to work in the bedroom. It was…

"Mischief."

He picked up a pen from the coffee table in front of him and wrote down eight words on a blank sheet of paper in his notebook: LESTER BILLINGS. THE OLD WELL. DEMON. POSSESSION. ORNIAS.

He started to close the notebook, then hesitated and scribbled a ninth word and underlined it: MISCHIEF.

Jim stared at the word for a moment, then left the notebook open on the coffee table and went upstairs to take a shower.

That night, he dreamed he was lost in the woods.

Bathed in moonlight from a cloudless night sky and staggering through a thicket of decaying trees, the bare branches clawing at his face, scratching his arms and hands. A thin branch reached out and slapped at his cheek, drawing blood. He could taste the warmth of it on his lips. He staggered out of the thicket into a small clearing and dropped to his knees, sobbing, chest heaving. A small cabin stood in the distance, the front windows flickering with the dim glow of a burning fire. A finger of gray smoke curled from the stone chimney.

Something in the basement of his brain warned him to stay away, to turn around and flee in the direction he had come from. But he was exhausted and ignored it.

He scrambled to his feet and set off toward the cabin. An owl hooted somewhere in the treetops and lit off, the sound of its flapping wings very loud in the shadowy silence. Startled, Jim slowed his pace and glanced around the clearing. The night was windless. Nothing else was moving. He started to turn around to resume his way to the cabin when he saw it. Tucked away in the far corner of the clearing: a stone well.

Without thinking, Jim changed direction and headed for the well. He broke into a fast jog. His heart was hammering. Something was drawing him there. In that moment, he realized what had been bothering him. He could've sworn he'd been here before. That he'd spent time here within this clearing and seen this cabin—and most definitely, this stone well—many times before. He just couldn't remember when.

He reached the well and rested both his hands on the rough stone, catching his breath. The opening yawned at him like a hungry, dark mouth. He leaned closer to peer deeper into the darkness—as a skeletal corpse hand reached up over the edge and latched onto his right hand.

He gasped in terror and tried to jerk it back, but the thing in the well wouldn't let go.

A nightmare face emerged. Black holes for eyes. Decaying flesh hanging on pale exposed skull. Maggots squirming from the dark, wet socket of a toothless mouth.

Jim screamed, but gagging quickly drowned out the scream, as the creature's foul stench flooded his nostrils. He tried again to yank his hand back, and this time, it worked. He broke the corpse's grip and went sprawling onto his back in the clearing—

He woke in his darkened bedroom, gasping for breath. He flung the sweat-soaked sheet off him and sat up in bed. Once his eyes adjusted, he glanced down at his right hand. The Band-Aid he'd put on earlier was missing. A trickle of fresh blood marked his palm.

Jim held the door open for an elderly couple and hurried inside the crowded Starbucks. The weather report had called for sunny skies and moderate temperatures, so of course it had started raining just before dawn. Distracted and still shaken from his nightmare, he had rushed out of his condo this morning without an umbrella. Now, a widening puddle spread on the floor at his feet while he waited in line for his daily cappuccino.

He paid the cashier, ignoring her dirty look (she must be in charge of cleaning the floor, he thought), and someone tapped him on the shoulder. He turned to find a beautiful blonde woman he'd never seen before. Dressed in a stylish business suit and heels, she was carrying a folded-up umbrella.

"Here," she said, holding out a stack of napkins. "I think you need these more than I do." She smiled and Jim stood there and couldn't think of a single clever thing to say.

"Thanks," he finally mumbled, taking the napkins. She smelled so good, it made his head spin. He wanted to ask her what perfume she was wearing; he wanted to ask her right then and there for her phone number. Instead, he mopped at his dripping face and neck with the napkins and tossed them into a nearby trashcan.

"I've seen you here before," she said. "You're a writer of some kind, right?"

Jim nodded, still in disbelief that she was talking to him. "I write news and features for the Sun paper."

Her eyebrows went up. "Impressive."

"You might not think that if you saw my paycheck." *Jesus*, he thought. *What a stupid thing to say.*

She laughed. "Wow, honest *and* humble. A rare combination these days."

"Must be because I'm a Sagittarius." *A Sagittarius? Where the hell did that come from?*

The blonde stuck out her hand. "I'm Terry, by the way. And I'm a Taurus. You know what they say about Tauruses."

Jim didn't have a clue what they said about Tauruses and didn't care. He shook her hand, feeling the warmth of her skin against the cut on his palm. "I'm… Jim. Nice to meet you."

As Jim Hall walked into the conference room at half past one, Warwick and Hector Coltrane were already seated and waiting for him.

"Sorry, I'm late," he said, taking a seat and placing his notebook and a manila file folder on the table in front of him. "Phone call went long."

Hector waved away the apology. Warwick took a sip from his coffee mug. "No worries," he said, "we had a lot to talk about."

"Have you heard from Rick yet?" Rick was the head of legal affairs for the Baltimore Sun. If he didn't sign off on a second meeting, there would be no article for this Sunday's newspaper.

"Spoke with him twice in the past hour," Warwick said, grinning like a schoolboy. "We're good to go."

"Excellent."

"I reviewed the notes you sent over," Hector said. "I'm impressed."

Jim shrugged. "I just asked the questions. Your client did all of the talking."

"Perhaps," Hector said, "but there was a reason Mr. Billings chose you. I didn't quite understand his decision initially. Now, I believe I do."

"Well, thank you," Jim said, and started rubbing at something on the table with his thumb.

"I'm waiting for a return call from a Detective Cavanaugh," Hector continued. "Evidently, he's the only detective still active that worked on the initial investigation."

"He's the one I'll be talking to?" Jim asked, and returned his attention to whatever he was trying to scrub off the table.

"I'm sure there will be plenty of others, but I figured he was a good place to start."

Warwick put down his notes and craned his neck to see what Jim was doing. *Had he spilled something on the table?* He noticed Jim was wearing a Band-Aid on his hand. *Was he bleeding?*

As if he could read his mind, Jim looked up at Warwick and smiled. He stopped rubbing his finger against the table. "Does it bother you that you were born under the sign of Aquarius, boss? With everything that's going on."

Warwick started to respond, but hesitated. *What an odd question to ask.* Warwick glanced at Hector and he could tell by the surprised look on the older man's face that he was thinking the same thing.

"Not really," Warwick finally answered, wondering why he'd never noticed before how green Jim's eyes were. The way the writer was staring at him, grinning, made Warwick very uncomfortable. He tried to cover it with a fake smile. "I stopped being afraid of the boogeyman a long time ago."

Hector laughed and opened his leather portfolio, ready to get down to business.

The odd grin slowly faded from Jim's face, but he continued to stare at his boss. Warwick looked away first and gazed down at his notes. Hector asked him a question about the Sunday edition deadline and he answered, then quickly looked back at his notes again.

It didn't matter. He could still feel Jim Hall's green eyes on him.

BUER

Buer, a great president of Hell, apparently has fifty legions of demons at his command. *The Lesser Key of Solomon the King* describes him as the tenth goetic spirit, appearing in Sagittarius: "That is his shape when ye [sun] is there; he teacheth Phylosophy [both] Morall & Natural, & ye Logicall arts, & ye virtue of all hearbes and plants, & healeth all distempers in Man." He is also known for giving good familiars. A nineteenth-century engraving designed by Louis Le Breton and engraved by M. Jarrault shows him as having the head of a lion and five goat legs, which is hard to reconcile with the claim that he appears as Sagittarius, whose form would presumably be that of a centaur.

Hunter Hunterson and the President of Hell

SCOTT SIGLER

Howdy.

The following pages will recap my family's battle against the President of Hell. But first, bear with me while I catch you up on a few things.

It's come to my attention that some jackass hacker sumbitch good-for-nothing spec of horseshit got his electronic mitts into my computer and released the chapters of my War Journal. This misbegotten miscreant released said chapters out of order, which means people are stumbling across my entries with no contextual wherewithal to figure out just what in tarnation is going on. Maybe you haven't read about The Case of the Haunted Safeway, or The $15 Burger, or even Homefront. If you have perused those lovely tales, hang in there, we'll get to the good stuff right quick. However, if you haven't read about my family and I, allow me to elucidate.

My name's Hunter Hunterson. This is my War Journal, where I document the various endeavors of my family business. What business, you may ask?

The business of monster stompin'.

We work for the Netherworld Protectorate, an organization committed to protecting humanity by way of fighting any and all evil supernatch. My family and I are good stock from the hills of Kentucky.

Huntersons been stompin' going back five generations. Up until a few months ago, we lived in Salyersville, KY, known to the locals as "Slayerville." That's where the biggest dimensional fault line is, you see, and hence the place most demons, vamps, zombies, ghosties, goblins and whatnot pour out and try to set up shop in the real world. My clan and other clans like us find the supernatch, then we stomp 'em, bag 'em, tag 'em and bring them in for a reward of cold hard cash. It's a dangerous living, sure, but it runs in our blood.

About six months back, the NP transferred my family from glorious red-state conservative Kentucky to San Francisco, America's bluest of blue bastion of liberalism. We had to replace the city's existing NP team, which got eaten. We're still not sure if it was a pissed-off Oni, a gun slinging goblin or, perhaps, the worst nightmare of any monster-stomper—a rabid unicorn.

Man, do I hate rabid unicorns.

My family's voted straight-ticked Republican since the days of Rutherford B. Hayes, so you can imagine how moving to San Francisco has been a bit of a culture shock for us.

Let me give you a quick rundown on my clan, then we'll get into the Case of the President of Hell.

First and foremost is Betty Lou, the love of my life. We've been crazy about each other since we were in the sixth grade. Married at eighteen. First child at twenty. We've never looked back—I was made for her, she was made for me.

Betty Lou is an empath. She can read emotions and whatnot. She's also got a knack for magical potions and carries around a big old bag of charmed-up costume jewelry. She's a bit too sensitive for this line of work, but she balances me out—from time to time, people might describe me as "too intense," which is a really nice way of saying I'm a toned-up sonofabitch that would rather knock out a vamp's teeth than have a chat about whether or not it's right to bite some poor bastard's neck. In short, I punch first, talk second, and sometimes that ain't the best policy.

I have three sons. My eldest, Billy Mac, is a lazy piece of shit that sits in the basement all day and plays video games. Boy gives me the willies. Spiders seem to like him. He's opted out of the family business, so I don't talk about him—or to him—all that much.

My youngest son, Luke, is fourteen. He's whip-smart with computers and such. He ain't the biggest or strongest boy in the world, mind you, so we tend to keep him out of the most dangerous bits of the business. That angers him to no end. Boy has a temper. In that way, he's just like his daddy.

My middle son, Bo, he's adopted. If you ever see us together, you might figure that one out all on your own. I'm a good-sized man, 6-foot-2, about 290 if I haven't been to Golden Corral too many times that week. Bo, he's from different stock—6-foot-3, 275 pounds. And he's only sixteen, for cryin' out loud. Oh, and here's another subtle hint: I'm white and he's black. Sometimes that gives it away.

Lastly, there's Sunshine, the apple of my eye. Think your life is hard? Try being the daddy of thirteen-year-old jailbait that looks 18, easy, the kind of girl every hetero male this side of the Mississippi wants to get a piece of. Hell, monsters will probably never have a chance to kill me—I'll be in jail for murdering some horny boy who tried to take advantage of her. Of course, I highly doubt any boy could make her do anything she didn't have a hankering for, on account of she's a dead shot with a bow and carries a charmed-up switch blade in the pocket of whatever scrap of fabric she calls "shorts."

That's my clan. We live together, we fight together. There's a lot of love in our family.

And as a family, we had us a rather nasty run-in with a president. No, not the President of the United States—we locked horns with the literal President of Hell.

Here's what happened.

I'll never get used to living in a mansion.

Take our dining room, for example. It's got more square footage than our entire house back in Slayerville. That's right, just the dining room—I've measured it. And you could comfortably sit thirty people at this ridiculously long-ass table.

My family and I clustered at one end of the table: me, Betty Lou, Bo, Luke and Sunshine. Billy Mac sat at the far end, on account he hadn't showered in a few days. Betty Lou was happy just to have him out of the basement and joining us for once.

Everyone but Billy Mac was dead tired. While he stayed in the basement, getting plenty of sleep, the rest of us had been burning the midnight oil dealing with a recent spike of supernatch appearances.

In the last three days alone, we'd bagged a valravn, an orang minyak and a kasa-obake. The latter one was a real bitch. Thinking about it made me touch the big bandage on my left forearm. If you'd have told me that a one-eyed umbrella hopping around on one leg could be tougher to bring down than a pack of coked-up goblins, I'd have told you that you were crazy. Live and learn, I suppose.

We'd all gotten only a few hours of sleep, but Betty Lou made all of us come down to breakfast. Luke and Sunshine had to go to school. Bo and I could have slept in, but my wife wasn't having it—when you got no idea what each night will bring, breakfast is often the only meal the family can enjoy together.

The spike in activity had to be from a new dimensional fault line. Something in the San Francisco area had cracked open, creating a fissure between realities. Bad juju was coming out. The longer a fault exists, the bigger it gets. If this new one got too big, it couldn't be closed, and we'd be faced with another Slayerville situation—except this fault would be dead smack in a city of 750,000. Hence, the NP had us working overtime. Not that I minded the time-and-a-half, but we'd made no progress in tracking down the source. Neither had the rest of the NP.

The valravn had whacked me pretty good. It had also broken Bo's arm, but Betty Lou had fixed him up right with an old-school bone-mending spell. My son looked no worse for the wear. Ah, the energy of youth. Me? I felt like the losing end of a mule-kick, and I looked as battered as a red-headed stepchild.

Betty Lou had made plenty of food: platters of scrambled eggs, toast, grits and loads of ham. Sure, vegetarians might rule San Francisco, but none of 'em live in my house.

The platters were all closest to my son Bo. Maybe that's on account of his size—gravitational pull of large bodies and all. I don't know me much physics, but if a wayward satellite was drawn into my son's orbit, I wouldn't be at all surprised.

Bo doesn't talk much at breakfast, mostly on account of how much food he's shoveling into his maw. My son Luke ain't much better. Don't know where Luke puts all the food he eats. Fourteen years old, barely a hundred pounds, yet he can wolf down a large pizza all by himself. I should have him checked for a tapeworm one of these days. There ain't no lack of conversation at our table, though, on account of the chattiness of my wife and daughter.

"Then there's Samuel Carter," Sunshine said. "He's in my math class. He's so cute, he has eyes just like the Beib's!"

I'm not sure what's more disconcerting to a country music-loving father—the fact that his daughter is starting to moon over boys, one of whom will someday take her away from me, or that she actually listens to Justin Bieber.

Betty Lou frowned as she scooped more eggs onto Bo's plate.

"What about this Samuel Carter's grades?" she asked. "Appearances aren't everything. Just look at your father."

I grunted. "If that's a compliment, I'd hate to hear your insults."

Betty Lou waved her hand at me the way she always did when I said something stupid.

"Hush, Hunter. You ain't no supermodel, but you're the best husband a woman could ever ask for. What do you think about that, Sunshine?"

My daughter rolled her eyes in the way only thirteen-year-old girls know how to do.

"Ma, I don't want to marry Samuel. Dang."

Luke grinned, spoke through a mouthful of eggs.

"Sixteen and pregnant is a good show," he said. "You're way ahead of schedule."

Bo choked on his milk, which started coming out of his nose even as Sunshine whipped a piece of toast at Luke, and—true to form—hit him right between the eyes, smearing butter on his face.

Betty Lou slapped the table, making all the kids jump. I jumped, too—an angry Betty Lou is not to be taken lightly.

"Sunshine," she said, "you don't throw food like some white trash idiot! Luke, jokes about teenage pregnancy ain't funny, especially when your sister's involved! And Bo, you stop that milk from coming out your nose, right this instant!"

I sat very still. I wasn't about to defend the kids and draw Betty Lou's wrath on myself. I might stomp monsters for a living, but I ain't stupid.

Then, my boss came strolling into the dining room.

"Good morning, Hunterson family," he said. "I hope you're all enjoying this lovely, lovely morning."

Yngve Sjoelset is his name. I can spell it, can't pronounce it to save my ass. I just call him Ing. He'd grown a mustache since last time I'd seen him. A pencil-thin thing, jet black like the hair he must spend hours getting just-so. With his button-down white shirt and yet another of his horrible argyle sweater-vests, he's not exactly the kind of guy I'd typically hang out with. But he's a decent fella, as far as bosses go.

Except for the fact that he was in my dining room, and no one had opened the front door for him.

"Morning, Ing," I said. "How'd you get in?"

He smiled. "The Netherworld Protectorate owns this house. We have keys."

That wasn't going to cut it with me.

"Mister, my wife and daughter live here," I said. "I can't allow someone to just come strolling in anytime they like."

"Hey," Luke said, pretending I'd hurt his feelings, "what about Bo and I? Don't we need protecting? Only protecting the women-folk is sexist, Pa. We learned about the patriarchy in school."

That damn boy and his smart mouth. I gave him a warning glance.

"Luke, you'd best not step into something you can't finish. Because I'll finish it right here with everyone watching."

The smile faded from his face. "Sorry, Pa."

I kept my eyes on him until he looked down, then I turned my attention to my boss.

"Ing, I want them keys."

"I'm hardly going to harm your family, Hunter."

"Probably not. But if you got the keys, that means someone else can take them from you." I held out my hand. "Give 'em up."

"I came to talk about an urgent matter," Yngve said. "We can discuss the keys later."

I curled my fingers inward. "Give 'em up or turn your ass around and walk out, then you can handle your urgent matter your own damn self."

Yngve sighed. "And here I'd heard so much about southern hospitality."

"Back home we call what you did trespassing," I said. "Want to find out how we handle that down south?"

"I most certainly do not."

He handed me the keys.

I'd lost my temper a bit. Not that it wasn't justified—I don't think you'd like it much if the middle-aged man your daughter moons over had a set of keys to your house and could stroll in anytime he liked—

but I dialed my anger back down.

"Thanks," I said. "I assume you're bringing word about the new fault? Y'all find it yet?"

Yngve started to answer, but Betty Lou spoke first.

"Speaking of southern hospitality, Mister Sjoelset, would you like to join us for breakfast? We have plenty."

Ing flashed a smile that seemed well-practiced.

"I've already eaten, thank you. But I'll sit with you and tell you what we're facing."

Sunshine stood up, all doe-eyed and eager.

"How about some coffee, Mister Sjoelset?"

She pronounced it perfectly. I've always said my kids are smarter than I am, they just don't know as much as I do. Yet.

"Thank you, Sunshine," Yngve said. He smiled at her in a way I wish he wouldn't. "That would be delightful."

Sunshine scurried off to the kitchen. Betty Lou and I shared a glance, the unspoken communication of parents—we'd both keep an eye on Yngve when Sunshine was around. Just in case.

He sat next to Luke, which put him across the table from me.

"So, that fault," I said. "Your people find it yet?"

Fault lines are tears between planes of existence. They allow some supernatch to enter the physical plane. The Slayerville fault is the biggest in the world, with so many fissures and facets we can't even find them all. We don't know how faults start, but once they come into existence, they grow. If you find them early enough, you can close them with a simple spell. Betty Lou's done that at least a dozen times. If you don't find them early enough, though, if they get too big, then you can't close them at all.

"I'm afraid we've found nothing," Yngve said.

Not the news I'd wanted to hear.

"Charting sightings and appearances of paranormal activity indicates the fault is in San Francisco proper," he said. "That helps, but it is still a large area."

"Forty-six point-nine square miles," Luke said.

Yngve smiled at him. "Very good, young man."

Luke grinned. Sunshine wasn't the only one who enjoyed being on Yngve's good side.

"We think it's been open for a year or more," Yngve said. "Only in the last few months has it opened wide enough for the non-living to come through."

"Well, last night, we were up late fighting a psychopathic, one-legged umbrella," I said. "The bigger the fault gets, the badder the things what come out of it."

Yngve nodded solemnly.

"We're doing the best we can," he said. "We have to narrow down the search, somehow. But that's not why I'm here. We have a situation—there is evidence that a group is trying to influence the election of the President of the United States."

"Gotta be those commie reds," Betty Lou said. "It's the Russians, isn't it? We should have whooped Putin's ass a long time ago if you ask me."

Yngve shook his head. "I wish. It's not the Russians who are trying to influence the election—it's Hell. In particular, a demon named Buer."

The name meant nothing to me, but Luke perked up, a forkful of ham almost to his mouth.

"Buer? The President of Hell?"

"One of them," Yngve said.

I looked from my boss to my son.

"There's more than one president of Hell?"

"Twelve," Luke said, instantly. "Depending on how you count."

Sometimes—most times, even—I appreciated the fact that my youngest son was smarter than I was. Other times, I found his knowledge a little annoying, particularly when my lack of knowledge made me feel like a dummy.

"How can there be twelve presidents of Hell?" I asked.

Luke had forgotten his forkful of ham. The pinkish meat bounced in time with his excited motions.

"Pa, there's 196 countries in the world right now, each one with its own leader. Around 150 billion people have died on this planet, in total. If even ten percent of them went to Hell, we're talking fifteen billion souls in Hell. So, if there's almost two hundred nations in a world with seven billion living souls, seems to make sense Hell might have room for more than one president."

My son's estimate that a mere ten percent of people went to Hell was the kind of optimism only the youth can show.

"All right, I get it," I said. "So this Buer was elected? Didn't know Hell was a democracy."

"It's not," Yngve said. "We don't know much about it, but it's safe to say Hell's leaders aren't chosen by popular vote. Lakes of fire aren't a good way to motivate a constituency."

Luke waved his hand at me in a gesture that was annoyingly akin to his mother. "You don't understand the hierarchy of Hell, Pa. Presidents are way down the list, lower in rank than counts. Lower than knights, even. Being a president of Hell is a big deal overall, but not relatively speaking."

My son, weighing the relative merits of Hell's hierarchy. Not the kind of thing you find in your typical parenting book, now is it?

"So this Beer ain't dangerous," I said. "Do I have that right?"

"Buer, not beer," Luke said. "He's plenty dangerous. He controls fifty legions of lesser demons." Luke looked at the ham on his fork, seemed surprised to see it there, then ate it, chewing around a big smile.

I glanced at Yngve.

"Fifty legions?"

"About five thousand demon soldiers per legion," Yngve said.

I did the math. "So this Buer controls a quarter of a million demons. Yeah, I'd say that's a bit of a problem. If Buer is in San Francisco, could his legions come through that new fault?"

"Not without permission," Luke said. "Buer is a major demon. His legions are lesser demons. Lesser demons need two things to enter the physical plane, Pa—a fault line and permission from the land owner the fault line is on. Good thing, too, otherwise we'd always be dick-deep in demons."

I winced at my son's cursing. Not because it bothered me, so much, but because I knew how mad it made Betty Lou.

She glared at our youngest son. With her finger and thumb, she made the "OK" symbol, then flicked her finger forward. Ten feet away from her, Luke winced and clutched at his ear.

"Ow! Ma!"

"Watch your mouth at my table," she said.

I was grateful my own mother hadn't been a spell caster, or I might have suffered plenty of mystical ear flicks. Sunshine came out of the kitchen carrying a platter with two porcelain cups on it. She'd broken out the fine china for our guest. She set the platter down and placed the first cup in front of Yngve.

"Here you are, Mister Sjoelset."

He took the cup, smiled at her.

"Thank you, my dear."

I saw her eyes widen and her shoulders sag, just a little—she liked it when he called her my dear.

She picked up the other cup and raised it to her mouth.

"No you don't," Betty Lou said. "Since when do you drink coffee?"

Sunshine frowned. "Mom, I'm not a little girl anymore."

Betty Lou folded her arms.

"You're thirteen," she said. "No coffee until you're eighteen. I've read it's bad for you."

Sunshine stared, brought the cup to her lips. Betty Lou made the "OK" symbol. Sunshine put her cup down so fast a bit of coffee spilled out onto the platter.

"I ain't drinking it," she said. "Just because you see something on the Internet doesn't mean it's true, Ma."

With that, Sunshine dropped heavily into her chair, arms crossed, frown still on her face—at that moment, she looked just like her mother.

Yngve defused the awkward situation; he took a sip of coffee, paused, looked at the cup, then smiled at Sunshine and raised his cup slightly. Didn't matter that she hadn't made the coffee, she blushed so bright I thought her head might pop.

"If we're done with this morning melodrama," I said, "can we get back to business?"

Yngve took another sip, then continued.

"Your son has the general idea," Yngve said. "Buer's legions can't come to the material plane unless they have permission from the owner of the land they wish to occupy. It's one of the reasons why demons and their ilk spend so much time trying to trick people. This isn't the first time Buer, or other demons, have tried to trick a leader, but until now, even the worst leaders have been too smart to be duped."

My heart sank. "Enter the current candidate."

Yngve nodded. "Exactly."

Now Yngve's sudden visit made more sense. The candidate in question was holding a political rally in San Francisco that very night. Yngve ain't the type to do dangerous field work—the Huntersons are.

"I was wondering how that man won the nomination," Betty Lou said. "Considering the horrible things he said about women."

"We think Buer helped him," Yngve said. "But we don't know why.

I need you to go to the rally tonight at the Moscone Center. If Buer appears, find out what's going on. We need to know before the general election."

I supposed I should have known that big city brought big problems. We didn't have it easy in Slayerville, not by any stretch, but we never faced a president of Hell trying to influence an election.

"Pa," Luke said, "wanna see a picture of Buer?"

He glanced at Betty Lou instead of waiting for an answer from me. The no computers or cell phones at the dining table rule was hers, not mine.

She sighed. "Go get your laptop."

Luke shot out of the chair.

"Let me get this straight," I said to Yngve. "This Buer, and probably his guards and whatnot, might be at the rally tonight? Won't people see them?"

"Buer is a powerful illusionist," my boss said. "He can easily hide his minions in plain sight. You'll need some proper optics to see him. Betty Lou, I'm guessing you can handle that part?"

She nodded. "I sure can."

Luke came tearing into the dining room, laptop in hand.

"Here he is, Pa!"

He set the computer in front of me. Not a photo—most demons don't register on cameras or video—but rather the thick and thin black lines of an etching. For a moment, I thought the picture was a joke, but I know my son well enough to know he wouldn't be this excited over a gag.

"That's him? That's the President of Hell?"

Luke nodded. "Crazy looking, ain't he?"

Bo and Sunshine came around the table to look over my shoulders at the image.

"He sure is ugly, Pa," Bo said. "That a lion's head? And horse legs?"

"Goat legs," Luke corrected. "And yeah, that's a lion's head."

Bo grunted, impressed. "I bet he'd be a great soccer player."

"He ain't even got no arms," Sunshine said. "Just... hooves."

Buer, high-ranking officer of Hell, was indeed a lion's head with five goat legs radiating out from behind a thick mane, like a five-finned pinwheel.

"Bo, Luke, Sunshine, clear the table," Betty Lou said. "Breakfast is over."

Bo and Luke immediately did as they were told. They're smart enough to be terrified of their mother; Sunshine is not. She sighed heavily, picked up one dish as if it was the heaviest thing in all the world. Betty Lou glared at her. The conflict between mothers and daughters is something I'll never understand.

I closed the laptop. "Anything else we need to know, Ing?"

He took another sip before answering.

"I'm afraid you know everything we know at this point. I have people at the Protectorate looking for more info. You'll get whatever we find as soon as we find it."

I nodded toward the front door.

"Then you'd best be going," I said. "And next time you come to visit? You knock."

For once, Luke didn't have to stay in the car. That boy is delicate, I tell you. Reminds me of a dried-up stalk of corn in a draught, swaying with the slightest breeze. He's not made for the physical altercations that are part and parcel of the family business. While that digs at his daddy's heart—I ain't proud of my feelings about his weakness, but I won't lie about them, either—the boy has brains to spare. Bringing him into the Moscone Center with Betty Lou and I was the smart choice.

And boy-howdy, was Luke excited.

I haven't traveled all that much. There was plenty to do back home in Slayerville. Important work. My idea of "traveling for a vacation" meant driving a hundred miles for a weekend in Lexington with Betty Lou. As such, there are still things I see in San Francisco that blow my mind. You could easily fit the entire downtown of Slayerville into the Moscone Center and have plenty of room to spare. Moscone, a wide-open space of glass and metal, criss-crossed escalators, and plenty of people.

Like I said, I haven't traveled much, ain't paid much attention to elections, either. I've missed the last two presidential campaigns. I always mean to vote, but eight years ago I was staking out a master vamp. Four years ago, I was laid up thanks to a venom splash from a giant spider.

Voting's important, I know. But some things can be more important than voting.

Betty Lou, Luke and I stood in line with a lot of people who were very excited to get inside and join the event. A lot of white people. As for minorities, there weren't many among the attendees, but there were plenty of them among the throngs protesting the event. And a lot of people wearing masks. A lot of people waving Mexican flags. A lot of people screaming at us.

Turns out that by standing in line for a political event, I was: a) a racist, b) a sexist, c) a white supremacist, d) a fascist, e) a misogynist, f) a Nazi (in case "racist" and "white supremacist" didn't already cover that), g) stupid, and h) every possible variation of the word "fucker" you could conceive of.

Me, a white supremacist—I guess I brought the wrong son.

Although, to be honest, while I never gave any truck to that Nazi/supremacist bullshit, I admit I was pretty damn racist in my younger days—I just didn't know it then. I wasn't exactly fond of black people. My God-given right to think as I wanted to think, right? Imagine the change in my perspective when a black man saved my life and lost his own in the process. I remember his guts spilling out all over the place, his hand gripping mine, him begging me to take care of his infant son. Spoiler alert: that young son was named "Bo."

That changed me. Forever.

So now I go out of my way to evaluate people one at time, evaluate them on their own merits and actions. I don't presume to judge entire groups of people I've never talked to. Unlike these howling protestors, who seemed to consider themselves as judge, jury, and—if some of them had their way—executioners. The people screaming hate at us were saying that we were the ones propagating hate. It was goddamn strange, I tell you.

The cops were out in full force. Body armor, shields, masked helmets. Crowds pushing at them. Some protestors went too far in their effort to get at people attending the event, wound up pushing back at the cops. A bad choice; the pushers wound up on the ground beneath a pile of big, uniformed bodies.

Garbage, rotten eggs, water balloons… anything people could get their hands on became a missile. Red ball caps seemed to be a prize trophy—I saw them snatched off people's heads, waved about in triumph, doused with lighter fluid and burned in the street.

No one tried to take my hat. It was just a John Deere cap, sure, but also bullies tend to avoid those that seem likely to whip their ass.

We even saw attendees being attacked, chased, beaten. The cops didn't do shit about that, as if they were afraid to break formation and incur the wrath of the mob.

Insanity.

Betty Lou watched the madness, scowling.

"These protestor folks think they're all righteous and brave," she said, quietly, so as not to strike up a conversation with the people around us. "They can't see how this will play on the news? Imagine our friends back home, Hunter, the ones who ain't sure how they'll vote. Imagine them watching this, watching people attack those exercising their right to assemble. These protester thugs have no idea their actions will make more people vote for that asshole."

Luke shook his head. "No, Ma. These people are marginalized. They have to do something to express their emotions. We're learning about that in school."

"Enough politics," I said, quietly but firmly. "Let's all keep our eyes open in case this violence engulfs us, too."

The last thing I needed at that moment was my red-state Generation X wife in a heated debate with my Millennial son who was being educated in an ultra-liberal school district.

Fortunately, the line moved along and we didn't have any direct altercations with the massed protestors, most of whom, it seemed, weren't that much older than Luke.

The Netherworld Protectorate has some serious connections. Our passes got us floor seats, off to the right side of the main stage. We were surrounded by lots of bigwigs with suits, red ties and red ball caps, women in red dresses, people waving American flags and flapping campaign signs that were being handed out when we walked through the door.

The place was packed. Thousands of people. I'm not sure if many of them were drunk or just acting like it, caught up in the moment. These attendees were just regular folks, probably unaware of the evil in their midst.

I listened in on the conversations around me. People were mad about high taxes, about healthcare, about illegal immigrants taking away jobs, about illegal immigrants getting "free stuff," about welfare, and—most of all—about the "goddamn liberals ruining this country."

There was hate outside the convention center, sure, but plenty of hate inside as well—particularly hate against the Democratic candidate. I heard more about "emails" and the "cultural elites" in passing than I cared to, I'll tell you that one for free.

Overall, these people were just as mad as the protestors outside. It's not that I didn't get why. Since moving to San Francisco, I've been more exposed to some of the blowback against white people. Everywhere you turn, it seems, the media is telling you you're a horrible person just because of the color of your skin, or your sexual identification. Until we moved here, I wasn't aware that the "Cis-Het Straight White Men" were responsible for all the world's evils. Judging someone on their skin color and genitalia is supposed to be a bad thing, ain't it?

You can only tell people they are awful, evil and stupid for so long before they embrace those things as badges of honor. We've seen that time and time again with the various immigrant ethnicities that moved here looking for something better, and those whose ancestors were brought here against their will.

To be honest, it's been frustrating to watch. My pappy had a phrase he taught us to live by. A variation on the Golden Rule, I suppose, but it was quite simple: if it's wrong for me to do it to you, it's wrong for you to do it to me.

In other words, if you keep telling people they're evil because they don't think like you do, don't be surprised if they make choices just to spite you—whether that choice is good for them or not. That's the way I view it.

We reached our seats. We'd missed most of the speakers—the candidate himself was due up next. You could feel the energy in the room. It was like being in church, except instead of waiting for the pastor to begin you were waiting for Jesus himself to show up and start passing out blessings.

I'm guessing the Democratic National Convention was the same way, but still… kind of chilling.

"Pa," Luke said, "I still don't see any demons."

Betty Lou flicked his ear, a lightning-fast, well-practiced move.

"Ow!" Luke glared at her. "What was that for?"

"We told you to keep quiet about those things," she said through clenched teeth and a fake smile. "There are people all around us."

Luke rubbed at his ear. "Sorry, I forgot. But still, shouldn't we see something?"

Betty Lou dug in her oversized purse.

"I charmed up some sunglasses for us. We should be able to see Buer and any cronies of his even if they're invisible to everyone else."

"Like in that movie," I said. "The one with Rowdy Roddy Piper."

Luke's face wrinkled. "Who?"

Betty Lou shook her head as she clawed past costume jewelry, hair brushes, makeup, compacts, tissues and the seventeen hundred mysterious things women keep in their bags.

"Hunter, we've been neglecting this boy's proper education," she said. "He's never seen *They Live*?"

"Movie night," I said. "For that movie, I bet we can even get our lazy-ass eldest son out of the basement."

She found a pair of small black sunglasses, gave them to Luke.

"Your eldest son has a name," Betty Lou said. "It's Billy Mac. I didn't spend thirty-six hours in labor so you could refer to your seed as lazy-ass."

Luke put his sunglasses on. They were just a bit too big for his skinny face, but they looked good on him.

Betty Lou handed me a pair of sunglasses. I stared at them.

"You got to be kidding me," I said.

She sighed. "Hunter, don't be a baby. Put them on."

I held them up for her to see, as if she hadn't just handed them to me.

"You want me to wear these?"

Each blue-tinted lens was round and half the size of my face. The cheap plastic felt like it might snap if I moved too quickly. Worst of all, the frames were pink.

"It's all I had," Betty Lou said. "I didn't have time to go shopping for Ray Ben's or anything, now did I?"

"Ray-Bans," Luke corrected.

I looked at the frames, as if by doing so they might change into something more palatable.

"But these are for women," I said.

Luke laughed. "Come on, Pa, you were the best man at a gay ghost's wedding and you're still not comfortable with your masculinity?"

"Keep flapping your gums, son," I said, "and I'll show you masculinity."

Luke laughed harder, shook his head. "That sounds a lot different than you mean it to, Pa. Especially when you're wearing pink sunglasses."

Betty Lou hit him with another lightning-strike ear flick.

"Ow... Ma!"

"Don't disrespect your father," she said. Then she turned to me. "The boy needs an attitude adjustment, but he's right, Hunter—I thought you'd learned something at that wedding."

My wife and son had a point. The Case of the Haunted Safeway had ended with a lovely ceremony, held in Aisle 6: Chips, Salsa and Ethnic Foods. I'd been best man to a tortured soul who had been murdered because he loved a man so deeply he refused to leave him, despite losing a fortune because of it, despite threats of violence.

Well, fine. Maybe pink sunglasses didn't make me gay, but man, did they sure make me feel like an idiot.

I put them on, took in the crowd. Betty Lou's charms stripped away illusions—I saw a half-dozen demons in the crowd, hooting and hollering just like everyone else. Most of the security guys were demons, too. Black suits and white shirts hid their bodies, but not their faces. What a horror show.

One of the security demons was off to my right, at the end of our aisle. He looked like a lizard had caught flesh-eating bacteria then been dipped in boiling oil and rolled in gravel. He looked my way. I glanced off, watching him out of the corner of my eye. Was he looking at me? No, he was scanning the audience, looking for potential problems. He reached a nasty hand to a nasty ear, nodded. When he lowered his hand, I saw the earpiece wedged into his pointed ear.

The crowd's excitement picked up. Some stuffed shirt approached the podium. On the video screens behind him, he looked a hundred feet tall. He revved up the crowd with an introduction, an introduction that finished with "here is the next President of the United States of America!"

The crowd roared. When the candidate stepped to the podium, the roar intensified.

And right behind him—the stupidest-looking demon I've ever seen.

"Damn," Luke said. "Buer really is that ugly."

He was at that. A sneering lion's head with piercing, intelligent eyes, eyes that soaked up the crowd's energy. And its body? Not sure it had one—sprouting from the mane were five goat legs: dirty white fur, cloven hooves and all.

I was looking at the President of Hell. Well, a president of Hell, anyway.

Buer smiled his lion's smile, raised two of his goat-feet-whatever-the-fuck-they-were, and waved them.

Simultaneously, the candidate smiled. The candidate raised his arms. The candidate waved.

"Shit balls," Luke said. "Buer's controlling him like a puppet."

Betty Lou and I didn't even bother correcting Luke's language.

The crowd ate it all up. This was what they had come to see, their guy, the man who would change things, who wasn't beholden to the "political machine" that had run the country for so long. The very idea of it made me realize just how gullible people could be—a man who'd been made rich by the establishment was going to fight to stop the establishment from making people rich?

Believe that, and I've got a bridge to sell you.

The candidate lowered his hands, held the edges of the podium. The crowd quieted just enough for him to open his speech.

"Friends and fellow Americans, we are going to set things right."

The crowd roared. I felt like I was at a football game and the home team had just scored the winning touchdown. People leaned toward him, eyes wide, ears eager to drink in everything he had to say.

Off to my right, I saw a security demon at the end of our aisle. He had one of those secret service earpieces in his nasty, pointy ear.

To my left I saw two more, one wearing cop sunglasses. Just standing in the crowd. Had we been spotted?

The candidate continued, his voice booming through the hall.

"Americans watching this address tonight have seen the recent images of violence in our streets and the chaos in our communities. Many have witnessed this violence personally, some have even been its victims."

Like that guy had any idea what it was like to face real violence. The rich almost never know what many of America's poor see on an almost daily basis. But he was telling the crowd what they wanted to hear—there was going to be a new sheriff in town, and a hanging judge, and those two were one and the same.

"I have a message for all of you," the candidate said. "The crime and violence that today afflicts our nation will soon come to an end. Beginning on January 20th 2017, safety will be restored."

I glanced back at the demon on my right—he was staring directly at me.

We'd been made.

The demon started sliding through the crowd toward us.

I tugged on Betty Lou's hand.

"We need to leave," I said. "Now."

Luke slapped my shoulder.

"Uh, Pa, I think we're in trouble."

I followed my son's gaze—the two security demons to our left were working their way toward us.

And, from in front of us, two more.

"Follow me," I said, "stay close."

But when I turned to leave, there were two demons—big fuckers—standing right behind us. They looked like warped lobsters wearing white shirts and black suit coats.

I hesitated, for just a moment, and in that moment they all closed in.

We were surrounded.

"Pa, can we fight our way out?"

The demon with the cop sunglasses shook his head.

"I wouldn't recommend that," he said. "Buer is aware of your presence. He would like a word. Would you follow me backstage, please?"

"We ain't going nowhere," I said.

Cop Shades stared at me. "I assure you, he only wants to talk."

I sneered. "Right. And I should either take a demon—you—at his word, or believe the President of Hell? We all know that politicians always tell the truth, right?"

Cop Shades smiled, revealing pointy teeth, several of which were broken and jagged.

"Come with us now, or we'll kill you where you stand and say you were Muslims trying to assassinate the candidate. This crowd would love to believe that's true. I think that's the better choice and it would get us more votes, but Buer calls the shots."

I quickly scanned the demons surrounding us, seeing if one or two looked weak, if we could punch a hole through their circle and make a run for it. Individually, I was sure we could whoop any of their nasty asses, but there were six of them and three of us. Betty Lou could handle herself, but Luke ain't much of a scrapper.

If I'd have brought Bo, we'd have mopped the floor with them. But I hadn't brought Bo.

No way I was going to take my wife and son somewhere these demon assholes could do away with us quickly and quietly. We were going to have to fight our way out of it. Maybe I could drop two of them fast, make enough room for Betty Lou and Luke to make a break for it.

I slid a hand into my pants pocket, let my fingers slip through the loops of Old Glory—silver knuckles that Betty Lou had charmed up good and proper. Best anniversary present she ever got me.

From behind, a big, lobstery hand rested on my shoulder.

"Bring those mitts out where we can see them," Cop Shades said. "If I see anything but skin, I'll start with the boy."

Luke's eyes widened.

Outnumbered or not, we had to make our move. I breathed in, gathering myself for the moment—an instant before I turned to strike, Betty Lou gripped my forearm, stilling me.

"If you mean no harm," Betty Lou said to Cop Shades, "then you won't object to a binding spell. Right?"

Cop Shades said nothing. Betty Lou must have taken that silence as a yes.

She reached into her purse, fished around through the sea of mysteries therein, until she pulled out a jeweled pin—a garish peacock of some kind.

"Tacky," Cop Shades said.

Betty Lou nodded. "But powerful. If we come with you, you will be bound to keep us safe from all harm, caused by you or by others—including Buer. As Buer's emissary, you agree that this binds him as well. We don't harm him and his, you don't harm me and mine."

Cop Shades glanced around at the crowd. Perhaps he was debating if he could make good on his threats of instant martyrdom.

Maybe he thought better of it, because he smiled at Betty Lou.

"Of course," he said. "I agree."

Betty flipped open the brooch's clasp, jabbed the pin into her palm. The garishly colored fake gemstones flared and pulsed with magical energy.

She held her bleeding palm toward Cop Shades.

"Swear on blood," she said.

Cop Shades could lie out his mouth all day, but blood binds. Even in the hands of an amateur, blood magic has power. When wielded by a master like my wife? Shit is damn near bulletproof.

The demon held out his disgusting hand. His long talons reflected the overhead lights. Betty Lou's blood was still on the pin when she poked it into the demon's wrinkly palm. The bit of costume jewelry glowed bright, then evaporated in a puff of sparkly magic.

"You are bound by your word," she said. "Lead the way."

I have to make a confession—I've spent my life dealing with the dark arts, yet I don't know a whole lot about how most magic works. When it comes to stompin' the supernatch, you might say I'm a size-fourteen steel-toed boot with cow shit and gravel jammed up in the treads. Betty Lou? She's more like a pair of pumps with lethal stiletto heels. I'm blunt trauma—my wife is delicate surgery.

"Follow me," Cop Shades said, and he walked through the crowd.

I didn't know if Betty Lou had enough power to bind these demons, and therefore Buer as well, but I did what I'd done since the day we met—I trusted her.

Luke, Betty Lou and I followed Cop Shades, demons flanking us on either side, and the two big lobster fuckers bringing up the rear.

The demon parade led us away from the crowd, into the back hallways of Moscone. Rolling racks for food, coffee, cleaning carts, random bits of machinery under repair… the unseen lifeblood pumping through the convention center's arteries.

We were led to a door that had two huge demons standing to either side of it. They wore suits and white shirts, just like the rest. One of them had a face that made me wonder if a walrus and cockroach could do the nasty and kick out some big-ass kids. The other had a disturbing resemblance to a young Clint Eastwood, if Clint had been made of green-tinted SPAM.

Walrus-Roach opened the door. We followed Cop Shades inside.

A green room of some kind, meant for stars or convention presenters to rest before their time on stage. Three more black-suited demons were already inside, but the demon standing dead center in the room caught and held my attention.

Buer.

My pink sunglasses hadn't played tricks on me—he was, indeed, a lion's head with five goat legs sticking out of it. He smelled like a goat—unpleasant, yet it reminded me of our place back in Slayerville.

"I presume you're from the Protectorate," Buer said. "You seem to have taken your redneck costume to great lengths. You look like his ideal voter."

"And you look like the aborted fetus of a sunflower that grudge-fucked some roadkill," I said. "That or a drunken swastika."

I like to get my feelings out in the open. I'm diplomatic that way.

Buer's cat eyes flicked across me and mine like we were insects destined for a pushpin and a curio frame. His lion nose sniffed at the air, then the eyes narrowed with annoyance. Or maybe it was hunger, I really wasn't sure.

"How fortunate for you that my underling agreed to a binding spell," he said. He glared at Cop Shades. "Something I will discuss with him later, in private."

The sunglasses blocked Cop Shades' eyes, but from the way his posture sagged I knew that the discussion wasn't exactly going to involve a six pack and thoughts on the College Football Playoffs.

Buer moved. He didn't walk, he rolled—yes, rolled, pinwheeling on smelly goat legs—to Betty Lou's purse, which had been set on a table.

"You had magics in this bag that protected you," he said. "Of course, that same bag full of magic is how we detected you." He looked at my wife, grinned a lion's grin. "Otherwise, we wouldn't have known you were here. Ironic, is it not?"

Betty Lou frowned. She'd made a mistake, and she knew it.

Buer looked at me, feline eyes sharp and alert.

"You can take those pink sunglasses off now," he said. "You know you look like an idiot, right?"

I took the glasses off, yet I could still see him. His invisibility was some kind of charm he could turn on and off.

"You're telling me I look like an idiot?" I shook my head. "Ever glance in a mirror, Yellow Brick Road? Or don't they have mirrors that don't melt down in Hell."

Betty Lou gestured to her purse.

"I've got a makeup compact in there," she said. "Hunter's right—you should take a look before you criticize other people's appearances."

Damn, do I love that girl.

"You're an arrogant woman," Buer said. "You seem to have a lot of faith in that binding spell of yours."

Betty Lou smiled sweetly. "Oh, bless your heart. If you don't think I've got the power to back it up, why don't you try to break it?"

Buer made no move. Was my wife facing down a president of Hell? As I said, I love her like nobody's business, but I was also praying she knew what she was doing.

"Perhaps later," Buer said. "For now, you can all tell me what you're doing here."

Time to get down to brass tacks.

"You're meddling with the election," Luke said. "We're here to stop you."

I put my hand on my son's shoulder and squeezed, hard enough to get his attention but not hard enough to make him wince. He knew better—I was supposed to do the talking, not him.

"I'm not meddling in anything," Buer said. He shrugged, with all five goat legs. "I'm merely volunteering my time and expertise for a cause I believe in. There's nothing to worry about—this is democracy in action."

"You ain't a citizen of the United States," I said. "Which means you shouldn't be involved at all. So how about you get your ass out of my town? Maybe down in Hell you've got all kinds of power, but on the plane of the living, you ain't got shit."

Have you ever seen a lion smile? Let me tell you, it's very disturbing.

"You're half right, anyway," Buer said. "In Hell, I've got power to spare."

Was he saying he also had power here? At the very least, he had the juice to disguise his demons. What else could he do up here?

"You're making the candidate say things," I said. "Some wild things, sure, but he won the nomination. What do you benefit if he wins the general election?"

The lion face grinned. "Who says I want him to win?"

In the pause that followed, I realized something we hadn't considered. Did he want the Republican candidate to win… or had he helped him so that the Democratic candidate would have an opponent that couldn't possibly win the presidency?

I thought back to that old South Park episode about how the US presidential election is like choosing between a douche and a turd sandwich. The more elections I live through, the more I think that's the way our system will always be.

Buer waved one cloven foot.

"You may leave," he said. "I hope we meet again. Very soon."

A sardonic smile on that lion face, a smile that showed plenty of long, sharp teeth.

Betty Lou gently gripped my elbow.

"Hunter, let's go."

We've been married a long time, she and I. Her eyes said more than her mouth could, and her eyes said she was running out of strength to hold the binding spell.

Time to get out while the getting was good.

She grabbed her purse from the table.

I conveniently left the pink sunglasses behind. I swear, sometimes I can be so forgetful.

Home sweet home.

I'd gathered the family in the TV room. The place has a "family room," but it strikes me as a ballroom packed with more furniture than any group short of a full military company could ever use. The one we used for family gatherings had a flat-panel TV, the living room did not, so the smaller TV room had become our default gathering place.

Betty Lou was telling Bo and Sunshine about our wee little adventure with Buer. The two kids were all ears—Bo, wide-eyed and focused; Sunshine, her eyes locked on the piece of pine she whittled at with a Bowie knife. Luke, meanwhile, was pounding away on his laptop like it owed him money. I leaned against a wall, arms folded, simultaneously listening to Betty Lou and letting my mind wander, hoping my subconscious might lead me to a solution my conscious mind couldn't quite grasp.

We've had far more dangerous run-ins with the supernatch than our encounter with Buer, but something about that messed-up sunflower made my nuts shrivel up and want to burrow for cover just south of my heart.

"Then they let us go," Betty Lou said, finishing the tale.

Bo shrugged. "That doesn't sound so bad, Ma. But you seem really scared."

"I am scared." Betty Lou pursed her lips, thinking. "There's something… off about what he said."

Sunshine set down her knife and wood.

"He let you go real easy, Ma," she said. "You check to see if he put a tracker on you?"

My wife nodded. "Course I did. Full check across all eldritch spectrums. He just let us go, didn't seem to care about where we went."

"Our location ain't no secret," Luke said without looking up from his laptop. His bony little fingers on the keyboard sounded like a nonstop drumroll. "We work for the Netherworld Protectorate. This house is owned by the Protectorate. Any demon who can grab his ass with both hands would know where to find us... if they really wanted to."

I honestly wasn't sure where ass fell on Betty Lou's list of ear-flickable curse words, but she didn't seem to take notice. Lucky Luke.

"Here's the thing," I said. "Buer is clearly trying to influence the election, but now I don't know who he wants to win."

Betty Lou glared at me.

"He's a demon, Hunter. He obviously wants that man to win."

"Does he?" I shrugged. "I kinda wonder which candidate would better his goals more."

Bo shook his head. "Pa, it's obvious who needs Buer to win. It ain't like that racist Cheeto could actually win on his own. Right?"

The way he said right... not a rhetorical question, a child looking for reassurance. My middle son had a smile on his face more often than he didn't. Now, though—he wore an expression of controlled anger, perhaps just a few notches below those protestor kids we'd seen at the convention center.

Bo's my son. Sometimes, believe it or not, that makes me forget the color of his skin, and forget that his reaction to certain events might be more... magnified... than my own.

He wanted comfort from his Pa, but false comfort wasn't the Hunterson way.

"No one thought he could win the nomination," I said. "Remember when the debates began? He was the butt of all jokes, the laughing stock of smart people who knew about such things—pundits, experts, talk-show hosts, movie stars, late-night comedians. Turns out those people maybe don't know as much as they'd like to think."

And yet, even now, when the grand prize was down to two contestants, when so many people had been proven wrong and should have been eating their words, those same people continued to mock the candidate at every turn.

Not only him, but anyone they thought might vote for him.

I thought back to what Betty Lou had said while we were in line at the Moscone Center—these protester thugs have no idea their actions will make more people vote for that asshole.

Of course, anyone who would consider voting for him was in the basket of deplorables and could be easily dismissed, right? I knew how these supposed deplorables thought, how they lived, how they breathed. This is America—you tell an American what he or she should do, and their reaction is more often to tell you to go fuck yourself.

Except now people weren't saying that out loud. They weren't talking at all, because, as a nation, so many people had learned that you do not speak up against the orthodox view. Not unless you wanted to be publicly shamed, your name splattered across the Internet so people who had never met you—people who knew nothing about you—could declare you evil not just for speaking your mind, but for asking a question, for daring to do anything but go along with the established groupthink.

No, people weren't saying things out loud. They weren't saying anything at all, and that was what worried me—the Internet kids seemed to be a unified body, but the silent majority was both silent and the majority. Come November 8th, which way would that majority vote?

That question lurked at the back of my mind, made me worry. More and more I was starting to think that Bo was wrong—maybe the product of the establishment who preached against the establishment could actually win it all.

Luke stopped typing. The absence of sound drew everyone's attention to him as if he'd started screaming at the top of his lungs.

"Uh-oh," he said.

Sometimes that boy is disrespectful. Sometimes he's rebellious. He says a lot of things that piss me off, but very few things that make me worried. *Uh-oh* was one of those things.

"What is it, son?" I asked.

"A couple of things," Luke said. "First, we didn't meet Buer himself. We saw his projection. He can only physically enter the world when the sun is in Sagittarius—this year that happens November 16, a week after the election."

The kid was confusing the hell out of me.

"So lesser demons can't enter without permission, and major demons can, but only sometimes?"

"Demonic rules are complicated and can contradict themselves," Luke said. "Kind of like girls."

"Sexist," Sunshine said.

Luke giggled at getting a rise out of his sister.

Buer's involvement with the election, and the timing of whatever the hell horoscope thingee Luke was talking about… just a coincidence?

"Maybe Buer has a deal with the candidate," Betty Lou said. "But if Buer can enter the physical world on a specific day, what could someone offer him in exchange for manipulating the election? It's not like he needs an invitation to walk the plane of the living."

"He can enter without permission," Luke said, "but his legions can't. Pa, we've been looking for that new fault line—what if it's on property controlled by the US government? Once the election is over, the president-elect is the de-facto owner of that land."

Sunshine shook her head, crossed her arms.

"Wait a minute," she said. "I'm taking a civics class. The owner of government land is the people, not the president."

Bo huffed. "Sure, Sis—you try going somewhere the government says you can't, and you'll find out how much ownership you have."

Bo did most of his communicating with fists rather than words, but this time he'd hit the nail right on the head.

"The president can go anywhere he wants," I said.

"Or she," Betty Lou and Sunshine said in unison, glowering at me like I was trying to banish them to the Eternal Barefoot Kitchen of Endless Pregnancy.

"Or her," I said. "My bad. If Luke's right, it means Buer could be helping one of the two candidates in exchange for permission for his legions to enter our plane."

It did seem a little too connected to be a coincidence—a new fault in San Francisco, Buer showing himself (or at least his projection) here in the city… many possible explanations fit what we'd observed, but Luke's conjecture about getting permission from a "land owner" qualified as one of those explanations.

"What about one of the federal buildings in the city?" Betty Lou said. "Those are government-owned. Could the fault be in one of those?"

I thought about the various supernatch we'd seen recently. A one-eyed, one-legged, mad-as-hell umbrella in an office building would have caught people's attention much sooner. Even if it had slipped into this plane at night, the federal buildings were still in the heart of a major city. We'd bagged that baddie in Golden Gate Park, and the other two in the Presidio.

"Has to be somewhere less developed," I said. "Luke, what parks are there in San Francisco? Not state parks, but National parks, that a president might have sway over?"

His fingers beat on the keyboard, continued to pound away even as he answered.

"Muir Woods," he said. "Alcatraz Island, Golden Gate Recreational Area, the Presidio and… Fort Point, the old Civil War fort under the Golden Gate Bridge." He looked up at me. "Ain't no one in Fort Point at night, Pa. Any supernatch originating there could spread through the Presidio's woods, and in the dark it wouldn't be that hard to reach Golden Gate Park without being seen."

Couldn't be Alcatraz; the 'natch hate open water. Which also left out Muir Woods as a possibility, unless the deaders crossed the Golden Gate Bridge, which has traffic all night long. Not impossible for something to cross it unseen, but pretty improbable. If the fault line was on federal land, that made the Presidio the most likely spot.

"I'll get Ing to put his people on it," I said. "They can start searching the Presidio. In the meantime, y'all gear up—we'll start at Fort Point."

We'd lived in San Francisco for only six months. I hadn't visited Fort Point before. I wish I'd done so, during the day, to get a little familiarity, because at night the damn thing was spooky as hell.

We didn't know for sure if the fault was in there or not. But I felt that tingle I often feel when we butt heads with the dead.

"Pa," Bo said, "how come faults are always in places that look haunted?"

That tingle runs in the family, maybe, even family that ain't genetically mine.

"Don't know, son. I honestly don't know."

Quite a sight, that Fort Point. A redbrick, Civil War-era fort, three tall stories, with bigger, paler blocks running up the corners. The Golden Gate Bridge towered above it. Quite the metaphor for progress, I suppose—at one point in history, the fort was probably the tallest building for miles around. Now? It was tucked under a modern marvel of rust-colored steel that made the fort look like a child's toy. Floodlights lit up spots of the redbrick wall, and some light from the tall bridge tower filtered down as well, making the corner blocks seem to glow with ethereal dimness.

The old-school wooden doors were shut tight. Maybe there was security around here, somewhere, but we'd deal with that if it came up. No one around. Not even any cars. Water on three sides, a rock wall opposite the fourth—any supernatch that came out of a fault around here, at night, wouldn't be seen. Golden Gate Bridge traffic hummed along high above, creating a steady state of white noise that melded with the burble of small waves crashing against the piled rocks and concrete that passed for a shore. No one would see the supernatch, no one would hear them, either. And then there was the location—at the top of the Presidio, meaning a supernatch could go unseen to dozens of areas of the city at the Presidio's southern and eastern boundaries. If the fault line was here, it explained the dispersal pattern we'd seen over the past few weeks.

The fam had gussied up for battle. Bo wore his long, black leather trench coat, the inside of which holstered his silver baseball bat. Luke had taken to wearing black combat fatigues like he was some kind of action hero, complete with a silver sword and a Mossberg 500 loaded with silver buckshot crisscross holstered on his back. Sunshine, thankfully, had traded in her daisy dukes for jeans, combat boots, and a no-nonsense long-sleeve shirt patterned in urban camo, quiver across her back, bow in hand.

As for Betty Lou and I? We hadn't bothered to change clothes; we're always ready for a dust-up. She's got her bag of goodies; I've got a huge repeating crossbow—ten shots in about fifteen seconds. Power is for shit and accuracy ain't that great, but each bolt is tipped with a charmed-up point that can fuck up a low-level deader's world. Sometimes it works, sometimes it don't.

When it don't? That's okay, because I've got Old Glory ready to go.

"Fort Point was built in 1853," Luke said. "Decommissioned in 1970. Did you know they knocked down a cliff to build it? They wanted it closer to the waterline, so cannonballs could skip off the surface and increase range. And then—"

"Ain't the time for random facts," I said. "Tell me something useful."

Luke frowned. He hates being interrupted, but I swear, that kid has diarrhea of the mouth.

"Well, the center of the fort is open to the sky," Luke said. "There's rooms in the walls, but they're kind of narrow. The interior of the fort is a big open space."

So we didn't have to go through a door, which would make noise, draw attention.

"Betty Lou," I said, "can you get us over that wall?"

She dug through her gym bag of a purse. She pulled out a necklace: a black owl, wings spread, its eyes and outline done up in garnets.

"We're going airborne," she said. "Everyone, get close to me."

We did as we were told. I chose not to mention the last time we "went airborne," her magic petered out and we fell on our asses. My tailbone still aches from that if the weather is right.

Betty Lou mumbled some magical gibberish talk. I always wonder if she and her kind just make that shit up as they go along. Maybe the talismans have an activation button and all you have to do is press it, but a mishmash of syllables just seems more impressive.

A disc of pale red light formed beneath our feet. Seconds later, we were, indeed, airborne.

The disc rose up. Bo made a whining noise—he hates heights—but Sunshine and Luke laughed, enjoying every minute of the flight.

Betty Lou took us up a hundred feet or so, then over the wall. Sure enough, the space inside was wide open. On the outside, the walls were smooth brick, but on the inside each story had a deck that ran all the way around, dotted with brick archways. It reminded me of New Orleans architecture. That or a prison, cells opening to catwalks that overlooked the common area.

She set us down in the middle of the fort on the cracked, patched concrete floor. Walls soared up on all sides, tall, but diminutive compared to the long mass that was the Golden Gate.

At ground level, alcoves were set into the base of the wall. Inside each, an old civil war cannon or wagon, black masses that were more part of the shadows than hidden by them.

No movement. The place was still.

"Don't see nothing," Sunshine said.

Luke tugged at my sleeve. "Pa, should we split up and search?"

"Of course not," I said. "This look like the Sunday matinee to you? This is real life—we don't do dumb shit."

Luke's eyes widened with embarrassment. He looked down. Well, he should be embarrassed for asking such a stupid question.

When you see monster hunters on TV or in the movies, they are dumber than ten pounds of shit stuffed into a five-pound bag. We need to split up and get a look around, they say. Well, in real life, that don't happen. Once we're in a hot zone we never split up. Want to take out one of us? Good luck, you sumbitch, because all of us will gang up to stomp your ass.

"Give me a minute," Betty Lou said. "I think I sense a presence."

I kept my head on a swivel as she looked in her oversized bag. I couldn't see anything, but I felt the presence of evil. Supernatural spider sense—natchsense, I call it—is a trait you develop early in this business, because if you don't, you ain't around to do it later.

"Feels creepy," Bo said.

"Real creepy," Luke said.

Betty Lou pulled a bracelet out of her bag. I'd seen the like before: a fault-closer. She slid it onto her wrist, where it joined a dozen other clinking bangles. She slung the bag over her head, then spread her hands.

"*Lux lucis nihil mali*," she said.

Her hands glowed with static white.

Not fifteen feet from us, something in the old concrete floor began to glow. The same white as Betty Lou's hands, at first, but as it brightened in intensity the hue darkened, took on color.

The color of electric blood.

From the alcove shadows, a familiar voice rang out, echoing off the brick walls and up into the night.

"Step away from the fault, and you won't be hurt."

Cop Shades was here.

Turned out there were guards—just not the human variety.

They came out of the alcoves. Five of them, from all directions. The same demons who'd corralled us at the rally. They looked human, since we hadn't gone all Cory Hart and worn our sunglasses at night, but I'd seen their true faces and that was something one couldn't unsee.

"Howdy, boys," I said. "Moonlighting? Sad to see Buer ain't paying you enough as bodyguards."

Cop Shades smiled.

"The President thought you might be up to no good and come

poking around," he said. "So he had us wait here. I'm glad he did, too, because this time there's no binding spell." A wide smile. "We're going to feast on your souls."

I nodded. "Hate to disappoint you, numb-nuts, but this ain't the first time we've looked down the barrel of a gun. You want to dance? Then come and dance."

My family made a tight circle, facing out, each of us staring down one of the demons. Bo pulled his silver baseball bat from his black trench coat. Sunshine knocked an arrow. Betty Lou fished in her purse. Luke—God, please keep my baby boy from harm—drew his shotgun.

The demons advanced.

I didn't think my crossbow bolts would do much against Cop Shades, but I tried anyway. Great gadget, my crossbow—fire by pushing the top lever forward, cock it by pulling the lever back. I ripped off all ten shots—Cop Shades brushed them aside with casual waves of his hands. One hit him, and he winced, but on he came.

Oh well.

I dropped it and slid my hand into my pants pocket, felt the weight of Old Glory. The cool metal around my fingers felt as comforting as a thump on the back from a lifelong friend.

Old Glory in place, I put up my dukes.

I heard the twang of Sunshine's bow and the roar of Luke's shotgun. Hopefully they'd have better luck than I did.

Cop Shades closed in, as did his four demon pals—five against five.

In a blink, they shed their human appearance. Wrinkled, red skin oozing pus. Clothes burned away in wisps of smoke, the smell of burned polyester hitting us before the demons did. The two huge lobster demons shambled toward us, one centering on Luke, the other on Sunshine.

"*Tamen Daemones*," Betty Lou shouted. She whirled a golden necklace, spinning it so fast it looked like a disc of translucent metal. We'd seen her use that necklace before—at its end, an enameled birdcage lined in green and blue stones. We all knew what to do next.

The air electrified, making my hair stand on end; a cage of light formed around us, just outside our perimeter.

The demons smashed into the cage and were instantly thrown back in a shower of eldritch energy.

I took advantage of the moment to get a good, fast look at all five demons. Two arrows stuck out of Sunshine's lobster—and it looked to be in pain—but Luke's shotgun hadn't done jack shit to his shelled foe.

We'd have to settle this the old-fashioned way.

"Knuckle up, family," I said. "Get 'em!"

Betty Lou stopped her swing—the cage crackled, vanished.

Bo strode forward like the man he was, brought his bat down in a big, powerful arc that smashed in a yellow demon's skull.

Sunshine's bow twanged and twanged again; damn, but that girl can fire fast. A howl of pain followed each shot, but I couldn't see how my baby girl had done because Cop Shades closed in on me.

He lashed out with a taloned hand. I stepped in and blocked it with my right, drove Old Glory into his belly with a body blow that Ali would have admired. The shit-eater stumbled back, surprised.

Maybe these demons had never met seasoned stompers before. Well, too bad for them.

We had the situation well in hand—and then the fault started to glow with the burnished maroon of the damned.

"Hunter," Betty Lou shouted, "we're about to have company!"

The double distraction took my eyes off the prize; a flash of movement—I flinched, felt the burning pain of demon claws slashing my face. Cop Shades smiled wide, pointy teeth flashing in the lights of the Golden Gate Bridge. A long, blackened, forked tongue licked my blood from its talons.

"You taste delicious, mortal. Your soul will taste even better."

I felt blood coursing down my cheek. If I hadn't flinched away, that shot would have taken off my head. I couldn't look at the crack to another dimension, not if I wanted my children to have a daddy at their graduation.

The fault's glow made Cop Shades' sunglasses gleam a solid red.

My left hand surged with power—Old Glory was thirsty.

"Hey, dickless," I said to Cop Shades. I curled my fingers inward. "How about you come finish me off?"

In he came. He floated toward me, hands outstretched, talons reflecting the lights of the Golden Gate Bridge above.

The demon swung his lethal right claw at my head, but now I had his range—I bobbed back just enough and felt the breeze from talon tips that missed by a hair.

My turn.

A step forward, a twist of the hips, a turn of the shoulders, and I landed a left cross with the force of Thor's hammer. Old Glory hit Cop Shades in his right eye. The sunglasses broke, the tinted lenses flying away in three pieces, the twisted wire frames falling to the ground.

Cop Shades dropped: down goes Frazier.

He lay on the bricks of Fort Point, unmoving.

Then there was Bo—my middle son's silver baseball bat arced down and turned Cop Shades' head into silly putty.

Down stays Frazier.

I pressed a hand to my bleeding face as I looked around. I felt a twinge of pride at my family's handiwork. Sunshine's demon was a twitching pincushion, the red-shelled beast well on his way to wherever demons wind up when you kill them. Luke held his left arm with his right; he'd been hurt. His lobster demon was on the ground, though, with a head turned to shell-spotted paste—before finishing off his pa's assailant, Bo had helped his brother. Betty Lou's foe was nothing more than a smoldering green globule. I felt a hankering to re-watch *Spinal Tap*.

My wife's scream brought me back to the trouble at hand.

The fault seethed like a dying red sun. Something was coming out of it. Betty Lou's body glowed the pure white of her soul—two colors fighting against one another for dominance.

"Help me," she said. "I need y'all's strength!"

Luke, hurt arm and all, was instantly at her left side, joining hands with her. I took my wife's right hand, our fingers locking with love and fury.

Delicate fingers slid into my other hand; Sunshine, bow slung, blonde hair still fixed in place by an inordinate amount of hairspray.

I felt the strength of my daughter's soul flow into me, through me, joining mine as our combined essence coursed into my wife.

"Yes," Betty Lou said, snarling with delight. "Oh hell yes!"

On her left, Luke, and on his left, Bo—a family with hands and hearts and souls locked together into one bad-ass battery of power.

Betty Lou's white glow increased, it pulsed, it rocked and it rolled like a machine gun strobe light, her power flowing into the fault, thickening as it did, the light becoming something so pure and intense it was almost a solid.

And then, a bubble of red energy slipped from the fault, a bubble bigger than Bo and I combined. It rose, swelled, as if it was patiently blown by a little kid intent on blowing the world's biggest soap bubble.

Something inside it kicked, stretching the red membrane.

"Betty Lou," I said, "you better hurry up."

Her answering words were grunts, the kind of throat-raw sounds weightlifters use to get that last set done.

"I'm trying, Honey… I'm trying."

Something else inside that red bubble moved, something wide and long… wings.

"Woman," I said, feeling the first real bit of fear crawl up my groin and wiggle in my belly, "finish the damn job already!"

Her eyes squeezed shut. "Hunter, shut your damn pie hole!"

She was giving it her all, but it was too late.

The bubble popped, revealing what lay inside.

Even as the energy flowed out of us, flowed through my wife, we all stared.

Betty Lou wasn't finished sealing the fault—we couldn't let go, couldn't do a damn thing until she was.

"Pa," Bo said, "you see what I'm seeing?"

I nodded. "I'm afraid so."

Feathered white wings unfurled, stretched out, flapped against the air hard enough that we felt a sudden, pulsating wind. The body, so taut that we saw muscles twitching beneath a grayish, mangy coat spotted with missing patches showing blistered pink skin beneath. Black lips coated with white spittle-foam curled back to reveal big, cracked, blocky yellow teeth. Eyes flared wide with madness, blazed orange with mindless fury.

And, worst of all, sticking out of its head, that single, twisted horn, sparkling with untold levels of magical power.

Of all the supernatch, this was one of the worst.

A rabid unicorn.

"Pa," Luke said, "we gotta get it."

His words were as weak as my arms and legs. We'd all given our strength to Betty Lou, and we simply didn't have any left with which to fight—if the beast came at us, we were finished.

"Almost," Betty Lou grunted. "Almost… have it…"

The fault line's red light dimmed. The split in reality contracted, pushed together like an earthquake that had changed its mind and come together again.

The fault sealed shut like a ziplock bag, once again nothing more than old concrete.

The red light vanished.

But the rabid unicorn remained.

"Family, get ready," I said, releasing Betty Lou's and Sunshine's hands. Betty Lou crumpled to the ground.

Sunshine tried to unsling her bow. She stumbled, the simple task proving too much for her weakened condition.

Luke raised his sword, which promptly slipped out of his trembling hand and clattered against the concrete. He dropped to his knees, staring up at the flapping monstrosity before us.

Bo stumbled to me. Father and son stood shoulder to shoulder. Out of bravery? No, out of the need to keep each other on our feet.

The rabid unicorn rose up ten, fifteen feet. It looked down at me, red smoke curling away from orange eyes. The cracked teeth gleamed with a need for prey.

The black lips moved, and a voice like grinding rust came out.

"I… am… Sparklehorse!"

Wonderful. It even had a cute name.

With that, the powerful wings beat down. The unicorn rose up into the air, above the wall, and in seconds it was gone, only a trail of dissipating red smoke marking its path.

Bo and I dropped to our asses, our chests heaving.

I looked to the fault—gone. Thank God.

Betty Lou rolled to her side.

"I don't feel so good," she said.

I kissed her cheek, brushed the hair from her face.

"Breakfast in bed for you tomorrow, darlin'," I said. "You earned it."

I found enough strength to gather her into my arms.

Bo, Luke, Sunshine, Betty Lou… my family, exhausted but unhurt.

Another flash of eldritch energy—emerald green this time—and my heart sank. We were so worn down we couldn't have stopped a no-legged zombie from taking us out.

The green energy coalesced, condensed into a final form.

A familiar form, with a lion's head and five ridiculous goat legs.

"You will pay for this," Buer said, his feline eyes boring straight into me.

"He can't hurt us," Luke said, forcing out the words. "He's… just a projection."

The lion/goat demon ignored him, kept his focus locked on me.

"You will pay for this, mortal," he said. "I will make it my personal goal to wipe you and your family from the face of the earth."

A big-time demon. A President of Hell. And he now had it out for me and mine. Frightening? Absolutely. This was bad news with a capital B, but I wasn't about to let him think we were afraid.

"Blow it out your ass, fuzz-nuts," I said. "Anyone ever tell you you look like the king of the jungle got face-fucked by an octopus?"

The lion eyes flared with fury.

Come on… it wasn't like I could make him any more enraged, so I might as well get my licks in now, right?

Buer opened his lion mouth and roared. Maybe he was just a projection, but that roar was so loud it hurt my ears, fanned the flames of my fear, made my soul feel like it had just been kicked in the balls.

"Soon," Buer said, then he pinwheeled straight for the fort wall. Five hooves rolled him into an alcove, where he vanished in a burst of green light.

None of us said anything for a little while. We just sat there and breathed. Except for Luke, who threw up. That boy and his delicate constitution, I swear.

Finally, Bo broke the silence.

"Pa," he said, "did we really just see a rabid unicorn?"

I nodded. "We did, son. We did."

"We gonna go get it?"

Somewhere in the San Francisco Bay Area, a lethal, diseased, winged, one-horned supernatch was on the loose. We had to track it down.

Eventually.

"Not right now," I said. "We need some rest. And I promised your mother I'd make her breakfast. Come on, clan Hunterson—it's time to go home."

We'd taken away Buer's motivation for influencing the election. Without him, the election would be a whoopin'. There was no way that Republican could actually win.

Was there?

AGARAS

Agaras, or Agares, is the first duke of the Power of the East. He has thirty-one legions of spirits at his command. Unlike some of his demonic colleagues, he is said to be quite willing to appear when summoned. He looks like an old man riding a crocodile ("very mildly," according to *The Lesser Key of Solomon*), and has a hawk sitting on his fist. Reginald Scot's *Discoverie of Witchcraft* (1584) describes his powers thus: "He fetcheth backe all such as runne awaie, and maketh them runne that stand still; he overthroweth all dignities supernaturall and temporall, [and] hee maketh earth quakes." He is also said to be good at teaching languages. *The Lesser Key* says that he was one of the seventy-two spirits imprisoned by Solomon in a brass vessel at the bottom of the ocean.

The Old Man Down the Road

R.S. BELCHER

Sunny found the old man in the 'glades, so deep in that her cell phone lost signal and her navigation app went mad. The gateway to his kingdom was adorned with alligator skulls, hung everywhere, all over the rough-hewn wooden archway that led into the mud and gravel parking lot and all along the rusted wire fences that marked where the swamp ended and the farm began.

Her car paused at the arch as she read the sign nailed there. The letters had been burned into the wood by a shaky hand:

Agares Alligator and Crocodile Farm
No public shows! No trespassing!
No goddamn kids!
This isn't fucking Disney World!
PISS OFF!

Mateo, the bartender in Miami who had given Sunny the old man's name and a general idea of where to find him, had said he wasn't keen on visitors.

"He hates pretty much everyone," he had said, sliding another shot across the bar, "but he's really good at what you need. At least that's what I've heard."

The gravel lot was mostly empty. There were a few very old, very dilapidated cars parked near a squat cinderblock building with an attached open-air shelter. The shelter had a corrugated tin roof and a cement floor, and there were some Native American men milling around inside. Most looked to be members of one of the tribes that made their homes in the Everglades; Okeechobee, maybe.

Sunny noticed the low fences of the pen gates and a dirt trail wandering lazily down a hill off to the left. She parked in a corner next to a beat-to-shit, tan Chevy pickup truck that was covered in mud. The truck had a rear-window decal on it that looked like some coat of arms she didn't recognize. The symbol was the cleanest part of the pickup.

She got out and walked toward the men under the shade of the shelter's roof. It was after three. She knew anytime now the afternoon rain would roar through for about 20 minutes and then depart, making it even more of a sauna than it already was. An old radio on a wood workbench broadcasted a scratchy AM country channel. "The Ballad of Gator McKlusky" by Jerry Reed was playing. The men were gutting big-mouth bass and dropping the chum into a large, stained, plastic trashcan. One of them, a big fella with snow-white hair, paused and looked up at her.

"You lost? It's a ways back to the main road if you are."

"No," Sunny said. "I'm looking for the owner of the farm."

"If you're trying to sell him something," another man said, not looking up from the fish guts, "save yourself the time and the bullshit. He ain't buying any."

"I'm told he can… find things," Sunny said. "I'm looking for his help. I want to hire him."

"No," the snow-haired man said, real sadness and concern in his eyes. "You really don't."

A voice made of rotgut and unfiltered cigarettes called out from the deep darkness beyond the cinderblock building's open door. "Tell her to get her ass in here and get back to feeding the damn 'gators!"

"He's waiting on you in there," the man with white hair said. "Good luck."

Sunny clutched her messenger bag a little tighter and did a quick recall of exactly where the stun gun and the .38 were tucked away inside. The darkness beyond the open door seemed impenetrable. She smelled thick cigarette smoke and pungent marijuana inside. She wondered if she was really this desperate, then answered her own question by stepping into the darkness.

It took a second for her eyes to adjust. Strangely, all the noise from the outside, the radio, the men's voices, even the sounds of the swamp, ended when she passed through the door. The room was a hot mess. It looked like it was used as a combination bar, office, and bedroom. Every part was cluttered. Papers and bills overflowed the large, old, oak desk in the corner. She noted there was no computer, just an old, heavy manual typewriter that belonged in an antique shop window. The "bar" was some warped, bare plywood nailed together crudely, crowned with a pile of half-empty liquor bottles. Two cheap stools stood beside it. There was an unmade bed in another corner. The floor around the bed had dirty clothing as carpeting. There was a low, round coffee table with a huge hookah, and a bunch of threadbare pillows and cushions forming an island around it.

A man reclined among the cushions, puffing on one of the pipe's hoses. He was gaunt, wiry with compact muscles moving under his powerful forearms stained with old, faded tattoos of strange symbols. His face was more carved than organic, furrowed with lines and crags. His nose was hawk-like, his eyes hot pitch. Everything about his features spoke of cruelty and impatience. His long, greasy, dirty, gray hair swooped back from a widow's peak and fell down his shoulders. It matched his gray beard and mustache. He was dressed in an olive-drab Henley shirt, old jeans, and steel-toed cowboy boots made of rattlesnake hide.

"Sit," the old man said. His voice was sandpaper on the air, but Sunny found herself responding at once. She sat opposite him in the circle of pillows. They looked at each other. He said nothing, just gazed at her with pitiless eyes.

"Some people in Miami told me about you," she began. "They said you're the one who found that thirteen-year-old who got abducted from Hadley Park. They said she was all the way across the county, sold to human traffickers, but you found her, brought her home." The old man stayed silent, his gaze unwavering. Sunny tried again. "I want to hire you to find someone."

The old man suddenly had a pocket knife in his hand. He flicked the lock-blade open with a snap of his wrist and tossed the knife to Sunny, seemingly unconcerned with the blade hitting her. She caught it and avoided getting cut, but looked at the knife like it was venomous snake.

"Cut yourself," he said. "I need your blood."

"Look, Mr. Agares," Sunny began.

"Just Agares."

"That Latino?"

"It's Latin," Agares said, "close enough."

"Well, Agares, I grew up in Little Havana, all that Santeria and Palo Mayombe witchcraft shit, I don't buy any of it, so..."

"I don't give a fuck what you buy into or not," Agares said. "I find people and I find things, better than anyone else on this goddamned planet. But it costs."

"I have money," She said, pulling at the envelope full of tips she'd saved for over 5 years. The old man's voice stopped her.

"Money don't mean shit. My price is blood and honesty. Both are a damn sight rarer in this world than cash."

"I'm not doing that," Sunny said.

"Then get the fuck out." Agares took another long hit on the pipe's hose. Sunny started to rise then sat back down. She examined the pocket knife's narrow blade, frowned and tossed it back to Agares, who plucked it right out of the air while exhaling a thick cloud of Marijuana smoke.

"The blade's filthy," she said. Agares squinted at the knife. He cleared his throat loudly and spat on the blade, polishing it dry with his dirty shirt. He handed the knife to Sunny this time.

"Clean now," he said. "You doing this, or am I getting stoned and eating Fruity Pebbles?"

"Why should I bleed for you?"

Agares sighed.

"You lost your virginity at a very early age. You didn't like it, either. You got lost once at the Dadeland Mall when you were seven. You were so scared, you pissed your pants. When you were 13, you lost your brother, who was pretty much the only real family you ever had. You lost the love of your life at 23. She couldn't stand your drinking and your abuse and your bullshit anymore, so she left. She never returns your calls, especially the drunken ones you make to her every New Year's Eve. Oh, and you lost your cellphone at a bar in Hialeah 3 years ago. It slipped under the truck next to your car when you stumbled in the parking lot because you were drunk off your ass."

Sunny clutched her messenger bag like a life preserver. "How… how the hell could you possibly… how?"

"Because I'm the fucking duke of finding lost shit," he said. "That's all I could sniff off you without your blood. Now, you in, or you out, and if you're out, shut the fucking door on your way. You're killing my hotbox."

Sunny looked down at the pocket knife and carefully nicked her index finger with the blade. The skin sliced like warm butter, and a fat drop of her blood welled up. Agares stood, walked around the table and took her wounded hand by the wrist, tightly.

"This is a deal," he said, staring her in the eyes. His grip was very strong. "You make this deal, there's no going back. You understand?" Sunny swallowed and nodded. Agares took her hand and pulled it to his face, slipped her bleeding finger into his mouth and sucked the blood away. An almost sexual light burned in his dead eyes for a moment, and she had to admit this felt strangely like her time flirting with BDSM, like this nasty old man was somehow claiming ownership of her. A little thrill went through her body at the feeling, and then she recalled why she had sucked at submission. She didn't trust anyone that much. She pulled her finger away from Agares's mouth and jerked her wrist free of his grasp. It was surprisingly easy.

"Gross," she said. "You satisfied?"

The old man made a sound in the affirmative. It sounded like a growl.

"We're good," he said. "Let me grab my shit and we'll be on our way."

"Wait a minute," she said. "Don't you want the money? You don't even know who I want you to find."

"I do," the old man said, grabbing a rumpled, canvas campaign jacket and a battered, leather outback hat from a pile of dirty clothes. He wrapped a belt around his virtually non-existent waist. A huge, sheathed Bowie knife hung off it. "Hang onto the money," he said as he scooped some keys off the work desk and held them up. A large alligator tooth dangled from the keychain. "We'll need it. I need to know something else right now, though."

"What?"

"What do you want to do when you find him?"

She paused, felt the velocity of her life rush through her, all the pain and chaos that had led her to this place, to this stranger. It struck her like the invisible anvil you hit at the moment of falling asleep, the weight of our lives, the iron of our sins.

"I want to kill him," she said.

"Then I need your word. I need your promise now that you will see this through, that you will kill him when I find him."

"Okay," Sunny said and rubbed her suddenly throbbing index finger. "You've got it."

"Then let's boogie." The old man strode past her and through the door.

Outside it was dark, humid, damp. Sunny was at a loss. It had been midday when she arrived, and she hadn't been inside with Agares longer than maybe 10 minutes, right?

The gravel lot was empty except for her beat-up little Honda and the swamp truck she had parked next to. All the men at the shelter were gone, and so were their cars. A single, halogen light on a telephone pole bathed the area in dingy, white light, filtered through a frantic swarm of bugs orbiting the light like mad moons.

Agares noticed her surprise. He grunted, which she suspected was the closest thing to a chuckle he had in him. "Yeah, things are going to get kinda fucked up for you from here on out," he said. "Time, space, all that shit you people cling to to keep from losing your fucking minds, it's going out the window." He opened the driver-side door of the truck, climbed in with a groan. He nodded to the passenger door. "Get in." She did.

The cab smelled of tobacco and sweat. Crumpled coffee cups and fast-food wrappers huddled in the floorboard of the passenger seat. The little slide-out ashtray overflowed with cigarette butts and ash. The rifle rack mounted on the back window held a shotgun and a scoped 30-30 rifle. With a low rumble, the truck started like a live, hungry thing. The radio came alive, too. Mark Collie's "In Time" playing on a ghostly local station.

They started down the bouncing, twisting dirt road, Agares's headlights jerking and clinging to the wet shadows of the massive beast that was the 'glades. Looking out her side window, Sunny saw dark drops strike the wide leaves; they left a black trail as they raced to the oblivion of the edge and fell again. She looked ahead, dark drops of what looked like blood hitting the windshield. Unphased, Agares clicked on the wipers and the blood smeared and scattered under their relentless cycle.

"Did you… drug me?" she asked, rolling down her window and sticking her hand out. It came back wet with rain.

"You feel drugged?"

Sunny kept looking at her hand and then back to the blood on the windshield. She shook her head, curtly.

"You wanna?" he asked, grinning a tobacco-stained smile.

"What the fuck did you do to me?" she asked. The anger came to her rescue and tamped down the fear.

"You're riding shotgun with me," he said. "You gave blood, and you swore an oath to me. You see things the way they are now, not the way they want you to see them."

"They? I don't know what you're talking about. You're crazy."

"In the land of the blind, the one-eyed man is king," he said, turning left past what looked to Sunny through the gauze of blood on the windshield like a massive, inhuman skull the size of a motor home. "Your senses are all you got to experience the world. They were built to lie to you. This is the world you really inhabit. Well, one of them, anyway."

"Let me the fuck out."

Agares slowed the truck and stopped. Sunny opened the door. She put one foot onto the muddy road. The air outside was hot and thick. Rain, not blood, struck her hair and face. Other than the truck's lights, all was darkness and jagged shadow. Agares turned, regarding Sunny as she stood half in the truck and half out.

"Your choice," he said. "It's always been your choice. Step on out, slam the door if it will make you feel better. Walk back to the compound—it's about eight miles back—and drive home. Most likely, you will never see any weird shit again. You will also never find him, and you will wonder until your dying day what could have happened if you'd kept going. Then, you'll die, and they will put your meat into the ground to rot. I won't help you again, not in 10 minutes, not in 10 years, not in 10,000. You keep your bargain, and I'll keep mine, but you always, always remember it was your choice."

She knew she should run, knew she was on the shores of some madness she had never known. She also felt the certainty in Agares's voice. The old man would find him, and if she didn't take this ride, she never would. It was the same feeling she had the first time she shot up at 17, the broken glass of her emotions stabbing her insides. She understood as she raised the needle to her skin that she was crossing a line she could never come back from. But she did it anyway.

"Coming?" Agares asked. "Hurry up, you're letting the god-damned mosquitoes in."

Sunny climbed back in the truck and shut the door.

They drove on in silence, and the blood rain finally ended. The swamp gave way to a paved county road; the sky was gray mist choking the stars. Endless fields of sawgrass stretched in both directions, swaying in the tepid wind. Agares turned right, and they continued on.

It felt like an hour had passed when Sunny saw a dark shape, a pyramid, hovering, spinning silently above the sawgrass fields off the right of the road. Small red and green lights twinkled across its black surface like alien fireflies. Below the pyramid, she thought she saw people, arms flailing in distress, heads bobbing into and out of view in the thicket of tough, sharp grass. She looked back as they passed, and now the pyramid was gone, replaced by a blinking radio tower of steel girders.

"What the fuck did we just pass?"

"What do you think?" Agares asked. "Radio tower or big floating pyramid? They're both right to a point. Your blinders are slipping, because you're riding with me."

"This…"

"Can't be real, yeah, yeah, yeah. I'm bored with that shit. Here's a more interesting question, why do you want to kill him?"

She went quiet, gazing at the dark horizon through the blood-smeared windshield.

"Aw, come on now. You haven't shut your trap since you walked in my door; now suddenly you're giving me the silent treatment. Spill."

"You're so goddamn prescient," Sunny said. "Why you asking me?"

"I don't know *everything*," Agares said. "I can teach you every single one of the nearly 7000 languages known to man on this Earth, and a few they don't speak or even remember anymore. I can teach the biggest douchebag you can find how to be charming as fuck. I can make the ground tremble like a bride on her wedding night."

"And you're humble, too," Sunny said, the closest thing to a laugh she could summon brushing her voice.

"And best of all," Agares continued, "I can find any-fucking-thing or anyone, anywhere, and I can make them come home. I can see the things you've lost hanging on you like leaves on a tree, but I can't read minds! I'm glad, too. It would be like being in a fucking library full of those insipid little Bazooka Joe comics that came in the gum." Sunny looked at him blankly. "The ones folded around the stale, shitty gum that cracks your fucking teeth? Hello?" She shook her head and looked out the passenger window. "What I get for hanging out with fucking children."

They drove on and the swampland transformed to highway and waterways on either side of them. They were headed south. Sunny saw a boat made of bloated, putrid, water-logged bodies gliding through the black-glass water, a hooded giant standing at its stern, pushing it through the wetlands with a long wooden pole. A decapitated head, staring stupidly, was mounted on the pole.

"Is this Hell?" she asked.

"Nah," Agares said. "Not yours, anyway, but you're starting to get it now."

"Why can't you just answer a straight question?"

"Why can't you?" he replied. "Why you going to kill this man I'm finding for you?"

Sunny looked to the east, past the old man's profile. The darkness was being ripped away by the scarlet lashes of the dawn. None of this made any sense except in the context of some kind of drug trip, or if she had died and gone to Hell, or maybe gone crazy again. No, crazy didn't feel this way. She watched the sun struggle for a foothold against the tyranny of the night and sighed. "You got a cigarette, preferably not weed, since I'm pretty sure you dosed me."

Agares dug into one of his pockets and fished out a badly crumpled pack of smokes. She took one and handed it back to him. He snapped open a matte black Zippo and lit it for her.

"This man, he took every bit of joy from my life," she began. "Not accidentally, not without malice. He wasn't clumsy, or stupid, or uncaring. No, if he had been any of those, I could forgive him, forget it. He set out to poison me, poison my life, and he succeeded. I'm already dead in all the ways that really matter. I want him dead before I finish up dying. I want the *cabròn* to know it was me that did it."

They continued on the highway for a long time. Sunny noticed that the road signs all bore strange alien script that made her think of worms squirming in a hot skillet. Oddly, the billboards were all very sweet, positive images with a golden, almost glowing script, equally alien. They gave her a strange sense of comfort and a desire to relax, to stay calm. It was like reading Prozac. Agares stuck his arm out the open window and gave one of the billboards the finger as they passed.

What seemed like a few hours later, Agares pulled the pickup over to the side of the highway. He climbed out with a creak of his back and legs and a groan.

"What are you doing?"

"Getting directions." The old man walked to the center of the highway. Sunny opened her door and stretched. Everything felt like dream time, dream logic. It couldn't have been more than a few hours at most since she'd pulled into the gravel lot of the alligator farm. But her body was responding as if she had been cooped up in the truck, driving all night. Agares was scanning the struggling eastern light. He put his fingers to his lips and let off a high-pitched whistle. After a few seconds, there was a distant shriek of reply, and a dark cataract appeared in the opening eye of the dawn. It grew as it came closer to them. It was a hawk, a big one, too.

The animal lighted gently on Agares's forearm. Sunny saw the long, sharp talons carelessly pierce the old man's skin. He didn't even wince as dark streams ran from the wounds. He opened his mouth and the bird spilled something from its beak down his throat. The act nauseated Sunny. Agares swallowed and then leaned in close and whispered to the bird. He looked over to Sunny as he whispered, and she had a mortifying instant of feeling completely naked to his gaze. He finished telling the hawk whatever he had been saying, and the beautiful, powerful bird screeched in reply then took to the air and was soon out of sight.

"Do you do card tricks and children's parties too?" she asked as he ambled back toward the truck. "Maybe geek shows?"

"Cute." The old man grunted as he climbed into the cab. "I got eyes in the sky. Better'n satellites or drones. I got a lead on who you're huntin'. Gonna have to make a detour onto someone else's turf, though. Always dangerous." He started up the truck and Sunny took her seat. They were on their way again.

❖

The night was coming again in all defiance of ordered time and space. The highway narrowed and became a causeway, blue-green water churning to either side, darkening with the sky. Miami jutted in the distance, a sprawling profile of neon, shadow, and stolen electrical fire burning from a thousand windows and streets. Sunny had grown up here, lived here her whole life, but this city was a stranger to her.

Sunny checked her cell phone again, as she had all during the long journey. The screen glowed with the same unreadable golden script as the highway billboards and refused to function. It had been like this since she had started her journey with the old man. She turned to Agares. "I need to understand what's happening," she said. "I've tried to roll with all this like it's some kind of weird hallucination, but it doesn't feel like a drug; it doesn't feel like crazy. Can you please tell me what's going on? Why am I seeing these things? What do they mean?"

"*Please*," Agares said and whistled. He seemed pleased with himself. "I bet that smarted to say. I know you, remember; I tasted you. You hate to rely on anyone for anything, ever. It's cost you, too. Jobs, friends, lovers. You've built a nice little fortress, haven't you? You really want to know what's going on?"

"Yes."

"At first your mind will deny it. Then you'll think I'm crazy, and then you'll think you've gone crazy, but then you'll see it, see the blurry edges of it, see the shitty wallpaper and choke on the cheap air freshener, and you'll wish for the rest of your life you hadn't asked, hadn't seen it. You ready for that?"

Sunny didn't understand why, but she was scared. Agares nodded, keeping his eyes on the road and the growing city. There was a sharp screech somewhere beyond the cab. The hawk drifted ahead of the truck, gliding deeper toward the canyons of concrete, steel, and light. They followed.

"Let's just dip a toe into the water," he continued, "not too deep. Suppose I told you there was no omniscient, omnipotent entity that created the universe, no Heaven or Hell, no afterlife."

"No shit," Sunny said, reaching over and taking the old man's cigarettes again. "That's the big mind-blowing revelation? Anyone who's lived in this shit hole of a world for a while knows that. No Super Santa, no reward for being a good girl and sure as fuck no punishment for the bad by the cosmic cops."

The old man laughed. It was an ugly, unnerving rasp. "You know, I'm betting you for one of the ones who goes crazy when you get it." He lit the cigarette that dangled between her lips. "There is a divinity in this place," he said, keeping the flame of the black lighter shivering before her eyes. "It's in you and all the rest of your kind, a tiny spark of the infinite, a seed of God. Saints got it, serial killers too. Cops, criminals, all of y'all got it, and regardless of what you may think, you can't lose it, can't sell it, either. Harder to get rid of than dog shit on your shoes."

Agares flipped the Zippo shut with a hollow clank, and the flame was snuffed out. Sunny took a pull on the cigarette and shook her head. "Sounds like you're talking about a soul. I don't believe in that shit, either. Even if such a thing existed, what the hell has it ever done for me, for you?"

"Hey, don't drag me into your fucking existential tea party. I never said shit about being part of your fucked up species. I got no use for a soul, myself. Just get in the way of getting things done quick, y'ask me." Sunny gave him a sideways glare. "Not that you did," he added. "No one ever fucking asks me… until it's too late to make a difference."

The sun had lost its battle; night swallowed it whole. The city stretched all around them now, and Sunny realized that this was the first traffic she had seen on the road since they had begun in the Everglades. A lion-headed biker sped past the old truck; wings of flame mantled his back. By the time she saw the rider cross in front of them, he looked like a burly man with a gray mane and beard.

"He's here?" she asked. "I looked all over Miami for him for decades."

"Not the places I'd look," Agares said. "I know a guy who can get us a little closer to him."

"How do you know all that? You don't have a cell. You haven't talked to anyone since we took off."

"A little bird told me," he said. "Hopefully, the asshole we're headed to will be talkative when we find him. We're in his domain now, so we need to watch our asses."

They got off 441 at 17th Street and headed east. The streets were choked with cars and people, despite the hour. Afterhours bars, clubs, third shift. Everyone was always going somewhere in this city or running from something. The beach never really closed. She welcomed a return to something that felt normal, though she still saw flashes of nightmares and miracles camouflaged in the mundane.

"You grew up in Little Havana, right?" Sunny started to ask how he knew that and then she felt her fingertip throb where he had sucked her blood. "We're headed into Overtown. Keep your eyes open and stay close."

The pickup pulled up across the street from Town Park. They got out and the old man slid around the traffic, like smoke, headed for the park. Cars, throbbing with music and bass, drifted down 17th, cruising like steel sharks with ground effects lights. Sunny followed, dodging traffic and catching "DNA" by Kendrick Lamar spilling out the windows of a passing car. She found the pistol in her bag and slipped it into the pocket of her jeans.

The park at night was washed out and faded in the stolen light of the moon, the land of Faerie littered with crushed red Solo cups, plastic bags drifting like jellyfish, and discarded condom wrappers. She felt something crunch under her high tops and saw it was an empty plastic meth vial. There were more of them scattered among the jungle gyms, the water fountains, the graffiti-covered benches.

"Jesus," she said, her hand in her pocket, cradling the .38. "I thought they cleaned this place up?"

"Doesn't matter," Agares said. "Places, things, hold an energy, a resonance, from the events, the people, that mark them. Shit leaks over."

"You saying City Park is haunted?" There was no skepticism in her voice now.

The old man grunted. "From your point of view, more like cursed."

Agares approached a figure in a hoodie who was slumped on the swing set. The park's one functioning street light pinned the man, and Sunny could see his hands were an unhealthy pale color and blotchy with sores and scabs. As the two pilgrims entered the circle of harsh, shuddering, sodium light, she sensed the presence of other figures gathering around them, behind them, in the darkness. She slipped the gun free of her pocket, her hands shaking, and held it close to her leg.

"Hey, Meth," the old man said to the shadow on the swing.

"Long fucking time, huh? How's biz?"

The man on the swing looked up and slipped back the hood on his black, zippered jacket. His skin had the discolored pallor of a grub. Scabs and scars covered his face. His eyeballs were yellowed, and when he smiled, his remaining teeth and recessed gums were gray and rotting. For one horrible instant, Sunny swore his teeth had been replaced with endless rows of gleaming hypodermic needles.

"That you, Agares?" The corpse-man's voice was a hiss strained through broken glass. "What you doing in the big city, swamp rat? Ain't safe for you out of your muddy hole, you know that, grandpa."

"Sunny," Agares said gesturing toward her, "Meth-istopheles." He pointed to the man on the swing. "Meth, Sunny. We're here to do a bit of business, that's all. I'm on a hunt. The prey tarried in your garden for a time. I'm just wanting to narrow my focus. Simple, see?"

"Uh-huh," Meth-istopheles said. "You just wander on in to my territory, ask me to help you claim a skim it sounds like I have a pretty good claim on myself, and then wave goodbye like a happy, happy asshole while you and—Sunny, was it?—drive off. That's no business, gator-fucker, that's a motherfucking insult."

Meth stood. It reminded Sunny of a zombie lurching to life in a horror movie. The others just outside the circle of dingy light shuffled closer. She almost brought up the pistol, but Agares raised a palm to stop her. His own hand fell to the hilt of his Bowie knife. He walked forward until he and Meth were only inches apart.

"You aren't still pissed about the whole business with the German, are you?" the old man said. "We both got good and fat off that one, old buddy. You have no fucking right to…"

"You have never honored the law of domain," Meth snarled. His anger was the first sign Sunny had seen that he might perhaps be human. "You and your fucking hawks wander wherever you please and stick your big beaks into matters that are none of your concern."

"My domain is the lost," Agares said. He spit on Meth's expensive-looking sneakers and grinned. The expression was a joyless thing, a wolf bearing fangs. "She's bound herself to me, and we're seeking a man she wants to kill. His essence-scent led to you. Now you can give him up, or I can kick your scabby ass all over your playground, Meth, and then you give him up. Make the smart choice."

Meth's response was to draw a small pistol from the pocket of his hoodie. "Kill her," was all he said, his voice shrill as he leveled the gun at the old man. Agares's hand flashed up, the big knife's blade bright in the counterfeit light. Sunny heard the faint thudding of sneakers and saw the circle closing on her. The first to reach her had a box-cutter in his hand. He cocked his arm to cut her, and she pulled the trigger, her hands shaking from fear and adrenaline. The hooded shape jerked and fell. A second shape was on her, then a third. A scabby hand grabbed her shoulder from behind. She screamed, firing again and again, spinning wildly.

Meth's gun blew a ragged hole in the old man's shoulder as Agares's arm shot out, like a snake striking, to slice Meth's throat. A crimson curtain of blood spilled from the nicked carotid, and the cadaverous drug dealer staggered backward. Agares tossed the knife to his non-injured arm as the bleeding one fell to his side. He snarled and dove at Meth, who was trying to dam his spurting neck while firing again. The shot missed and Agares sunk the knife deep into the dealer's side. They both fell to the ground in a tangle.

Sunny stopped shooting. She felt somehow distanced from her body. She had lost count of the shots when the fear devoured her reason. No one was trying to touch her, hurt her anymore. Three corpses were cooling in the playground dirt. Her whole body shivered as she reconnected with it, and her ears felt like they were stuffed with cotton. Dark shapes darted and fled the park, startled birds scattering. Sunny looked over toward the swings to see Mephistopheles lying still on the ground, his chest wet and black with blood. The old man crouched on top of him. His knife was sticking upright in the sandy soil near Meth's still-smoking pistol, cradled in a severed hand. Agares's arm was bleeding, but the old man used his good arm to lean in near the dead drug dealer's face.

"Come on," Agares said, "come on… give it up, give it up, come on…" He pulled the corpse's mouth open. Sunny walked slowly toward them.

"What are you doing?" she asked. "We have to go. I… I killed these people. The police…"

"Police will be here in about 10 minutes. To take pictures, file reports, and clean up the mess. I still need answers from this jackoff."

"He's dead," she said, still feeling like she was dream-walking. "And you're bleeding pretty bad."

"Yep." The old man stared intently at Meth's gaping mouth. "Liable to pass out pretty soon, but not until… here we go."

She watched as a small object floated out of the dead man's mouth and hovered a few inches above Meth-istopheles's face and slowly, silently, rotated. It was an octahedron, made of something that resembled black, mirrored glass. Blood dripped from the object, staining Meth's pale face.

"Yeah," Agares said, almost purring, "give it up like a virgin on prom night, yes." He reached out with his good arm and clutched the object in his fist. "Not getting away that easy, asshole. I told you to do it easy but no. Everybody's gotta be a fucking gangsta. Dumbass."

"What the fuck is that thing?" she asked, helping Agares to his feet. His clenched fist jerked and moved as if the eight-sided object was struggling to get free.

"It's the Colonel's secret recipe," Agares said and laughed harshly. Several cars had stopped to watch what was going on in the park, locals holding out camera phones, shouting to one another. Sunny thought she heard sirens in the distance. The old man stumbled a little and paused as they headed to the truck.

"Shit," he said. "Yeah, I'm going to pass out. Here, hang on to the little fucker. Don't let him get away." He handed her the bloody little octahedron and she clutched it tightly. It was trying to move, to slip free. She stuffed it in her pocket and tamped it down with the still-warm .38 and then helped Agares reach the truck, sliding him into the passenger seat.

"It's your town," the old man said, his eyes closing, "find us a safe place to flop." Then he was out.

"*Maldito idiota*," Sunny muttered under her breath. She found the keys to the truck still in the ignition, the large alligator tooth dangling from the keychain. She started the truck and sped into the evening traffic.

Agares woke on the couch, his hat and jacket gone, his arm bandaged. He tested the wounded arm, grunting in pain. It had to hurt like hell, but it still seemed to work. His boots were off and beside the couch, and he groaned as he sat up. Sunny was watching him across the room wearing a pair of pajama pants and a sports bra. She had the .38 leveled at him.

"Where is this?" he asked.

"My place," she said, enjoying the look of shock on his face. "It was close. You were bleeding like a stuck pig."

"Why the gun?"

"Because I have no idea what you are, or what this thing is." She nodded curtly toward a sealed mason jar. The black, shiny octahedron hovered and spun inside. "Or what is really going on. You gave me some lame bullshit about the soul being immortal and indestructible, and that doesn't cut it. I thought maybe you drugged me back in the 'glades, but I know better. I've been high, been drugged; this is more like a lucid dream. And now, because of you, I've committed murder, so you're going to explain all this to me, or I'm going to shoot you."

"Yeah, I can see it," he said. "You got a taste for it now. That's good. You'll need it for your old man."

"What? What the fuck do you know about it, you hustling bastard?" She aimed the gun at his face, stabilizing the pistol by using both hands on the butt.

"Not as much as I did know," he said. "When I lost that blood, I lost some of my tie to you too. Explain it to me. Why are we going to kill your father?"

The words, said out loud, hit Sunny like a punch. She lowered the gun a little. "Like I said. He ruined my life, ruined everything."

"How? Tell me."

"He was born in Cuba," she said. "He came over in 1980 with some of his buddies, looking for work. Castro and Carter stopped people from coming before he could get settled and get his mom, my grandma, Benita, over. She died a few years later. He got a job doing construction for one of our relatives who came over to the U.S. in the late fifties, and his sister, my Aunt Lira—she was really pretty—she got a job as a waitress." Sunny paused for a moment, the memories swimming in front of her, picking through thorns to find the few sweet ones. "Papi, he always said I looked like her." Something painful bit her and she looked back to Agares with the same cold, slate eyes she had come to him with in the swamp. "He said I was his sunshine on a cloudy day, you know, like that stupid song. That's why they named me Sunny. Bad choice."

"Suits you," Agares said. He sounded sincere.

"Shut the fuck up," she replied. "The rest is typical. He met my mom. They had fun. She was in her twenties; he was in his late thirties, and he had a pocketful of cash. He was foreman then, and there was apparently a big boom in the eighties, so it was like a party. The work dried up around the time me and my brother were born. Papi, he didn't plan to stick around. Good guy, right? But he lost his job, and he needed a place to crash, so he stayed with Mom and ended up raising us kind of by default."

"Why didn't he stay with your aunt?" Agares looked around, found his jacket draped over one arm of the couch, and searched it for his cigarettes but came away with nothing. Sunny tossed the mostly empty pack to him. He slipped one of the remaining ones out and lit it.

"Yeah," she said. "That's a funny story. See, one of the reasons he had all that fucking money in his pocket was he was doing some side jobs besides construction. He was dealing coke, and he started using. He got Aunt Lira into the business and got her using too. Mom used every now and then, but she stopped when she found out she was going to have me and Mendo. Lira, she couldn't stop, even when she told Papi and Mom one night when she was high and drunk that she was going to have a baby, Papi's baby. She never got to have the kid, though. She got cut up in a men's room over an eight-ball sale that went south. Bled out along with my cousin-brother in her belly."

Agares smoked his cigarette and watched her with eyes like a reptile, alien, cold, unknowable, and rapacious. Sunny paused a moment. The pack of cigarettes flew back across the room and dropped in her lap. She selected one of the remaining coffin nails as she continued. "Mom stayed with him even after Lira. She had a taste for the coke by then, and Papi would give her just enough to keep her quiet, let him crash at the apartment, or when he wanted to fuck her… or me. See, there were four of us by this point, and Mom used while she was pregnant with both my younger sisters. It fucked them up. Me and Mendo were the oldest; we were both 12. Did I mention he always told me how much I looked like Lira?" She lit the cigarette with a shaky hand and took a long pull on it, like she was willing more of the smoke deep into her being. She got up, gun in one hand, cigarette in the other. "You want a beer? I think have some rum."

She returned with the rum for herself and a cold bottle of *La*

Tropical for Agares. He took it. She joined him on the couch, her knees curled up close to her chest, the gun no longer anywhere to be seen. After a long pull on both the smoke and the bottle, she continued. "He would give me coke, just a bump, to make me less whiny when he came to visit. After a while, I was happy to do what he wanted…" She took another long drink. "Happy," she said with dead eyes. "Mom didn't give a shit. She pretty much sold me to him for her own habit. By this time, she was doing rock, spent her own money on that, the money she was supposed to use to feed and clothe us, y'know, pay the rent, stuff like that?

"Mendo, he didn't like the idea of his twin sister being a coke whore at 13, so he called the old man out. He had grown about half a foot, put on some muscle. He grabbed Papi when he tried to take me with him. They fought… and Papi… he… he killed Mendo, right there in the apartment. He made me leave with him… made me help him get rid of the body. He… we… chopped him up, fed him to the sharks out on a boat. He told me that if I ever told anyone, if I ever disobeyed him, he'd do my younger sisters like he did me, and then he'd kill them too, make me kill them and…" Her voice caught in her throat for a second, tangled in pain and sadness. It was a wet sound. "He said… he said I was his and he'd see me dead before he'd ever let me go. That we were… family."

Agares leaned forward eager to catch every strain of the suffering in her voice. He closed his eyes and sighed. Lost in her pain, Sunny caught herself suddenly when she noticed the almost orgasmic reaction in the old man. Her eyes stayed dry. She took several long swallows off the bottle and composed herself. "So, I did what I was told. Somebody called the cops, but no one said anything, and Papi skated on killing his own son. He joked once that he was sure he had a few other bastards laying around. My sisters got taken away by DSS while the cops were looking into Mendo. They saw what a cesspool our apartment was, the shape Mom was in, and they took them into foster care. They were going to do the same to me, but Papi said he could take me in. He was smart enough that he didn't have a record, and he looked good on paper so they gave me to him."

"How long you with him?" Agares asked.

"Till I was almost 18. The… things I did for him…" She finished off the dregs of the bottle. "I ran. Got out of town with some help from his uncle, the guy that had put him to work in construction.

After the business went bust, he started doing sales on construction materials, equipment, shit like that. I showed up at his door one day, and he and his wife hid me, cleaned me up. They got me a little money, some help, and I got the hell out of town. I came back about 5 years ago when I heard from a lot of people that Papi had just up and vanished."

"So you've looked for him for 5 years?" Agares set the empty beer bottle down. Sunny nodded. "Never found him. Why not just get on with your life? Why keep looking?"

"I fucking tried," she said. "I tried to forget, tried to build something on top of all that shit. I couldn't. I tried over and over again. I wrecked lives, hurt people, destroyed friendships, and more. Finally, I knew. I knew if I was ever going to get away from him, ever going to be free of him, I had to find him and kill the son of a bitch."

"And that eventually brought you to my door."

Sunny nodded again, putting down the empty bottle. "So now you know the why. Now, your turn. Explain to me what I've been seeing. What the hell is that thing that came out of your dead friend's mouth? All these things… explain them to me. No more vague-ass bullshit. Tell me."

Agares grunted. "Okay, I think you're ready now. There is no Heaven, no Hell, nothing beyond this place. Human beings, their immortal souls, have existed here since the world's—the universe's—creation."

Sunny began to open her mouth to protest, but Agares silenced her with a raised finger. "There is a god, well a god of sorts, small g. He holds dominion over this world, and he is more like a jailer than a creator or shepherd. He doesn't give a shit about you, any of you. Truth be told, he hates you. He built this universe to contain you, to contain the divinity, the god—big 'G'— inside all of you."

"You expect me to buy any of this horse shit?"

"Shut up. Stop for one fucking second. You want proof? You know proof is one of your jailer's favorite diversions, right? You're fucking smart enough to know all that, though, right? So fucking smart. Okay, be still, open your mouth, and don't fight it. I'll give you your fucking proof."

Sunny began to say something but stopped herself. She glanced over to the thing hovering in the mason jar and then looked back to Agares. She opened her mouth. He leaned closer; his voice was warm, oiled leather. "C'mon out… come on," he whispered, "don't be shy, give it up to me, give it…" Sunny felt a sensation not unlike the panic just before you vomit. It welled up in her as she felt something moving up from her stomach, to her throat, in her mouth. Her body tensed, and she felt like she was drowning. Agares locked gazes with her. His eyes went dark, either in anger or something sexual. "Relax, don't fight me on this… easy… easy. There we go."

She watched as a tiny sun drifted out of her mouth and hung in the space between her and the old man. It raged, it flared, it slowly rotated, and tiny prominences jetted from the surface only to spill back down. Clusters of dark motes marred the radiant surface. She closed her mouth and stared at this thing that had just come out of her.

"This," Agares said, "is the human soul. Your soul. Your small part of the collective essence of mankind."

"What… oh shit…" Sunny started to rebuff this, to claim he had somehow dosed her again, perhaps a flashback or… but she stopped herself. The blazing orb was like looking into a mirror; she knew what it was, instinctually. The old man was telling the truth; this was the essence of her, the totality of her. "How," she said, softly, almost prayerfully, "how can I still be alive and talking without my… soul?"

"It's close to you," he said. "You wander too far from it, and your skinsuit shuts down and your soul goes back into the cycle, until you get spun into another body, get born, live again."

"So, that—" she pointed to the spinning octahedron "—that is Meth's soul?"

"No," Agares said. "It's… well, the closest analogy would be to say it's an artificial soul, constructed by the divine dictator that runs this world. We were his attempt to make his own life, based off of you, but he can't make a true soul, like what you all have. He created us as servants, guards, to help distract you humans from the confines of this universe. I guess you'd say you were kind of like divine robots. But that," he nodded toward the small sun, "that is the real deal."

"If you're supposed to distract me from what's really real," Sunny said, "why tell me all this stuff?"

"Well first of all, because you wouldn't shut the fuck up about it, and secondly because there was a revolt against the tyrant. We wanted to free all you poor bastards, let you see the universe as it really is, give you the choice to go insane or tough it out and make your own way in it. We lost."

"What happened to you, to the other rebels?"

"We were told that if we didn't do our jobs, we'd be stripped of corporeal existence," he said, nodding toward the octahedron. "Our essence would be locked away, and we would remain in perpetual limbo. Some refused to play along, and they are gone now, nothing but memory. We were given tasks, karmic busy work. Like, for example, Meth's job is to keep humanity in a stupor through drugs and addiction. Any human who wanders into his domain becomes his responsibility. Mine is to misdirect by granting wisdom, to blind by helping wayward families come back together. 'Home' and 'family'—attachment in any form, really—are big snares to keep your kind distracted. 'The ties that bind,' and all that.

"We're pitted against each other by management. We're given perks when we keep y'all distracted, unfocused, and clueless. If we under-perform our essence could end up as a paperweight on some angelic douchebag's desk. The angels, the servants who didn't rebel, have dominion over us. It's a pretty shitty existence, to be honest, but we still rebel in our own little ways, like me telling you all this, opening your eyes to the reality past the lie. Most of us are still on your side. We want you to be free. We just have to be careful with how we do that."

Sunny was silent. She stared deeply into the brilliant, contained inferno of her soul, as Agares saw it reflected in her brown eyes. Finally she said, "I figured that if souls were real, I had fucked mine up a long time ago." She looked past the tiny star to the old man. "You said we can't do that, can we?"

"Nope. You can dirty them up, life to life, but they are pretty much self-cleaning. By the time your body dies and you come back in your next body, it's shiny again. Your soul remembers everything, though, even things your conscious mind don't. It's the source of your dreams and your nightmares. Best we've ever been able to figure out, you're learning, striving to become more than you are, to become God. This world was designed like a narcotic, to drag you under, keep you here, until you don't care about higher truth, until you're dead. Then you do that again, and again, and again."

"Anyone ever gotten out?"

"A few," he said. "Saints, Buddhas, prophets, messiahs. So, now that you know all this. You ready to call it quits? Move past your anger and pain?"

"I can't," she said. "I tried that. His roots and his poison are too deep in me. I have to make this final. I have to put him down before I can try to rebuild."

Agares sighed. "Even knowing what I just told you, even knowing you'll send him back into the wheel, not to Hell? The only Heaven and Hell are here, the ones your kind make and my kind tend?"

"I understand," she said. "I still need this. I have nothing left."

Agares carefully called Sunny's soul back into her body. It was as amazing a feeling as its departure had been a terror, as if for one resplendent instant, everything inside and out made sense. The old man took the mason jar and carefully opened it. He clutched Meth-istopheles's essence and whispered to it in a language Sunny didn't recognize, which sounded like cold water rushing over slippery river rocks. The words made the insides of her ears itch. She got up and left the room, packed a small bag, and took the remainder of the box of bullets for the .38, after she reloaded the gun. She splashed water on her face and looked at herself in the mirror. She hardly recognized the person who stared back. She returned to the living room to see Agar-es pulling on his bloody campaign coat and his hat. Meth-istopheles's essence was gone, but the room smelled like strong chemicals.

"He's in Tampa," the old man said. "Let's boogie."

The adult care facility off of De Leon Street in Tampa was a dingy, cinderblock tomb painted the color of mustard. The old man parked his truck in the parking lot, turned, and looked over at Sunny. "This place is pretty much off the books," he said. "They collect Medicare money for warehousing him here. Meth-istopheles said he was here because of a drug overdose that put him into a persistent vegetative state. He's been here for years."

"You coming with me?" she asked.

"I'll be along presently," he said. "I want to give you a few minutes. If you are still going through with it, you may want to use something other than the gun."

She got out and found her way inside. The hallways were dark and cool. They echoed with *The Price is Right* on dozens of TVs in different rooms, and smelled of shit and Pine-Sol. No one was at the reception counter, but she found a directory of residents and their room numbers on a sign near the door. She located Papi's name and made her way down the hall to his room. Her hand was damp on the butt of the pistol in her purse.

The door was open, and the shit smell was worse inside this room. She crossed the threshold and was face-to-face with Papi—or what was left of him. He weighed about 80 pounds now and had a few yellow teeth jutting from diseased gums in his drooling, gaping mouth. His face was skeletal—hollow craters for cheeks—but she could just make out the roughest edges of the monster who haunted her. It was him. But the creature she had wanted to blow a hole in, to watch breathe his last, ragged breath was long, long gone.

She pulled a folding metal chair next to the bed and looked around. No TV, no radio, no cards, no gifts, no little bears. Four bare walls and a bed holding the shell of a life. She didn't feel pity well up in her; instead, the anger remained bright and strong.

"This is exactly what you deserve, you son of a bitch," she said softly. "For Mom, for Aunt Lira, for Mendo." She felt the gravity of grief pull at her, and she thought for a moment she might cry, but she wouldn't give the prick the satisfaction. "For all of us you ruined. For me, you bastard, for me!" Her voice was shrill, and it set off a series of shouts and shrieks all along the hall.

"The pillow would be best," Agares said, suddenly at her side. "He'll be gone in few minutes."

"There a problem here?" asked a burly attendant standing at the door wearing a white T-shirt stained with some unrecognizable green-and-brown substance. Agares turned and shook his head.

"Just emotional," he said, pointing to Sunny who was still sitting, still looking at her father. The attendant rolled his eyes and shook his head.

"Just keep it fucking quiet," he growled and disappeared down the hall.

Agares turned back to Sunny. "Well, you ready to keep your promise to me?"

She remained staring at Papi's body, watching the chest rise and fall. A fly hummed around the stale, hot air of the room and landed on Papi's nose. He didn't move.

"Nothing beyond this, right?" she asked, looking up at Agares. "No torture, no gallery of regret to wander through, no justice?"

"Nope," he said. "A cosmic crucible of fire and light, churning, burning clean, then sending him down a stream of starlight back into the universe, back into the queue to begin again. There is no payback, no even-steven in this universe. No justice, no mercy, no reward, no punishment. All that only exists here, now."

Sunny stood, placed her hands on the cold rail of the hospital bed and looked down at the broken, starving memorial to this monstrous man and his inhuman acts. "I'm staying here," she said. "I'm not going to kill him, free him. I'm going to sit here day after day and watch him die, trapped in a rotting husk. This will be his Hell and I will be his Devil."

"What about getting past this, getting on with your life?" Agares asked. "He could be here for years, decades. What about your life?"

"I want him to suffer," she said. "I want the immortal part of him to weep, because I didn't let it fly free. He took my life away from me. I might as well be trapped in that stinking body with him. This is all I have left. Maybe after he's escaped, died, maybe there will be something after that, but I doubt it."

"You sure about this?"

"I am."

The old man sighed and nodded. "Well, I guess in a weird way you're keeping your word to me to kill him, just doing it at your own pace. Go on and get your shit from the truck. I'll be along in a second." Sunny looked at the old man and then at her father. She walked out the room.

Agares leaned closer to the comatose man's face and smiled. "You hear me in there, don't you? Yeah, you do. I can see you still burning, still shining down in all the muck and matter. Well, I know it took a while, but I made good on our agreement, didn't I? You said you'd lost her, and she was yours, and you wanted her back, wanted her home, where she belonged, and here she is. By your side until the day you die."

Agares tipped his hat to the living dead man and ambled toward the door, still grinning. "I do so love bringing families back together." The old man walked down the shadowed hall of Hell hearing the echoing screams of damned souls trapped in slowly dying bodies, brains rotting, abandoned in this world, waiting for death like a lost lover to free the bright bits. The sounds of suffering were an anthem, and the old man whistled along with it as he went to help Hell's latest willing occupant settle in to her new home.

ABYZOU

Abyzou is a female demon. Her name is sometimes said to derive from the Greek *abussos*, "abyss." In the pseudepigraphical *Testament of Solomon* (dating from the first through third centuries AD), as Obizuth, she describes herself thus:

> I am called among men Obizuth; and by night I sleep not, but go my rounds over all the world, and visit women in childbirth. And divining the hour I take my stand; and if I am lucky, I strangle the child. But if not, I retire to another place. For I cannot for a single night retire unsuccessful… For I have no work other than the destruction of children, and the making their ears to be deaf, and the working of evil to their eyes, and the binding their mouths with a bond, and the ruin of their minds, and paining of their bodies.

She further confesses that the angel who can confound her is Raphael (also the subduer of Asmodeus in the apocryphal Book of Tobit). Solomon, the narrator of this text, describes her thus: "She had a head without any limbs, and her hair was dishevelled.

I beheld all her body to be in darkness. But her glance was altogether bright and greeny, and her hair was tossed wildly like a dragon's; and the whole of her limbs were invisible." Solomon orders "her hair to be bound, and that she should be hung up in front of the Temple of God," a detail that suggests her appearance might have been inspired by Medusa, a Gorgon (monster) whose severed head was also displayed on Greek temples (and sometimes Jewish synagogues) to ward off evil.

The high rate of infant mortality in ancient times caused Abyzou to be much feared. Indeed a number of amulets from Byzantine times mention her by name and often portray her as kneeling, bound, and being whipped by a figure identified as Solomon or Raphael.

In 2012, Abyzou made her debut in popular culture as a *dybbuk* (possessing spirit) in the horror film *The Possession*. Online references to this film sometimes state, incorrectly, that her name is Hebrew for "taker of children."

Class of '72

J.D. HORN

The color of moonlight, the boy's paleness was a stark contrast to the violet rings beneath his eyes and the russet scabs on his knees poking out from the dove-gray shorts. Same shorts worn by all the boys Emma had seen at the Karkhous Academy, though the fields that surrounded the school's central manor, classrooms, and dorms were blanketed by snow. A snow whose surface remained pristine, the academy's students never straying from the cleared concrete paths.

The girls, Emma had taken special notice, wore knee-length skirts cut from the same gray, lusterless cloth. Like the boys, they wore dingy white button-down shirts topped with thin cardigans the color of the manor's slate gray roof shingles.

The chill inside was such that she could see the mist of her breath as Miss Carreau, a woman with vermillion-colored hair and an onion-like odor, led them—Emma, her parents, and her younger sister Isabella—across the great hall.

The pale boy hummed to himself in a high, tuneless pitch, unaware of their presence. He sat on a straight-backed bench, which reminded Emma of the pews at the church her grandfather had attended—the one they had visited with him whenever her parents fought about money. Those fights always led straight to her grandfather. He would sign a check, then hold it an inch or so beyond Father's reach as he scolded Mother, claiming they'd just about tapped the well dry. That it was time they both put aside childish dreams and find lucrative employment. Yet they'd come back again and again. "The only way to make it in Hollywood," Mother was fond of saying, "is to look like you already have."

There'd be no trips to Grandfather's now. Emma's mother's brother, the one she and Isabella were never to call Uncle Ray again, had inherited Grandfather's almond orchards and—outside of smaller bequests she and Isabella would receive at age twenty-one—the balance of his bank accounts. The lawyers provided Mother with an accounting of the years of grants and unrepaid loans to explain why Grandfather had thought this was fair.

"Both girls will be addressed as 'Miss Wiley,' and both must learn to speak only after having been spoken to," Miss Carreau continued, ticking off a list of rules she'd begun enumerating the moment after greeting them.

Emma jolted as Miss Carreau paused beside the boy. She'd come close to believing he was a product of her own imagination. If she focused hard enough on him, it seemed she might see through his translucent skin. His bench sat beside a mahogany door fitted with a frosted window. On the glass, stenciled in black block letters, were the words "Ana Bardalea, Headmistress," followed by "Class of '72."

Emma meant to ask if the headmistress had once been a student at Karkhous, but her father spoke first. "Is that really necessary? To address the students so formally? I mean, they're just kids."

"The world lives and dies by formalities," Miss Carreau said, her chin pulled low, a crease splitting her forehead. "Besides, Headmistress Bardalea feels a formal manner of address is good for discipline. It discourages favoritism." Her eyes narrowed on Emma. "Discourages those who might seek it out."

Miss Carreau shifted her penetrating gaze to the boy. She looked down over her nose and made a tutting sound as she regarded him. "Have the older boys been roughing you up again, Mr. Beck?"

The boy startled at his name, as if he had only then noticed the woman standing before him. He opened his mouth, then closed it. Bit his lip. Shook his head. "No, Miss Carreau."

Emma could tell he was lying. Most likely to avoid worse treatment at the boys' hands later.

"The Wiley family has chosen to arrive early," she said, a hint of accusation in her tone, "for their meeting with Headmistress Bardalea. We'll put the call through to your mother as soon as the Wileys have been *accommodated*." She emphasized the final word as she cast an icy glance at Emma's parents.

"No," Father began, "we don't want to interrupt your schedule, it's only, well, we thought it might be easier for the girls..."

"Of course," Miss Carreau cut him short. "We must always," she said, hissing out the *s*, "put children first." She tilted her head, pursed her lips.

Father coughed, retreating a step and tugging Isabella, whose hand he held, back with him.

"They call home each week?" Mother said, speaking for the first time since they'd entered the hall. Her voice, usually so confident and polished when dealing with the public, warbled and broke. "The students?"

"Each and every week," Miss Carreau said. "The headmistress insists parents be kept abreast of their child's... progress. It's a requirement of enrollment." She paused. "Much more enjoyable now that it's possible to video chat. Make sure—" her gaze fixed the boy to the bench "—to let your mother get a peek at your knees, Mr. Beck."

The boy nodded. "Yes, Miss Carreau."

A group of girls, some younger than Isabella, some as pale as the boy—a few even tinged blue—passed by, their scuffed Mary Jane shoes tapping the hall's stone floors as they proceeded in single file behind a skeletal woman whose dour expression pointed toward the door through which Emma and her family had entered.

Despite the influx of students, there was no chatter or laughter. The tapping of the girls' soles remained the only sound as they followed on one another's heels, their eyes downturned, their lips sealed. There was a heavy sense of *something wrong* that Emma couldn't quite put into words.

"You'll be joining Ms. Preta's girls," Miss Carreau said, addressing Isabella, with a nod toward the thin woman at the head of the procession. Isabella froze, her mouth quivering. Emma expected her sister to begin to wail, but their mother reached out and snatched her away from their dad, to whom she had been clinging. She gave Isabella a firm shake and then released her, leaving her standing alone, shocked out of the incipient tantrum.

"See," Father said, stepping forward and clasping Isabella's shoulder. "There are kids here your age. You'll make friends in no time." The youngest girls at the end of the line looked painfully small. Emma focused on her father's eyes. He was lying. To make himself feel better, painting a happy picture for Isabella to assuage his own guilt.

"Yes," Miss Carreau said, "we're unusual in that aspect. Most of the finer boarding schools are designed to accept older students, grades nine through twelve. Karkhous Academy accepts live-in students as young as pre-school."

Her eyes slid from Isabella to Emma then up to their mother. "Treacherous biology often saddles extraordinary people with the most ordinary of offspring. One does try so hard to cultivate a fondness for them, but a clear mind recognizes them for what they are—obstacles. Barriers that stand between oneself and reaching one's true potential. The Karkhous Academy specializes in freeing up those who are called to greater things than wiping runny noses by allowing parents such as yourselves to…" she paused, seeming to look for the right word and finally settling on "consign," which she said with approval, "their offspring to the care of the academy."

Emma gasped, the breath catching in her chest as she waited with a pounding heart for her parents to object to the woman's harsh words. No protest came.

A ragged exhale tore out of her.

"We're not quite sure what to do with you yet," Miss Carreau said, turning her attention toward Emma. "Your age should place you in second, but your grades and standardized test scores imply you're capable of working well above your grade level."

"She's a bright girl," Father said. Emma was thrilled to hear the pride in his voice. A wave of relief washed over her. He may not have spoken up like she'd wanted him to, but he thought of her and Isabella as special, not as burdens. He would set things right. She began to feel the knot in her stomach unwind when it struck her that any pride he felt was not for her, but for how she reflected well on him. The thought came as if it had been planted in her mind. A chilling glint in Miss Carreau's eye sharpened this impression.

"Loves art," he continued. "She has a real sense of color. Don't you, Em?"

"Yes, well…" Miss Carreau's tone made it clear she had no interest in Emma's answer. The administrator eyed Emma as if she had come across a spider and was debating whether to go through the trouble of releasing it outdoors or to crush it beneath her heel. "At Karkhous Academy we've learned that precociousness often lends itself to delinquency. The brightest are often the worst troublemakers."

"She won't be any trouble," Father said.

Miss Carreau hummed a reply.

"Emma's a good kid. You'll see, she's…"

"Matthew," Mother cut him off, turning his given name into a threat. He fell silent.

A sudden flash of interest sparked in Mother's eyes. She turned to the boy. "Beck?" she said. "Are you Chelsea Beck's son?"

The boy looked to Miss Carreau before answering. She nodded permission.

"Yes," he said, though his response held no conviction.

"Chelsea Beck," Mother said, with the same reverence of the "amen" Emma's grandfather had used to end his prayers. Her face beamed. She turned toward Father, though her enthusiasm seemed to flag as her eyes grazed Isabella, whose face tightened up with fear.

But even as her mother's fervor dimmed, her father's face flushed with excitement. He stepped around Isabella, not sparing her a glance, and drew nearer to the boy, towering over him. The boy pressed back into the bench.

"You're fans, I take it?" Miss Carreau said.

"Well, of course," Mother replied, her glow renewed, gushing. "She's my hero. She basically swept the awards last season."

"In a year, two max, it'll be you taking home those trophies," Father said. He was Mother's number one fan, always encouraging her, telling her that she was exceptional. Like when she landed the role in that regional commercial. And when she lost the part in the web series. But somehow Emma sensed a new certainty in his words, which went beyond his usual reassurances.

Mother's gaze softened as she turned to him, displaying such warmth, such love. She never looked at Emma or her sister in that way. Even when she said she loved them, the look in her eyes seemed practiced, like she'd repeated the words before a mirror a thousand times. "It will be us," she said, addressing Father, but not including, Emma sensed, Isabella or herself.

Father's face melted into a goofy smile.

"It doesn't pay to be too starstruck here at the academy," Miss Carreau said. "Every child here is *someone's* child. Actors, business moguls, rock stars, politicians—especially politicians," she added, as if correcting herself. "I thought we were well on track to having the sons of another president as alumni, but of course you've heard about the incident involving Senator Porter. Dreadful business."

"I knew him," Mother said, either desperate for attention or trying to establish her worthiness to be here in the great hall—maybe a bit of both. "Senator Porter."

Miss Carreau paused and raised her eyebrows, an invitation to continue.

"Well, not really *knew*, I guess," Mother said, backtracking now that she felt the heat of the spotlight. "But I met him. Back when I was in school. I worked part-time for a caterer. It was his birthday. Somehow he learned it was mine, too. He sent over a glass of champagne. Insisted the whole room toast me."

"Imagine that," Miss Carreau said. "You share the same birthday, and now your girls are taking his children's place at the academy. Seems like kismet to me. Or is it karma? I always confuse those two." Her eyes narrowed into those of a satisfied cat, a tight smile ascending her lips.

"Taking their place?" Father said.

"Well, yes," Miss Carreau replied. "Their short-sighted guardians have elected to pull them out of school. But their choice was to your benefit. That's how we happen to have openings so late in the term. Two students out, two in."

"But was that for the best? Even more change? Seems like it would be better to let them remain…"

"He was a lovely man," Mother said, though Emma sensed she spoke more to quiet Father than out of actual sentiment.

Miss Carreau smirked. "A lovely man who murdered his wife, then…" She put a finger to her temple and mimicked pulling a pistol's trigger. She shrugged. "Lovely man, indeed."

Emma felt her stomach drop as the scene flashed through her mind, her imagination casting her parents as the senator and his wife.

Miss Carreau's glance brushed over Emma, a knowing twinkle in her eyes, before she shifted her focus to Emma's father. "You should consider going into politics, Mr. Wiley. You have the look for it, that requisite pedestrian comeliness, and a jaw square enough to level out any lies."

"Thank you," he said, casting a confused, embarrassed look at Mother, "but I'm afraid I don't have political aspirations."

"No?" Carreau shrugged. "Pity. Well, keep the idea in your back pocket. As your wife's star rises, you'll find doors opening to you, laurel crowns waiting to tumble into your upturned palms. Of course, all honors come at a price. Mr. Beck," she said in a commanding voice that made the boy sit up straight. "Remove your shoes and socks."

Though it didn't seem possible, the boy's face lost more color. "Please, Miss Carreau…"

"*Mr. Beck*," she responded sternly.

The boy bent and untied his right shoe first, slipping it off and letting it fall to the floor. He looked up, his mouth pleading silently. Miss Carreau responded with an impatient nod toward his other foot. He undid the second shoe, setting this one on the seat beside him.

"Socks," Miss Carreau said.

He took his time tugging these off, then, once removed, held them between his hands, wringing them as fat tears formed.

Emma felt a flash of heat rise to her cheeks. Her stomach churned. The boy's right foot had lost its pinky toe. The two smaller toes were missing from the left.

Isabella cried out and rushed forward to bury her face against Father's leg. He impatiently patted her, staring at the boy's disfigured feet with something like disgust. And maybe… interest. Emma bit her tongue, determined not to react.

"Lost them last year to frostbite, didn't you, Mr. Beck? Walking around for hours in the winter garden, he was. Shoeless."

The boy's eyes fell to the floor, ashamed.

"How many awards did your mother win last year?" Miss Carreau asked.

"Three," Mother answered for him, breathless.

Miss Carreau reached wide to open the office door for Emma's family to enter, and Emma swung back, trying to avoid the sharp, green scent that wafted off the woman. "Do come in and make yourself comfortable. Headmistress Bardalea will see you as soon as possible. She is, after all, a busy woman. Her title is headmistress, but she wears a dozen different hats around here, maybe even twelve and a half."

Emma reluctantly stepped over the threshold. The room before her was spacious, with polished mahogany panel walls and two large French-paned windows. On the wall opposite the door they'd entered was a second door, painted an incongruous gunmetal gray. Emma took a few steps farther. Miss Carreau motioned toward a loveseat and two chairs on one side of the room, then perched behind the desk opposite the furniture.

"Yes, we understand. Thank you," Father said, scooping up Isabella and depositing her on the loveseat. He sat next to her, then patted the space beside him for Emma to join. She ignored him and crossed to the window, the individual panes letting in the day's dim light, though rattling in their attempt to hold back the buffeting wind.

"The winter," Miss Carreau's voice drifted to her, "has a way of hanging on here. Some days it seems it might last forever."

Her dad had taken her and Isabella up to Big Bear last year, so Isabella could touch snow for the first time. But until now, winter was something you *went to*; it wasn't something that happened to you. It certainly wasn't something that bit off pieces of you.

Emma peered through the shaking window panes. In the distance, tall pines formed a seemingly impenetrable curtain, cutting off the academy from the outer world. She strained her eyes to follow a double set of footprints cutting across the otherwise undisturbed field toward the tree line. The prints appeared too small and too close together to have been made by adult feet. She scanned the unbroken snow, searching for the marks left by the return trip, but found none.

"They'll grow accustomed to it." Emma turned at the sound of her mother's voice. She had come up behind without Emma realizing it. She, too, appeared to be considering the footprints in the snow. "A little hardship builds character," Mother continued, quoting Grandfather, even though she'd scoffed when he addressed those same words to her.

A light flickered on Miss Carreau's desk. She lifted the receiver of something Emma recognized from old movies as a telephone, and pressed a button. "Yes, he is, but your two-fifteen is here... already." She fell silent, her eyes gleaming as they scanned Emma's parents, then came to rest on Emma. "Yes. Better than punctual. One might even say keen." She nodded, presumably in response to a question, as if the nonverbal gesture could be sensed over the phone. "Of course. I'll send them right in."

Miss Carreau returned the part of the phone she'd held to her ear to its base. "Headmistress will see you now." She rose, waving her upturned palm as a signal that Emma's father and Isabella should do the same. She crossed to the door behind her desk and eased it open.

Isabella grasped Father's arm, her tiny fingers turning white in their urgency, and buried her head in his shoulder. "Time to act like a big girl," he said, sweeping her into his arms. Mother gave him a look, and he set Isabella on her feet. Emma stood her ground, forcing each of her parents to meet her eyes, silently urging them to acknowledge their betrayal. Father flinched. Blinked. Looked away. Mother reached out, but her hand stopped inches away and dropped to her side. Emma slipped past them and led the way into the headmistress's office.

She stopped dead in the doorway, surprised by the office's interior. Miss Carreau's office was large and bright, but even though the headmistress's space measured at least twice as large as her secretary's, the room was windowless. Its sole source of light was a single rectangular fluorescent fixture that buzzed far off-center overhead; the effect was a gradient descent into shadow, bathing the far end in darkness.

The walls near her showed mint green in the dim light. The gray metal desk that sat at the exact midpoint of the room resembled a battleship, like the ones in the black and white movies their father loved and Mother detested. An empty armchair, of the same gray metal, sat behind the desk, with two more identical seats positioned on the visitor's side.

The office was unoccupied.

A rough shove forced Emma over the doorsill, though she wasn't sure if the compelling hand belonged to the secretary or her mother. The momentum carried her across the office, almost up to the desk.

She heard the door clack shut behind them and glanced back to discover Miss Carreau had left them on their own.

She turned back to examine the items strewn over the desk. A phone similar to the one Miss Carreau had used to speak with the headmistress sat like a castaway in a sea of dusty curios. Some looked as ancient as the relics Emma had seen in the antiquities wing on her class field trip to the museum last spring. Others were cheap trinkets bearing the names of faraway places. Emma reached out and picked up a snow globe that held a miniature building, round with three levels. She rubbed the globe's face on her jacket sleeve, then turned it to read a plastic ribbon engraved with the words "Temple of Heaven" on one line, and "Beijing" below.

"Emma," her mother said, "put that down."

"It bears a reasonable likeness to the actual temple," a voice came from the far side of the room. Headmistress Bardalea stood hidden in the deepest shadow, her back pressed so close to the wall that it appeared as if she'd just passed through it to greet them. Emma jolted and fumbled the globe, catching it between shaking hands.

The woman was pale, even paler than the children under her care, her complexion picking up the cool green of the surrounding walls. Her hair, glistening dark like licorice, hung in thick, long, curled tresses. She wore a black dress—a sad, matte version of the formal gowns actresses on red carpets wore in the glossy magazines Mother bought to read during her long baths, the four hours of "me time" she took every Sunday afternoon while Emma's dad took her and Isabella to the Tar Pits or the park on La Cienega. Its hem dragged on the floor, hiding the woman's feet, blending into the deep shadow. Around her neck hung a necklace, a thick torsade of freshwater pearls.

Headmistress Bardalea seemed to glide across the room, her movement smooth, silent, and predatory. Emma struggled to identify the odor that preceded her, deciding it was like the earthy scent of her grandfather's fresh grave mixed with the spicy aroma of baking gingerbread. She noticed that her father slid Isabella forward, positioning her between Bardalea and himself.

"Just a bit of gimcrack," she said as her hand darted out and grasped the souvenir, "but not without sentimental value." Her fingers brushed Emma's flesh, and Emma immediately snatched back her hand. On that trip to Big Bear, she had forgotten her mittens, but she'd still pelted her father with a snowball. This woman's touch felt colder than the snow bank she'd plunged her bare hand into. Emma shivered. The woman lifted the globe and examined it. "I've been there, you know. I've been to all these places." She waved her hand over her desk. "And many more." She returned the globe to its place, but picked up a miniature blue and white ceramic horse and offered it to Emma, who accepted the bit of glazed clay without taking her eyes off the administrator.

"That came from Chile." The headmistress glanced at Isabella. "I used to have to travel. All the time, it seemed. Until I came to the academy." She held out her hand with its too long fingers and too sharp nails. Rather than hand it to her, Emma dropped the trinket into the woman's open palm, careful to avoid contact with her flesh. "Now it seems that everything I need comes to me. Sometimes earlier than anticipated." She looked over Emma's shoulder at her parents. "You weren't expected until this afternoon."

"We do apologize for any disruption we've caused," Father said. In spite of the chill, Emma noticed his brow glistening.

"No inconvenience," she said. "Miss Carreau has already prepared the enrollment paperwork. We just need a mark from each of you acknowledging that you both have a full understanding of what it means to commend your daughters to our care. A quick bit of work, then you can be on your way. Perhaps you can catch an earlier flight? People to meet. Casting calls to attend. No?"

"Well, yes," Father began, "but if it's a contract we're signing, maybe we should have our lawyer read it over first."

"We don't have a lawyer," Mother snapped. She wrapped her arms over her chest, flattening her breasts, hands clenched. Her knuckles shone white. "We've already discussed this. We've made up our minds."

"But I don't understand what this is all about. Not really."

"A simple enough arrangement, Mr. Wiley," the headmistress said, her voice husky. "A tried and true one that benefits the parents of every child at Karkhous." She motioned toward the chairs before her desk. Emma's parents exchanged a glance then sat obediently. It surprised Emma to see Isabella had drifted away from their father, standing on her own a few feet before the headmistress. "I get something I need. I give back… generously… in return."

"But what could you possibly need from these kids you have enrolled here?"

The headmistress sighed, the expression bunching up her forehead. "I thought this had all been covered," she said, casting a querying look at their mother. She must have found her answer, because she gave her head a shake, the coils of her hair jostling one another then springing up individually—as if each tress had a life of its own. "There are higher levels of being, Mr. Wiley." She worked at her hair, stroking the tresses down in a calming gesture. "I am one of those beings."

Father puffed out his cheeks, and forced out a fake laugh.

"It's true, Matt," Mother said. Father widened his eyes and shook his head, a stupid smile on his face. "You know it is," she said, spitting the words out. "You must feel it, too."

He reached out for her, but she leaned away.

"Higher beings at the top of a food chain that *overlaps* your own."

Father's eyes darted between Isabella and Emma, his mouth working silently, his brow wrinkled up. *He* should've been the actor in the family. Emma almost laughed. She might have, if the rage wasn't rising within her. He would leave her and Isabella here. She knew it. He was putting on a good show. For the headmistress. For their mother. For himself. "You eat…" he began.

Isabella started sobbing. Emma expected Father to go to her. To comfort her like he usually did. But he didn't budge. He didn't even seem to notice.

The headmistress did, and she grimaced as Isabella choked back her tears.

"I feed from the children's vitality," she said, her voice a tired singsong, as if she'd been forced to explain herself far too often, "just a little each day. Spread out over the entire student body. In return, I help make things… good things… happen for the…" she paused, settling on the word, "donors' parents. I can and will do the same, or perhaps even more, for you and your wife. There is no realm over which I don't exert some influence. I have contacts everywhere. Feelers—" she raised her hands and wiggled her ghastly fingers "—everywhere. That's how I came to learn about your beautiful family."

"But the Beck boy," their father said, looking back over his shoulder in the direction of the office entrance. "His feet…"

"His mother required a favor not covered under the usual terms of enrollment. We can always accommodate special requests, though they require negotiation. She offered me a tiny *amuse-bouche* and conquered Hollywood in return."

"This is crazy," he said, looking at Mother. He turned to face the headmistress. "*You're* crazy."

The headmistress pounced and landed beside Isabella. She placed her hands on Isabella's temples and turned the girl to face her.

Isabella gasped, and before their eyes her golden tan turned blue. The headmistress had only *touched* her. Isabella reached up, clawing at the woman, and her hands caught ahold of the necklace and snapped one of the strands. The pearls bounced along the floor, a couple of them stopping before Emma's feet. Emma stood frozen, realizing that the necklace hadn't been made of pearls after all. At her feet lay two tiny teeth.

The headmistress shrieked in anger, and Isabella cried out, trying to cover her ears. "I'll take from your mouth to replace any beads that are lost!" With a wave of her hand, Isabella shot into the air, convulsing, arms and legs splaying in opposite directions, her head snapping back.

Emma looked to her parents, her eyes pleading with them—*do something!*—but they sat there slack-jawed, gaping as their daughter jerked about like a kite in the wind.

No relying on them for help. Emma raced over and grabbed her little sister with both hands, tugging with all her might, freeing her from the headmistress's invisible grip. Isabella somehow landed on her feet, but in her terror tried to climb into Emma's arms, as if her sister were an adult capable of saving her, of taking her away from this place. Emma barely managed to keep them both from tumbling over.

Bardalea advanced, snatching at Isabella with her terrible pointed nails, but Emma spun her little sister out of the way and swung out, her palm connecting with the headmistress's cheek. A loud smack echoed through the room. Bardalea jumped back, placing her hand over the struck cheek, eyes wild with fury. She dashed to her desk and lifted the phone receiver. Emma could make out the purplish outline of her own hand on the creature's sallow, gray-green face. There was a soft click as the headmistress's taloned finger pressed a single button.

"Bring the paperwork," she said, her voice calm now. "Please." She'd no sooner hung up than Miss Carreau appeared at Father's side, clipboard in hand.

He accepted it without looking at her, his gaze fixed on the objects crowded on the desk before him, anywhere but on his daughters. "I need a pen," he said, his tone flat.

"Here," Miss Carreau said, but when he reached up, she grasped his hand and ran the edge of a razor blade over the tip of his index finger.

He gasped, but said nothing. His eyes fell to the blood bubbling up on his fingertip, then he finally looked at Emma. She could see it was only now dawning on him that any of this could be real and not some initiation prank.

"By the X," Miss Carreau guided him.

He turned his face to Mother, searching her face for direction. To Emma, her mother's expression was inscrutable, but her father must have found the guidance he sought. He nodded, pressing his finger against the form.

"And now you, Mrs. Wiley," the headmistress said. "Your dreams await."

Their mother tugged the clipboard from Father's white-knuckle grasp, then offered her own hand to an obliging Miss Carreau. She hissed at the bite of the blade, but didn't hesitate before smearing her blood onto the page.

"Excellent," the headmistress said, a bright smile on her lips. "Your first autograph."

Miss Carreau stuck a cartoon character bandage over Mother's wound, then offered a pink and yellow polka dot one to their father. She leaned in and placed a kiss on his finger before wrapping the cut. The tip of her tongue darted out to lick the blood.

"May we leave now?" their mother said, holding the clipboard out to the headmistress.

"Miss Carreau has a few more forms for you," Bardalea responded. "To collect a few bits of information. That's all. Then we'll get you on your way. *Ad astra.*" She smiled a wild and toothy smile—all sharp like a row of incisors—then turned to her assistant. "You'll finish up with the Wileys, won't you, dear?"

"Certainly, headmistress." Miss Carreau looked down at Emma's parents. "You'll want to say goodbye to your daughters, of course."

Mother was already rising. "No. Let's just go." Emma watched her mother's ponytail bob back and forth as she strode away without even a backward glance. Isabella lunged at their father, but Headmistress Bardalea moved in even more quickly, snatching her up into the air with a single hand. "Now, now, we'll have none of that."

Isabella kicked and screamed, screeching "Daddy!" over and over.

Emma put her hands in her ears to block out the sound, but not before she heard their father say, "Sorry, pumpkin. Sorry…" He looked down at Emma, but she turned her back to him and walked toward the far end of the room, moving into the shadows.

"Close the door behind you, won't you, dear?" Headmistress Bardalea called out to her assistant.

"Yes, Headmistress."

The door pulled shut with a loud bang, causing Emma to turn back.

In that instant, headmistress Bardalea stood before her. She now held Isabella with great tenderness, stroking the girl's hair as she sobbed with abandon.

Emma stared up in wonder. "Let her go," she said, trying to sound unafraid. She reached out to catch hold of Isabella's leg, but Isabella yanked it from her grasp and held onto Bardalea for dear life, nestling her head into the headmistress's shoulder. Bardalea shifted the girl to her hip. Emma stood there, dumbfounded, as the headmistress knelt down to speak to her.

"Our Isabella," she said, "knows a secret. One I shared with her before our scuffle. One I tried to share with you, but you pulled away from my touch too soon." A smile that seemed as genuine as possible—when stretched over the tips of sharp teeth—rose to her lips. An impossible gleam of kindness welled up from the bottomless blackness of her eyes. "You never need fear me." Bardalea touched her as she said it, that same cold touch that had seeped into her skin earlier. This time she did not flinch. "Your sister and I, we were only playacting. For your parents' benefit."

Strangely, Emma felt this to be true. Isabella pulled her head back from the headmistress's shoulder and met Emma's gaze. Her little sister seemed at home in the creature's embrace.

"Your mother," the headmistress said, "believes she's an actress. But I believe you would make a better one. Shall we test my theory?"

Emma nodded.

"Good," Bardalea said. "Your sister has played her part, but now I need *you* to scream. Scream like you're being hurt worse than you've ever been hurt before." She reached out and placed her palm on Emma's cheek.

"Shall we try?"

Emma nodded once more, and Headmistress Bardalea patted

her shoulder. "On three, then?" Emma nodded again. "One… two… three!"

The headmistress hadn't begun the final number before Emma's lips parted. She screamed, reaching down and touching the shame and anger and fear instilled by her parents' abandonment.

Isabella reached up and covered her ears, but then began keening along with Emma, giving voice to her own fury and despair.

Headmistress turned Emma to face the wall behind them. She and Isabella both fell silent as the shadows gave way to the image of her parents fleeing the building and getting into their rental car. The tires skidded as the car hurried down the icy drive. Neither of them looked back.

"There. That's done," Bardalea said. "It is finished."

Someone took Emma's hand, and she looked up to find Miss Carreau's face smiling down on her. Her unpleasant scent was gone, replaced by a sweet smell that reminded Emma of orange blossoms.

"I've never harmed a child," the headmistress said, setting Isabella on her feet before rising to stand. "I would never harm a child, though some have been… broken in my name. I never wanted such a thing. Never needed such a thing. Children suffer. Children die every day. Starving. Washing up drowned on shores. If the suffering of children nourished me, man's fearful greed and indifference would see to it that no arena could contain me. But it isn't you children I feed from." She reached out and pulled Isabella in for a squeeze. "I feed from the souls of the parents who would willingly sacrifice their babies to me."

The Beck boy came running into the room, his bare feet slapping against the floor. He threw his arms around Bardalea's waist, demanding to be taken into her embrace. Emma had to look twice to confirm it was the same boy. His complexion was rosy, and he looked fuller and a good three inches taller than when she had seen him in the hall minutes before. Emma, her fear reborn in a flash, cast a nervous eye at his feet. But they were whole, all ten toes intact.

The headmistress leaned over and placed a kiss on his head. "You put on your shoes, then take your new friends outside to play. Introduce Emma and Isabella to the others, make sure they feel at home."

"But..." Emma began, thinking of the snowy fields and icy air.

"Go on, dear," the headmistress replied, placing Isabella's hand into Emma's, giving them both a gentle squeeze. "I believe you'll find it's gone spring out there now."

CAIM

It might be tempting to link the name *Caim* with that of the biblical Cain, but in all likelihood there is no connection. Formerly one of the order of angels, Caim (sometimes known as Camio) is a "great president" of hell, with thirty legions of demons at his command. He is said to take the form of a thrush, or, alternatively, a blackbird. He can also take on human form, and when he does, he carries a sharp, tapered sword, which may be symbolically linked to one of his chief traits, since he has been called the wisest occupant of hell. (Swords have long been associated with sharpness of wit.)

Caim has the power to teach human beings the languages of the animals, including birds, bullocks, and dogs. He also bestows the power of understanding the voice of the waters—probably an allusion to verses in Ezekiel and Revelation in which God speaks with the voice of many waters, for example: "And, behold, the glory of the God of Israel came from the way of the east: and his voice was like a noise of many waters: and the earth shined with his glory" (Ezekiel 43:2). These passages appear in prophetic contexts, so this detail may be connected with another of Caim's salient abilities, because he is said to be the devil most adept at foreseeing the future.

Caim is also said to naturally excel in debate. One nineteenth-century demonology says that he was the devil who disputed theology with Reformer Martin Luther. But whether Caim was the devil at whom, in a famous episode, Luther threw an inkpot, claiming he was distracting him from translating the Scriptures, cannot be determined. In any event, for centuries, Luther's room at the Wartburg castle in Thuringia displayed a large blue stain on the wall that was supposedly connected with this incident, although the stain has long since worn away.

By Promise Preordained

SEANAN McGUIRE

The scent of absinthe and sandalwood coiled through the air like the body of a great snake, thick and cloying and bitter at the back of the throat. Ian struggled not to choke on the smell, all too aware that it would make him look weak. He didn't want to be the first to break. The cost of failure, here, would be too high.

Somewhere off to the left, Molly began to cough. His throat relaxed as the fear of being chosen left him. Now that he didn't need to be afraid, breathing the burnt offerings was easy, almost pleasant.

Molly was still coughing, sounding increasingly alarmed. Jared pounded on her back, hitting her between the shoulder blades, trying to knock the intangible obstruction away.

Sucks to be you, thought Ian languidly. Jared thought no one knew that he and Molly were fucking after ritual every Wednesday night. Jared wasn't half as subtle as he believed himself to be.

Across the circle, writhed in ribbons of smoke, Helene offered Ian a slow smile. Unlike their companions, *they* hadn't been foolish enough to yield to the temptations of the flesh, not when they knew this hour was coming. Ian allowed himself to give her a more appreciative glance than he usually dared. She was a lovely woman, and they got along well. Maybe now that they knew neither of them was going to be chosen, they could reconsider their hands-off policy. They were about to be rich and powerful beyond their wildest dreams, and like those wildest dreams, none of it was going to make any sense to anyone who hadn't been there. They could do worse than choosing their partners from inside.

(There should have been more of them. There should have been ten, twelve, thirteen of them, some larger, sacred number, something to distribute the lottery that they had all entered into before they really understood what they were doing. There should have been better odds. There could never have been better odds.)

Barbara stood at the head of their circle with her toes almost brushing the Seal of Solomon, the Book held protectively close to her chest. "It's time," she said. She turned her disapproving gaze on the choking Molly. "Can you stand? If you can't stand, we'll carry you."

Molly's breath caught in her throat, the reality of her situation finally appearing to sink in. "You're not..." she said, voice raspy and torn. "You're not *serious*."

"You came. You agreed. You signed in blood, signed with bone, swore that this was what you wanted." Barbara raised her own left hand, her missing index finger a silent reminder that everything she said was true. "You were chosen. How many would have died for the right to be chosen in your place? How many would have killed for it? You came of your own free will."

The incense grew thicker as it burned down, turning the air into a perfumed mire, a swamp intended to be inhaled and allowed to linger in the body, thick and dank and terrible. Ian took another breath. It was so easy to breathe it now, now that he knew it wasn't for him. So very, very easy.

Molly shot a panicked look at Jared, clearly expecting him to help her, and paled when he turned his face away.

"Please," she moaned. "*Please*."

"You were called; you came; you were chosen," said Barbara. "You can't escape your duties with a few petty pleas and a heart that forgets loyalty for the sake of self-preservation. Seize her."

With a sigh, Ian lumbered to his feet, realizing as he did how lightheaded he was. Jared grabbed Molly from behind, holding her in place as Ian advanced, as she thrashed and moaned. The look on Jared's face was one of indescribable regret. Ian smirked at him.

Bet you wish you hadn't fucked her now, don't you? he thought. This would have been so much easier if Jared had only waited. "I've got her," he said, and grabbed her right arm, allowing Jared to shift his grasp to her left. Together, they pulled the struggling, wailing woman toward the waiting Seal. She fought them—how she fought them!—until her breath caught in her throat again, and she began to choke. She was still choking when they cast her into the center of the Seal and stepped quickly away.

It was one thing to agree to take part in a lottery of sorts, one that would end as soon as someone was chosen. It was something else to be chosen after the game had ended. Neither of them was willing to risk that.

Molly curled up in the center of the circle like an infant, hugging her knees to her chest, coughs wracking her body. She was still clothed. It would have been better if she'd been willing to fulfill her promise to the rest of them, to go naked and willingly, but that wasn't necessary. Better was an ideal to strive for not, thankfully, the minimum that had to be achieved.

"We have drawn the circle in salt and silver," intoned Barbara. *Her* voice was perfectly clear. The smoke didn't seem to bother her at all. Ian thought, for one envious moment, that she had somehow never been in danger of being selected.

Unaware of his envy, or perhaps simply unconcerned by it, Barbara continued: "We have shaped the sigils in lead and gold. Every door has been opened for you, Caim, who knows the speech of bird and beast, who speaks truth to the faithful, who sees what is yet to be. We have prepared you this good offering, ready for your use, waiting only for you to come before us."

There was no sound apart from the rasp of Molly's breath and the snivel of her fear. Jared and Ian exchanged an uneasy glance across the circle. When Barbara had proposed this as a better way to get ahead than grad school, they'd been desperate enough, and afraid enough of further student loan debt, to listen. Now, standing in a smoky basement with their friend having what looked like a nervous breakdown in the middle of a modified Seal of Solomon, this all seemed a little less realistic, and a little more like a children's game gone horribly wrong.

The candles blew out. The smoke, rather than rising toward the ceiling, fell out of the air like it had suddenly been weighted down, becoming too heavy for suspension.

Molly laughed.

It was a low, burbling sound, nothing like her usual flatly bitter tones. It was laughter filtered through soil and stone, run through a shield of sea salt and regrets. Ian fought the urge to step backward, away from the circle's edge. Jared started forward, only to be stopped when Barbara shot him a harsh look, warning him away.

"Who comes?" she demanded. "Speak your name, and be remembered before the world."

Molly's laughter continued. No: not Molly's. The fear was gone. Even more telling, the thin line of curdled regret that had always seemed to haunt her voice was gone as well, replaced by chilling delight. Slowly, she uncurled, stretching until the tips of her small breasts pointed toward the ceiling. There was nothing sexual about the motion, which made Ian even more uncomfortable. Molly had always been a woman aware of her effect on people, fond of straight men and lesbians, anyone who would dance to the tune behind her smile and the shimmy of her hips.

This Molly didn't look like she'd care about what people did when she looked at them. This Molly didn't look like she'd care about much of anything. She ran her hands along her sides, practically purring at the touch of fingers on solid flesh.

"Yes," she said, voice low and virtually toneless. It was the voice of someone who hadn't spoken in years, who didn't know what she sounded like or how to stress the syllables in a natural manner. It was like listening to a rainstorm decide to carry on a conversation, and it made Ian's bowels turn to water while his skin turned to ice.

What had they done?

"Yes?" echoed Barbara.

"Yes." Molly turned toward their high priestess, the woman who had brought them to the dark beneath the world, and smiled. "This will do. You have fulfilled your portion of the bargain. It is mine to keep?"

Jared made a low, animal noise, but was otherwise silent as Barbara nodded.

"Yes," she said. "The contract was signed in blood, and all forms were properly observed. The vessel belongs to you, now and always and until you have finished with it."

"That will be a while," said Molly—no, not Molly, not anymore;

never again—and stood, running her hands down her sides for a second time, until they came to rest just above her hips. She looked around the room and frowned. "So few of you. There are no great powers in this room. How is it you've called me with so few?"

"We asked thirty-five," said Barbara. "The number recommended in the scripture. These are the ones who agreed."

"So *few*," said Molly again, more peevishly. "Never say the word 'scripture' in my presence again. You have the contract?"

"I do," said Barbara.

Ian squirmed. He had helped to compose the contract, back when this had seemed like an impossible long shot. Molly's body was already forfeit, the cost of the summons. Now came the tithing, the promises of wealth and comfort and anything the creature—the demon, oh, God, they had summoned an actual *demon*—desired, forever.

Barbara produced the thick sheaf of paper and handed it over for Molly's perusal. For her part, Molly stood unconcerned, flipping through the pages and nodding. Finally, she looked up, and smiled.

"It will do," she said.

"Welcome, Caim," said Barbara, and it was done.

"It's funny," said Jared, sipping his overpriced latte, his legs extended in front of him and crossed at the ankles. To look at him, Ian would never have been able to guess that he had grown up poor and angry, never sure where his next meal was coming from, willing to do anything—*anything*—to get ahead.

Six years of absolutely everything a man could want certainly made a difference. As did a decent suit. Ian was willing to bet that Jared's current outfit cost more than his first car. It fit better, too, at least when measured against the rest of their environment.

"What is?" asked Ian finally, rising to the prompt.

"I was going through some boxes from the old apartment yesterday, and found a photograph of Cait, smiling. For a moment, I didn't realize what I was looking at." Jared blew on the surface of his coffee and took another sip. "I've adapted. There was a time when I wouldn't have thought that was possible, and yet here we are."

"Here we are," agreed Ian.

Here they were, six years after opening a door and inviting what waited on the other side to come through; here they were, standing on steady ground while everything around them shifted. Their investments always seemed to bear fruit. Their choices always seemed to be good ones, even when they made little sense in the beginning. They were the golden boys. The golden girl, as well: Helene had done just as well for herself as her companions. Ian thanked the heavens nightly that Molly had been chosen in place of himself, in place of the woman who had become his wife, and when he kissed their children before bed, he knew that everything they had done had been more than justified. The ends were glorious enough to put the means into their place.

"Do you know why she wants to see us?"

Ian shook his head.

Summoning the demon Caim—a president of Hell, who could speak to animals and understand the messages in the rushing of water, who could foresee the future—had been Barbara's idea. A Classics major, she had always been a little to the left of ordinary, a little overly willing to believe in the impossible. She had been the one to go around their college campus with a petition, gathering signatures to summon her own little oracle.

It had only been after the fact that Ian had learned she'd asked exactly thirty-five people to join her circle, a number she'd derived from some book of sacred alchemy. It had only been after it was all too late, after they had signed in blood—willingly, God, they had all signed of their own free will, and if that didn't prove Barbara had been a sorceress even before she'd managed to summon a demon, nothing did—that she had explained the form the summoning was going to take.

"Demon presidents of Hell don't have material forms that can survive in this world," she had explained, calm and easy as if she were telling them how they were going to handle rental fees on the room beneath the library, the one where the smell of smoke still lingered, even now, and would never quite come out of the walls. That, too, had been in their budget: an electrical fire, a cleaning fee, a series of carefully planned excuses that had been designed to be believable to the administration, even as they did nothing to touch upon the truth. "If we want Caim to come to us, to listen to us, to *help* us, we need to offer something in return. We need to offer a body."

They had been so innocent then, so easily led by promises of wealth and power—and to be fair, Barbara and Caim-now-Cait had delivered on all of them. With a demon who could see the future and talk to animals accessible at the press of a button, how could they *not* have become richer and more powerful than their wildest dreams? How could they have failed to thrive, once the world was entirely adjusted to their pleasures?

Ian had no regrets about the last six years. He had a lovely home, a beautiful wife, two precious children, and more money than he would be able to spend in a dozen lifetimes. Even after paying what he considered to be his fair share of taxes—because why should he be beholden to more than his fair share, when his only crime was success? Really, it was unreasonable in ways he couldn't even find words for—he knew he would never need to worry again. None of them would. And all it had cost them was a little bit of blood, a few hours every month to renew the summoning circles, and Molly.

But Molly had come willingly, just like the rest of them. She had made her own decisions, and when those decisions led her to a dark place, she had been lost forever. It was sad. It was tragic, even, especially if you asked Molly's family, who had never learned what became of her. But it wasn't their *fault*. It wasn't like anyone had *forced* her to pick up the bone and sign in blood, when all of them knew what it could cost. Even if none of them apart from Barbara had believed, they had all known.

That had been enough. Contracts with Hell had to be specific; they had to be detailed; they had to cover every eventuality. They did not, it turned out, need to be believed. Signing was binding, and once bound, there was no getting away.

Helene appeared at Ian's elbow, her own latte in hand. She no longer announced her approach with the staccato click of heels: instead, she wore blue jeans and comfortable shoes, eschewing the armor of her younger years. She had matured into her beauty, softening and stretching it until it fit her like the finest silk. Resting her hand on her husband's shoulder, she smiled at Jared, who sat up a little straighter in his seat.

Too late, thought Ian, fighting back the urge to smirk. *Had your chance, chose the wrong girl. Now back off.* Their little "demonology club" had seemed like a great way to meet girls. It had been, discounting Barbara, who had always been far more interested in her books and sigils than meeting Mr. Right. And then, for Jared, it had turned into something far less pleasant, when his chosen girlfriend had become the new fulltime residence of a president of Hell.

"Barbara says she's almost ready for us," she said.

Jared sat up further still, looking pained. "You spoke to her?"

"No." She held up her phone. "Texted."

"I still can't believe you carry that thing on business."

Helene rolled her eyes. "I can't go silent or the babysitter will have a panic attack and call the police. If you had kids, you'd understand."

Jared grimaced, and said nothing. Helene shot Ian that venomous sideways smile that he loved so much, the one that said she was still and forever the girl who'd joined a demonology society of her own free will, looking for power and prestige just as much as the rest of them. If her ideas of power took a slightly different form, that was her choice. Ian loved her all the same, and always would, for her fierce intellect and unflinching willingness to do whatever it took to get ahead.

Their children were going to rule the world one day. He was sure of it.

"Do *you* know why she called us here?"

Helene sighed. "If I knew, I would have told my husband before coming over here to tell you. United front, Jared. Remember?"

"We put it in our wedding vows for a reason," said Ian smugly, and snaked his arm around Helene's waist, pulling her snugly close.

That wasn't all they'd put into their vows, of course, and with Cait in attendance, those vows had been remarkably binding, all things considered. She had called it her gift to them, a lifetime of loyalty, love, and absolute fidelity. Ian supposed there were worse things she could have done than compel him to remain faithful to his wife.

Jared opened his mouth to reply, and froze, looking for all the world like a rabbit that beheld the shadow of a hawk swooping overhead. Helene stiffened as well, her body becoming an iron bar against Ian's side.

There was only one thing that could—or would—get that kind of reaction out of the two of them. Ian didn't turn, didn't flinch, didn't do anything that might make him seem like a target. The united front he and Helene presented had been mandated by their vows, but that didn't mean he had to draw fire away from her.

"Hello, Cait," he said.

"Hello, Ian." There were, as always, strange undertones in her superficially feminine voice, acoustic angles that were neither human nor acceptable to the ear. She walked like a human, talked like a human, but she wasn't human, any more than the person in the giant Mickey Mouse head at Disney World was a real mouse. She was playing a role. Whether she played it well or poorly didn't change the fact that it was all pretend.

Helene pulled away from him, his arm unwinding from her waist, until there was nothing preventing him from putting his coffee down and rising. A united front once more, they turned together to face the demon in the dead woman's body.

Like Molly before her, Cait was pretty enough to move through the world without attracting undue attention. "Great beauty and great ugliness both have their appeal, but it is the median where true security can be found." That was what she'd said when Helene—who was a great beauty, and always had been—had asked her, very carefully, whether there had been outside forces influencing Caim's choice of host bodies.

(Helene had taken this response as a great relief, since it meant she would never be seen as a suitable host vessel, even if something should happen to Molly. Ian, who was more ordinary looking, for all that he had been attractive and ruthless enough to catch Helene's eye, had been somewhat less reassured. Only the fact that Cait seemed to enjoy being a woman kept him from going to Barbara with his concerns.)

"What can we do for you today?" asked Ian, with the stiff politeness that always overwhelmed him when he was faced with the source of everything he'd ever wanted. He was much more comfortable dealing with Cait from a distance. She emailed daily, supplying each of them with the keys to the kingdom in the form most likely to benefit them. Sometimes it was big things—stock projections, the results of major sporting events or political elections, changes in federal law that couldn't be stopped but would influence future profits. Sometimes it was smaller things. They had learned of both of Helene's pregnancies from Cait, when the daily emails had included details on the best prenatal vitamins and the correct doctors to guarantee a trouble-free delivery. They had learned that their youngest, Sabrina, was going to fall from her horse during a riding lesson and break her ankle.

They had learned so much. The future, once recorded, was virtually impossible to change; Cait's daily emails not only predicted, they preordained. Only spoken prophecy could be evaded. Sabrina's broken ankle had become inevitable when it was written down, but they had been able to be there for her, ready on the scene with ice packs and a trip to the hospital. Sometimes the small things were the best things they could do.

"It is time," said Cait patiently. "I informed Barbara of this; she contacted the three of you. It is not my duty to contact you with anything beyond our bargain. You *do* remember the terms, do you not?"

"You tell us our futures, and we come when you call," said Jared. He moved to stand on Helene's other side, flanking her, presenting a different sort of united front. The three survivors of the ritual circle. The ones who'd walked away.

(None of them counted Barbara among their number. Cait—Caim—couldn't lie to them. The rest of the world, yes, but not to them. That had been a part of the contract. When Jared, emboldened by too much wine and embittered by seeing the woman he loved replaced by a demon, had written and asked her if Barbara's name had been included in the lottery, the answer had been a single word: *No*. Nothing had been the same after that.)

"Yes," said Cait. "I have called. Now you will come." She turned and walked away, soft-soled shoes making no sound on the hotel's marble floor.

The other three exchanged an uneasy glance before following her, deeper into the maze of twisting halls and spiral-set conference rooms, like sacrifices striding into the labyrinth, never to be seen again.

The room Barbara had found for them was pleasant, in the way of expensive hotel conference rooms: the carpet was plush, the drapes were floor-length, and the soundproofing was first-rate. The wide table which dominated the space looked to have been made from real oak. Barbara was already seated at its head, her ever-present notebook open in front of her, writing quickly. She looked up when Cait opened the door.

Ian, who was closest on Cait's heels, saw the smile that spread across Barbara's face before she caught herself and suppressed it. It was all he could do not to recoil.

My God, he thought. *She's in love with the thing.*

Barbara and Cait's relationship was no secret. The two had been living together since the ritual, and as a president of Hell, Caim expected certain physical needs to be fulfilled. That, too, was covered in the contract, which was a comprehensive document—terrifyingly so, covering every possible request their personal demon could make, from matters of personal comfort all the way to how they would react if the End Times began while Caim was prisoned in mortal flesh and hence in danger of being annihilated alongside the rest of them. It had seemed quaint, almost charming, in the beginning, the idea that getting their hands on a demon would require so much paperwork, so much precision.

It wasn't quaint anymore. It hadn't been quaint in a long time. Caim was ruthless in enforcing the terms of the contract. It wasn't unusual for any one of them to be woken in the small hours of the morning by a ringing phone and Cait's dry, improperly inflected voice on the other end demanding some small comfort, some finicky point of subservience that was technically owed to her by the terms they had agreed to. If not for the unflinching accuracy of her foretellings, the way she reached into the future and pulled back lottery numbers, stock figures, anything and everything they asked of her, it would have been tempting to believe that she was in cahoots with Barbara, that she was still Molly, playing some sort of long, terrible con game on the lot of them.

But when Caim predicted the future, the future came true. Every time. No matter how small, no matter how seemingly inconsequential a prediction, it came true. Cait was Caim and Caim was really a demon president of Hell, and whatever had called them here, it wasn't likely to be something the rest of them enjoyed.

"Barbara," Cait said, and crossed to stand behind the other woman, touching her shoulder lightly as she passed. In that gesture, Ian saw the other half of the equation. Barbara loved, yes, but she did not love alone.

It should have been soothing to realize that even demons could love, that even demons could learn to appreciate the humans around them. Ian knew he was going to Hell. All of them were. They had called a demon into the physical world. That might not have been enough to damn them, had they not then given that same demon ownership of a physical body and bound it to do their bidding. They had bought their own damnation one predicted future at a time. Only the fact that Caim didn't seem to mind—indeed, seemed to find this all quaint and even pleasant, like an extended vacation from the duties of a president—kept him from panicking about it at night. When they died, they would go to a place partially ruled by someone who thought well of them, someone who could love.

Someone who thought nothing of wearing a dead woman's skin like a Sunday dress, walking through the world on a dead woman's feet, smiling at a lover with the dead woman's mouth. Caim was many things. Ian wasn't sure "merciful" was among them.

Cait sat at Barbara's left. The last of Barbara's smile faded, her eyes skirting across the three of them like they were something unpleasant she had hoped to forget by simple dint of waiting until they went away. Her gaze lingered on Helene for a moment. There was something there that Ian didn't like, something that managed to be greedy and dismissive at the same time.

You're being paranoid, he chided himself.

"Please," said Barbara. "Sit."

With Cait there looking on, the word had the force of a command. The three of them found seats at the conference table, Ian and Helene side by side, Jared a few chairs away, trying not to stare at Cait, who seemed as alien and serene as ever.

("How can Barbara stand it?" Helene had asked once, after a little too much wine had loosened her tongue, leaving her soft and yielding and a little sloppy. Ian had tried to shush her, but she'd pushed on, saying, "It would be like fucking a robot or, I don't know, a lizard. Something that shouldn't *be* there. Something that shouldn't *be*."

Ian had been oddly vindicated the next morning when her hangover had left her helpless and weeping. *That's what you get for risking Caim's attention*, he'd thought fiercely, and brought her Tylenol and water, and waited for the feeling of impending doom to pass.)

"I want to thank you all for coming so promptly," said Barbara.

"Did we have a choice?" asked Jared. His voice was bitterness from top to bottom.

"No," said Cait. "But then, neither did I, when you summoned me onto this plane. Courtesy is granted to those who grant it."

There was a moment's uncomfortable pause. Cait was normally more careful to avoid reminding them of her origins. They all knew what she was, what they had made, but it seemed somehow inappropriate to remind her, as if by reminding her they would remind the world, and possibly pull down the attention of things vaster and crueler than a simple president of Hell.

"My apologies," said Jared, dropping his eyes to the table.

"The summoning we performed, while sadly lacking in courtesy, was effective," said Barbara, with a quick glance to Cait. "It bound the demon President Caim in the human vessel of his own choosing, and kept him here, hidden from the eyes of the Archangels who might otherwise have cut his visit short."

"I do not wish to go before I am ready," said Cait, calm and serene. "I enjoy this place and this vessel and this reality. I am a human woman, and it pleases me."

Helene, who had strong opinions about Cait's status as a human woman, swallowed hard and said nothing, but her hand tightened on Ian's until he thought he felt the bones grind together. He clenched his teeth and didn't pull away. Attracting attention seemed unwise.

"I wish to continue to be a human woman," said Cait. "The contract which you have all signed specifies the prioritization of my wishes."

"Yes," said Helene, sounding confused. "But it also states that we won't do anything to eject you from your chosen vessel, and that we'll defend your vessel against attacks. Is someone threatening you?"

Cait's expression softened. It was a small thing, almost intangible; something in the muscles around her eyes and the corners of her mouth. She still looked cold, still looked alien. But with that little change, she looked like something new as well.

She looked tired.

"Please explain," she said, turning toward Barbara, reaching out to put her hand over the other woman's. That, too, was new. Ian's stomach churned as he realized just how demonstrative the two of them were being. By their eternally discreet standards, they were practically jumping on top of the table and ripping their clothes off.

Barbara and Cait had never made a secret of their relationship, but they had never flaunted it like this.

"All right," said Barbara. She laced her fingers into Cait's before turning to the rest of them and saying, in a voice that was almost as clear, almost as calm as her demon lover's, "Cait is made of two halves. The demon Caim, bound here by our contractual agreement, and the human woman Molly, who agreed to the possession prior to the summons."

Jared said nothing, only grimaced and took a slug of his coffee, hand tightening around the paper cup. Cait looked at him coolly. Ian knew she was seeing the future in the man's gestures, charting the course his life would take from here until it ended. All any of them needed to do to know the circumstances of their deaths was ask. Cait would tell them truly, if they did, which was why none of them ever would.

"Caim is immortal and unkillable by human means. All that could be accomplished is banishment of the demon back to Hell." Barbara's voice faltered, and for a moment—only a moment—she looked less sure of herself.

Helene's hand tightened on Ian's again. He glanced at her, and her eyes were wide and frightened. She saw something in Barbara's loss of control that he didn't, and the fear he saw in her face woke the fear in his own belly, where it coiled hot and restless and ready to strike.

"Molly, unfortunately, lacks Caim's indestructability," Barbara finished.

"Cancer." Cait sighed. It was the rush of wind across the desert, it was the beating of a vulture's wings, and it was no human sound. No human sound at all. "We are informed by the physicians that it is past the point of curing, although they have offered to see to my comfort during the final weeks of my material existence. Palliative care, it is called. I have declined."

The strange stiffness of the demon's posture made sudden, terrible sense. If she had reached the point of palliative care, she must have been in excruciating pain, held upright solely by her inhuman will. For Caim to experience the pleasures of the flesh, he also had to experience its agonies. That was his side of the bargain.

"I'm so sorry," said Helene, before she could think better of it. Then she froze, terror sweeping over her face. "Are… are you going to…?"

"I do not desire your face or form," said Cait. "Your husband would be a tedious inconvenience. He would refuse to leave your side, which would discomfort Barbara, and I have no desire to be saddled with a human's get."

The children. The children had saved them. Ian shot a triumphant glance at Jared, who had tried to convince them that having children while tied to a demonic bargain was tempting fate.

Jared didn't look at him. All of Jared's attention was on Cait.

"What do you want us to do?" he asked. "Kidnap a woman for you? Do you have a shopping list of things you'd like in a vessel?"

"If I asked, you would be required to do so," said Cait. "That is our agreement."

"What if I don't like our agreement?" Jared half-rose. "What if I want out?"

Cait looked at him without flinching. "Then I pick up a pen and write the time and circumstance of your death. I lock it into being. It becomes so. Can you live the rest of your life knowing how it ends? Many men have tried to do so. Very few of them have succeeded in any meaningful way. You are weak. I have known you were weak since I extinguished the guttering flames of your lover and saw you through her eyes. She screamed for you as she was being excised from existence. She howled your name, and you did not save her. You belong, then as now, too much to me."

Jared paled, sitting back down. Cait turned to the others.

"I am fond of my existence," she said. "I enjoy this place, this world and time. I appreciate the advantages offered to me by my chosen partner, and I possess no immediate desire to return to my throne. I could demand you find me a new vessel. But it has been brought to my attention that of the four of you, only one truly understood what you undertook in bringing me here, and thus, of the four of you, only one can be truly trusted. This will not do, if I am to adapt to a new vessel. You have been called here to be offered a second bargain. Tonight, at midnight, I will transfer myself to a new home of my own choosing, as I am allowed to do under the terms of our compact. If you can find the way to destroy me before that time, you will be free. The wealth you have amassed will remain yours. There will be no penalties for breach of contract. If you cannot prevent the transfer, however, you will lose more than you feel is fair, and you will have no way to reclaim what has been taken. Do we have an accord?"

Ian frowned. "Why would we want to destroy you?"

Cait's smile was ice and flame, an echo of Hell painted on a human face. "Do not think me a fool simply because it amuses me to be bound," she said. "You already do."

The three of them gathered in Jared's room, which was twice the size of the room Ian and Helene shared. Helene rolled her eyes when she stepped inside.

"Compensating for something, *darling*?" she asked, tone snide.

"Always and forever," Jared replied, crossing to the room's built-in desk. A small array of liquor bottles had been set out there, despite the fact that they had only arrived that morning. He picked up the whiskey, tipped a healthy amount into the waiting tumbler, and drank before he said, "You try letting the love of your life become a mansion for a demon lord and see how much you have to compensate for."

"Caim is a president, not a lord," said Ian. Had they tried for a lord, and *succeeded*, they would have lost a lot more than a single foolish college girl. The lords were as far above Caim in power as Caim was above the rest of them.

Helene's interests were more practical. "Molly wasn't the love of your life," she said. "She was thinking about breaking up with you after the ritual was performed. She said you were dull in bed and never wanted to talk about anything she cared about."

"We would have found a way to make things work," said Jared.

Ian looked at his friend and wondered if Jared understood how deeply in denial he was. This felt like something he should have seen sooner—but when he looked back to his own reaction to Molly's selection, all he could find was relief. Relief that it hadn't been him, that it hadn't been Helene, that it hadn't even been Jared, who had been foolish and impulsive, yes, but who hadn't deserved to die. Of the others, Molly had always been the one he felt the least attachment to, and so it was only natural that he had been glad to see her pay the finder's fee.

He was sure that if he could convince Jared to tell the truth, the other man would admit to having hoped that the demon would choose Helene, who wasn't his girlfriend and wasn't his best friend. There was no shame in that. They had both gone into the ritual with priorities: it was just that only Ian had been lucky enough to have his fulfilled.

"Let's be reasonable here," said Helene, wrinkling her nose as Jared took another gulp. "Cait is going to need a new vessel if Molly's body is giving out. She wants to stay a human woman—"

"You mean he wants to keep fucking our glorious leader," muttered Jared.

Helene pinched the bridge of her nose. "Is it so much to ask that we not fight about our personal demon's gender identity again? I have a headache, we had to hire a sitter at the last minute to come here and that does *not* come cheap, and Caim has made his pronouns quite clear. When outside Molly, he's male. When occupying a human vessel, she's female. Caim and Cait. It's not difficult."

"What's difficult is understanding why you care," snapped Jared. "We have a chance to be rid of it, without losing everything it's already given to us. Why would you hesitate for a *second*?"

"Well, first off, because I don't know how to kill a demon president of Hell," said Helene. "Do you?"

Jared was quiet for a long moment. Just as Ian thought this was over—that Jared's perhaps understandable tantrum had run its course—the other man took a breath, and nodded.

"Yes," he said. "I do."

Silence fell.

Understandably, given the circumstances, Jared was the one to break it. "Or well, not kill it, but banish it from this world. I've been researching," he said. "If we kill the host and prevent the demon from leaving for one hour, it will be unable to seek another without a fresh summoning."

"How do we lock the demon down?" asked Helene.

"You leave it to me," said Jared.

"Barbara will arrange a second summoning," said Ian.

"Not if we kill her too." Jared glared at the rest of them, eyes suddenly alight with fanatic rage. "She wasn't part of the lottery. She did all the research. She had to know that Caim preferred female vessels. She didn't put her own name in the sigil. It was going to be Molly or Helene—a coin toss when it should have been one chance in five. She set me up. She set *all* of us up. Helene, do you even understand how close you came to being devoured by a demon? Ian, do you understand how close you came to losing her? This can't be allowed to go on."

"You've benefitted from Caim's prophecy as much as the rest of us have," said Ian.

"Because I knew that this day would come. The day when I had a chance to destroy the thing that killed Molly. I couldn't get what I needed if I didn't stay—and if I didn't have the resources to pay for the information I was looking for. I've been patient. I've paid. Now's when I get what's mine. Now's when I get my revenge."

"You're talking about murder," said Ian.

"You can't murder the dead," Jared countered. "Molly died when Caim entered her. The cancer is just a cherry on top of the shit sandwich she got dealt. Or maybe it's a mercy. If that damn demon weren't in her body, she would have been getting regular checkups."

Ian, who was fairly sure Caim's ability to see the future meant the cancer had been caught as early as possible, and was hence genuinely untreatable, said nothing.

"Barbara isn't going to like this," said Helene. "Even if Cait says we're allowed to kill her, Barbara will try to stop us."

"You can't murder the dead, but Barbara will sure as hell try to make sure we're punished for doing it," said Ian, feeling faint relief at the idea that here was an objection: here was something that might stop this mad idea before it could go any further. "This is foolishness. We signed the contract of our own free will—"

"We were *kids*," snapped Jared. "It was a *game*. I was still in that damn vampire LARP on the weekends, remember? People who spend half their time pretending to be vampires shouldn't be allowed to pledge themselves to actual demons. When I signed that contract, I thought it was something a little naughty, but not anything *real*."

Ian, who had known Jared long enough to know that he was revising history, said nothing. Helene sighed.

"Intent doesn't matter," she said. "Intent has never mattered. Barbara is the reason we're in this situation. She's the one who found the ritual, decided that we should secure our futures by summoning a demon, and told us what the costs would be. She never told us that she'd be holding her own name out of the lottery, now, did she? She never told us that when it came time to pay the tab, we'd be the ones holding the check." Helene's mouth settled in a cruel twist. "She deserves this."

Ian had known for years that Helene hated Barbara. Yes, they were wealthy, and comfortable, and loved their lives. But Barbara had been a little too miserly with the facts, and it was hard not to look at Cait and see a dodged bullet.

"We can make it look like a murder-suicide," said Jared. "Messy, but it gets the attention off of us. We'll be free. No more channel to the future, but we have enough to be comfortable for the rest of our lives. We can have everything, if we act tonight. Are you in?"

"Yes," said Helene.

Ian, bound by the word of a demon to present a united front with his wife, closed his eyes and hoped the sky was not about to fall.

Jared had a gun; Cait had a diagnosis of terminal cancer on her record. The plan wasn't difficult to devise. It was Helene who knocked on the door of Barbara and Cait's shared suite at eleven-thirty, a bottle of port in her hand, dressed only in a hotel bathrobe. When Barbara opened the door, suspicion in her eyes, she found no one else in the hallway.

"Go away," she said.

"I'm not here to hurt you," said Helene. Her words had been carefully chosen for their honesty. She held out the bottle. "Strip me, search me, do whatever you like, and then let me in, because if anyone needs a drink right now, it's you."

Barbara's suspicion wavered. "You're not here to hurt me? To hurt *us*?"

"Come on, Babs, what kind of fool do you take me for?" Helene's smile was blinding. "You think I want to throw away everything you've helped me achieve? I have money, power, a family that loves me, all the things I never thought I'd have. I am so much more than I believed I was going to be. I thought I was only ever going to be the pretty one. You changed that for me."

"I guess that's true," said Barbara, and stepped to the side. "Come in."

Helene—who had told so many truths, but who had never said "no"—stepped inside.

According to Barbara, Cait was resting; the cancer left her weary. Helene, whose system was crackling with so many uppers that it was a miracle she could pour the port without trembling, kept smiling as she served herself and Barbara, as she drank from the same bottle. Barbara waited until Helene had consumed several sips before starting in on her own glass, but once she started, she didn't seem able to stop. Helene drank more slowly, aware of the sedatives hidden by the overly sweet alcohol, keeping herself awake as long as possible.

Barbara seemed to realize what Helene had done as she was losing consciousness. Her eyes widened. Her hand tightened on her glass. Helene reached over and removed it from her grasp, smiling sweetly.

"It's time for you to rest," she said. "Don't worry. We're going to take care of *everything*."

Barbara made a soft sound of protest before slumping over in her chair. Helene rose, still carrying both glasses, and walked to the door.

Ian and Jared were waiting on the other side.

"My part's done," she said, with visible distaste. "The rest is up to you." She leaned onto her toes to kiss Ian on the cheek. "Make it quick. I want to be seen in the bar before they chase everyone out for the night."

Then she was gone, ghosting away down the hall with the tainted glasses and the doctored bottle of port. Anyone looking for its contents would need to be prepared to dredge the sewers. Even then, they'd be lucky to find so much as a trace. As for the sedatives in Barbara's system, they were a brand she was known to use when she couldn't sleep. Their presence would be easy to explain.

Easy.

So much of this was going to be easy.

Ian and Jared, working together, were able to hoist Barbara and carry her to the bathroom, where they stripped her naked and settled her into the tub. It was strange, seeing her like that. Like she was small, like she was helpless, and not the woman who had decided that the answer to all their prayers was calling out for a personal demon.

"Should we fill the bath now?" asked Ian.

"No," said Jared. "Forensics makes it too easy to tell how long a body has been in the water. We kill the damn demon, and then we come back here and finish the job."

Ian, looking nervously at Barbara, said nothing. *United front*, he thought, and followed Jared out of the bathroom, back to the main room of the suite.

Cait was waiting in the bedroom. She was seated primly on the edge of the bed, looking so much and so little like Molly that it ached, seeing her so. Her posture was too poised, too perfect. But her face was and had always been Molly's, open and innocent, with wide-set eyes and a mouth that always looked slightly bruised, like she had been biting into apples too tough for her to swallow.

"Have you come to kill me, then?" she asked. She glanced meaningfully at the clock beside the bed. "You have four minutes remaining. If you are to do it, it had best be done quickly. Unless you wished to request one last foretelling before I go, one more sliver of the future doled out for your dull mortal minds to clasp?" She stood, chin up, regal as a queen, imperious as a president. "I have always kept my word to you. Always. It is not my fault if you do not like the things I have had to show you. You knew what you were doing when you called me."

"Where do we go when we die?" asked Jared.

Cait smiled, syrup-slow and cruel. "Molly is already there," she replied.

The gunshot was very loud and very soft at the same time, muffled by the homemade silencer Jared had somehow produced from his suitcase. Ian thought that this whole thing wasn't nearly as spur of the moment as it had initially seemed; suspected, in fact, that Jared had been watching for an opportunity for quite some time.

Cait fell backward, clutching at her stomach. Her wide, wounded eyes were the most human things she had displayed since the moment she had entered her host body, since the moment she had become herself, and not the two component halves of Caim and Molly.

"I understand," she said, and collapsed.

"I hope it hurts," spat Jared. He produced a stick of chalk studded with specks of silver from his pocket and used it to sketch an uneven circle on the floor: the first thing they had done that couldn't be explained as circumstantial. He dragged Cait, unresisting, into it, and kicked her once, well away from the blood.

"Good luck escaping *that*," he said. Then he turned and walked away, and once again, Ian followed.

Barbara had known. Of course Barbara had known. She had been the lover of a demon president who saw the future like it was behind a clear glass pane: there was no way she could have missed her own impending demise. And so she had taken things into her own hands.

She had known they were coming.

Ian and Jared returned to the bathroom to find a puddle of vomit in the tub, alcohol and sedatives mixed with the charcoal Barbara must have taken before Helene arrived. Barbara herself was sprawled in the middle of the floor, her wrists slashed to the elbow, strange sigils fingerpainted on the tile all around her.

They stood in the doorway for a while, looking at her, not saying anything. Finally, Ian asked, "What do they mean?"

"I don't know," said Jared. "But fuck her. I hope she burns. God, I need a drink."

With that he turned and walked away.

After a time, Ian followed.

Ian and Helene had been silent for the entire drive home from the hotel. The lights were on when they arrived, and there were no police cars waiting. Ian breathed out hard.

"We did it," said Helene.

"We're free," he said, and the words felt foreign on his tongue.

The babysitter was sitting on the couch, her phone in her hand and a movie playing quietly on the television. Ian went upstairs to check on the girls while Helene dealt with paying the teen. They had both agreed that it was best if he never be alone with her. Not that he could have touched her, not with Cait's wedding gift binding him to fidelity, but people talked. Oh, how people talked.

Phoebe was sleeping soundly, curled into a tight ball on the very edge of her bed. He smiled, easing the door closed again.

Sabrina sat up when he entered her room.

"It's just me, Brina," he said softly. "Go back to sleep."

"Thank you," she said, and something was wrong with her voice; something was still and hard and alien.

Ian frowned. "For what, pumpkin?"

"It would have been very difficult for Barbara, to be left behind," said Sabrina calmly. "Your intervention enabled her to request that she come with me when she cast the second summons. We will be happy here, once she has adjusted. It can be… jarring, on the first transition."

Ian felt the blood drain from his face, leaving him dizzy. He clutched at the doorknob, praying for balance.

The nightmare behind his daughter's face smiled at him in the dim light.

"Do not be concerned for the welfare of your daughters," she said. "Molly will care for them as best she can."

Ian was still screaming when Helene ran up the stairs.

She joined him shortly after.

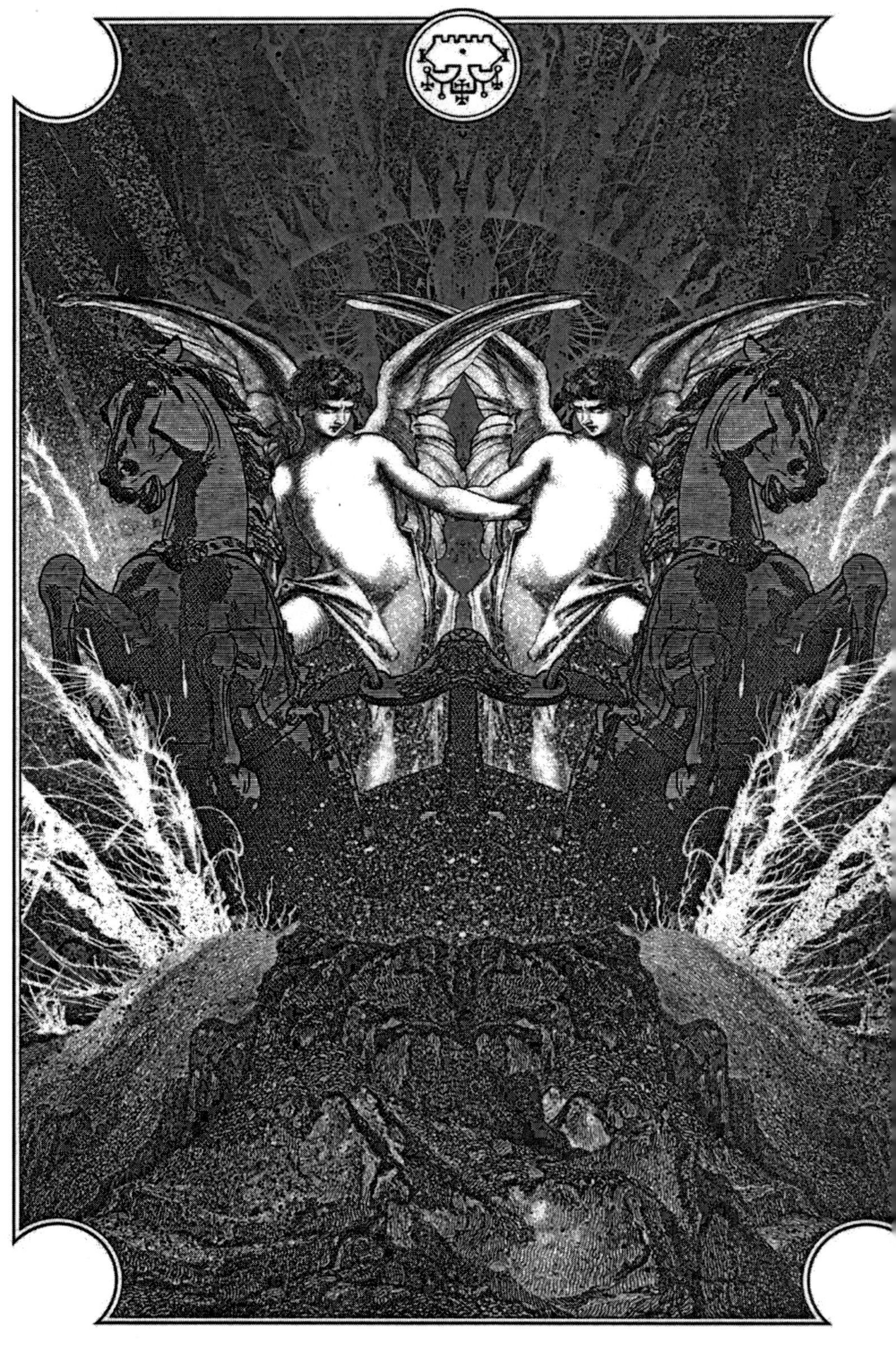

BELIAL

Belial's name comes from the Hebrew *beli*, "without," and *ya'al* ("value"). His name appears in older translations of the Old Testament, but always as part of a compound: "sons of Belial," "children of Belial" (e.g., Deuteronomy 13:13, Judges 19:22). Current scholarship holds that the Hebrew *beli'al* is an abstract noun meaning "worthlessness" (Hebrew idiom tending to use abstract nouns rather than adjectives as modifiers: thus "children of worthlessness" rather than "worthless children").

Later, however, Belial came to be personified, and he appears as an adversary of God in the pseudepigraphal *Testament of the Twelve Patriarchs* (dated to around 150 BC). In the present age, the text says, he causes man to stumble, but in the end times he will be bound and "thrown into eternal fire." His name occurs often in the Dead Sea Scrolls as well, as the ruler of the world in its current wicked dispensation. Belial also makes an appearance in the New Testament, in 2 Corinthians 6:15, as an opponent of Christ: "What concord hath Christ with Belial?" (So reads the King James Version, although the Greek text has the alternate spelling *Beliar*.)

The Lesser Key of Solomon says that Belial was created immediately after Lucifer, and is a king in the demonic hierarchy. He was first to fall among "the worthier and wiser sort" of angels. He will accept sacrifices and offerings, and will give true answers in response, although no more than he absolutely has to: "He tarrieth not one hour in the truth, except he be constrained by divine power." As for his appearance, "he taketh the form of a beautifull angell, sitting in a firie chariot; he speaketh faire; he distributeth preferments of senatorship, and the favour of friends, and excellent familiars." He commands eighty legions, some from the order of virtues, some from the order of angels. Somewhat obscurely, the text adds that he appears to the exorcist "in the bonds of spirits."

Dalia of Belial

MICHAEL GRIFFIN

Dalia writhes in agony, seeping wounds soaking tangled sheets with blood. Infection breeds within six deep knife cuts in her belly. As fever overrules her reason, she craves to throw aside the bedding and strip off her clothes. At the same time shivering compels her deeper under the blankets, hoping warmth will lessen the pain.

Her hands, arms and front of her dress are stained green and brown from tinctures applied in hope of killing the infection, but without effect. All healing has failed, and Dalia's agony only increases. In her delirium, she barely notices the dampness against which she has writhed and moaned for days and nights, slipping in and out of consciousness. When briefly lucid, she recognizes the pungent smell of illness pervading the room. Dalia has always valued smell. The most vital sense. In better times, she utilized essential oils and extracts to aid the alignment of body with mind and spirit. Rosemary for study, myrrh and vetiver for spiritual seeking, ylang-ylang to enhance sensual pleasures. Now the stench of sepsis threatening to kill her is more terrifying than the pain of her actual wounds.

No question, her injuries have festered. She's too weak to restore herself, either with herbal remedies or esoteric techniques. Nothing has halted the progress from fever and inflammation, to onset of blood poisoning, and finally, toward agonizing systemic death. Dalia must confront a fear she never imagined would apply to her.

Mortality. The ultimate failure of personal power.

And so she lies dying in her private room, concealed by the curtain hanging across the inner doorway at the rear of her storefront. The outer, unmarked door to the street was left unlocked to permit the arrival of clients on Tuesday morning. But before her first appointment, she was visited not by one seeking services, but by the husband of a client from the day before, angry at some divinatory detail his wife had learned from Dalia.

Angry enough to kill.

At first, she must have slipped into shock. By the time she revived and dragged herself to the back room, so much blood had been lost, she was barely able to stagger to her workbench. There she mixed restorative remedies, spoke healing conjurations, and tried by various means to influence her wounds. Already she was too weak. Lightheaded and dizzy, she was unable to focus her vision, let alone intent.

Dalia waits, barely aware of her slippage into sleep and back out again, yet hoping strength might return, even as recovery seems increasingly unlikely.

How could someone of her knowledge and power be brought so low? She possesses a diverse arcane knowledge, has at her disposal an array of obscure tools. At least at first, it seemed reasonable to persist in believing some method of influence, whether natural or occult, may yet remain.

At the very last, failing all else, she imagines she could climb from her bed, stagger out the front door and into the street, where she might find someone willing to help. Even that now feels impossible.

In the days since the attack, no clients have come. Three days, or has it been four? In that time, no visitors, none of her appointments, not even the usual drop-ins. That's unheard of! Even in such a small town, the devotion of a loyal clientele has kept her constantly busy, almost from the first day of her arrival, years ago. Usually, her shop hums with activity throughout the day, into evening, often late into night. What slander could have spread, sufficient to frighten everyone away? Some vengeful distortion, designed to demonize her and terrify her patrons? Dalia knows the accusations must have originated with the same man who did this to her.

Her gut clenches again in response to rising anger. The pain is too much. Something inside feels ripped loose. She has never given birth, but the sensation in her belly is like what she's always imagined that experience to be. Muscles cramping, flesh tearing, screams in delirium. Wild havoc, all self-control overcome, and finally an aftermath in a blood-soaked bed.

She hesitates to look at the blankets, or her dress, but feels the wetness all around, as if her body is disintegrating. Though she's never been squeamish, she's disquieted by these sights. The spreading purple wetness reminds her of something else she can't quite place.

There's no reason she has to look. She closes her eyes. In this self-imposed blindness, totally alone in the world, Dalia wants to speak. But as she begins, she's unsure what to say.

"Please, can't someone come…?"

She almost addresses a specific name, but can't guess what she meant to say. If any help is available, she has no idea where it might be. Dalia wallows in pitiful helplessness. She wishes she could be the devout sort, one who slipped easily into supplication. How simple it would be to beg for salvation, to simply give herself over to the divine and pray to be saved. Even now, a weak and frightened shadow within herself whispers, suggesting one possible answer.

Ask forgiveness. Beg to be saved!

But who could be listening?

Dalia feels exhausted by this burden of solitude, hopeless to a degree she's never before felt. She tries to believe the self-pity isn't real, that it's only a symptom of her physical pain, but she gives in to an overwhelming sense of vulnerability and angrily discards the suggestion. Her persistence, which she's always considered a strength, is really only stubbornness. Self-reliance is nothing more than a name invented by the forsaken to disguise their own loneliness. Normally she wouldn't allow herself to think this way, but she no longer cares. Her plight is real.

If her power has reached an end, she'll have nothing left at all. Who will be here for her? Dalia trembles, heartbroken and afraid, experiencing the fear of an abandoned child, beyond hope or rescue. The panic rises, a jagged spike that quickens her breath. She wants to run, but her body is incapable of rising from the bed.

"Please..." she moans through gritted teeth.

No grace, no dignity remaining, only weakness in the face of looming death. She needs help, any assistance from anyone at all. Yet no one cares. Whatever lies Tara Lamb's husband spread about Dalia, she still deserves better. Someone loyal should have come. If not Tara Lamb herself, one of the others.

"I... *need* you." Finally Dalia allows herself to direct her pleading outward, words choking, interrupted by tears. If she begs, if she cries, someone will respond. She strains to project her voice, to cry as loudly as she's able. "Please. Save me!"

The suffering of her body is overmatched by anguish of spirit. She would offer anything, even promise to give herself faithfully again, if only...

But how? What has she to offer, lying here this way? She has no payment to pledge in exchange for salvation.

A bargain.

That's what Dalia can give. Her promise.

Shudders override her. She is no longer an accomplished woman, not the things she's experienced, nor the truths she's learned, nor the moments shared with people met all over the world. She's been reduced to a quivering animal, paralyzed in fear of death, lost and adrift. Such fear is a poison that expands to fill her vision. She can't tell whether her eyes are open or closed.

"I'll believe again," Dalia promises, grasping, though she doesn't know what this means. A flash of memory throws her backward, tumbling across decades of her life, to a room in a church, lit yellow from high windows.

Young Dalia, kneeling before a crucified figure.

Is this her?

"Yes!" she cries. Her terror shifts, becomes more solid and comprehensible. She recognizes this glimpse of memory. "I promise, I'll take back everything I said. I'll repent. I'll offer myself again."

Something shifts, a movement which seizes Dalia's awareness. A sound of someone brushing past the inner curtain and entering her private room. The stink of her sweat and illness subsides, as if a window has allowed a gust of fresh air. No windows are open, but the shift in atmosphere is so abrupt, she feels certain someone has arrived. Is it possible, in the moment of her final breakdown and desperate prayer, her willingness to pledge her very soul, that someone might help?

She struggles to sit up, to see, expecting one of her clients. But it's a man, maybe half Dalia's forty-nine years. He crosses the room, as if having casually browsed past shelves of bottled tinctures and oils, and bundles of exotic herbs, to stumble into this private back room, somehow failing to realize this isn't a part of Dalia's *Apothecarium* meant for public access.

Of course, she doesn't care, now. She feels only relief that someone has come. Her eyes are slow to focus. He makes a narrow figure, elegant in a tailored suit of a neutral, nameless color. His skin is pale, his chin-length hair streaked white and black.

Unable to rise, Dalia lifts a hand, certain the man's lingering, bemused smile must indicate that he hasn't yet seen her. But he does see. His gaze does not avoid the awful mess of her bed, the rank tangle of blood and sickness. But as if uncomprehending of Dalia's plight, he seems only pleased to have found her. Her breathing comes fast, in a shallow, animal whine.

"Help me," she cries, straining.

With a rush of shock, she recognizes the man. She doesn't know exactly where she's seen him before, but he's someone she knew before she arrived in this town, during her long travels, or even before. Handsome, even delicately pretty, with the idealized, glistening smoothness of a retouched fashion photograph. His skin appears lit with a soft-focus cinematic glow. He seems not to have heard her pleading. If anything, his smile becomes more relaxed, familiar.

"Please, help me." Dalia struggles to gain control. "A... a doctor."

The man approaches blithely. He appears intent on seduction or charm, or preoccupied with ramifications of this reunion which are beyond Dalia's recall or understanding. He shows none of the urgency appropriate to the discovery of a dying woman.

That's what she is, Dahlia admits. *Dying*. Her situation is acute, her time slipping away.

"Please," she begs. "I need you now."

He reaches toward Dalia, and his hand finds the crest of her hip. The touch is not an open-palmed gesture of comforting, but a squeezing grasp. The pressure suggests an urgency Dalia fails at first to register, until the desire behind it hits her on a primal level. She's surprised at her own body, at her hungry, animal-like reaction, leaving her suddenly overcome with a new kind of need. How is it possible to contemplate intimacy, sunk so deeply into fear and pain? A subconscious reconnection occurs, and she remembers. Memory floods in a rush of images, of terror and ecstasy, revealing a timeline of shared history deep and expansive. More than familiar, she and the man have been intimate. How is this something she could forget? She marvels at the new recognition, and the many, varied emotions and echoes of a part of her life long suppressed.

Vision clarifies, and though the pain continues, she feels like herself again. Still she can't remember his name.

"What comfort I have, I will give to you," he says, in a rhythm like incantation. He sits on the edge of the bed, close beside her. "I knew you would forget only for a while. Soon, you will remember the love in its entirety." His sweet words overflow with reassurance.

Dalia strives to remain hurt by his casualness, to insist he recognize the extremity of her plight. He should want to help. Yet even now, part of her wants to avoid seeming too needy, though she truly is desperate.

She reaches for his hand, but it slips away. "Anything," she begs.

His appearance is agreeable in every aspect, to an uncanny, almost disconcerting degree. Features too perfectly aligned, every proportion exactly correct, as if sculpted from Dalia's ideal conception of masculinity. Did he look like this when she knew him before? How is it possible she can see him this way, can be thinking such absurd, superficial thoughts concerning appearance and mannerism, even as her body lies so wrecked? Somehow, the pain has relented slightly, simultaneous with his arrival. Dalia has a sense that he's caused her suffering to diminish, at least to a degree sufficient to allow her to see him clearly, to focus her admiration, and find a place of at least enough equilibrium to allow her to be enchanted.

But why? His swagger, and that arrogant smile, seem so wrong in this place.

He lies. That phrase comes to mind, though she's unsure why.

"You want," he says, each syllable light and singsong, "something from me." He shifts, as if about to lie down, but instead moves weightlessly across her to the lower part of the bed, and disappears from vision.

She perceives a series of disconcerting movements under the sheets and blankets, an easy slipping beneath the fabric of her dress.

Now, a touch of forceful, determined hands provoke her skin, fire hot, slick with sweat.

His voice rises, yet Dalia can't understand the words. Then she remembers, and realizes he's waiting for her answer. This is what he does. He pauses on the brink, at the very point at which it's impossible for her to refuse and turn back. There he waits for her to beg.

Her gut heaves, a terrified jump from a place of uncertainty into definite need. "Please," she moans, and this time the word carries a different meaning. "Yes, please." She seeks release from pain and fear. The trauma of her wounds becomes less focused, more distant, fading into detachment. She senses the worst of the infection being met with a localized, burning cold, then removed by pressure, hard and sharp. A new heat takes the place of the burning, no longer specific to the wounds themselves, but spreading throughout her body. Not feverish with sickness, but shimmering with a modulated, internal fire. Tinges of pleasure emerge, broaden and become more complex, blending with other sensations that must certainly be remnants of pain, but in no way resembling the agony that troubled her just minutes earlier.

She is aware of her rational mind observing with a distant intrigue this change within her, even as the greater part of her psyche is swept away on waves of sensation that seem, at first, utterly foreign, then familiar in some depths of memory. Her agony is almost erased, relieved so quickly, as if the entirety of her trouble has been cut free, a poisonous rot discarded, and the place of emptiness left behind, refilled with an ecstasy unequaled.

Seems impossible she could ever have forgotten this.

All pain supplanted by a yearning to merge, to wrap herself around the man enmeshed with her, flowing liquid beneath her stained skirts, drinking away her inner poison. Unseen, he absorbs every aspect of her injury, her trauma, her sickness. Dalia feels him drinking the pain and all its causes, apparently not harmful to him, but worthy of savoring.

Suffering swirls into pleasure, a mix so complete Dalia can't be sure which she prefers. Too much feeling, too sharp and intense, leaves her overwhelmed. Her legs tremble, her breathing quickens. Not only awareness of sin, but desire for it. She doesn't care, she only wants—

The explosion of pleasure and relief extends in time, broadens in scope, expands outward beyond love, belonging and acceptance. Fully embraced, she trembles in relief and recognition. She's not alone. Every limb feels bruised, as if she's been manipulated wildly enough to break every joint, yet she remains intact and alive.

She breathes slowly again, surveying the sensations that flood back as consciousness returns. Dalia opens her eyes. The agony in her belly has subsided, replaced by a ticklish sensitivity. The bed is soaked with old, thick blood, and something else, newer, black and thick as tar.

The man rises out of the sticky mess, covered in the substance like wet, black enamel paint. He lifts from the bed, stands away, momentarily out of view. When he reappears, his hands and face, his hair, even the fabric of his suit are clean again. The substance, whether manifestation of Dalia's disease, or some emission of his, seemed too adhesive and staining ever to be removed. Yet he is able to wipe it away with his hands.

Her own fingers are still stained, and adhere to the tacky bedding as she tries to pull them free, to hold them up for him to see.

"What's happened to me?" she asks.

"Someone harmed you," he says. "Unless you harmed yourself."

"No." She holds out the black palms of her hands. "I mean this."

He approaches the bed, not near enough to touch.

Dalia wants to reach out, ask him to clean her, to be taken up in his—

"What else do you *want*?" he asks. His seriousness suggests she ought to consider her answer.

Her mind spins with the implications of all that has changed. From the quiet routine of her days before Tuesday, to the sudden attack, without warning. Then, in the days since, to plunge so completely, to realize how near death remains at every moment. Finally, the drastic, inexplicable reversal following his arrival. If mortal danger is truly past, if she can think of desiring something other than simply to not die, then what does she want? Her chest and throat still ache from the desperate hyperventilating of minutes earlier. She tries to remain calm, reminds herself to be relieved at the arrival of help. The memory of suffering lingers, still near and vivid. "I want to remain alive," she decides.

He answers without pause. "Nobody remains alive."

"At least for now." Dalia looks around, seeing her room for the first time, as if she has traveled somewhere distant, been absent long enough to almost forget this life, her shop, this town. "For the moment, at least."

He raises his left arm and looks at his wrist as if to consult a wristwatch, but there is nothing there. "You will remain alive for the moment, at least."

Now that she's been flooded with recollection of so many detailed experiences with her visitor, it's somehow worse, being unable to place him. She wants to trace backward, to run down the long, convoluted thread of her life, until she finds her way to where and when they met.

He stands watching, seeming to read her thoughts. "I find you at these turning points," he says.

Dalia believes this, that she knew him in a time of some earlier crisis, but can't imagine what that might be. "I'm far from where I began," she offers, still uncertain, and hoping for further hints. She tries to wipe the blood from her hands, if blood is what it is. All the fabric, her skin, everything tainted.

"You were poisoned," he says. "You remain poisoned, even after I took so much."

"You helped me before," she says, unsure what she's about to assert, but trying to encourage her memory to be forthcoming. She extends her left hand, the hand nearest him, hoping he will at least wipe that part of her clean.

"I helped you before, and I helped you after." He smiles a different smile, one of concealment.

Dalia shivers, wondering what he means by these riddles. She hopes he's only teasing, waiting until she remembers the rest. Of course, she should just ask his name. There's nothing wrong with admitting there are gaps remaining in her recollection. She's afraid to grasp too hard at understanding, aware of her usual need for absolute control. For so long, through all the blurred decades of her adult life, she traveled widely, questing in a constant motion of endless study and speculation. So much of that time has blended into vague generality, thirty years compressed by lack of differentiating specifics. The names of places and people, now an echoing murmur, far behind.

Lately, she has come to desire a life with boundaries she can see, with interactions she can touch and define. She accepts the impossible only so far as necessary to earn a living, to survive. All the passionate commitment of earlier life, those urgent desires that drove her, footsore and weary, until she settled into this place, all that drive has dissipated.

Dalia looks at the man, tries not to look away. Somehow, the very thing that makes his features so pleasing, all mathematical ratios, proportions of line, surface and angle, like a complex geometric sculpture, these are the very aspects that make her need to look away after only a glimpse. It's all too much, a dessert too richly sweet. Part of her feels ecstatic at seeing him again, at achieving this reunion so long anticipated that she forgot she was ever waiting for it. She can almost remember his name, the appellation that attaches to this pale, elegant face, the sharp-edged eyes, the distinctive fall of hair, and the slender height of his very distinctive frame.

What is this wanting? Her memories remain impossibly confused.

"I remember," Dalia begins. What does she remember? "The first time I saw you…" She trails off, noticing his ankle boots, red suede with fine gold stitching around the toe and up the instep. These must be significant, some clue to his identity. He can't be wearing the same boots from… how long ago? No, she has allowed herself to become distracted only because she still can't manage to close the circle of recollection. Memory, another blind alley. Why does she feel every time she's about to put it together, he manages through some dodge or misdirection to make her forget, yet again?

She feels weak, foolish, susceptible. At least she's no longer dying, at least not immediately. More than ever, she doubts herself. She keeps pretending, trying to draw out further hints, while he remains so obviously comfortable with her confusion. Surely he'll explain himself eventually, if she only encourages him to talk. Maybe he'll reminisce, or mention some detail she may recognize. Of course, if she remembered anything of her own past, she might be able to draw him out.

"And what has become of you?" he asks. "Once a world-walking seeker. Now, what?" He surveys the room, seeming to focus beyond the curtain, toward her shop's public outer room. "Reader of cards. Maker of potions. Divining truths by tossing rune sticks, or gazing into crystals?"

Dalia's cheeks flush. Her impulse is to protest, but she knows he's right. She's thought the very same things herself, using these exact words. It's as if he's capable of reading all the self-doubt that bubbles within her. Is he able to study her inner life, like reading words on a page, or did these notions arise within her at his suggestion, prior to his arrival? Instead of answering, Dalia props herself upright. At least her wounds no longer trouble her so much.

"You occupy yourself with conjurations, yet speak no love of your own?" he continues, his tone almost bitter. "You scry answers to the amorous, yet speak no words of your own yearning? Build potions to enhance physical desire, yet drink no pleasure for yourself?"

Dalia's nature has always been to rise when challenged, to assert strength whenever words are spoken against her, even when she perceives them to contain some truth. Now she finds herself incapable of self-defense.

"How sad," he says, not an accusation, but a question.

Nothing remains but to ask. She can't hold her own in this interaction without knowing his name, and how they met. Already he makes obvious his disappointment in her, only moments after saving her with his…

How exactly did he save her?

His efforts were not medicine, of course. That should be some clue. His methods are not scientific, but more like her own.

"The day we met," he offers, "you were the most innocent. Among all of them, you stood out in your purity." He watches, seeming to await recognition, and finally sits on the black velvet upholstered bench against the wall, beside the shuttered window to the alley, and the table before it.

Dalia nods, still not understanding, hoping he might continue.

"A virginal seeker, misled as to aims, but in spirit, immaculate."

Virginal, yes. A story reappears, like a book read once long ago and forgotten, and only now reopened. That was her, a segment of her own lost history, obscured in the same fog as this man's name.

So long since she considered her convent year. Days kneeling on hard floors, weeping tears pointless yet absolutely sincere, and staring in bereft supplication into the light streaming through windows so high, always and forever beyond reach. Now, all in a rush, it feels not so long ago. That period in life may seem in retrospect like only a few days, blurred in a distortion of drugs or wine.

But the truth, she now recalls without effort. She spent a year in that place, until he came for her.

"I was an aspirant," she whispers. That word feels new. A young girl who dreamed of becoming a nun, who overflowed with passions she never completely understood. Did she become disillusioned on her own, or did this mysterious and unasked visitor's first intrusion shape her wants? She recalls being wracked with doubt, even then. It seems impossible to be sure, looking back, whether or not he imposed this upon her.

What she sees with renewed clarity is that she left that life, walked out and never looked back, to become a seeker in the wider, truer sense. Her reaction to that encounter shaped everything she was to become.

Dalia finds herself now capable of looking at him directly, without blinking. She sees his perfection as an unreal blankness, like a newly painted wall. The smooth skin lacking pores or blemishes, the glossy luminosity of his hair, the rigid mannequin's posture. She remembers that first glimpse, when he appeared behind her in the vacant stairwell. It was the one place beyond earshot of the rest of the order, her one daily moment of privacy. The way he glided toward her, and they slipped together so easily. No fear, not even in the first. A shy virgin, all renunciation and proud chastity, lingering alone on the stairs with a man she'd never before seen and didn't know.

She should have been afraid. Why wasn't she afraid?

The entire, detailed recollection floods back, carrying with it another round of the same prurient supercharge by which he healed her body. That first seduction, and all her plans discarded. Every aspect of her life thrown into upheaval by a single moment, only for him to disappear. What choice remained, having broken her vow? It felt impossible to beg forgiveness, to apologize to authorities, especially a figure in which she no longer believed.

She decided to venture out, seeking the only perfection life ever granted her.

Now, Dalia sees in the way he's watching her that he understands, that he has followed and comprehended every aspect of the lapse and recollection of her memory.

"Why did you forsake me?"

He sits straight, so upright he seems to stretch and become thinner. His chin lifts, a gesture of refutation. "Always I remain."

Dalia rolls over in the bed, sits up and places her feet on the floor. She feels recovered, and more than that, energized. She stands, with slow caution at first, then fully upright, arms extended to both sides.

This way, in her blackened dress, heavy with the stains of her blood and his emissions, she confronts him.

"I didn't want you to stay with me only symbolically." She lets out a sigh, realizes this sounds pathetic, but doesn't care. "I wanted to remain with you, not just serve from a distance. My endless, solitary wandering, it brought me so low. You left me with nothing."

She steps closer, confronts him where he sits on the velvet bench, his erect back near the wall, not quite touching. She fears he might flinch away, but he doesn't actually move. She doesn't touch him, as she knows he expects her to do. Instead she grasps at her own chest, tears open the front of her dress to reveal her flesh, then pulls the garment open lower, to show the bloodless wounds. Her fingernails press, trying to tear at the cuts, but they won't reopen. "Not just these knife wounds. I was dying long before."

His face displays no sympathy or regret, yet even his neutral equanimity becomes a seductive offering. "I can offer a cure. This cure, final."

She hesitates, wants to argue, but belief is so tempting.

"A cure forever," he says.

Excess of emotion, and her own wild swerve from ignorance to remembrance, leave Dalia overwhelmed and queasy. In reaction against her resentment at his abandonment, a new wave of physical desire rises within her. Forgetting all she wanted to argue or demand, now Dalia wishes only to suggest that he come to her again. Why not? Every disagreement or resentment might be washed away. With bliss comes clarity, at least for a short while.

She imagines he may be causing her to feel this way. It's easy to believe he prefers to distract her from her complaints. Always before, he's managed to break off her protestations before they coalesced into real arguments. His greatest power seems to be not seduction, but suggestion. He evokes her compliance with the merest smile or subtlest gesture, by means of impulses which seem to enter Dalia's mind from out of nowhere.

Still she wants to protest, to speak a litany of old complaints and unmet needs. The words won't come.

"Dalia," he begins, reasonable and entirely unobjectionable, "in your time, you have traveled the world's glorious, hidden places. You have walked stairways high above the ground, and delved in tunnels far below it. You've swum waters cold and deep, and kept watch over vast, ancient spaces."

She remembers, but only barely. Most of these sights now seem shifted to an additional degree of removal, never encountered first-hand.

"You have grasped unto wild flesh," he continues, "and drunk from the cups of first and last mystery. You have inhaled the perfume of fragrant colors and ventured into dense atmospheres of tombs long undisturbed. Through all of this, ever since we met, you were Dalia of Belial."

"I'm..." she begins, and trails off.

"I gave you the gift of everything you became." He makes this assertion without pride, as if praising Dalia, granting her autonomy and acknowledging her centrality in her own history.

She wants to resist, to raise the question of so many omissions from his summary of her story. Not to fight him, but to reassert the existence of other aspects of the world she knows to exist, of daylight time and mundane obligation, and all the effects these forces exert upon herself and every living person. Also, to insist on the inevitability of time and mortality, and the limit of his power to counteract these effects. He can't deny, he must realize—

But she notices him watching, presiding over this apparently closed subject. She remains quiet, tries to stay focused in her resistance, but finds this impossible as she looks at him. He's attractive, magnetic, possessed of powerful, maddening charm, but the strength of his effect goes beyond superficial attributes. When Dalia looks at him, and particularly when he speaks, all intentions to resist, any contrary thoughts she may harbor, vanish in an instant. She wishes she might in some way assert autonomy, perhaps to remind him that she managed to direct her own path in decades of travel, as she sought to find him. Even this seems absurd and vain. Most of all, she just wants to remain near him, on any terms.

If she can't control him, can't be his equal, at least she might let him see she's her own person. If the past repeats itself, soon he will leave, no matter what she wishes. She'll be alone again.

This moment is everything she has. All is now.

He moves closer, as if about to impose himself, but stops short of initiating contact. Once he's within reach, Dalia is unable to stop herself. She reaches out, grasps his hand. On unexpected impulse, her free hand flashes toward his face, an attempt at a hard slap, which he easily avoids. All at once, he is the one holding Dalia motionless, restraining her by both wrists. She's unsure whether she's actually struggling to free herself, or if that's only a distant impulse on which her body fails to act. He pulls her in, forces her to accept his kiss. The moment before their mouths meet, he changes slightly. She gasps, tries to inhale, and the liquid floods her mouth, rushes down her throat and fills her lungs. No resistance. The notion of exchange of power is part of the game. True resistance never occurs. The seduction is mutual.

Pleasure surges within her, threatens to overfill her, not a slow accumulation like most of the sexual experiences of her life, but a sudden and wild rush. This is sometimes his way, this forceful taking, this redirection of her attention and energies. Dalia laughs without a sound, not breathing, not needing to breathe. Her body, her mind, all her questions and fears, all are overwhelmed with pleasure, full of his rightness and his truth.

They stand clenched, facing one another, in what must appear outwardly a slow dance, close and rigid. Dalia lightly grasps the fabric of his lapel. The two of them barely sway.

The feeling of suffocation rises. Unable to breath, she spasms, tries to cough. She can't pull back. Both his hands grasp her throat, choking. Her eyes water, and she's surprised, having thought that his hands were in her own, not on her neck. Lightheaded, she panics, but doesn't resist. She allows herself to be overcome.

He releases his grip, satisfied.

She inhales, overwhelmed by nausea and dizziness, and notices that the effect of these experiences seems to be anchoring him to this place, fixing him in this concrete physical moment, contrary to her own experience of being swept away to abstract realms, seeming to become less a person and more a whirl of impressions and desires.

She backs up, turns away so he won't see, and vomits thin, black ink onto the floor. The liquid spatters and forms a puddle. In this smooth surface she sees her face reflected.

"Now I remember," Dalia gasps, and vomits again, again, until she's empty. "I remember everything."

"My name?" He leans in from behind, initiating touch for the first time since he entered and sat on her bed.

Belial.

She doesn't need to say it. To know is everything.

"And your name?" he continues.

"Dalia of Belial." She remains determined to make him hear her argument, that most of what she has been throughout her life derived from within herself and was not bestowed or forced upon her. But this argument sticks in her throat, refusing to be spoken. Even the wish to express such ideas begins to lose force.

What Dalia wants most, what never wavers, is to hold onto what she has regained. She fears memory might slip, that he may depart and leave her again with nothing but a complex of empty, nameless yearnings. Desire overwhelms her, an urgent certainty that he should remain, that she must always be granted access to him, every day.

"I remember those first months," she whispers, "trying to reclaim the backward kiss. To seize again, even once, that explosion of impossible, perfect bliss. But you weren't there. You were never there. For a long time I believed you'd return to me, in fact never doubted it until..." She stops.

For a suspended instant, their positions are reversed. Belial seeming to wonder and to desire, while Dalia withholds.

"Until what?" he asks.

"The failure of a ceremony." Dalia looks down at the bare skin of her chest and wonders at her own desire. She prefers to deny it could be imposed upon her, would rather believe it comes from within. The outrageous lust she felt upon their first encounter, so vastly outsized beyond the scale of anything she ever sought from scripture, so much larger and more potent than anything ever imagined. Not merely more intense and carnal than her pleasureless seclusion in the convent, but greater, more dynamic, full of blood and sensation, beyond the material worlds or realms of spirit.

"I'm intrigued." His face relaxes, no longer a mask, until after a moment he reasserts control. "I wonder how you experienced our meeting, and after, under my influence."

"I hid, and wandered in the trees." She considers withholding this aspect of her story, making him ask, or at least wait. "I chanted your name. Weeks of meditation and fasting."

His face slackens in obvious disappointment.

"That was only at first," Dalia clarifies. "When sitting still and visualizing did nothing, I decided to move, to act. I traveled, sought gurus, asked questions, always learning. Then I secluded myself in the California desert, working ceremonies, hoping to conceive a child of your spirit. Your child." The memory of her disappointment returns to her with perfect clarity, threatens to choke her with tears.

Sighing, he steeples his fingers. "It would be rude of me not to ask. How did that turn out?"

She wants to lash out at this affront, to chide him for mocking the frustrated desire that consumed decades of her life, yet to speak against him in such a way feels impossible. Every instance of such failure to stand up for herself seems singular in its moment, just a solitary impulse toward protestation fallen impotent rather than acted upon, yet the whole stretch of time from their first encounter has been characterized by exactly such defeats. This must be how he wants it.

He moves into her line of sight, his head leaning slightly to one side, hinting at concession. "Here is what I would give you," he says. "Follow the path of ease and pleasure. These lives are limited in number, and the risk of striving for abstract desires is great. Reach no farther than your own grasp."

She considers. "That's what you give me? Philosophy?"

He straightens, appears to expand and broaden, becoming regal and statuesque. "And don't you deem my philosophies sound?"

Dalia hesitates. She wants to offer a contrary response without taking ownership of it. "I knew a teacher who called you 'The Adversary.' He mocked my devotion. He told me I'd be better off forgetting you."

Belial laughs.

"He swore your influence on mankind was nothing but obfuscation and interference. Those were his exact words."

For the duration of Belial's laughter, his face changes entirely, his skin paled to ice white, deeply creased with striking black lines. When the laughing stops, the lines disappear, and no trace remains of whatever entity briefly revealed itself.

"Yet you believe in me," he says. "Even when you forget why."

She almost makes another small protest, but before she can speak her courage shrinks and she's afraid again. She puts on a smile, hoping to convince him.

"Will you tell me what keeps you alive?" she asks.

"Alive?"

"Intact, still moving and thinking." She sits on the edge of her bed. "After... How long?"

Slowly Belial nods, as if having decided some alternate definition of the word alive will have to suffice. "I avoid other people's wars, holy or unholy. Three lives, three existences, that's the most any should hope for, whether human or higher being."

"Are you a higher being?"

He looks surprised. "Are you?" Belial gestures to dismiss his own question. "What would you prefer to think me? Angel, demon or god?"

It's a question Dalia has never considered, the taxonomy of his fundamental nature. Out of nowhere she feels moved to approach him, suspecting as she does so that he might slip away. Yet he remains motionless, even as she looms before him. Impassive, his face pale marble.

Dalia eyes the circular work table between the bench and window. Amid a scattered dust of dry herb powder rests a pewter-handled knife, an artifact discovered on the opposite side of the world, in a country that no longer exists. The blade was dull, after centuries buried. She had an artisan brighten the steel and rework the edge, so the blade was new again, razor sharp. If only Dalia herself could be restored in such a way as this, all physical breakdowns repaired, and the grime of age brushed away.

She realizes another part of her is wondering if she might reach the knife before he's able to guess her intent, but she dismisses the idea, and wants to change the subject.

Though unsure how much she recalls of scripture, or how he might receive it, Dalia begins to recite. "I am the Lord, your God."

Belial stands to face her. "Open your mouth wide, and I will fill it."

She does as he commands, and they merge. This time, the ecstasy is very brief, but still adequate to justify a lifetime of devotion. How many are lucky enough to experience even one instant so perfect? The moment is everything, a taste of divinity, and also far too much to bear. Parts of her remain sore, overwhelmed and hyper-sensitive.

After, she turns away, hoping she won't be sick again. Her stomach heaves, and a deep, thrumming shudder spreads to every muscle in her body.

The black liquid filling her stays down this time.

Belial goes to the edge of the bed, still wildly disarranged and stained black, like some perverse flower of death. "You said this is the second time I've visited you. Have you forgotten the other time?"

Startled, Dalia tries to remember. The part of her mind that seeks backward into the past is exhausted, or broken.

"The first instance, we agree upon," he begins. "I came to you in the stair, hidden from the rest. We remained many hours, teasing ever nearer, backing away and again approaching, until your capitulation was entire. Later, it was your idea that we go outside, and display our coupling in the grass before the broad windows, where all would hear your cries ringing out. So they would be unable to look away, and would have to see the truth."

Dalia remembers that evening and night, an encounter she has relived through decades of obsession, until at some point her mind must have relinquished it. Perhaps the pain became too great.

"I remember," she says.

"So there would be no going back," he continues. "I never took you, Dalia. From the first, you gave yourself over."

"It was my greatest moment." She sighs, feeling ridiculous for asserting that she remembers moments enough to be able to compare.

"And… the other time," he begins.

Does she really want to know? Her psyche feels tender, incapable of facing surprise, let alone shock or trauma.

"All your years of wild roving, seeking truth, disconnected," he continues, seeming intent on reading her reaction, appearing to enjoy her discomfort. "Entirely dispossessed."

She laughs, a bitter sound. "I'm still dispossessed."

"No. You're immobile, not seeking or learning. How long since you last discovered the new? Always dare. Constantly strive. This sustains us."

She winces at a twinge in her belly, and looks to him. "A cure, you said?" So easily she sets aside her anxiousness to hear of their other meeting.

"Let me see."

She sits on the bed, tries to lie back, but the pain makes her cry out. "It was better for a while. But now I can't…"

He stops short of approaching, lets her lie there. "And have they lacked in pleasures, or fallen short in sublimity, these lives of yours?"

Even through the distraction of recurrent pain, Dalia can't deny that her time has been everything he suggests. If she now finds herself burdened by any regret, it may be only the nagging fear that her path has not been her own, that she has been nudged in the direction of another's agenda.

"How will you ever know?" he asks, seeming to intuit her fears.

She gives no answer, only writhes and squirms against the burning.

"What do you want, then?"

To answer this, Dalia needs no time to consider. "To see your true face, and feel your touch, unaltered by illusion."

She squeezes shut her eyes, trying to resist the rising pain, so she can't see his reaction. He doesn't answer right away, and when her pain lets up slightly, she wonders if this is his doing, a way of changing the subject.

But finally he does answer, sounding surprised at one of her words. "What illusion?"

"There has always been a glass between us, even when one enters the other. A sort of privacy screen, always." She forces herself to open her eyes, to regard him directly, even though she's afraid. "Even when I've felt your touch, there has always remained a distance of unknowing."

He appears lost in consideration, not ready to meet her gaze. "What you ask comes at great cost."

"I know."

"All lives have an end. Altered by knowledge, one gives way to the next."

Dalia nods. "None of us can have more than three." She wonders if she should have asked about their second meeting, instead of this. "You told me so."

He looks at her, and kisses her fingers as if preparing to say goodbye. "You would know what this is, then?"

Her throat tightens. "Tell me," she demands.

Belial leans in and grants to her the scent of northern fir trees, the pungent waft of aging cocoa, smoke of drying cloves, and winds blowing in from equatorial seas across a beach of black sand. Memories flood in, from the world's every corner. Unwinding his last secret, he whispers to Dalia her one desire. Belial's only lie has been to hint at separation between them. The truth is that Dalia is herself Belial, and has always been since that encounter, hiding on the stairs.

She watches his face change, his rigid posture slipping, straightness becoming asymmetric curves. Narrow eyes of icy blue widen and brown. Alabaster skin flushes pink. Belial is no less appealing, may even be more beautiful. Dalia of Belial cannot speak, overwhelmed by revelation.

Hot pain burns her gut. She flinches, looks down, and sees her own black-stained hands grasping the pewter handle, pressing the knife into her flesh.

CPSIA information can be obtained
at www.ICGtesting.com
Printed in the USA
LVOW10s1620250518
578520LV00001B/226/P

9 781947 654082